"LOOK OUT!" TEX YELLED.

A bullet ripped through Tex's side, and he drove his horse into Hoppy's, slamming his friend aside, hoping to spoil the killer's aim.

Off-balance, Hoppy's own shot went wide, and he did not know if he would have time for another. The ambushing outlaw was crashing down on them, blood in his eyes, charging through the undergrowth in a headlong rush, his guns blazing.

His ears ringing, Hoppy tried for another shot.

BUCK PETERS, RANCHMAN

Clarence E. Mulford

TOR

A TOM DOHERTY ASSOCIATES BOOK
NEW YORK

BUCK PETERS, RANCHMAN

All new material in this edition copyright © 1993 by Tom Doherty Associates, Inc.

Cover art by Carl Cassler

A Tor Book
Published by Tom Doherty Associates, Inc.
175 Fifth Avenue
New York, N.Y. 10010

Tor ® is a registered trademark of Tom Doherty Associates, Inc.

ISBN: 0-812-52499-3

First Tor edition: July 1993

Printed in the United States of America

0 9 8 7 6 5 4 3 2 1

Introduction

IN JUNE 1991 Bantam published the first of Louis L'Amour's acclaimed Hopalong Cassidy novels, *The Rustlers of West Fork*. Since then, publishers tell me there has been a tremendous ground swell of enthusiasm for Hopalong and his friends. Readers around the country want to know more about these Bar-20 boys—and above all, want more of their books.

Consequently, Tor Books is bringing back the original novels, written by Clarence E. Mulford, the man who created Cassidy and company. It's a good thing too. These are really first-rate books, full of true grit and pulse-pounding action, the kind of books you can't put down.

If you liked Louis L'Amour's Hopalong Cassidy novel—*The Rustlers of West Fork*—you'll *love* this one. This is no imitation, but the real thing.

A lot of western writers—people like Richard S. Wheeler, Earl Murray, Al Dempsey and yours truly— when we get together for a few beers, we sometimes talk about books. We talk about the books that inspired us; the authors who made us love the West and even want to write ourselves. For whatever it's worth, it's a short list. And for a lot of us, the guy at the top is Clarence Mulford.

Clarence, old hoss, wherever you are, here's a Lone Star beer to you.

—Jackson Cain,
author of *HELLBREAK COUNTRY*
and *HANGMAN'S WHIP*

Contents

CHAPTER I

Tex Returns

JOHNNY NELSON reached up for the new, blue flannel shirt he had hung above his bunk, and then placed his hands on hips and soliloquized: "Me an' Red buy a new shirt apiece Saturday night an' one of 'em's gone Sunday mornin'; purty fast work even for this outfit."

He strode to the gallery to ask the cook, erstwhile subject of the Most Heavenly One, but the words froze on his lips. Lee Hop's stoop-shouldered back was encased in a brand new, blue flannel shirt, the price mark chalked over one shoulder blade, and he sing-songed a Chinese classic while debating the advisability of adopting a pair of trousers and thus crossing another of the boundaries between the Orient and the Occident. He had no eyes in the back of his head but was rarely gifted in the "ways that are strange," and he felt danger before the boot left Johnny's hand. Before the missile landed in the dish pan Lee Hop was digging madly across the open, halfway to the ranch house, and temporary safety.

Johnny fished out the boot and paused to watch the agile cook. "He's got eyes all over hisself—an' no coyote ever lived as could beat him," was his regretful comment. He knew better than to follow—Hopalong's wife had a sympathetic heart, and a tongue to be feared. She had not yet forgotten Lee Hop's auspicious initiation as an *ex-officio* member of the outfit, and Johnny's part therein. And no one had been able to convince her that sympathy was wasted on a Chinaman.

The shirtless puncher looked around helplessly, and then a grin slipped over his face. Glancing at the boot he dropped it back into the dish water, moved swiftly to Red's bunk, and in a moment a twin to his own shirt adorned his back. To make matters more certain he deposited on Red's blankets an old shirt of Lee Hop's, and then sauntered over to Skinny's bunk.

"Hoppy said he'd lick me if I hurt th' Chinaman anymore; but he didn't say nothin' to Red. May th' best man win," he muttered as he lifted Skinny's blankets and fondled a box of cigars. "One from forty-three leaves forty-two," he figured, and then, dropping to the floor and crawling under the bunk, he added a mark to Skinny's "secret" tally. Skinny always liked to know just how many of his own cigars he smoked.

"Now for a little nip, an' then th' open, where this cigar won't talk so loud," he laughed, heading toward Lanky's bunk. The most diligent search failed to produce, and a rapid repetition also failed. Lanky's clothes and boots yielded nothing and Johnny was getting sarcastic when his eyes fell upon an old boot lying under a pile of riding gear in a corner of the room. Keeping his thumb on the original level he drank, and then added enough water to bring the depleted liquor up to his thumb. "Gee—I've saved sixty-five dollars this month, an' two days are gone already," he chuckled. He received sixty-five dollars, and what luxuries were not nailed down, every month.

Mounting his horse he rode away to enjoy the cigar, happy that the winter was nearly over. There was a feeling in the air that told of Spring, no matter what the calendar showed, and Johnny felt unrest stirring in his veins. When Johnny felt thus exuberant things promised to move swiftly about the bunkhouse.

When far enough away from the ranch houses he stopped to light the cigar, but paused and, dropping the match, returned the "Maduro" to his pocket. He could not tell who the rider was at that distance, but it was wiser to be prudent. Riding slowly forward, watching the other horseman, he saw a sombrero wave, and spurred into a lope. Then he squinted hard and shook his head.

"Rides like Tex Ewalt—but it ain't, all right," he muttered. Closer inspection made him rub his eyes. "That arm swings like Tex, just th' same! An' I didn't take more'n a couple of swallows, neither. Why, damn it! If that ain't him I'm going to see *who* it is!" and he pushed on at a gallop. When the faint hail floated down the wind to him he cut loose a yell and leaned forward, spurring and quirting. "Old son-of-a-gun's come back!" he exulted. "Hey, Tex! Oh, Tex!" he yelled; and Tex was yelling just as foolishly.

They came together with a rush, but expert horsemanship averted a collision, and for a few minutes neither could hear clearly what the other was saying. When things calmed down Johnny jammed a cigar into his friend's hands and felt for a match.

"Why, I don't want to take yore last smoke, Kid," Tex objected.

"Oh, go ahead! I've got a hull *box* of 'em in th' bunkhouse," was the swift reply. "Couldn't stay away, eh? Didn't like th' East, nohow, did you? Gosh, th' boys'll be some tickled to see you, Tex. Goin' to stay? How you feelin'?"

"You bet I'm a-stayin'," responded Tex. "Is that Lanky comin'?"

"Hey, Lanky!" yelled Johnny, standing up and waving the approaching horseman toward them. *Pronto!* Tex's come back!"

Lanky's pony's legs fanned a haze under him and he rammed up against Tex so hard that they had to grab each other. Everybody was talking at once and so they rode toward the bunkhouse, picking up Billy on the way.

"Where's Hopalong?" demanded Tex. "Married! Hell he is!" A strange look flitted across his face. "Well, I'm damned! An' where's Red?"

Johnny glanced ahead just in time to see Lee Hop sail around a corner of the corral, and he replied with assurance, "Red's th' other side of th' corral."

"Huh!" snorted Lanky, "You've got remarkable eyes, Kid, if you can see through—well, I'm hanged if he *ain't!*"

After Red came Pete, waving a water-soaked boot. They disappeared and when Tex and his friends had almost reached the corral, Lee Hop rounded the same corner again, too frightened even to squeal. As he started around the next corner he jumped away at an angle, Pete, still waving the boot, missing him by inches. Pete checked his flow of language as he noticed the laughing group and started for it with a yell. A moment later Red came into sight, panting heavily, and also forgot the cook. Lee Hop stopped and watched the crowd, taking advantage of the opportunity to gain the cook shack and bar the door. "Dlam shirt no good—sclatchee like helle," he muttered. White men were strange—they loved each other like brothers and fought one another's battles. "Led head! Led head!" he cried, derisively. "My hop you cloke! Hop you cloke chop-chop! No fliend my, savee?"

Skinny Thompson, changing his trousers in the bunkroom, heard Lee's remarks and laughed. Then he listened—somebody was doing a lot of talking. "They're loco, plumb loco, or else somethin's wrong," and he hopped to the door. A bunched crowd of friends were tearing toward him, yelling and shooting and waving sombreros, and a second look made him again miss the trousers' leg and hop through the door to save himself. The blood swept into his face as he saw the ranch house and he very promptly hopped back again, muttering angrily.

The crowd dismounted at the door and tried to enter *en masse*; becoming sane it squirmed into separate units and entered as it should. Lee Hop hastily unbarred his door and again fled for his life. When he returned he walked boldly behind his foreman, and very close to him, gesticulating wildly and trying to teach Hopalong Cantonese. The foreman hated to chide his friends, but he and his wife were tired of turning the ranch house into a haven for Chinese cooks.

As he opened the door he was grabbed and pushed up against a man who clouted him on the back and tried to crush his hand. "Hullo, Cassidy! Best sight I've laid eyes on since I left!" yelled the other above the noise.

"Tex!" exclaimed Hopalong. "Well, I'm damned! When did you get here? Going to stay? Got a job yet? How'd you like the East? Married? *I* am—best thing I ever did. You look white—sick?"

"City color—like the blasted collars and shirts," replied the other, still pumping the hand. "I'm goin' to stay, I'm lookin' for a job, an' I'd ruther punch cows for my keep than get rich in th' East. It's all fence-country—can't move without bumping into somebody or something—an' noise! An' crooked! They'd steal th' fillin's out of yore teeth when you go to talk—an' you won't know it!"

"Like to see 'em fool *me*!" grunted Johnny, looking savage.

"Huh! Th' new beginners'd pick you out to practice on," snorted Red. "That yore shirt or mine?" he asked, suspiciously.

"They'd give you money for th' fun of taking it away from you," asserted Tex. "Why, one feller, a slick dresser, too, asks me for th' time. I was some proud of that ticker—cost nigh onto a hundred dollars. He thanks me an' slips into th' crowd. When I went to put th' watch back I didn't have none. I licked th' next man, old as he was, who asks me for th' time. He was plumb surprised when I punched him—reckon he figured I was easy."

"Ain't they got policemen?" demanded Red.

"Yes; but *they* don't carry watches—they're too smart."

"Have a drink, Tex," suggested Lanky, bottle in hand. When the owner of it took a drink he looked at his friends and then at the bottle, disgust pictured on his face. "This liquor's shore goin' to die purty soon. It's gettin' weaker every day. Now I wonder what in hell Cowan makes it out of?"

"It *is* sort of helpless," admitted Tex. "Now, Kid, I'll borrow another of them cigars of yourn. Them Maduros are shore good stuff. I wouldn't ask you only you said you had a—"

"D'ju see any shows in th' East?" demanded Johnny, hurriedly: "Real, good, bang-up shows?"

Skinny faded into the bunkroom and soon returned, puzzled and suspicious. He slipped Tex a cigar and in a few moments sidled up close to the smoker.

"That as good as th' Kid's?" he asked, carelessly.

Tex regarded it gravely: "Yes; better. I like 'em black, but don't say nothin' to Johnny. He likes them blondes 'cause he's young."

It was not long before Tex, having paid his respects to the foreman's wife, returned to the bunkhouse, leaned luxuriously against the wall and told of his experiences in the East. He had an attentive audience and it swayed easily and heartily to laughter or sympathy as the words warranted. There was much to laugh at and a great deal to strain credulity. But the great story was not told, the story of the things pitiful in the manner in which they showed up how square a regenerated man could be, and how false a woman. It was the old story—ambition drove him out into a new world with nothing but a clean conscience, a strong, deft pair of hands, and a clever brain; a woman drove him back, beaten, disheartened, and perilously near the devious ways he had forsaken. He could not stay in the new surroundings without killing—and he knew the woman was to blame; so when he felt the ground slip under his hesitating feet, he threw the new life behind him and hastened West, feverish to gain the locality where he had learned to look himself in the face with regret and remorse, but without shame.

In turn he learned of the things that had occurred since he had left: of the bitter range-war; of his best friend's promotion and marriage; and of Buck Peters' new venture among hostile strangers. The latter touched him deeply—he knew, from his own bitter experiences, the disheartening struggle against odds great enough to mean a hard fight for Buck and all his old outfit. Something that in Tex's heart had been struggling for weeks, the vague uneasiness which drove him faster and faster toward

the West, now possessed him with a strength not to
be denied. He knew what it was—the old lust for
battle, the game of hand and wits with life on the table, could not be resisted. The southern range was
now peaceful, thanks to Buck and his men, thanks
to Meeker's real nature; the Double Arrow and the
C80 formed a barrier of lead and steel on the north
and east, a barrier that no rustler cared to force.
Peace meant solitude on the sun-kissed range and
forced upon him opportunities for thought—and insanity, or suicide. But up in Montana it would be different; and the field, calling insistently for Tex to
come, was one where his peculiar abilities would be
particularly effective. Buck needed friends, but
stubbornly forbade any of his old outfit to join him.
Of course, they would disregard his commands and
either half or all of the Bar Twenty force would join
him; but their going would be delayed until well after the Spring round-up, for loyalty to their home
ranch demanded this. Tex was free, eager, capable,
and as courageous as any man. He had the cunning
of a coyote, the cold savagery of a wolf, and the
power of a tiger. In his lightning-fast hands a Colt
rarely missed—and he gathered from what he heard
that such hands were necessary to make the right
kind of history on the northern range.

Finally Hopalong arose to go to the ranch house
for the noon meal, taking Tex with him. The foreman and his wife did not eat with the outfit, because the outfit would not allow it. Mary had
insisted at first that her husband should not desert
his friends in that manner, and he stood neutral on
the question. But the friends were not neutral—they
earnestly contended that he belonged to his wife
and they would not intrude. Lanky voiced their attitude in part when he said: "We've had him a long
time. We borrow him during workin' hours—we
never learned no good from him, so we ain't goin' to

chance spottin' our lily white souls." But there was another reason, which Johnny explained in naive bluntness: "Why, Ma'am, we eats in our shirt sleeves, an' we grabs regardless. We has to if we don't want Pete to get it all. An' somehow I don't think we'd git very fat if we had to eat under wraps. You see, we're free-an'-easy—an' we might starve, all but Pete. Why, Ma'am, Pete can eat anythin', anywheres, under any conditions. So we sticks to th' old table an' awful good appetites."

So Hopalong and Tex walked away together, the limp of the one keeping time with that of the other, for Tex's wounded knee had mended a great deal better than he had hoped for. Hopalong stopped a moment to pat his wolf hounds, briefly complimenting them to Tex, and then pushed open the kitchen door, shoving Tex in ahead of him.

"Just in time, boys," said Mary, "I hope you're good an' hungry."

They both grinned and Hopalong replied first: "Well, I don't believe Pete can afford to give us much of a handicap today."

"Nor any other time, as far's I'm concerned," added Tex, laughing. "We'll do yore table full justice, Mrs. Cassidy," he assured her.

Mary, dish in hand, paused between the stove and the table. She looked at Tex with mischievous eyes: "Billy-Red tells me you love him like a brother. Is he deceiving me?"

Hopalong laughed and Tex replied, smiling: "More like a sister, Mrs. Cassidy—I can't find any faults in him, an' we don't fight."

Mary completed her journey to the stove, filled the dish and carried it to the table; resting her hands on the edge of the table, she leaned forward in seeming earnestness. "Well, you must know that we are one, and if you love Billy-Red—" finishing with an expressive gesture. "Those who love me call me Mary."

Tex's face was gravely wistful, but a wrinkle showed at the outer corner of his eyes. "Well," he drawled, "those who love me call me Tex."

"Good!" exclaimed Hopalong, grinning.

"An' I'm thankful that my hair's not th' color to cause any trustin' soul to call me by a more affectionate name," Tex finished. He ducked Hopalong's punch while Mary laughed a bird-like trill that brought to her husband's face an expression of idolizing happiness and made Tex smile in sympathy. As the dinner progressed Tex shared less and less in the conversation, preferring to listen and make occasional comments, and finally he spoke only when directly addressed.

When the meal was over and the two men started to go into the sitting-room, Mary said: "You'll have to excuse me, Mr.—er—Tex," she amended, smiling saucily. "I guess you two men can take care of each other while I clean up."

"We'll certainly try hard, Mrs.—er—Mary," Tex replied, his face grave but his eyes twinkling. "We watched each other once before, you know."

As soon as they were alone Hopalong waved his companion to a chair and bluntly asked a question: "What's th' matter, Tex? You got plumb quiet at th' table."

The other, following his friend's example, filled a pipe before he replied.

"Well, I was thinkin'—couldn't help it; an' I was drawin' a contrast that hurt. Hoppy, I'm not goin' to stay here longer'n I can help; you don't need me a little bit, an' if you took me in yore outfit it'd be only because you want to help me. This ain't no place for me—I need excitement, clean, purposeful excitement, an' you fellows have made this part of th' country as quiet as a Quaker meetin'. I've been thinkin' Buck needs somebody that'll stick to him—an' there ain't nothin' I won't do for Buck. So I'm goin' to pull my freight north, but *not* as Tex Ewalt."

"Tex, if you do that I'll be able to sleep better o' nights," was the earnest reply. "We'd like to have you. You know that, but it might mean life to Buck if he had you. Lord, but couldn't you two raise hell if you started! He'll be tickled half to death to see you—there will be at least one man he won't have to suspect."

Tex considered a moment. "He won't see me—to know me. I'm one man when I'm known, when I've declared myself; I can be two or three if I don't declare myself. One fighting man won't do him much good—if I could take th' outfit along we wouldn't waste no time in strategy. Th' rest of th' population, hostile to Buck, would move out as we rode in—an' they wouldn't come back. No, I'm playing th' stranger to Buck. Somebody's goin' to pay me for it, too. An' th' pay'll not be in money but in results. I won't starve, not as long as people like to play cards. I quit that, you know; but if I do play, it'll be part of my bigger game."

"I feel sorry for th' card-playin' population if you figger you ought to eat," smiled Hopalong, reminiscently.

"If I'd 'a' knowed about Buck, I'd 'a' gone to Montana 'stead of comin' here, an' saved some valuable time," Tex observed.

"But as far as that goes, Tex, they can't do much before Spring, anyhow," Hopalong remarked, thoughtfully. "An' it's yore own fault," he added. "We wanted to send you th' news occasionally, but you never let us know where you was. We'd 'a' liked to hear from you, too."

"Yes, I reckon I've got time enough; besides, I need th' exercise," agreed Tex.

"How is it you never wrote?" asked Hopalong, curiously.

Tex left his seat and walked to the door. "Take a walk with me—this ain't no place to tell a story like that."

"I've got somethin' better 'n that—I want to go down to th' H2 an' see my father-in-law for a couple of minutes. Never met him, did you? We can ride slow an' have lots of time. Be with you in a minute," and Hopalong hastened to ask his wife if she had any word to send to her father. He joined Tex at the bunkhouse, now deserted except for Lee Hop, and in a minute they left for the H2. As they rode, Tex told his story.

"This is going to be short an' meaty. When I left here I struck Kansas City first, then Chicago, spending a few days in each of them. I'd heard a lot about New York, an' headed for it. I hadn't been there very long before I met a woman, an' you know they can turn us punchers into fool knots. Well, I courted her four days an' married her—oh, I was plumb in love with her, all right. She was one of them sweet, dreamy, clingin' kind—pretty as hell, too. I had a good job by then, and for most a year I was too happy to put my feet on this common old earth. I never gambled, never drank, and found it not very hard to quit cussing, except on real, high-toned occasions. But I never could get along without my gun. Civilization be damned! There's more crooks an' killers in New York than you an' me ever saw or heard of. Once I was glad I had it—didn't have to shoot, though. Th' man got careless an' let his gun waver a little an' was lookin' at th' works in *mine* before he knowed it. He didn't want no money— what he needed was a match, an' he was doin' it to win a bet—or so he palavers. I takes his stubby .32

an' kicks him so he'd *earn* that bet, an' lets him go. I had to laugh—him stackin' agin *me* at that game!

"Well, I got promoted, an' had to travel out of town every two weeks. I'd be gone two days an' then turn up bright an' smilin' for my wife to admire. Once I was wired to come back quick on account of somethin' unexpected turnin' up, an' I lopes home to spend that second night in my own bed. I remember now that I wondered if th' wife would be there or at her mother's.

"She was there, but she wasn't admirin' *me*. I saw red, an' th' fact that I didn't go loco proved that I ain't never goin'. But th' trigger hung on a breath an' *he* knowed it. He was pasty white an' couldn't hardly stand up. Then th' shock wore off an' he was th' coolest man in town.

" 'What are you goin' to do about it?' he asks, slowly. 'Yo're wife loves *me*, not you. She's allus loved me—you never really reckoned she was in love with *you*, did you?'

"*I* was shocked then, only I was wearin' my poker face an' he couldn't see nothin'. 'Why, I did think, once in a while, that she loved me,' I retorts. 'I certainly kept you hangin' 'round th' gutter an' *sneakin'* in, anyhow. When I get through with you they'll find you in that same gutter.'

" 'Goin' to shoot me? I *ought* to have a chance. I ain't got no gun—you see, I ain't wild an' woolly like you,' an' he actually grinned!

" 'What kind of a chance did *I* have, out of town an' not suspectin' anythin'?' I asks.

" 'But she *loves* me; don't you understand? She was *happy* with me. What good will it do *you* if you kill me an' break her heart? She'll never look at you again.'

" 'I reckon she won't anyhow,' I retorts. 'Leastwise not if I can help it. Look here: Don't you know you deserve to die?'

" 'That's open to debate, but for brevity I'll say yes; but I want a chance. I gave *you* a chance every time I came here—you didn't take it, that's all.'

" 'I'll get you a gun, damned if I won't,' I replied, an' backed toward th' valise where my big old Colt was. But he stops me with a sneer.

" 'I said a *chance*! You was *born* with a gun in your hand, an' it'd be pure murder.'

" 'I'm glad somethin's pure,' says I. Then I remembered that old valise again. Remember th' last thing I did for you an' Peters before I quit, Hoppy?"

Hopalong thought quickly. "Yes, you an' Pete put in two days settin' poisoned cows in th' brush on th' west line. Did a good job, too. Ain't been bothered none by wolves since."

Tex chuckled. "There was a bottle of yore stuff in that warbag an' it was half full. I don't remember puttin' it there, but there she was. So I takes it an' holds it up for him to look at, readin' th' label out loud. That was th' only time my wife says a word, an' she says *his* name, sorrowful; then she goes on lookin' from him to me an' from me to him.

"He laughs at me an' sneers again. 'Think I'm goin' to eat that?' he says.

"I don't answer. I'm too busy workin' with one hand an' watchin' him. I knowed he didn't have no gun, but there was chairs an' bottles a-plenty. I got down a bottle of bitters an' poured some of it in a couple of glasses. Then I drops in some pain-killer an' stirs it up. It doesn't mix very well, so I pushed th' remains of their supper to one side an' slips th' two glasses under th' table cloth, holdin' one edge of it in my teeth so it wouldn't touch th' glasses an' let him follow 'em. If they'd been cards I'd 'a' spread 'em monte-fashion under his nose—but they wasn't.

" 'Now, you skunk—take your pick an' don't wrangle no more about yore chances. An' you drink it before I drink mine, or I'll blow yore cussed ribs loose!'

"I had given him credit for havin' a-plenty nerve, but now I sees it wasn't nerve at all—just gall. He was pasty white again, almost green, an' his little soul plumb tried to climb out of his eyes. I was a whole lot surprised at how he went to pieces an' I was savagely elated at th' way he was a-starin' at that cloth. He looks at me for an instant and then back at th' little shell game on th' table an' he says in a weak, thin voice: 'How'd I know—you'll drink—yourn?'

" 'You ain't supposed to be knowin' anythin' about my habits while I've got this gun—an' it's gettin' plumb heavy, too,' I retorts. 'You've been yellin' about an even break, an' there it is. An' if it'll hurry things any I'll pick up my glass now an' drink it as soon as I see yore glass empty, an' yore Adam's apple bob enough. We won't have to wait very long before we get results. You'll pick yore glass an' drain it or you'll stop lead.' An' I didn't care, Hoppy, which one he got—I was worse'n dead then—what th' hell did I care about livin'?

"I reached out to get my glass as soon as he had his'n an' I laid th' gun on my knee, knowin' he didn't have no weapon, an' that I could get th' drop before he could swing a bottle or chair. But I knowed wrong. He was a liar. As I touched my glass his hand streaks for his hip pocket. I gave him th' liquor in his eyes an' lunged for his gun hand just in time. Then I lets loose all th' rage that was boilin' in me an' when I gets tired of punishin' him, I throws him at th' feet of th' woman, picks up both guns, gets what personal duffle I need, an' blows th' ranch. His face was even all over, his nose was busted, his teeth stuck in his lips, an' he had a broken gun-wrist that gave somebody a whole lot of trouble before it worked right again, if it ever did. I'm glad I didn't shoot him—there was a lot more of satisfaction doin' it with my naked hands. It was man to man an' I played with him, with all his extra twenty pounds. By God, I can feel it yet!"

During the short pause Hopalong looked steadily ahead with unseeing eyes, his face hard, his eyes narrowed, and a tightness about his lips that told plainly what he felt. To come home to that! He realized that his companion was speaking again and gave close attention.

"I don't know where I put in th' next week, but when I got rational I found myself in a cell in a Philadelphia jail, along with bums and crooks. I found that I'd beat up a couple of policemen when I was drunk. When I got ready to leave th' town I didn't have a whole lot of money, so I played cards with what I had an' left th' town as soon as I had my fare—which didn't take long. That bunch never went up agin' such a well trained deck in their lives."

This time Hopalong broke the silence that ensued, his hand dropping unconsciously on his friend's arm in warm, impulsive sympathy. "By God, what a deal! It's awful, Tex; awful!"

"Yes, it was—an' it ain't exactly what you'd call a joke right now. But I ain't worryin' none about th' woman—she killed my love stone cold that night. But when I think of how things *might* 'a' turned out if she'd been square, of th' home I'd 'a' had—but hell, what's th' use, anyhow? Now what hurts me most is my pride an' conceit—an' th' way I turned to th' drink an' cheatin' so easy. It makes me mad clean through to think of what a infant I was, how I played th' fool for th' Lord knows how long; an sometimes I want to kill somebody to sort of get square with myself. Up north I'll be too busy tryin' to make fools out of other people to do much in th' line of sympathizin' with myself—an' too busy an' cautious to break back to drink an' cards. That was one of th' things drove me back here—there's a whole lot more temptation facin' a man back East, an' 'specially a feller that's totin' a big load of trouble."

"Don't it beat all how different luck will run for different people?" marvelled Hopalong, thinking of his portion.

"That was runnin' in my mind while I was eatin'," replied Tex. "Reckon I *did* get sort of quiet. But I'm plumb glad th' right kind of luck came yore way, all right."

They rode on for a short time, each busy with his own thoughts, and then Hopalong looked up. "We're goin' up to see Buck just as soon as I feel th' ranch is in proper shape. I've got to get th' round-up out of th' way first. You see, we ain't had no honeymoon trip yet."

"Yo're lucky again; I never could see no joy in hikin' over th' country changin' trains, livin' in hotels, sleepin' in a different bed every night, each one worse'n th' one before, lookin' after baggage, an' workin' hard all th' time. I've often wondered why it is that two people jump into all that trouble just as soon as they get into their own little heaven for th' first time." Then Tex's face grew earnest. "Now, look here, Hoppy: You ain't goin' up to see Buck till I tell you to come. I know you, all right; just as soon as you land you'll be out gunnin' for th' bunch that's tryin' to bust Buck's game. You ain't single no more—yo're a married man, an' when a man's got a wife like yourn he naturally ain't got no cussed business runnin' 'round puttin' hisself in th' way of gettin' killed. You let yore gun get plumb dusty an' when you want any excitement, go out an' try to make water run up hill, or somethin' simple like that. You handle th' trouble that comes to you, an' don't go off a-lookin' for it."

They spent the rest of the time in discussing the status of the married man, and when Mary afterward learned of the stand Tex took she shared more of her husband's affection for him. After a short stay at the H2 they turned homeward and went thoroughly into the matter of Tex's ride north. It was agreed that extra precaution would do no harm, and in order to have no blunder on the part of any one, they decided that it was best not to say anything about where he was going. Hopalong was greatly pleased and relieved now that he knew that his old foreman would have some one to help him fight his battles on that cold, distant range; but he did not appear to be as cheerful about it as was his companion. Tex looked forward to the trip with all the eagerness and impatience of a boy and it showed in his conversation and actions.

When they reached the ranch house at dusk they found Mary cooking a very small meal, and she waved them off. "You an' Billy-Red can't eat here to-night: yo're goin' to eat with th' boys in th' bunkhouse. I wouldn't spoil your fun for anything. Now you get right out—I mean just what I say!"

"But, girl—" began Hopalong.

"Now I've made up my mind, an' that's all there is about it. I can get along without you this once—I won't do it again, you know—an' I want you boys to have a rousin' good time all by yoreselves. I want th' boys to like me, Billy-Red, to feel that I ain't changed *everythin'* by bein' here. Now you clear out—Lee knows all about it, an' I cooked some goodies this afternoon for th' feast. Johnny cleaned out th' cake tins an' scraped th' bowls I mixed th' fillin' in—I had to drive him away. Look! There he is, leanin' up against that tree watchin' for me to set somethin' out to cool. He purty near got away with a pie—oh, he's terrible! But he's a good boy, just th' same."

Tex turned, emitted a blood-curdling yell and started for the anxious Johnny, Hopalong close behind, while Mary stood in the door and watched the fun, laughing with delight. The outfit piled out of the bunkhouse, caught sight of Johnny pounding towards them, and joined in, much to the Kid's disgust. They did not know anything about the affair, but they did not have to know—Johnny was legitimate prey for all, at any time and under any conditions. The fleeing youngster was nearly caught twice as he dodged and doubled, but once past them, he drew away with ease. When the winded and laughing pursuers finally stopped, he circled around to the nearest corral, found a seat on the gate and watched them straggle back to the bunkhouse, deriding them with cheerful abandon, dissecting them with a shrewd and cutting tongue. He took them up in rotation and laid bare their faults and weaknesses until they leaned against the wall and laughed at each other until the tears came. Then he turned to ridicule.

"An' there's Skinny," he continued, slowly and gravely, while he rolled a cigarette. "Th' only way you can see him, except at noon, is to look at him in front, or at his feet. Why, I grabbed a broom in th' dark one time an' shore apologized before I realized that it wasn't him at all. When he sits down he looks like a figger four, an' I'm allus a-scared he'll get into one pant's laig by mistake. When he eats solid stuff he looks like a rope with a knot in it—it's scary watchin' them knots go down—looks like he was skinnin' hisself. You can't tell whether he's comin' or goin'—th' bumps is all alike. His laigs is so long he looks like a wishbone an' I'm holdin' my breath most of th' time for fear he'll split. When he goes huntin' all he has to do is to stand still so th' game won't see him; it wanders up to see what's holdin' up th' hat. He put Pete's pants on once when he fell in th' crick—after he fell in—an' lifts my hat when I saw th' ridin' skirts. His laigs are beautiful—except for them knobs halfway down where they hinge. An' when he swallers a mouthful of water he looks like a muscle dance. Why, I got into his bunk one night by mistake an' spent five minutes a-tryin' to smooth out a crease in th' blanket. Then he wakes up an' tells me to go over an' scratch Red for a change. Tells me to git off'n him, 'cause I'm flattenin' him out. That can't be did, an' he knew it, too.

"What *you* laughin' at, Red? You ain't got no laugh comin'. Every mornin' you sit on th' bunk an' count yore clothes an' groan. You put yore hat on first an' yore boots next. Then you takes off th' boots so yore socks can get on. Then th' boots go on again. Then they come off again to let yore pants go on, after which on go th' boots again. Then you take yore hat off to let th' shirt slip over yore head an' it goes right back on again. I've seen you feel around for yore suspenders for five minutes before you remembered they was under th' shirt."

"Yo're another! I don't wear no suspenders!"

"No, you don't. Not now, but you did. You quit 'em 'cause they cost a dollar a pair an' kept gettin' lost under th' shirt. Now when you dress up you lift *my* suspenders. Tex never saw you in love. I did; lots of times; about twice a month. You put th' saddle on th' corral wall, close th' horse, an' mount th' gate. You eat coffee with a knife an' sugar th' water. When I wake up first I see you huggin' th' pillow, which is my old coat wrapped around my old pants. If anybody says 'patience,' you bust yore neck a-lookin' for her. What did you do up to Wallace's that time when his niece came on to visit at his ranch? Wallace told me all about it, an' all about th' toothbrush, too. Lemme see if you remember good. Didn't you—"

"You never mind about me rememberin'," Red shouted, grabbing up a bucket of water off the wash bench and starting for his tormentor. Johnny leaped down and backed off, dodging behind the corral wall. As Red made the turn he fell sprawling, the water affectionately clinging to him. When he arose and looked around Johnny was entering the bunkhouse door and the rest of the outfit clung together trying to hold themselves up, and voiced its misery in wails. At that moment Lee Hop buck-jumped around the corner on his trip from the cook shack to the corral, his favorite place of refuge when the ranch house was cut off from him, and he saw Red too late. When he was able to think he was minus a shirt and Red was carrying him under one arm and the shirt under the other.

"Now, you heathen—get that grub on th' table or I'll picket you an' Johnny to th' same stake!" Red threatened, grimly.

"Him get clake. His stealie pie. Alle same in klitchen. Eat chop-chop!" wailed the cook. He was promptly dropped and looked up in time to see a rush for the cook shack. But Johnny was placing the delicacies on the table and close scrutiny failed to discover anything wrong with them, notwithstanding the suspicious manner in which his tongue groomed his teeth.

The supper was a howling success, and unlike the usual Bar-20 meals, was prolonged, and fun seasoned every dish. Even Lee Hop, incapable as he was of grasping most of the points in their rapid flight, and not wholly in sympathy with certain members of the outfit—even his countenance lost its expression of constant watchfulness; his mouth widened into a grin whose extremities were lost somewhere in the region of his back hair; his eyes gleamed like jet buttons in a dish of mush; and his moisture-laden skin shone until, altogether, his head resembled nothing so much as a pumpkin-bogie, a good-natured one, with an extra large candle lighted inside. He was tempted now and again to insert a remark in the short openings, but experience checked him in time. When the crowd filed into the living room it was to tell tales of men living and dead; stories that covered a great range of human action, from the foolishness of "Aristotle" Smith to the cold ferocity and cruelty of Slippery Trendley and Deacon Rankin. The hours flew past with astonishing speed and when Tex looked at his watch he stared for a moment and returned it to his pocket with a quick, decisive movement.

"It's past midnight, fellows, an' I'm ridin' on in the mornin'," he remarked, arising.

The crowd looked its amazement and then vociferously announced its regret. These men held it a breach of etiquette to question, and because there were no "whys" or "wherefores," Tex felt impelled to explain. He was going on to see old friends, but he would return. The Bar-20 was his range and he would get back as soon as he could. In deference to his wishes and to let him get as much sleep as possible, the outfit quietly prepared for rest, and Hopalong, bidding them goodnight, departed for the ranch house.

Breakfast over the next morning, Tex rode north, followed by an escort of friends of which any man would have been proud. Hopalong and Mary rode at his side and behind in a compact bunch came the boys. They stopped when the river trail was reached and Tex shook hands all around.

"I'm sorry to leave you, Hopalong," he said earnestly; "but you know how it is: I've been away quite a spell and things happen quick out here. You'll see me again this Summer an' I'll come to stay if you want me. Mary, I'm mighty glad to see he's got such a good foreman—he's needed one a long time; an' I can see a big improvement in him already."

"Reckon you might profit by the example—must be girls a-plenty out in this country who'd make good foremen," she replied, laughing.

Tex's face showed no trace of hurt as the chance arrow sped to the mark; he laughed, pointing at Johnny. "I reckon there are; but the Kid wouldn't give me no show."

"We'll answer for him, Tex," chuckled Red. "We cured him once before an' we'd be shore glad to do it again."

"Yep—kept him in the hills, starvin' an' freezin' for a whole month," sweetly added Skinny.

Johnny flushed and squirmed but had no time to retort, Pete and the others being too busy talking to Tex to let him be heard. Finally Tex backed off, raised his hat, and with a bow and a smile to Mary, wheeled and loped off along the trail to run Spring a race to Montana. Every time he looked back he waved in answer to his friends, and then, swiftly mounting a rise, was silhouetted for an instant against the white clouds on the horizon and as swiftly dropped from sight, a faint chorus of yells reaching him.

The outfit turned slowly to return to their ranch and when they missed their foreman, they saw him sitting silent where they had left him, his wife's hand on his arm. He could still see Tex against the sky, clear cut, startlingly strong and potent, and he nodded his head slowly. "He's needed up there, an' he's the best man to go." Turning, he was surprised to find his wife so near and he smiled joyously: "Wouldn't go an' leave me all alone, would you, Honey? Yo're shore a thoroughbred an' I'm plumb proud of you. Race you to th' bunch!"

CHAPTER II

H. Whitby Booth Is Shown How

IF ANY man of the Bar-20 punchers had been brought face to face with George McAllister he would have suffered the shock of his life. "Frenchy?" he would have hesitated, "What in —? Why, Frenchy?" And the shock would have been mutual, since Frenchy McAllister had been dead some months, a fact of which his brother George was sorrowfully aware. Yet so alike were they that any of Frenchy's old friends would have thought the dead come to life.

A distinguishing feature was the eyeglasses which George had long found necessary. He took them off and laid aside his book as the butler announced Mr. Booth.

H. Whitby Booth entered the room with the hesitating step of one who has a favor to ask. A tall, well-set-up man of the blonde type of so many of his countrymen, his usual movements were slow when compared with the nervous action of those in the hustling city of Chicago. Hesitation gave him the appearance of a mechanical figure, about to run down. Mr. McAllister's hearty welcome did not seem to re-assure him.

"Ah—Miss McAllister—ah—is not at home," he volunteered, rather than questioned.

The older man eyed him quizzically. "No," he agreed, "she and Mrs. Blake are out somewhere; I am not just sure where. Shall I inquire?"

"No, oh no. I rather wanted to talk to you, you know—that is—ah—"

"Sit down, Whitby, and relieve your mind. Cigars on that table there, and some whiskey and fizz. Shall I ring for brandy?"

"Awfully good of you, really. No, I—I think I'll go in as I am. The fact is I want Margaret—Miss McAllister—and I thought I'd ask if you had any ob-jections."

"Margaret has."

"Oh, I say!"

"Fact, she has. Might as well face the music, Whitby. The truth is just this: It's less than a week ago since Margaret was holding you up as a horrible example. Margaret comes from a line of hustlers; she has not had common sense and national pride bred out of her in a fashionable school; and she looks with extreme disfavor on an idler."

"But I say, Mr. McAllister, you don't think—"

"No, my boy, I don't think where Margaret is concerned—Margaret thinks. Don't misunderstand me. I like you, Whitby. Confidentially, I believe Mar-garet does, too. But I am quite sure she will never marry a man who does nothing and, as she ex-pressed it herself, lives on an allowance from his fa-ther."

"Then I understand, sir, you have no objections?"

"None in the world—because I believe you will strike your gait before long and become something of a hustler yourself. But let me tell you, Margaret doesn't deal in futures—I'm used to it—but she insists on a fact, not a probability."

Whitby drew a breath which was largely expressive of relief. "In that case, sir, I'll try my luck," and he arose to say good night.

"You know where to find them?"

"Rather! I was going there when I had spoken to you."

"I see," said Mr. McAllister, somewhat grimly, remembering the other's greeting. "Sit down, Whitby. The night is young, you can't miss them, and I am so sure of the badness of your luck that I should like to give you a little encouragement to fall back on." Whitby resumed his seat and Mr. McAllister puffed thoughtfully at his cigar for a few moments before speaking.

"Not to go too far back," he began, "my grandfather was a boy when his father took him from Ireland, the birthplace of the family, to France, the birthplace of liberty, as the old man thought. Those were stirring times for that boy and the iron of life entered into him at an early age. He married and had one son, my father, who thought the liberty of this country so much better than that of France, that he came here, bringing his young wife with him; the wife died in giving birth to my younger brother, John. All that line were hustlers, Whitby. They had to be, to keep alive. Margaret knows their history better than I do and glories in it. You see?"

Whitby nodded mournfully. He was beginning to lose confidence again.

"My father would have been alive today but for an unfortunate accident which carried off both him and my mother within a few days. My brother and myself were found pretty well provided for. My share has not decreased. In fact I have done very well for a man who is not avaricious. But I had to fight; and more than once it was a close call, win or

lose. Margaret knows all that, Whitby, and the dear
girl is as proud of her father, I do believe, as of any
who went before him. Her mother left us very soon
and Margaret has been my companion ever since
she could talk. Are you beginning to understand?"

"I am, indeed," was the reluctant acknowledgment.

"Very good. Then here is where you come in."
His face clouded and he was silent so long that
Whitby looked up inquiringly. The motion aroused
McAllister and he continued:

"My brother was strange. I have always thought
his birth had something to do with it; but however
that may be, he was, in my opinion, peculiar in
many of his ways. The choice of his path in life was
quite on a par with his character: he invested every
dollar he had in land out West, he and a partner
whom I have never seen, bought and paid for land
and stock at a time when Government land was
used by any one without payment of any kind and
when livestock raising was almost an unknown in-
dustry, at least in that part of the country. But that
wasn't all. He went out to the ranch and took his
delicate young wife with him, a bride, and lived in a
wild region where they saw only Indians, outlaws,
and those who were worse than either." His face
hardened and the hand he laid on the table trembled as he turned to face his listener. "Worse than
either, Whitby," he repeated. "The Indians were bad
enough at times, God knows, but there is excuse for
their deviltry; there could be no excuse for those
others.

"One reason John gave for going West was that
the life would bring health to his wife. It did so. A
few months' time saw her a robust woman. And
then John returned to the ranch one day to come
upon a scene that drove him crazy, I verily believe.
No need to go into it, though I had the details from

his partner at the time—John did not write me for years. They both started out after the murderers and wandered over a great part of this country before finding the chief fiend. Even his death brought no peace to John. He would never go back to the old place nor would his partner, out of feeling for him. After much persuasion I got them to put matters into my hands, but so many years had passed that I found the ownership in dispute and it is but lately that I have succeeded in regaining title. It was too late for John, who died before I came into possession, but his partner, a man named Peters, has gone up there from a Texas ranch to run the place. He is half owner and should be the best man for the job. But—and my experience with those Westerners places emphasis on that 'but'—I do not really know just what kind of a man he is. I am putting quite a large sum of money in this venture, relying upon Peters' knowledge and hoping for a square deal. And if he is the best man for the place, you are the best man I know to show me that. Don't interrupt.

"I know right well what Margaret will tell you tonight, and if you want to make her change her mind, you could have no better opportunity than I offer. My brother's history is an abiding grief with Margaret, and if you go out there and make good you will surely make good with her.

"That's all. If I'm right, come and see me tomorrow at the office. I will have everything noted down for you in writing. Commit it to memory and then destroy the notes; because you would be valueless if any one interested discovered you were acting for me. And don't see Margaret after tonight before you go."

He arose and held out his hand. Whitby grasped it as he stood up and looked frankly at him. "It's awfully good of you, Mr. McAllister," he declared. "You've left me deuced little hope, I must say, but there's no knowing where you are if you don't ask, is there? And if I come a cropper I'll try your way and chance it."

"You'll find my way is right. I've made mistakes in my life but never any where Margaret was concerned. Good night."

Whitby stood at the top of the steps, slowly drawing his right-hand glove through his gloved left hand, time after time, casting a long look before he leaped. The driver of his hired *coupé* eyed him with calculating patience, observing to himself that if this were a specimen of the average Englishman, England must be a cinch for a cabman. Whitby had not yet arrived at the leaping stage when another *coupé*, a private one with a noticeably fine team, stopped in passing the house, and a voice hailed him: "Hello, Whit! What are you mooning there for?"

Whitby smiled: for all his consideration he had been pushed in at the last. He slowly descended the steps while he replied: "Evenin', Wallie. I was just going to drop in on the Sparrows."

"Good enough! Me, too. Jump in here and let your wagon follow. Do you hear, you driver? Trail in behind—unless you won't need him, Whit."

"Oh, let him come along. I—ah—I may be leaving rather early, don't you know."

"That so? Me, too, I'm darned glad I met you, Whit. I'm in a regular blue funk—Brown is sulky as a bear. He's been driving me about for an hour, I should say, and he doesn't understand it. Fact is, Whit, I'm going to ask a girl to marry me tonight, and I don't want to, not a little bit; but if I don't, some other fellow will, and that would be—well, worse."

"By Jove! Marry you *tonight*! Do you fancy she will?"

"No, you 'bloomin' Britisher.' *Ask* her, not marry

her, tonight. For the love of Moses! Do you think it's
an elopement?"

"Well, I didn't know, you know," and his tone was
one of distinct disappointment. "You seem to be
pretty certain she'll have you."

"Oh! She'll have me right enough, but I've got to
ask first and make sure. There're too many others
hanging around to suit me."

"I say, old chap, I hope you won't mind my asking
but—it isn't Miss McAllister, by any chance, is it?"

Wallie turned in his seat and stared at the anxious
face of Whitby for a few moments, then he broke
into shouts of laughter. "You, too," he managed to
say; and at last: "No, you trembling aspirant, it isn't,
by any chance, Miss McAllister. Margie and I are
good friends, all right, but not in that way. Oh, you
sly Johnnie! Why, I'll bet a hundred you're up to the
same game, yourself. Own up, now."

"I think a great deal of Miss McAllister, a very
great deal. If I thought she'd have me I'd ask her the
first opportunity."

"And that will be in a few minutes. She's bound to
be there—and here we are. Wish me luck, Whit."

"I do, with all my heart, Wallie," and he was very
serious in his earnestness.

"Same to you, Whit, and many—no, not that, of
course." They were in the rooms by this time, both
pairs of eyes wandering, searching this way and
that as they moved toward their pretty hostess
whose recent marriage seemed to have increased, if
possible, her popularity with the male sex; she
stood so surrounded by a chaffing crowd of men
that they found difficulty in getting near her. They
did not linger, however, as each caught sight of the
object of his pursuit at the same time, and their
paths parted from that moment.

The maturity of Margaret McAllister's mind would
never have been suspected from her appearance.

The pale green satin gown, overhung with long draperies of silk-fringed tulle, the low round satin corsage being partly veiled by a diagonal drapery of the same transparent material, and ornamented—as was the skirt—with a satin scarf, tied with knots of ribbon and clusters of water-lilies—this formed a creation that adorned a perfect figure of medium height, whose symmetry made it seem smaller than it really was. The Irish temperament and quickness of intelligence were embodied in a brunette beauty inherited from her French ancestry; but over all, like the first flush of morning's light on a lovely garden, lay the delicate charm of her American mother. One of a group of girls, with several men hovering on the outer circle, she detached herself upon Whitby's approach and advanced to meet him.

"Good evening, Mr. Booth. Aren't you late?"

"Yes, rather." Whitby drew comfort from the fact that she had chosen to notice it.

"Aunt Jessie is over this way. She is complaining of the heat already. Perhaps you would better mention it."

"Mrs. Blake? I will. I've a favor to ask of Mrs. Blake. Let's join her."

Mrs. Blake was of that comfortable age, size, and appearance which expressed satisfaction with the world and its ways. She affected black at all times with quite touching consistency; doubly so, since gossip hinted at a married life not altogether happy. However, her widowhood did not permit derogatory remarks concerning the late Mr. Blake, who made up to her in dying all his shortcomings when alive; and she had proven a discreet chaperon for Margaret from the assumption of that position. Her most conspicuous weakness was endeavoring to overcome a growing embonpoint with corsets, and the tight lacing undoubtedly had much to do with her susceptibility to heat. Whitby was a favorite with

her and she greeted him warmly, closing her waving
fan to tap him with it now and again in emphasis.

But Whitby's purpose would not wait; as soon as
the chance offered he begged free, and arose to the
occasion with a daring that surprised himself. "I am
going to hide up with Miss McAllister for quite a
time, Mrs. Blake. If any one comes bothering, just
put him off, will you? That is, if Miss McAllister
doesn't mind."

"Mind? Of course she doesn't mind. Run along,
Margie, and for Heaven's sake, don't sit in a draft—
though I don't believe you can find one in this
house," and the fan was brought into more vigorous
action at the reminding thought.

"Well, I don't know, Mr. Booth," remonstrated
Margaret as they moved away. "They will begin to
dance very soon and I promised Wallie Hartman the
opening. You came in together, didn't you?"

"Oh, Wallie! Yes, he was pretty keen on getting
here but I rather fancy he's forgotten about that
dance, you know."

"What makes you say that? What mischief are
you two brewing?"

"Ah—it's Wallie's secret, you know,—that is, his
part of it is—I say, here's the very spot."

They had made the turn behind the stairs, where
a punch bowl stood; the space immediately behind
the stairs being too low in which to stand comfort-
ably upright, a mass of foliage was banked in a half
circle, outside of which the stand and punch bowl
were placed; inside, a thoughtful hostess had arranged a *tête-à-tête*, quite unnoticeable from without. Whitby's attention had been drawn to it by the
couple who had emerged upon their approach, the
girl radiant and the man walking on air, of which details Whitby was entirely oblivious. Margaret was
more observing and she looked after Wallie with a
dawning look of understanding and then at Whitby

with a quick glance of apprehension. There was no time to protest, even if she would, as Whitby had led her behind the leafy screen before she fully realized the import of his action.

Like many slow starters, Whitby, when once in movement, set a rapid pace. He came to the point now with promptitude:

"Miss McAllister, I arrived late because I called on your father before coming here, to ask his permission to address you. I must say he rather dashed my hopes, you know. He doesn't think I'm such a bad sort—he doesn't object in the least—but he seemed to fancy his daughter Margaret would. I—I hope he is mistaken."

She turned to him a face in which the eyes were slowly filling with tears, nor did she remove the hand upon which his rested, on the curving back of the seat. It was not her first proposal, by several, but there was a vibrating earnestness, an unexpected tenderness in this big, slow Englishman which told her she was going to hurt him seriously when she spoke. And she did not want to hurt him; with all her heart and soul she wished she did not have to hurt him.

"I'm not worthy of you, Margaret. I don't think any man is worthy of a good woman, and I'm just an ordinary man. But I'll *be* worthy of you, from tonight—and that whether you say yes or no.

"You know I love you. You must know I left London and came over here to follow you. But you don't know how much I care for you—and I can't tell you. I'm a duffer at this sort of game—like everything else—I never did it before—and 'pon my word, I don't know how. But if I could say what I feel, then perhaps, you might know better. What is it to be, Margaret? Wait a bit! If you feel doubtful, I'll wait as long as you want me to. But—but—I'm afraid it's no go." He sat looking dumbly at her, hop-

ing for some sign of encouragement, but there was
no misreading the answer in her face.

It was a long minute before she spoke. She was
unnerved by the hysterical desire to put her arms
around him and soothe him as she might a hurt
child. Something of her embarrassment was con-
veyed to him and with the wish to save her the pain
of refusing in words he started as if to rise. She
stopped him with a gesture.

"Wait. I *will* say what I want you to know. I like
you—no! not in that way; not the way a woman
should—the man she expects to marry. Perhaps if
you had been—I am not sure—but I could *not* marry
a drone. Oh! why don't you wake up! How *can* you
go on from day to day with no thought but self-
indulgence? You say you love me. Ask yourself: Is
not that merely a form of self-indulgence? Oh, I
know you would take care of me and defer to me
and let me have my way in everything—you are
that kind of a man—but to what end? That I might
be the more pleasing to you. Is it your purpose to
dawdle through life, taking only such pains as shall
make things more pleasing to you?"

"Is that all, Margaret? Is it only because you fancy
I'm a loafer?"

"But you are! You are! Oh! I don't know—I'm not
sure—"

"I'm sure!" the exulting certainty in his voice startled her. "I'm sure!" he repeated. "I may be a bit of
an ass in some things but no woman would care as
you care, what a man was or what he did unless she
loved him. You love me, Margaret, thank God! Give
me a chance. You're only a girl, yet. Give me a year
and if I go under, or you find I'm wrong, I'll thank
you for the chance and never blame you. Will you?"

Her heart was pounding in suffocating throbs and
she trembled like a leaf in the wind before the eager
intensity of his gaze. A strong will held her in check,

else she had given way then and there, but she faced him with a fine bravery. "Yes," she promised, "I will. Go away and make good."

"Make good! By Jove, that's what your father said. Make good—I'll not forget it." His head bent low in an old-fashioned but becoming salute while her free hand rested unfelt for an instant upon the yellow hair, a gesture that was at once a blessing and a prayer.

CHAPTER III

Buck Makes Friends

THE TOWN of Twin River straggled with indifferent impartiality along the banks of the Black Jack and Little Jill branches where they ran together to form the Jones' Luck River, two or three houses lying farther north along the main stream. The trail from Wayback, the nearest railway point, hugged the east bank of Jones' Luck, shaded throughout its course by the trees which lined the river, as they did all the streams in this part of the country: cottonwoods mostly, with an occasional ash or elm. Looking to the east, the rolling ground sloped upward toward a chain of hills; to the west, beyond the river, the country lay level to the horizon. On both sides of the trail the underbrush grew thick; spring made of it a perfect paradise of blossoms.

Boomerang, pet hobo of Twin River and the only one who ever dared to come back, left Little Nell's with his characteristic hurried shuffle and approached the wooden bridge where the Wayback

trail crossed the Jill, and continued south to Big
Moose. Boomerang was errand boy just now, useful
man about the hotel or one of the saloons when necessity drove, at other times just plain bum. He was
suspected of having been a soldier. A sharp
" 'tention" would startle him into a second's upright
stiffness which after a furtive look around would re-
lax into his customary shambling lack of backbone.
He had one other amusing peculiarity: let a gun be
discharged in his vicinity and there was trouble
right away, trouble the gunner was not looking for;
Boomerang would fly into such a fury of fighting
rage, it was a town wonder that some indignant cit-
izen had not sent him long ago where he never
could come back.

Coming to the bridge he looked casually and from
habit along the trail and espied a horseman riding
his way. He studied him reflectively a few seconds
and then spat vigorously at something moving on
one of the bridge planks, much as the practiced
gunman snaps without appearing to aim. "Stranger,"
he affirmed; "Cow-punch," he added; "Old man," he
shrewdly surmised, and shook his head; "Dunno
'im," and he glanced at the stain on the plank to see
what he had bagged. Among his other pleasing human habits "Boom" used tobacco—as a masticant—
there was the evidence of the fact. But he had
missed and after a wistful look for something to in-
spire him to a more successful effort, he shuffled
on.

The horseman came at a steady gait, his horse, a
likely-looking bay with black spots, getting over the
ground considerably faster than the cow-ponies
common to the locality; approaching the bridge he
was slowed to a walk while his rider took in the
town with a comprehensive glance. A tall man, lean
and grizzled, with the far-seeing, almost vacant eye
of the plainsman, there was nothing, to any one but

such a student of humanity as "Boom," to indicate his calling, much less his position in it. The felt hat, soft shirt and rough, heavy suit, the trousers pushed into the tops of his boots, were such as a man in the town might wear and many did wear. He forded the stream near the bridge at a walk. Pop Snow, better known as Dirty, cleverly balancing himself within an inch of safety in front of the "I-Call" saloon, greeted him affably: "Come a long way, stranger?" asked Dirty.

"From Wayback," announced the other and paused in interested suspense. Dirty had become seized with some internal convulsion, which momentarily threatened disaster to his balance. His feet swung back and forth in spasmodic jerks, the while his sinful old carcass shook like a man with the Chagas fever. Finally a strangled wheeze burst from his throat and explained the crinkle about his eyes: he was laughing.

"Wayback ain't fur," he declared, licking his lips in anticipation of the kernel of his joke about to come. "You can a'most see it frum here through the bottom uv—"

"How d'you know it ain't?" the horseman abruptly interrupted.

Dirty was hurt. This was not according to Hoyle. Two more words and no self-respecting "gent" could refuse to look toward Wayback through a glass—and certainly not alone. The weather was already too cold to sit fishing for such fish as this; and here was one who had swallowed the bait, rejecting the hook.

"Why, stranger, I been there," explained Dirty, in aggrieved remonstrance.

"How long since you been there? Not since two-at-once, was you? Didn't it used to be at Drigg's Worry? Didn't it?"

Snow lost his balance. He nodded in open-mouthed silence.

"Course it was—at Drigg's Worry—and now it's way back," and with a grim chuckle the stranger pressed in his knees and loped on down the trail to the Sweet-Echo Hotel.

Dirty stared after him. "Who in hell's that?" he asked himself in profane astonishment. "It's never Black Jack—too old; an' it ain't Lucky Jones—too young. He sure said 'two-at-once.' Two-at-once: I ain't heard that in more'n twenty years." His air-dried throat compelled inward attention and he got up from his box and turned and looked at it. "Used to be at Drigg's Worry, didn't it?" he mimicked. "Didn't it? An' now it's way back." He kicked the box viciously against the tavern wall. "Darn yer! This yer blasted town's gettin' too smart," and he proceeded to make the only change of base he ever undertook during the day, by stamping across the bridge to the "Why-Not."

The door of the I-Call opened and a man appeared. He glanced around carelessly until he noticed the box, which he viewed with an appearance of lively interest, coming outside and walking around it at a respectful distance. "Huh!" he grunted. Having satisfied himself of its condition he drawlingly announced it for the benefit of those inside. "Dirty's busted his chair," he informed, and turned to look curiously after Pop Snow, who was at that moment slamming the door of the Why-Not behind him.

Through the open door three other men came out. They all looked at the box. One of them stopped and turned it over with his thumb. "Kicked it," he said, and they all looked across at the Why-Not, considering. A roar from behind them smote upon their ears like a mine blast: "Shut that door!"

With one accord they turned and trooped back again.

The rider meanwhile was talking to his horse as he covered the short distance to the Sweet-Echo Hotel. "Wonderful climate, Allday. If twenty years don't wear you down no more'n old Snow you'll shore be a grand horse t' own," and he playfully banged him alongside the neck with his stirrup. Allday limited his resentment to a flattening of the ears and the rider shook his head sorrowfully. "Yo're one good li'l hoss but yore patience'd discourage a saint." He swung off the trail to ride around the building in search of a shelter of some kind, catching sight of Boomerang just disappearing through the door of the barroom. "Things has been a-movin' 'round Twin River since Frenchy an' me went after Slippery an' his gang: bridges, reg'lar hotels, an' tramps. An' oblige *me* by squintin' at th' stable. If Cowan'd wake up an' find that at th' back door, he'd fall dead."

He dismounted and led his horse through the stable door, stopping in contemplation of the interior. He was plainly surprised. "One, two, three, four," he counted, "twenty stalls—twenty tie-'em-by-th'-head stalls—no, there's a rope behind 'em. Well, I'm damned! He ain't meanin' to build again in fifty years; no, not never!"

Allday went willingly enough into one of the stalls—they were nothing new to him—and fell to eating with no loss of time. Buck watched him for a few moments and then, throwing saddle and bridle onto his shoulder, he walked back the way he had come and into the hotel bar. No one noticed him as he entered, all, even the bartender, being deeply intent on watching a game of cards. Buck grunted, dropped his belongings in a corner, and paused to examine the group. A grand collie dog, lying near the stove in the middle of the room, got up, came and sniffed at him, and went back and lay down again.

The game was going on at a table close to the bar, over which the bartender leaned, standing on some elevation to enable him to draw closer. Only two men were playing. The one facing Buck was a big man, in the forties, his brown hair and beard thickly sprinkled with gray; brown eyes, red-rimmed from dissipation, set wide apart from a big, bold nose, stared down at the cards squeezed in a big hand. The other man was of slight build, with black hair, and the motions of his hands, which Buck had caught as he entered, were those of a gambler: accurate, assured, easy with a smooth swiftness that baffled the eye. He was dressed like a cow-punch; he looked like a cow-punch—all but the hands; these, browned as they were, and dirty, exhibited a suppleness that had never been injured by hard work. Buck walked up to the bar and a soft oath escaped him as he caught sight of the thin, brown face, the straight nose, the outstanding ears, the keen black eyes—Buck's glance leaped around the circle of onlookers in the effort to discover how many of the gambler's friends were with him. He was satisfied that the man was playing a lone hand. There was a tenseness in the air which Buck knew well, but from across the hall came a most incongruous sound. "Piano, by God!" breathed Buck in amazement. The intentness on the game of those in the room explained why he had seen no one about the place and he was at a loss to account for the indifference of the musician.

At the big man's left, standing in the corner between the bar and the wall, was a woman. Her blonde hair and blue eyes set off a face with some pretensions to beauty, and in point of size she was a fitting mate for the big man at whom she stared with lowering gaze. Close to her stood the hobo, and Buck rightly concluded he was a privileged character. Surrounding the table were several men quite evidently punchers, two or three who might be miners, and an unmistakable traveling salesman of that race whose business acumen brings them to the top though they start at the bottom. Buck had gauged them all in that one glance. Afterward he watched the gambler's hands and a puzzled expression gradually appeared on his face; he frowned and moved uneasily. Was the man playing fair or were his eyes getting old? Suddenly the frown disappeared and he breathed a sigh of relief: the motion itself had been invisible but Buck had caught the well-remembered preliminary flourish; thereafter he studied the faces of the others; the game had lost interest, even the low voices of the players fell on deaf ears. His interest quickened as the big man stood up.

"I'm done," he declared. "That lets me out, Dave. You've got th' pile. After tonight I'll have to pound leather for forty a month and my keep." He turned to the woman, while an air of relief appeared among the others at his game acceptance of the loss. "Go on home, Nell. I won't be up yet a while."

"You won't be up at all," was the level-voiced reply.

"Eh?" he exclaimed, in surprised questioning.

She pushed past him and walked to the door. "You won't be up at all," she repeated, facing him. "You've lost your pile and sent mine after it in a game you don't play any better than a four-year-old. I warned you not to play. Now you take the consequences." The door slammed after her. "Boom" silently opened the door into the hall and vanished.

The big man looked around, dazed. No one met his eye. Dave was sliding the cards noiselessly through his fingers and the rest appeared fascinated by the motion. The big man turned to the bartender. "Slick, gimme a bottle," he demanded. Slick complied without a word and he bore it in his hand to the table behind the door, where he sat drinking alone, staring out morosely at the gathering darkness.

Buck dropped into the vacated chair and laid his roll on the table. "The time to set in at a two-hand game of draw," he remarked with easy good nature, "is when th' other feller is feelin' all flushed up with winnin'. If you like to add my pile to that load you got a'ready, I'm on." He beamed pleasantly on the surrounding faces and a cynical smile played for a moment on the thin lips of the man facing him. "Sure," he agreed, and pushed the cards across the table.

"Barkeep, set 'em up," said Buck, flicking a bill behind him. Slick became busy at once and Buck, in a matter-of-fact manner, placed his gun on the table at his left hand and picked up the pack. "Yes," he went on with vacuous cheerfulness, "the best man with a full deck I ever saw told me that. We crossed trails down in Cheyenne. They was shore some terrors in that li'l town, but he was th' one original." He shook his head in reminiscent wonder, and raised his glass. "Here's to a growin' pile, Bud," and nodding to the others, who responded with indistinct murmurs, the drink was drained in the customary gulp. "One more, barkeep, before we start her," he demanded. "I never drink when I'm a-playin'." Here he leaned forward and raised his voice. "Friend, you over there by th' winder, yo're not drinkin'."

The big man slowly turned his head and looked at Buck with blood-shot eyes, then at the extra glass on his table. "Here's better luck ner mine, friend— not wishin' you no harm, Dave," and he added the drink to the generous quantity he had already consumed. Buck waved his hand in acknowledgment, then he smiled again on his opponent.

"Same game you was playin', Bud?" he asked, genially.

"Suits me," was the laconic reply.

Buck raised the second drink. "Here's to Tex Ewalt, th' man who showed me th' error of my ways." The tail of his eye was on Dave.

The name of Tex must have shocked him like a bucket of ice water but he did not betray it by so much as the flicker of an eyelid. Ewalt and he had been friends in the Panhandle and both had escaped the fate of Trendley and his crowd more by luck than merit. Buck knew Dave's history in Texas, related by Ewalt himself, who had illustrated the tell-tale flourish with which Dave introduced a crooked play; but he did not know that Dave Owens was Black Jack, returned after years of wandering, to the place of his nativity.*

Buck shuffled the cards slowly and then with a careful exaggeration of the flourish, dealt the hand in a swift shower of dropping units. A sigh of appreciation escaped the observant group and this time Buck got results: at sight of the exaggerated flourish an involuntary contraction of the muscles hardened the deceptively boyish form and face of the younger man and the black eyes stared a challenging question at the smiling gray ones opposite before dropping to the cards he had unconsciously gathered up.

Luck smiled on Buck from the start. He meant that it should. Always a good player, his acquain-

---

*The boy and girl history of David Jones (Black Jack) and his sister, Veia (called Jill), was well known to some of the old timers who went to Montana in the first gold rush and stayed there. It was difficult to get them to tell it and one was sorry to have heard it, if successful.

tance with Tex, who had taught him all he knew of crooked plays, had made him an apt pupil in the school in which his slippery opponent was a master. With everything coming his way Buck was quite comfortable. Sooner or later the other would force the fighting. Time enough to sit up and take notice when the flourishing danger signal appeared.

It came at last. Dave leaned forward and spoke. "Cheyenne, how'd jackpots strike yer? I got ter hit th' trail before six an' it's pretty nigh time to feed."

"Shore!" assented Buck, heartily.

The pot grew in a manner scandalous to watch. "Double the ante," softly suggested Dave.

"Shore," agreed Buck, with genial alacrity.

"Double her ag'in."

"Double she is," was Buck's agreeable response.

Pass after pass, and Slick stretched out over the bar and craned his neck. At last, with a graceful flourish a good hand fell to Buck, a suspiciously good hand, while Dave's thin lips were twisted into a one-sided smile. Buck looked at him reproachfully.

"Bud, you should oughter o' knowed better'n that. I got six cards."

The smile faded from Dave's face and he stared at the cards like a man who sees ghosts. The stare rose slowly to Buck's face, but no one could possibly suspect such grieved reproach to be mere duplicity. It was too ridiculous—only Dave knew quite well that he had *not* dealt six cards. "Funny," he said. "Funny how a man'll make mistakes."

"I forgive you this once, but don't do it no more," and Buck shuffled the cards, executed a particularly outrageous flourish, and dealt.

"Ha! Ha!" barked Bow-Wow Baker. "Darn if they ain't both makin' th' same sign. Must belong to th' same lodge."

Chesty Sutton dug him in the ribs with an elbow.

"Shut up!" he hissed, never taking his eyes from the game.

Dave passed and Buck opened. Dave drew three cards to two high ones. Buck stood pat. Dave scanned his hand; whatever suspicion he might have had, vanished: he had never seen the man who could deal him a straight in that fashion. He backed his hand steadily until Buck's assurance and his own depleted cash made him pause, and he called. Buck solemnly laid down four aces. Four!— and Dave would have taken his oath the diamond ace had been on the bottom of the deck before the deal—and Buck had not drawn cards.

"They're good," said Dave shortly, dropping his hand into the discard. "If you're goin' to stay around here, Cheyenne, I'll get revenge tomorrer." He started to rise.

"Nope, I guess not, Bud. I never play yore kind of a game with th' same man twice."

Dave froze in his position. "Meanin'?" he asked, coldly.

"I don't like th' way you deal," was the frank answer.

"Darn you!" cursed Dave. His hand flew to his gun—and stopped. Over the edge of the table a forty-five was threatening with steady mouth.

"Don't do it, Bud," warned Buck.

Dave's hand slowly moved forward. "A two-gun man, eh?" he sneered.

"Shore. Never bet on th' gun on th' table, Bud. You got a lot to learn. Hit her up or you'll be late—an' down where I came from it's unhealthy to look through a winder without first makin' a noise."

"Yore argument is good. But I reckon it'd be a good bet as how you'll learn somethin' in Twin River you ain't never learned nowhere else." Dave sauntered carelessly to the front door.

"You ain't never too old to learn," agreed Buck,

sententiously. The front door closed quietly after
Dave and half a minute later his pony's hoofs were
heard pounding along the trail that led toward Big
Moose.

"Cheyenne, put her there! I like yore style!"
Chesty Sutton, late puncher for the Circle X, shoved
his hand under Buck's nose with unmistakable
friendliness. "*I* like th' way *you* play, all right."

"Me, too," chimed in Bow-Wow. "Dave Owens has
got th' lickin' of his life. An' between you an' I, Cheyenne, I ain't never seed Dave get licked afore—not
reg'lar."

The chorus of congratulations that followed was
so sincere that Buck's heart warmed toward the
company. Chesty secured attention by pointing his
finger at Buck and wagging it impressively. "But you
hear me, Cheyenne," he warned. "Dave ain't no quit-
ter. He's got it agin' you an' he's hell on th' shoot. I
ain't never heerd of his killin' nobody but he's right
handy spoilin' yore aim. Ain't he, Bow-Wow?"

"Look a-here. How often have I told you? You sez
so. He *is*. Don't allus leave it to me." Bow-Wow's
tone was indignant as he rubbed his right arm reflectively.

"Gentlemen, I'm not sayin' a word against anybody, not one word," and Slick glanced from man to
man, shaking his head to emphasize his perfect belief in the high standard of morality prevalent in
Twin River. "But I begs leave to remark that *I* like
Cheyenne's game—which it is th' first time in my
brief but eventful career that I seen five dealt cards
turn into six. You all seen it. It sure happened. Mr.
Cheyenne, you have my joyous admiration. Let's
celebrate. An' in th' meantime, might I inquire, without offense, if Cheyenne has a habit of complainin'
of too many cards?"

They had lined up before the bar and all glasses
were filled before Buck answered. Slick stood di-

rectly before him and every face, showing nothing beyond polite interest, was turned his way. But Buck well knew that on his reply depended his position in the community and the gravity of the occasion was in his voice when he spoke.

"Gentlemen, Mr. Slick was called. There's two ways of playin'. When I plays with any gentleman here, I plays one way. Dave Owens played th' other way. I played his game."

He glanced at the silent figure by the window, set down his glass, and started to cross the room. Chesty Sutton put out his hand and stopped him. "I wouldn't worry him none, Cheyenne. Ned Monroe's th' best boss I ever worked for but hard luck has been pilin' up on him higher'n th' Rockies since he lost his ranch. Better let him fight it out alone, friend."

Lost his ranch—Ned Monroe—Buck's intention was doubly strengthened. "Leave it to me," was his confident assurance, and he strode across the room and around the table in front of the window. The somber eyes of the big man were forced to take notice of him.

"Friend, it's on th' house. Mr. Slick is a right pleasant man, an' he's waitin'." A rapid glance at the bottle told him that Monroe, in his complete oblivion, had forgotten it. Ned eyed him with a puzzled frown while the words slowly illumined his clouded mind. At length he turned slowly, sensed the situation, and rose heavily to his feet. "Sure," was the simple reply.

At the bar significant looks were exchanged. "I'm beginnin' to *like* Cheyenne," declared Slick, thoughtfully, rubbing the palm of his left hand against the bar; "which his persuadin' language is fascinatin' to see."

"It sure is," Chesty Sutton endorsed promptly,

while the others about him nodded their heads in silent assent.

"Well, gentlemen," said Slick, "here's to th' continued good health of Mr. Cheyenne." Down the line ran the salutation and Buck laughed as he replaced his empty glass.

"I shore hope you-all ain't tryin' to scare me none," he insinuated; "because I'm aimin' to stop up here an'—who in hell's poundin' that pie-anner?" he broke off, turning to glare in the direction of the melancholy sound.

"Ha! Ha!" barked in his ear, and Buck wheeled as if he had been kicked. "That's Sandy," explained Bow-Wow Baker. "He thinks he's some player. An' he is. There ain't nothin' like it between here an' Salt Lake."

"Oh, yes; there is," contradicted Buck. "You an' him's a good team. I bet if you was in th' same room you'd set up on yore hind laigs an' howl." Bow-Wow drew back, abashed.

"Set 'em up, Mr. Slick," chuckled the salesman.

"Don't notice him, Cheyenne," advised Chesty in a disgusted aside. "He don't mean nothin' by it. It's just a habit. It's got so I'm allus expectin' him to raise his foot an' scratch for fleas," and he withered the crestfallen Bow-Wow with a look of scorn.

"You was sayin' as how you was aimin' to stop here," suggested Ned Monroe, his interest awakened at thought of a rising star so often following the fall of his own.

"Yes," acknowledged Buck. "If I find—"

Crash! Ding-dong! Ding-dong! The noise of the bell was deafening. Buck set down his glass with extreme care and looked at Slick with an air of helpless wonder, but Bow-Bow was ready with the explanation. "Grub-pile!" he shouted, making for the side door, grasping hold of Chesty's hand as he went out and dragging that exasperated puncher after him by strength of muscle and purpose. "Come on, Cheyenne! No 'angel-in-th'-pot,' but a good, square meal, all right."

Chesty Sutton cast behind him at Buck a glance of miserable apology, seized the doorframe in passing, and delivered to Bow-Wow a well-placed and energetic kick. Relieved of the drag of Chesty's protesting weight and with the added impetus of the impact of Chesty's foot, Bow-Wow shot across the wide hall, struggling frantically to regain his equilibrium, and passed through the door of the dining room like a quarter-horse with the blind staggers. The bell-ringing ended in a crash of broken crockery, succeeded by a fearful uproar of struggling and profanity.

The collie bounded to his feet, his hair bristling along his spine, and rushed at the door with a low growl. Ned caught him by the collar and held him. "Down, Bruce, down!" he commanded, and the dog subsided into menacing growls.

Chesty, at the door, snorted in derision. "Darn fool!" he informed those behind him. "He's tryin' to climb th' table. Hey, Ned; let th' other dog loose," he suggested, hopefully.

By the time the highly entertained group had gathered about the dining room door, the oaths and imprecations had resolved themselves into a steady railing. Bow-Wow sat sprawled in a chair, gazing in awed silence along the path of wreckage wrought by the flying bell; opposite him, waving a pair of pugnacious fists in close proximity to Bow-Wow's face, stood Sandy McQueen, proprietor of the Sweet-Echo. It appeared that he was angry and the spectators waited with absorbed expectancy on what would happen next.

"Ye gilravagin' deevil!" he shouted, "canna ye see an inch afore yer ain nase? Gin ye hae nae better manners na a gyte bull, gang oot to grass like thae ither cattle. Lord preserv's," he prayed, following the strained intensity of Bow-Wow's gaze, "look at the cheeny! A'm ruined!" He started to gather up the broken crockery when the roar of laughter, no longer to be restrained, assailed his outraged ears. He looked sourly at his guests. "Ou, ay, ye maun lauch, but wha's to pay for the cheeny? Ou, ay! A ken weel eneuch!"

The hilarious company pushed into the dining room and began to help him in his task, casting many jocose reproaches on the overburdened Bow-Wow. Slick returned to the barroom to clean off the bar before eating, and Buck went after him. "Hey, what have I struck?" he asked, with much curiosity. "He sounds worse'n a circus."

"He's mad," explained Slick. "Nobody on God's green earth can understand him when he's mad. Which a circus is music alongside o' him. When he's ca'm, he talks purty good American."

"You shore relieves my mind. What is he— Roosian?"

"Claims to be Scotch. But I dunno—a Scotchman's a sort of Englishman, ain't he?"

"That was allus my opinion," agreed Buck.

"Well—I dunno," and Slick shook his head doubtfully as he hung the towel onto a handy hook and stooped to come under the bar. "Sounds funny to me, all right. 'Tain't English; not by a hell of a sight."

"Sounds funny to me," echoed Buck. "I'm *shore* it ain't English. But, say, Slick; gimme a room. I'm stoppin' here an' I'd like to drop my things where I can find 'em."

"Right," said Slick, and he led the way into the hall and toward a bedroom at the rear. Chesty Sutton stood in the doorway of the dining room. "Better git in on th' jump, Cheyenne," he advised, anxiously. "Bow-Wow's that savage, he's boltin' his grub in chunks an' there ain't goin' to be a whole lot left for stragglers."

"Muzzle him," replied Buck, over his saddle-weighted shoulder, while Slick only grinned, "If I goes hungry, I eats Bow-Wow. Dog ain't so bad." Chesty chuckled and returned to the sulky Bow-Wow with the warning.

Despite Chesty's fears, there was plenty to eat and to spare. Little talking was done, as every one was hungry, with the possible exception of Ned, and even he would have passed for a hungry man. Sandy McQueen and the cook officiated and the race was so nearly a dead heat that the first to finish was hardly across the hall before the last pushed his chair back from the table.

An immediate adjournment to the barroom was the customary withdrawal, and Buck, doing as the others, found Ned in his former seat beside a table. Buck joined him and showed such an evident desire for privacy that the others forbore to intrude.

"Ned," said Buck, leaning towards him across the table, "it ain't none of my business, an' it ain't as I'm just curious, but was that straight, what you said about bein' broke?"

"That's straight," Ned assured him, gloomily.

"An' lookin' for a job?" asked Buck, quietly.

"You bet," was the emphatic reply.

"Chesty said as how he used to work for you. Was you foreman?"

"I was foreman an' boss of the NM ranch till them blood-suckers back East druv me off'n it—darn 'em."

"Boss, was you? Then I reckon you wouldn't refuse a job as foreman, would you?"

Ned's interest became practical. "Where's yore ranch?" he asked, with some show of eagerness.

"Why, I was aimin' to stop 'round here some'rs."

"Hell! There ain't a foot o' ground within eighty

mile o' where yo're sittin' as ain't grazed a heap
over, less'n it's some nester hangin' on by his fingers an' toes—an' blamed few o' them, neither.
Leastaways, none but th' NM an' Schatz's range,
which they says belongs to th' old Double Y, both of
'em."

"What's keepin' them free?"

"'Bout a regiment o' deputies, I reckon." He
smiled grimly. "It's costin' 'em somethin' to keep th'
range free o' cattle. Mebby you could lease it. That
McAllister feller ain't never goin' to get a man to
run it for long. Some o' th' boys is feelin' mighty
sore an' Schatz is a tough nut. It's goin' to be a
mighty big job, when he starts, an' that's certain."

"I'd like to see it. We'll go t'morrow."

Buck's careless defiance of the situation pleased
Ned. With the first evidence of good humor he had
shown he hit Buck a resounding slap on the back.
"That's you," was his admiring comment.

The door opened to admit the short, broad figure
of a man who, after a glance around the room, made
his bow-legged way to their table. His tone betrayed
some anxiety as he asked: "Ned, haf you seen mein
Fritz?"

"Nope," answered Ned, "I haven't, Dutch. Hey,
boys!" he called, "Anybody seen Pickles?"

A chorus of denials arose and Chesty sauntered
over to get details. "W'y, you durned ol' Dutch Onion, you ain't gone an' lost him again, have you?"

"Ach! Dot leetle *Kobold*! Alvays ven I looks, like a
flea he iss someveres else."

"How'd you lose him?" demanded Chesty.

Dutch stole a look askance at Ned and turned on
Chesty a reproachful face. He laid a glove on the
edge of the table. "Dot's Fritz. I turn 'round, like
dot," suiting action to word, in a complete turn, his
right hand reaching out, taking up the glove and
whirling it behind his back as he faced the table

again. He looked at the empty spot with vast surprise, in delicious pantomime.

The glove, meanwhile, had fallen against the nose of Bruce, who sniffled at it and then picked it up and carried it to Slick behind the bar, returning to his resting place with the air of a duty accomplished.

Dutch continued to stare at the table for several seconds. Then he glanced around and called: "Fritz! Fritz! *Komm' zu mir*—und Fritz iss gone," he finished, turning to those at the table an expression of comical bewilderment. He took a couple of steps in the direction where he supposed the glove to be. Bruce was just lying down. Dutch looked more carefully, stooping to see along the floor. A light broke in on him. He straightened up and excitedly declared: "Yoost like dot! Yoost like der glove iss Fritz: I know ver he iss bud I can't see him."

"Dutch, come here." Ned's voice was stern and Dutch approached with hanging countenance. "Where was you when you 'turn 'round like dot'?" asked Ned.

"Only a minute, Ned; yoost a minute!"

"Where?"

"In Ike's I was; yoost a minute."

"Ain't I told you to keep out o' there?"

Dutch moved his feet, licked his lips, and cleared his throat; words seemed to fail him.

While he hesitated the door opened again, something more than six inches, and Boomerang squeezed through. He shuffled up to Dutch and touched him on the shoulder. "Hey, Dutch, I been chasin' you all over. Pickles went home wit' Little Nell, see? An' she sent me ter tell you."

"Vat! mit dot—" he broke off and turned to Ned. "I begs your pardon, but Fritz, he iss leetle—he learn quick. Right avay I go." He was at the door when Slick hailed him.

"Hey, Dutchy, this yourn?" The other caught the tossed glove, and nodded.

"Yah, first der glove, soon iss Fritz," and the door closed behind him.

"Good as a circus," laughingly declared Buck. "About pay now—how would eighty a month hit you, for a starter?"

"Fine," declared Ned.

"Then here she is, first month," and Buck handed it over. "Will that be enough to square up what you owe?" he added.

"W'y, I don't owe nothin'," declared Ned.

"Well—now—I was just a-thinkin' 'bout th' lady as seemed right vexed when you dropped yore roll to Dave." He looked casually at Slick, behind the bar, while he was saying it.

"Little Nell? I don't owe her nothin', neither. It was my pile,—all of it."

Buck heaved a sigh of relief. "I'm right glad to hear it. Then you'll be all ready to hit th' trail with me in th' mornin'?" he asked.

"Shore; but s'pos'n you can't get th' ranch?" suggested Ned.

"I'll get it. An' when I get it I'll run it, too, less'n they load me with lead too heavy to sit a horse—then you'll run it." His smile was infectious.

"Cheyenne, I like yore style. Put 'er there," and he shoved a huge, hairy fist at Buck. "'Nother thing," he went on, "Chesty an' Bow-Wow was a-goin' over to th' Bitter Root. I'll tell 'em to hang 'round for a spell. Them's two good boys. So's Dutchy—when he ain't a-runnin' after Pickles."

"All right; you talk to 'em. See you in th' mornin'," and with a general good night, Buck went to his room.

Chesty and Bow-Wow joined Ned to have a "night cap" and say good-bye, intending to start early next morning. "No, boys, I've had enough," said Ned.

"I've took a job with Cheyenne, an' you boys better hang 'round. Find Dutch in th' mornin' an' tell him. An' I'm a-goin' to turn in, too. I'm cussed sleepy." The other two sat staring across the table at one another. The news seemed too good to be true.

"Ha! Ha!" barked Bow-Wow, "I never did like them darn Bitters, not nohow."

Chesty nodded his head. "Me, too," he agreed. "Son, there's a big time due in these parts: I feel it in my bones."

Seized with a common impulse they sprang to their feet and began a war-dance around the stove, chanting some Indian gibberish that was a series of grunts, snarls, and yells. Their profane demands for information meeting with no response, the others one by one joined them, until a howling, bobbing ring of men circled the stove, and, growling and barking at their heels, the dog danced with them. Slick looked on with an indulgent grin and the row did not cease until Sandy stuck his head in at the hall door. "Deil tak' ye!" he shouted. "Canna ye let a body sleep?"

A minute later the room had settled down into its customary decorum and Bruce, with a wary look about, now and then, was preparing to resume his rudely interrupted doze.

CHAPTER IV

The Foreman of the Double Y

BUCK CINCHED up his saddle on Allday and led him out of the stable. "Ned, this is shore one scrumptious hotel," he observed as he swung into his seat.

"It certainly is. Nothin' to beat it in Montany, I reckon," was Ned's hearty endorsement.

Buck shook his head as they passed through the gate together. "Most too good," he suggested.

"I dunno," Ned doubted, "th' branch from Way-back's shore to come down th' Jones' Luck, an' then Sandy'll rake in."

They had just turned into the trail when a rider passed them at speed, causing Ned's cayuse to shy and buck halfway to the Jill. The evener-tempered Allday only pointed his ears and pulled on the bit. "Reckon you could catch the feller, eh? Well, you couldn't," was Buck's careless insult. "If Hoppy could see that horse he'd give all he's got for him— bar Mary."

The horse merited his criticism. A powerful black,

well over fifteen hands, he showed the sloping thigh bones and shoulder of a born galloper, while the deep chest gave promise of long-sustained effort. His rider had pulled up at the general store just beyond the hotel and Ned joining him, Buck expressed his admiration. A moment later he added to it: "By th' Lord, Ned, *that's* a woman." The rider had dropped from the saddle and paused to wave her hand to Ned before she entered the store. Buck caught the glance from a pair of beautiful dark eyes that rested on him a moment before it fleeted past to his companion. The grave smile was well suited to the wonderfully regular features and when she turned and entered the store it was with the swinging step of perfect movement. Buck faced about with a jerk when he realized that he had actually turned in his saddle to gaze after her.

"Best horse in these parts an' th' finest woman," agreed Ned, "an' honest," he added, gruffly.

Buck stared at him, surprised. "Why, o' course! Anybody say different?" He unconsciously stiffened at the thought.

"Um—no, not as I *knows* of. Her daddy's a nester; got a quarter-section 'tother side o' Twin River, off th' trail a piece. Rosa LaFrance—pretty name, ain't it? Th' boys calls her the French Rose."

"Yes, 'tis pretty," drawled Buck. "What I'm askin' about is this recommendation o' character to *me*."

It was Ned's turn to feel surprised. He pondered as he looked at Buck. "I reckon I warn't exactly speakin' to you, Cheyenne," he explained; "more to myself, like. You see, it's this way: Dave Owens, he won that horse from McReady of the Cyclone, one night in Wayback. I wasn't there but I hears it's a regular clean up. McReady was in a streak o' bad luck and would a' lost ranch an' all but his friends hocussed his liquor an' Mac, he drops out of his

chair like somebody hit him with an axe. Next day
Rose rides into Twin River on that same horse. John,
that's her daddy, he never bought him; he couldn't.
Then how did she come by it? That's her business, I
says. That's one thing. For another, Dave Owens travels that way considerable, an' Dave ain't no company
for the French Rose. I'm too old to interfere or I durn
soon would."

Buck brooded on this situation for some time and
then burst into a laugh. Ned eyed him with stern
disapproval. "I was thinkin' of a cow-punch I know,"
explained Buck, in apology. "He'd interfere so quick,
there wouldn't be time to notify th' mourners."

Ned smiled in sympathy. "That'd do," he admitted, "but you can't jump in an' shoot up a fellow if
a girl's sweet on him, can you? It'd be just nacheraly
foolish."

"That's so," agreed Buck, "but if the French Rose
can look at that son of a thief and like him, then
Hopalong Cassidy has no call to be proud o' *hisself*."

"Eh?" questioned Ned.

"Th' name slipped out. But now's as good a time
as any to tell you. Did you ever hear o' Frenchy
McAllister?"

"Owner o' the Double Y?"

"Half owner—leastways, he was. Frenchy's dead.
You was cussin' his brother last night. I want to tell
you about Frenchy."

Buck told the story in terse, graphic sentences,
every one a vivid picture. He painted the scene of
Trendley's crime to the accompaniment of a low-
voiced growl of lurid profanity from Ned, who was
quite unconscious of it. The relentless hunt for the
criminals, extending through many months; the
deadly retribution as one by one they were found;
the baffling elusiveness of Slippery Trendley and

the unknown manner of his fate when run to earth at last—one scene followed another until Buck left the arch devil in his story, as he had left him in fact, bound and helpless, looking up at the pitiless face of the man he had injured beyond the hope of pardon, their only witnesses the silent growths of Texas chaparral and the grieving eye of God.

It was a terrible story, even in the mere telling of it. Buck's level voice and expressionless face hid the seething rage which filled him now, as always, when his thoughts dwelt upon the awful drama. Ned's judgment was without restriction: "By the Eternal!" he swore, "that hell-hound deserved whatever he got. Damned if you ain't made me sick." They rode in silence for several minutes and then: "Poor fellow! poor fellow!" he lamented. "Did you say he's dead?"

"Yes, Frenchy's gone under," answered Buck gravely. "You'd 'a' liked him, Ned."

"Yes, I reckon I would," agreed Ned. He looked at the other, considering. "Where do you come in?" he asked. Buck's narrative had failed to connect the newborn "Cheyenne" as "Frenchy's pardner."

"I'm Buck Peters," was the simple explanation.

Ned pulled his horse back onto its haunches and Buck wheeled and faced him. So they sat, staring, Ned inarticulate in his astonishment, Buck waiting. The power of coherent thought returned to Ned at last and he rode forward with outstretched hand. "Th' man as stuck to Frenchy McAllister through that deal is good enough for me to tie up to," he declared, and the grip of their hands was the cementing of an unfailing friendship. "An' I'd like for Buck Peters to tell Frenchy's brother as I takes back what I said agin' him."

Their way led through an excellent grassy country. The comparatively low ground surrounding Wayback rose gradually to Twin River and more rapidly after leaving that town. The undulating ground now formed in higher and more extensive mounds, rising in places to respectable-sized hills; usually the sides reached in long slopes the intervening depressions, but not infrequently they were abrupt and occasionally one was met which presented the broad, flat face of a bluff. The air was perceptibly colder but the bunch grass, hiding its wonderfully nourishing qualities under the hue it had acquired from the hot summer sun, was capable of fattening more cattle to the acre than any but the best lands of the Texan ranges with which Buck was familiar. Snow had not yet swept down over the country, though apt to come with a rush at any time. Even winter affected the range but little as a general rule; disastrous years were luckily few and far separated, so that the average of loss from severity of weather was small. The talk of the two naturally veered to this and kindred topics and Buck began stowing away nuggets of northern range wisdom as they fell from the lips of the more experienced Ned.

Studying the trail ahead of him, Buck broke the first silence by asking: "Ain't we near the boundary of the Double Y?"

"You'll know, soon enough. Th' first big butte we come to, some cuss'll be settin' there, hatchin' out trouble."

"That's him, then," and Buck pointed to the right where a solitary horseman showed dark against the skyline.

"Yep, that's one of 'em. Reglar garjun, ain't he?"

"Beats me how you let 'em stand you off, Ned," wondered Buck.

"Well, when we made good and sure you owned the range, Buck, there weren't no use in fighting. That McAllister would 'a run in th' reglar army next, damned if he wouldn't."

Buck chuckled. "He's sure a hard man to beat. I don't mind fighting when I have to, but I'm mighty glad it looks peaceful."

"We'll have fightin'. When I was turned off my ranch, it just about foundered me. I sold th' stock, every head, an' you saw where th' last o' th' cash went. But don't forget Smiler Schatz. He's a bigger man an' a better man nor I ever was, an' he's a-layin' low an' a-waitin'. He calculates to get you—I dunno how."

"An' I dunno how," mused Buck. "Say, Ned, I thought th' stage line ran through to Big Moose: there ain't no tracks?"

" 'Cause it crosses th' ford at th' Jack an' goes to th' Fort; then it swings round to Big Moose, an' back th' same road. Wonder who's that pointin' this way?"

Buck glanced ahead to see a moving speck disappear behind a knoll far along the trail. "Dunno; maybe another deputy," he suggested.

The distant rider came into sight again and Ned stared steadily at him. "No," he declared, "think I know that figger. Yessir! It's Smiler. I kin tell him 'most as far as I kin see him."

"That's the feller gave us the fight, ain't it?"

"Did his share—some over, mebbe. He's a hard nut."

"Well, I'm not bad at a pinch, myself, Ned; mebbe I can crack him." Ned smiled grimly at the jest and hoped he would be cracked good. Evidently there was no great liking between the quondam owners of the Double Y.

However, this was not apparent in their greeting. The steady approach had been uninterrupted and Buck looked with interest at the "hard nut" as they met.

In a land of dirty men—dirty far more frequently

from necessity than from choice—Schatz was a by-word for slovenliness nearly approaching filth. If he washed at all it left no impression on the caked corrugations of his smiling countenance. His habit of smiling was constant, so much a part of him that it gave him his name. And it had been solemnly affirmed by one of his men that he never interfered with his face until the dirt interfered with his smile; then he chipped it off with a cold chisel and hammer. This must have been slander: no one had ever seen him when it looked chipped. A big man, with a fine head, he sat in his saddle with the careless ease of long practice. "Hello, Ned!" he called, with a wave of the hand. *"Wie geht's?"*

"Howdy, Karl!" replied Ned. "How's sheep?"

"Ach! don't say it, der grasshoppers. Never vill dey reach Big Moose. Also, I send East a good man to talk mit dat McAllister to lease der range yet. Before now he say a manager come from Texas, soon. Vat iss Texas like Montana? Nodding. Ven der snow come—"

"Hol' on! This is th' manager, Mr. Buck Peters, half owner o' the Double Y, an' he's put me in as foreman."

"So—it pleases me greatly, Mr. Buck. Ned iss a good man. If you haf Ned, that iss different." He shook hands with Buck who took note of the blue eyes and frank smile of the blonde German, at a loss to discover where he hid that hardness Ned had referred to.

"Sorry I can't offer you a job," said Buck, matching the other's smile at the joke, "but from what I hear, one foreman will be a-plenty on the Double Y."

"It iss a good range—eggselent—und der iss mooch free grass ven you haf der Double Vy for der hard years; but dere iss not enough for you und for me, too, so I turn farmer. Also some of der boys, dey turn farmer. I take oud quarter-section alretty."

"Quarter-section! Turn farmer! You! Sufferin' cows! give me a drink," and Ned looked wildly around for the unattainable.

"Donnerwetter! Somet'ing I must do. To lend money iss good but not enough. Also my train vill not vait. So I say good morning und vish you luck."

Ned wheeled his horse to gaze after the departing figure and Buck sat laughing at his expression. "Luck," echoed Ned; "bad luck, you mean, you grinnin' Dutchman. Hell of a farmer you'll be. Now I wonder what's his little game."

"Aw, come on, Ned. 'Pears to me he's easy," and Allday sprang away along the trail.

"Easy, eh!" growled Ned, when he caught up, "he's this easy: him and me started even up here, 'bout th' same time. 'T wasn't long before he begun crowdin' me. Neither of us had nuthin' at first but when we quit he could show five cows to my one. How'd he do it?"

"Borrowed th' money and bought yearlin's," answered Buck.

"Yes, he did," Ned grudgingly admitted. "But I kep' a-watchin' him an' he allus branded more than th' natural increase, every round-up—an' I could never see how he done it."

"You—don't—say," was Buck's thoughtful comment. "Well, down our way when a man gets to doin' miracles on a free range we drops in on him casual an' asks questions—they don't do it twice"; and he unconsciously increased Allday's pace.

"Here, pull up," urged Ned; "this bronc's beginnin' to blow. That's a bang-up horse you've got there. No good with cattle, is he?"

"No," agreed Buck. "I got this horse because 'discretion is sometimes better than valler,' as Tex

Ewalt said when somebody asked him why he didn't shoot Hoppy. Most times I finish what I start, but once in a while, on a big job, it's healthy to take a vacation. An' I naturally expected to leave some hasty an' travel fast."

"Ain't nothin' could catch you, in these parts, not if you got a good start, less'n it's French Rose an' Swallow."

"Well, I wasn't aimin' to run far nor yet to stay long. That seems like it'd be th' ranch."

"That's her," agreed Ned.

The ranch house, rectangular and of much greater dimensions than Buck expected to find it, presented two novel features, one of which he noticed at once. "What's th' idea of a slopin' roof, Ned?" he asked.

"That's Karl's notion. See that upside down trough runs along th' high part at th' back? There ain't a foot o' that roof you can't slosh with a bucket o' water. An' you can shoot along th' walls from them cubby holes built out at each corner. Th' house is a heap bigger'n th' old one was; it used to set over yonder in that valley, but th' wipin' out o' Custer put th' fear o' God in Smiler an' he raised this place soon after. Five men could stand off five hundred Injuns."

"Where's th' water?"

Ned chuckled. "Wait till you see it. There's a well sunk at th' side an' you can pull it in without goin' outdoors if you wants to. Karl is one o' them think-of-everything fellers. He put th' ranch house on a knoll an' th' bunkhouse on another. Then, he figgers, if they wants to rush me they'll be good an' winded when they gets here. My shack is a pigpen 'long side o' this un', but I got it figgered out I needn't to stop if I don't want."

"How's that, Ned?"

"I could cut an' run any time—come night. I'll show you when we goes over there."

Bare as was the interior, the ranch house gave promise of comfort and the bunkhouse and the stable with its adjacent corral proved equally satisfactory. The fireplace of the bunkhouse was built over the bare earth and there they repaired to make a fire and eat the food they had brought with them. The added warmth was a distinct comfort but the smoke brought company on the run. They had scarcely begun their meal when a faint sound led Buck to saunter to the door and look out. Down the steep side of a high butte dropped a horseman with considerably more speed and no more care than a dislodged boulder; arriving at the bottom, his horse straightened out into a run that showed he was expected to get somewhere right away. Buck gravely bit into a sandwich the while he admired the rider's horsemanship; an admiration that was directed into another channel when the object of it slipped rifle from holster, pumped a cartridge into the barrel, and threw it forward in businesslike attitude. " 'Spects to have use for it, right so," mused Buck, and then, over his shoulder: "Better hide, Ned. Here come a garjun an' he's got his gun out."

"Th' hell he has!" rumbled Ned. "Come an' push me up th' chimley, Buck; I'm a-scared."

Buck strolled back to the fire and half a minute later the horse pounded up to the house, his rider sprang off and came through the door, gun first. He continued across the room with solemn countenance, set his gun against the wall, and went to the fire where he extended his hands to the blaze. "Howdy, Ned; howdy, stranger," was his easy greeting.

Ned, sitting cross-legged, smirked up at him.

"Howdy, Jack. You weren't going to run me off'n th'
range, was you?"

"Nope. Saw Cheyenne Charley headin' this way
'bout an hour since. Thought mebbe he'd burn her
up—Pipes o' peace!" His eyes widened as he gazed
at Ned's upturned mouth. "Bottled beer, or I'm a Injun. You lives high," and he swallowed involuntarily
as the inspiring gurgle stimulated his salivary
glands.

"I'm taperin' off on beer," explained Ned. "Got
three bottles, one for Buck and two for me. I'm big-
gest. But you can have one o' mine. Buck, this is
Jim's Jack, head garjun an' a right good sort. Buck
Peters has come to take charge of his own ranch,
Jack."

"Shake," said Jack. He glanced over the papers
Buck handed him and passed them back. All three
turned to look at the open door.

"Hang up a sign, Buck," advised Ned. "If we stops
here long enough we can start a hotel. Come in,
Charley."

The Indian stepped slowly in. "Cheyenne Charley,
Buck," said Ned; "off the Reservation for a drunk at
Twin River. You'd think he'd stop in Big Moose.
Reckon he's hungry, too; he—" Ned paused and his
eyes sought the object of Charley's steady and significant gaze. "Oh, that be damned!" he exclaimed,
swooping onto the third bottle of beer beside him
and holding it out to Buck. "He wants your beer.
Charley is a good Injun—I *think*—but 'lead us not
into temptation' "—and with the other hand he proceeded to put his share of temptation out of sight,
an example that Jim's Jack emulated with dignified
speed.

"Let him have it," said Buck, good naturedly. "I
never hankered much for beer, nohow." He passed
the bottle to the Indian, not in the least suspecting
what "an anchor he had cast to windward." The

other two exchanged a look of regretful disapproval.

Half an hour later they had separated, Buck and Ned going on to the more distant NM ranch, Jack to gather up his fellow deputies, and the Cheyenne hitting the trail for Twin River with a thirst largely augmented by the sop he had thrown to it.

CHAPTER V

"Comin' Thirty" Has Notions

UP FROM the south, keeping Spring with him all the way, rode Tex. The stain of the smoke-grimed cities was washed out of him in the pure air; day by day his muscles toughened and limbered, his lightning nerves regained their old spontaneity of action, each special sense vied with the others in the perfection of service rendered, and gradually but surely his pulse slowed until, in another man, its infrequency of beat would have been abnormal. When he rode into Twin River, toward the end of a glorious day, he had become as tireless as the wiry pony beneath him, whose daily toll of miles since leaving the far off Bar-20 was well nigh unbelievable.

Tex crossed the ford of the Black Jack behind the Sweet-Echo Hotel. Dirt had bespattered him from every angle; it was caked to mud on his boots, lay in broad patches along his thighs, displayed itself lavishly upon his blue flannel shirt, and had taken frequent and successful aim at his face; but two slits of sunlit sky seemed peering out from beneath his lowered lids, the pine-tree sap bore less vitality than surged in his pulsing arteries, his lounging seat was the deceptive sloth of the panther, ready on the instant to spring; and over all, cool as the snow-capped peaks of the Rockies, ruled the calculating intelligence, unscrupulous in the determination to win, now that it was on the side of the right, as when formerly it fought against it.

One glance at the imposing Sweet-Echo and Tex turned his pony's head toward the trail. "No, no, Son John, you'll not sleep there with your stockings on—though I shan't ask you to go much farther," Tex assured him. "I've seen prettier, and ridden cleverer, but none more willing than you, Son John. Ah, this begins to look more like our style. 'I-Call'— sweet gamester, I prithee call some other day; I would feed, not play. 'Ike's'—thy name savors overly much of the Alkali, brother. Ha! 'By the prickling of my thumbs, something wicked that way bums.' " He had turned to cross the Jill and saw Pop Snow basking in the failing sunlight. " 'Why-Not'— well, why not? I will."

"Come a long way, stranger?" asked Dirty, his gaze wandering over the tell-tale mud. He had come the wrong way for profit, but Dirty always asked, on principle: he hated to get out of practice.

Tex swung his right leg over his pony's neck and sat sideways, looking indolently at the pickled specimen who sat as indolently regarding him. "Plucked from a branch of the Mussel Shell," murmured Tex, "when Time was young"; and then drawled: "Tolerable, tolerable; been a-comin' thirty year, just about."

Dirty looked at him with frank disgust, spat carefully, and turning on his seat no more than was absolutely necessary, stuck his head in at the open door and yelled: "Hey, boys! Come on out an' meet

Mr. Comin' Thirty. Comin' is some bashful 'bout drinkin' with strangers, so get acquaint."

Scenting a tenderfoot half a dozen of the inmates strolled outside. When they saw the suntanned Tex they expressed their opinion of Dirty in concise and vitriolic language, not forgetting his parents; after which they invited Tex to "sluice his gills." One of them, a delicate-featured, smooth-faced boy, added facetiously: "Don't be afraid; we won't eat you."

Tex released his left foot from the stirrup and slid to earth. "I wasn't afraid o' bein' et, exactly," was his slow response; "I was just a-wonderin' if it would bite. I notice it's slipped its collar."

"Go to hell! Th' lot o' you!" screeched Pop, bouncing to his feet with surprising alacrity. "Wait till I buy th' nex' one o' you a drink—wait! That's all."

"Lord, Dirty, we *has* been a-waitin'. Since Fall round-up, ain't it?" appealing to the others who gave instant, vigorous, and profane endorsement.

"Pah!" exploded Pop. He faced about and executed a singular and superlatively indecent gesture with a nimbleness unexpected and disgracefully grotesque in so old a man; and then without a backward glance, he stamped off across the bridge to the I-Call. The others watched him in fascinated silence until he plumped down on his inevitable box, when the smooth-faced first speaker turned to his nearest neighbor and asked in hushed tones: "What do you think of him, Mike?"

"Fanny, me boy, if I thought I'd ever conthract Dirty's partic'lar brand o' sinfulness, I'd punch a hole in th' river—with me head," and he solemnly led the way in to the bar.

"Gentlemen, it's on me," declared Tex, "—for good and special reasons," he explained, when they began to expostulate. "Give me a large and generous glass," he requested of the barkeeper, "and fill it with 'Water for me, water for me, and whiskey for

them which find it agree.' You see, gentlemen, liquor an' I don't team no better'n a lamb an' a coyote. I must either love it or leave it alone an' I'm
dead set agin' spiritual marriage. Here's how."

"If I'd begun like that I'd be a rich man this day,"
observed Mike, when his head resumed the perpen-
dicular.

"If I'd begun like that I wouldn't be here at all," responded Tex.

"Well, ye'll have a cigar with me, anyhow. Putt a
name to it, boys, an', Fred, whisper: Pass up that
wee little box ye keep in th' locker. Me friend,
Comin', will take a good one, while he's at it."

A blue-shirted miner next him interposed: " 'T is
my trate. He'll hev a cigar with me, he well. Das'
thee thenk I be goin' to drenk with thee arl the time,
and thee never taake a drenk 'long o' me? Set un up,
Fred, my son, and doan't forget the lettle box."

Tex gazed curiously at the speaker. It was his first
meeting with a Cornishman and Bill Tregloan was a
character in more than speech. Wherever gold, or a
rumor of gold, drew the feet of miner, there sooner
or later would be Bill Tregloan. He had crossed the
continent to California on foot and alone at a time
when such an attempt was more than dangerous.
That he escaped the natural perils of the trip was
sufficiently wonderful; as for the Indians, there is no
doubt they thought him mad.

Bill had his way in paying for the order and
turned to lounge against the bar when his eye
caught sight of that which drew from him a torrent
of sputtering oaths and a harsh command. The only
one who had failed to join the others at the bar was
Charley, the Cheyenne Indian. He lay sprawled on
the floor against the opposite wall, very drunk and
asleep, and about to be subjected to one of the
pleasing jokes of the railroad towns, in this instance
very crudely prepared. The oil with which he was

soaked, had been furnished far too plentifully, and he stood an excellent chance of being well roasted when the match, then burning, should be applied.

The man holding the match looked up at the Cornishman's shout. He did not understand the words but the meaning of the action that followed was plain; and when the miner, growling like a bear, started to rush at him, his hand dropped to his gun with the speed of a hawk. Fanny promptly stuck out his foot. Tregloan went down with Fanny on top of him but it takes more than one slight boy, whatever his strength, to hold down a wrestling Cornishman. The flurry that followed, even with the added weight of numbers, would have been funny but for the scowling face of the olive-skinned man who stood with ready gun until assured the struggle had gone against his opponent. Then he slipped gun in holster and felt for another match. "Take him away," he said, with a sneering smile, "he make me sick."

"What did they do that for?" asked Tex of Mike. Neither had moved during the excitement. The rest were pushing and pulling Tregloan out of the saloon.

"That's Guinea Mike," was the explanation. "He'd murder his mother if she crossed him. First fair chanst I mane to break his damned back—an' if ye tell him so he'll kill me on sight."

"Interestin' specimen," observed Tex. Guinea Mike found another match and calmly lit it. Those not engaged in soothing Bill were looking in at the door and windows. Dutch Fred, behind the bar, was swearing good American oaths regarding the unjustified waste of his kerosene. Tex stepped away from the bar. "Blow that out," he said, dispassionately.

Guinea Mike looked up with a snarl. The two stares met and grappled. Guinea slowly raised the match to his lips and puffed it out, flipping it from

him with a snap of one finger so that it fell almost
at the feet of Tex. They watched each other steadily.
A solitary snore from the Indian sounded like the
rumble of overhead thunder. Slowly the hand of
Guinea descended from before his lips and in uni-
son with it descended the head of Fred until his
eyes just cleared the top of the bar. Guinea's hand
rested in the sagging waist of his trousers, a second, two—

The roar of the explosion was deafening. Guinea
Mike's right shoulder went into retirement and his
gun dropped from his nerveless fingers. Screaming
with rage he stooped to grasp it with his left hand
and pitched forward at full length, both kneecaps
shattered, at the mercy of this stranger who shot as
if at a mark.

The noise awakened Cheyenne Charley who
opened his eyes and smiled foolishly at the dis-
torted face which had so unexpectedly reached his
level. "Darn drunk," he observed, and immediately
went to sleep again.

Tex walked over and kicked the gun across the
floor. Irish Mike picked it up and handed it to Fred. "I
could a' killed you just as easy as I didn't, Guinea,"
said Tex. "I don't like you an' yore ways. It's just a
notion. So don't you stop. An' don't send any o'
yore friends. 'No Guineas need apply.' That goes, if
I has to Garibaldi yore whole darn country."

The spectators had filed back to the room and
were engaged in audible comments on the justifica-
tion and accuracy of the shooting, while they
busied themselves in the rough surgery which had
to serve. To the suggestion that he ought to be
taken to the doctor at Wayback, Fred interposed the
objection: "No, dake him to Nell's. Mike is a friend
mit her."

Pop Snow, attracted by the excitement, stood

peering in a window. Twin River crowded the room but Pop's resentment was still warm. A man rode up and stooped from the saddle to look over his shoulder. "Who's that? What's up?" he asked.

"'Taint nothin'; *only* Guinea Mike. See th' feller Fanny's hangin' onto? Well, that's him: Comin' Thirty has notions—an' I ain't never seen better shootin'."

Dave swung down, tied his pony to the rail and went inside to see the new bad-man of Twin River. It had been growing steadily colder during the past few hours; the wind, sweeping in from the west, held a sinister threat, the air a definite chill, and Dave felt he would be none the worse for a little fire-water. Dirty felt it also, but his senile annoyance had merely simmered down, not subsided, and he scurried back to the I-Call for cover until such time as he thought it fitting to go home.

It was very late when Dave turned a tired pony to pasture and entered the three-room cabin of Karl Schatz. The rough exterior gave no indication of the comfort with which the German had surrounded himself. Fur rugs covered the floor of the living room; the chairs and table had traveled many miles before landing here; a fine sideboard showed several pieces of fair china; mounted horns of various kinds were on the walls, one group being utilized as a gun rack, and between them hung several good paintings. A stove had been removed but in its place smoldered a wood fire, the fireplace jutting out from the wall. When Dave came in Karl sat smoking; on the table beside him lay an open volume of poems. "Vell?" he asked, as Dave dropped into a chair and stretched his legs wearily before him.

"Double Y has got a new bunch o' cattle. Hummers. Bought 'em out of a drove come up last Fall on Government contract; the Government went back on th' deal an' they was wintered up here. Got th' pick o' th' lot, I hear." Dave fell into silence and stared at the fire. Karl puffed thoughtfully while he looked at the black head whose schemes seemed coming to nought.

"Cameron's got back," continued Dave; "he's brought his money with him; took up his note at the bank; paid full interest." Another pause, with no comment from Karl. Dave continued to display his items of information in sections. "I met One-eye Harris at Eccles'.

"Th' Cyclone ranch has got some with th' itch. It'll mean a lot o' work—an' then some.

"LaFrance wants to bleed you for two hundred. Don't you. He'll get too rich to have me for a son-in-law."

Karl nodded his head. "Farming iss goot," he murmured, "—mit vasser." Dave glanced at him.

"Them new steers o' th' Double Y oughta fetch forty in th' Fall. Will, too."

"Farming iss goot," repeated Karl, "—mit vasser. Also, to lend money. But Camerons, dey pay und der money lies idle. Ven do ve eat up der Double Y, Dave?"

Dave glanced at him sullenly. "Why don't you let me kill that darn Peters? Are you afraid I'll get hurt?"

"Alvays I fear. I haf no one bud you, *du Spitzbub.* But kill him? Ach! Soon anoder manager come. Killing iss not goot, Dave. You must plan besser, *aber* I do id. Dat make you feel sheep, *du Schwarzer Spitzbub, vas?*"

"I'll get 'em. Guinea Mike's shot up."

"Vell, he iss anoder von likes killing. Who vas id?"

"Stranger. Reminded me of a feller, somehow—an' then, again, he didn't. Deals a slick hand at cards."

"Ach, cards! Alvays der cards! Who know dem besser as me? Who pay for dem so much? Cards und killing, dey are no goot."

"Well, let's roost," suggested Dave, and led the way to the inner room. Karl fastened doors and windows, put out the light, and followed him.

CHAPTER VI

An Honest Man and a Rogue

How to do it? That was the question that hammered incessantly at Dave's brain until he actually dreamed of it. Dreaming of it was the only satisfactory solution, for in his dreams matters arranged themselves with the least possible effort on his part and with little or no danger—though, to do him justice, danger was the consideration which had the least weight. But the dreams presented lamentable gaps which Dave, in his waking moments, found it impossible to bridge. Winter had given way to Spring and Buck Peters, aided by the indefatigable Ned, was rounding the ranch into a shape that already cut a figure in the county and would do so in the Territory before long.

The Double Y owed nothing to Dave. His animosity was confined strictly to Buck; but he knew that Karl was resolved to usurp ownership of the range he had come to look upon as his own. And

Dave had become imbued with the idea that his own interests demanded the realization of Karl's wishes.

Why the German had become interested in this handsome idler, so many years younger than himself, Karl could not have explained. True, he was alone in the world, he was a red fox where the other was a black one, while Dave's present sinfulness and inclinations were such as the elder man understood and sympathized with. Yet these were hardly reasons; Karl himself never would have advanced them as such. Perhaps he had it in mind to use him as a cat's-paw. Few of our likes or dislikes have their origin in a single root.

If only they could "eat up" the Double Y! Dave cursed the obsession which threatened his fortunes; he cursed the energetic Buck who was rearing obstacles in his way with every week that passed; and he cursed his own barren imagination which balked at the riddle.

No heat of the inward furnace showed in the cool gravity of his face. Sitting at a table in the crowded barroom of the Sweet-Echo, he seemed intent on mastering the difficulties of a particularly intricate game of solitaire. From time to time some of those at the same table would become interested, only to turn away again, baffled by their lack of knowledge.

The usual class of patrons was present, augmented in number, since the spring round-up was at hand and strangers were dropping in every day. Later in the evening, most of those present would gravitate to the lower end of the town where forms of amusement, which Sandy McQueen did not countenance, were common. To none of these did Dave give any attention, though he looked with interest at Tex Ewalt when he entered; the increased hum of voices and several loud greetings had taken his mind momentarily from his thoughts. Tex's reputation had lost nothing in force since the excitement of his advent.

Suddenly and for the first time Dave hesitated in his play. He looked fixedly at the Jack of Spades and removed it from the pile where it lay. He paused with it in his hand. The Jack of Spades was in doubt—so was Dave.

A querulous voice was damning Buck Peters. *"Donner und Blitzen!* Vas it my fault *der verruchter* bull break loose *und ist hinaus gegangen? 'Yah!'* says Buck, *'Yah!'* loud, like dat. Mad?—*mein* gracious! Vot for is a bull, anyhow? 'Gimme my time,' I say; 'I go.' 'Gif you a goot kick,' says Buck; 'here, dake dis and get drunk und come back *morgen.'* I get drunk und go back und break his darn neck—only for leetle Fritz."

"Leetle Fritz" sat swinging his legs, on the bar. He looked at his father with plain disapproval. "Ah, cheese it, Pap!" was his advice. "What's th' good o' gittin' drunk? Why can't you hol' y' likker like a man?"

A roar of laughter greeted this appeal, at which even Gerken smiled gleefully. He was glad that Fritz was smart, *"wie seine Mutter."*

Dave pushed the Jack of Spades back into the pack. He arose and sauntered over to the bar. "That's th' way to talk, Pickles," he endorsed, tickling the boy playfully in the ribs. "Yo're a-going to hold yore likker like a man, ain't you?"

"No sirree! Ther' ain't goin' to be any likker in mine. I promised mother."

"Bully for you!" Dave's admiration was genuine and the boy blushed at the compliment. Like many other rascals, Dave was easily admitted into the hearts of children and simple folk and women and dogs. Bruce, the collie, was nuzzling his hand at the moment and the broad foolish face of Gottleib was beaming on him. "Hi, Slick! Pickles'll have a lemonade. I'll have a lemonade, too; better put a stick in mine, I'm a-gettin' so's I need one. An' Pap'll have a lemonade, too—oh! with a stick, Pap, with a stick—I wouldn't go for to insult your stomach."

They drank their lemonades, Gottleib's face expressive of splinters, and a minute later Pickles sat alone while his father endeavored to win some of Dave's money and Dave endeavored to let him. Tex tilted his chair and with a fine disregard for alien fastidiousness, stuck his feet on the edge of the table and smiled. He almost crashed over backward at sight of a figure that entered the room from the hall. "God bless our Queen!" murmured Tex, "he's a long way from 'ome. Must be a remittance man come over the line to call on Sandy."

H. Whitby Booth swept an appraising glance over the company and, without a pause, chose a seat next to Tex. "Surprisin' fine weather, isn't it?" he observed, taking a cigar case from his pocket.

"My word!" agreed Tex, succinctly.

Whitby looked at him with suspicion. "Try a weed?" he invited.

"I don't mind if I do, old chap," and Tex selected one with a gravity he was far from feeling.

Whitby looked hard at him while Tex lit the cigar. It was a good one. Tex noted it with satisfaction.

"I say, are you chaffing me?" asked Whitby, smilingly.

It was a very good cigar. Tex had not enjoyed one as good in a regrettably long time. He blew the smoke lingeringly through his nostrils and laughed. "I'm afraid I was," he admitted, "but you mustn't mind that. It's what you're here for, the boys'll think—that is, if you don't stop long enough to get used to it."

"Oh, I don't mind in the least. And I expect to stop if the climate agrees with me."

"What's the matter—lunger? You don't look it."

"Not likely. But they tell me it's rather cold out here in winter."

"Some cold. You get used to it. You feel it more in the East, where the air's damp."

"I'm delighted to hear it. And the West is becoming quite civilized, I believe, compared with what it was."

"Oh, my, yes!" Tex choked on a mouthful of cigar smoke in his haste to assure Whitby of the engaging placidity of the population. "Why, no one has been killed about here since—well, not since I came to Twin River." Tex did not consider it necessary to state how short a time that had been. "Civilized! Well, I should opinionate. Tame as sheep. Nowadays, a man has to show a pretty plain case of self-defense if he expects to avoid subsequent annoyance."

"Ah, so I was informed. They seem quiet enough here."

"Yes, Sandy won't stand any disturbance. He's away tonight but Slick's got his orders. Know Sandy?"

"No. Is he the proprietor?"

"That's him: Sandy McQueen, proprietor, boss, head bouncer, the only—"

"I say, what's the row?"

Tex's feet hit the floor with a bang. Gottleib Gerken was shaking his fist in Dave's face, Dave sitting very still, intently watchful. *"Du verdammter Schuft!"* shouted Gerken, *"Mein Meister verrathen, was!"* He sent the table flying with a violent thrust of his foot: "I show you!"

Watchful as he was, Dave did not anticipate what was coming. As the table toppled over he sprang to his feet, the forward thrust of his head in this action moving in contrary direction to the hurtling fist of Gottleib, which stopped very suddenly against his nose. Dave staggered backward, stumbled over his chair and went crashing to the floor, where he lay for an instant dazed.

"By Jove! that was a facer," cried the appreciative Whitby. The others were ominously quiet.

The next moment Dave was on his feet, white with murderous rage. There was more than fallen dignity to revenge: Gottleib knew too much. Without the least hesitation his gun slanted and the roar of the discharge was echoed by Gottleib's plunging fall. A frenzied scream, feminine in shrillness, rang through the room. Dave's gun dropped from his hand and he sank to the floor; a whiskey bottle, flying the length of the room, had struck him on the head, and Boomerang, struggling with maniacal fury in the arms of several men, strove to follow his missile. At the other end of the bar the numbed Pickles suddenly came to life and leaped to the floor. Caught and stopped in his frantic rush across the room he kicked and struck at his captor. "Lemme go!" he shrieked, "lemme go! I'll kill the—" The men holding Boomerang ran him to the open hall door and gave him forcible exit and the stern command to "Git! an' keep a-goin'."

A sullen murmur swelling to low growls of anger formed an undertone to the boy's hysterical cries, as the men looked on at Tex's efforts to revive the stunned culprit. "Lynch him!" growled a voice. "Lynch him!" echoed over the room. "Lynch him!" shouted a dozen men, and Tex ceased his efforts and came on guard barely in time to stop a concerted rush. Straddling the recumbent figure, his

blazing eyes shocked the crowd to a standstill. With
a motion quicker than a striking rattler a gun in either hand threatened the waverers. "Dutchy's got a
gun," he rebuked them; "he was a-reachin' for it
when he dropped."

"That's correct," agreed a backward member. "Sure.
I seen him a-goin' for it," affirmed another. They gathered about Gottleib to look for the proof.

Suddenly the door was flung open and Rose
LaFrance stood in the opening. "What are you
doing?" she questioned. "What is the matter with
Fritz? Come here, Fritz."

The boy, released and subsiding into gasping
sobs, staggered weakly toward her. She drew him
close and folded him in her arms. The men, silent
and abashed, in moving to allow the boy to pass,
had disclosed to her the figure of the prone Gottleib
and she understood. "Oh-h!" she breathed and
looked slowly from one to another, her gaze resting
last on Tex, the fallen table hiding from her the man
he was protecting. Utter loathing was in her look
and the innocent Tex was stung to defiance by it,
throwing back his head and returning stare for
stare.

"You wolf!" she accused, in low, passionately vi-
brant tones. "Kill, kill, kill! You and your kind. Is it
then so great a pleasure to you? Shame to you for
mad beasts! And greater shame to the cur dogs who
let you do it." Her glance swept the averted faces
with blasting scorn. "Come, Fritz." She led the boy
out and the door was closed carefully after her by
a sheepish-looking individual whose position behind it and out of sight of those scornful eyes had
been envied by every man in the room.

"Well—I'm—damned!" said Tex, recovering his
voice.

" 'They that touch pitch will be defiled,' " observed Whitby, sententiously. Tex looked his resent-

ment. He felt a touch on his leg and glanced down.
Dave had recovered consciousness. "Get off me,
Comin'," he requested. "Who hit me?"

"Boomerang flung a bottle at you," informed
Tex. "How you feeling?"

"All serene. Head's dizzy," he added, swaying on
his feet. He walked to the nearest chair and sat
down. "Must 'a' poured a pint o' whiskey into me."

"Boom passed you a quart bottle," replied Tex.

Dave glanced at the inert form of Gerken as it was
carried out into the hall. "Sorry I had to do it," he
said, "but I had to get him first or go under. He
oughtn't to said I cheated him."

"I say, that's a bally lie, you know." Whitby's
drawling voice electrified the company. Those behind him hastily changed their positions. Dave, with
a curse, reached again for his gun—it lay on the
floor against the wall, where it had fallen.

"Drop it, Dave," came Slick's grating command.
"Think I got nothin' to do but clean up after you?
Which yo're too hot to stay indoors. Go outside and
cool off."

"You tell me to git out?" exclaimed Dave, incredu-
lously.

"That's what," was Slick's dogged reply. "The Britisher wants to speak his piece an' all interruptions
is barred entirely. An' don't let Sandy see you for a
month."

Dave walked over and picked up his gun. "To hell
with Sandy," he cursed. The door slammed open
and he was gone.

Slick slid his weapon back onto the shelf and proceeded to admonish Whitby. "See here, Brit, don't
you never call a man a liar 'less yo're sure you can
shoot first."

"But dash it all! The man is a liar, you know. The
German chap said 'You darn scoundrel! Traitor to

my master, eh!' There's nothing in that about cheating, is there?"

"Well, mebbe not," agreed Slick, "but comparisons is odorous, you don't want to forget that. Which we'll drink to the memory of th' dead departed. What'll it be, boys?"

CHAPTER VII

The French Rose

THE HOME of Jean LaFrance, a small cabin built principally of the ever-ready cottonwood, was located in a corner of his quarter-section, farthest from the Jones' Luck River, which formed one boundary of his farm. He had designs upon more than one quarter-section, not at that time an unusual or impossible ambition, in so far as homestead laws went. His simple plan regarding residence was to move the cabin or build against it as occasion arose. The rolling country sloped steadily upward from the river to the chain of hills farther to the east. These sent down several tributary streams, all unreliable during the warm weather with the exception of one which passed close to the cabin. The conformation of the land gave a view from the cabin of one long stretch of the trail from Twin River and several short ones; opposite the house, continuing to Wayback, the trail was lost sight of.

Thus Buck was plainly visible as he loped along

the trail on the morning following the Sweet-Echo tragedy, only no one happened to be observing him. As he disappeared behind the first rise, a pair of inquisitive young eyes, half closed in the effort of the mouth below to retain possession of far more than its capacity, arose above the level of the window sill and looked eagerly for an invitation to mischief. Seeing nothing that particularly called him, Pickles went out and into the barn.

Buck struck off the trail and rode along the path to the house. Spring had returned in force after its temporary retreat before the recent cold and the air bore whisperings of the mighty wedlock of nature; all about him the ecstatic song of the meadowlark held a meaning that escaped him, vague, intangible, but thrillingly near to suggestion; the new green of the prairie melted into the faint purple of the distant hills, beneath a sky whose blue depths touched infinity. It was a perfect day and Buck, on his errand of aid to the helpless, forgave the fences and the evidence of land cultivation which threatened the life of the range. Riding close to the door he raised his quirt—and paused.

Rivalling the meadowlarks there flowed the music of a mellow contralto voice in song. His hand dropped to his side. That the language was strange made little difference: the meaning of life almost was discovered to him as he listened.

> *"Earth has her flowers and Heaven her sun—*
> *But I have my heart.*
> *Winter will come, the sweet blossoms will die—*
> *But warm, ah! so warm*
> *Is my heart."*

> *"When the White King makes his truce with the*
>   *Gold—*
> *How dances my heart!*

All the sweet perfumes that float in the Spring
Rest close, ah! so close
In my heart."

"One day when Love like a bee, buzzing past,
Wings close to my heart,
Deep he shall drink where no winter can chill,
Content, ah! content
In my heart."

The low voice died away into silence; from afar
came the soft cooing of a dove, soothingly insistent
as the croon of a lullaby; the riotous call of the
larks arose in gleeful chorus; within the cabin were
the sounds of movement: footsteps, the pushing of
a pan across the table, and then a subdued pounding which sent Buck's thoughts whirling back into
the distant past to hover over one of his most sa-
cred memories. He sat perfectly still. How many
years had gone by since he had heard a good
woman singing over her household tasks! How very
long ago it seemed since his mother had made
bread to the tune of that same "punch, punch,
slap—punch, punch"! His stern face softened into a
tenderness that had not visited it since he was a
boy. Mother—The French Rose—it was a pretty
name.

Buck was not in the least aware of it but when a
man thus links the name of a woman with that of
his mother, it has a significance.

The faint nicker of a horse aroused Allday from
his apathetic interest in flies; he raised his head and
sent forth a resounding whinny in response; the
blare of it was yet in the air when Rose stood in the
open doorway.

I despair of picturing her to you, so difficult it is
to portray in words the loveliness of a woman's
beauty; and the charm of the French Rose was as

many-hued as the changing sky at sunset; the modulations of her voice ranged from the grave, rich tones of an organ to the melting timbre of a flute, pitched to the note of the English thrush; her very presence was as steadfastly delightful as the fragrance of a hay field, newly mown. In a long life I have known but one such woman and this was she.

First, then, she harmonized. The simple gown, turned in at the throat, with sleeves rolled high on the arms for greater freedom in her work, the short skirt impeding but little her activity of movement, covered a form meant by God to be a mother of men; and the graceful column of her neck supported a head that did honor to her form. Luster was in every strand of the black hair, against which the ears set like the petals of a flower; the contour of the face, the regularity of the features, were flawless, unless for an overfulness of the lips in repose; the natural olive complexion, further darkened by the suntan from her outdoor life, could not conceal the warm color of the blood which glowed in her cheeks like the red stain on a luscious peach; and the mystery of her dark, serious eyes had drawn men miles to the solving—in vain.

So she stood, silently regarding Buck, who as silently regarded her. When she had first come upon him, in those few moments of unaccustomed softness when the hard mask of assertive manhood had been slipped aside, her questioning gaze had probed the depths of him, wondering and warming to what it found there. Her smile awoke Buck to a sense of his rudeness and he swept off his hat with the haste of embarrassment. "I've come for Pickles," he blurted out, anxious to excuse his unwarranted presence.

"Is it—is it M'sieu Peters?" she questioned.

"That's me," admitted Buck. "Can I have him?" He smiled at the absurdity of his question. Of course she would be glad to get rid of such a mischievous little "cuss."

Rose considered. "Enter, M'sieu Peters. We will speak of it," she invited.

"I shore will," was the prompt acceptance. Buck's alacrity would have called forth hilarious chaffing from the Bar-20 punchers. It surprised himself. She set out a cup and a bottle on one end of the table and hastened to the other with an exclamation of dismay: *"Hélas, mon pain!"* and forthwith the "punch, punch!" was resumed, while Buck stared at the process and forgot to drink.

"Why do you take Fritz from me?" asked Rose.

Buck resumed his faculties with a grunt of disgust. "What's th' matter with me?" he asked himself. "Am I goin' loco or did Johnny Nelson bite me in my sleep? What was that: *'Take* Fritz?' "

This was seeing the matter in a different light. Buck ran his fingers through his hair and looked helpless. He poured himself a drink. "Take Fritz? Take anything she wants? Why, I'd give her my shirt. There I go again—" and he savagely, in imagination, kicked himself.

"You see—I sort o' reckoned," he faltered. "Dutch bein' one o' my boys—Pickles—Fritz—ought to be taken care of, an'—"

"So—and you think I will not take care of him?"

"Oh, no; ma'am. Never thought nothin' o' th' kind. You stick yore brand on him an' we'll say no more about it. Yore health, ma'am."

Rose packed the dough into the pan and set it aside. Buck watched her with rueful countenance. "Now you've gone an' made her mad," he told himself. "Guess you better stick to cows, you longhorn!"

She returned to her place and sat opposite him, her flour-stained arms lying along the table. "You shall take him, M'sieu Peters," she declared.

To Buck's remonstrance she nodded her head. *"Mais oui*—it is better," she insisted. "He grow up a man, a strong man—yes. Only a strong man have a chance in this so bad country. Yes, it is better, I call him."

"Let me," Buck interposed, and stepping to the door he cried out a yodelling call that brought Fritz scampering into the cabin with scared face: it was his father's well-known summons. Rose called him to her and put her arms about his shoulders.

"M'sieu Peters has come to take you with him, Fritz. You will go?" she asked him.

"Betcher life," said Pickles.

Buck grinned and Rose laughed a little at the callous desertion. *"Eh, bien, m'sieu*—you hear?" she said to Buck, and then, to the boy: "It please you more to go with M'sieu Peters than stay with me—yes?"

"Betcher life," repeated Pickles. "Yo're all right, but I want to be a cow-punch an' rope an' shoot. Someday I'll get that damned ol' Dave Owens for killin' dad."

"Dieu!" Rose was on her feet, gripping Fritz so hard that he squirmed. "Dave kill—Dave—"

"Sure, he done it! Who'd yeh s'pose?" Fritz wriggled loose and stood rubbing his shoulder. Rose stood staring at him until Buck pushed him out of the room, when she sank back into her chair, covering her eyes with one shaking hand.

Outside Buck was questioning Pickles. "You rid yore daddy's bronc over, didn't you? Can you rope him? Bully for you. Get a-goin' then. We want to pull out o' here right smart." Pickles was off on the run and Buck slowly entered the cabin. He went over and stood looking out the window. "I wouldn't take it so hard," he ventured. "These sort o' mistakes is bound to happen. An' it might a' been worse. It might a' been Dave went under."

Rose flung out a hand towards him. "I wish—" she began passionately and then caught back the words, horrified at her thought.

"Course you wish he hadn't done it. He hadn't oughter done it. Dutchy was a good man—an' a square man—an' Dave ain't neither—though I shore hates to hurt yore feelin's sayin' so."

"*I* know him. He is bad—bad. No one know him like me." The deep voice seemed to hold a measureless scorn. Buck wondered at this.

"Well, if you know him I'm right glad. I figgered it out you didn't."

"I know him," she repeated, and this time she spoke with a weariness that forbade further remark.

They remained thus silent until Fritz rode up on the Goat, shouting out that he was ready and long since forgetful of a scene he had not understood. Buck turned from the window. "Good-bye, ma'am, I reckon we'll drift."

Rose came forward with extended hand. "Good-bye. You will guard him? But certainly. When you ride to town, maybe you ride a little more and tell me he is well and good. It is not too far?"

"Too far! Th' Double Y ain't none too far. I reckon you forget I come from Texas."

They waved to her just before they dropped from sight down the last dip to the trail. She was watching when they came into view again at the first gap and watched them out of sight at the end of the long stretch before the bend. Then she turned back into the room and removing the demijohn and cup from the table, she stood looking at the chair where Buck had sat. *"Voilà, un homme,"* she declared, patting gently the rough back of the chair: "a true man. They are not many—no."

CHAPTER VIII

Tex Joins the Enemy

TEX SLUNG a leg over Son John and ambled away from Wayback, in the wake of Dave. His adroit and unobtrusive observance of Dave had been without results unless there were something suspicious in the long conversation held with a one-eyed puncher who rode away on a Cyclone-brand pony. Tex, however, was by no means cast down; he could not hope to pick up something every day and he already had learned the only quarter from which trouble might come to Buck. He delayed action in the hope that something tangible might turn up; and he fervently hoped that it might be before Hopalong found himself footloose from the Bar-20. Tex was quicker with his gun than most men but he possessed a real artist's love for a reason why action should occur in a certain way; if he were also able to show that it could have occurred in no other way, he found all the more satisfaction in the setting.

A loud splash in the nearby river brought his head around in the direction of the sound; through a break in the foliage a broad patch of water, seen dimly in the dusk of the evening, showed rapidly widening circles. "Walloper," commented Tex, immediately resolving to emulate that fish in the morning. "Though I certainly hope old Smiler won't come to the water below me for a drink: nice mouthful of mutton I'd make for his wolf fangs. What in thunder!—" his pony had plunged forward as if spurred. Tex got him in hand and whirled to face the unknown danger. The rush of the river, the steady wind through the trees, the elusive chirp or movement of some bird—only familiar sounds met his ear and there was still light enough to show only familiar objects. "Why, you white-legged, ghost-seeing plug-ugly!" remonstrated Tex. "Who do you think is riding you? Johnny Nelson? Then you must be looking for a lesson on behavior about now. Get along."

He rode slowly, not wishing to overtake Dave before he settled in Twin River. Tex had as much right as Dave to be riding from Wayback but he wished to avoid arousing the faintest hint of suspicion. There was no other place along the trail for Dave to stop, except the LaFrance cabin. Strange how opinions differed regarding the French Rose: from the extreme of all-bad to that of all-good. Judicious Tex, summing up, concluded her to be neither—"Just like any other woman: half heart, quarter intellect, and the balance angel and devil; extra grain of angel and she's good; extra grain of devil and she's bad." Tex, not knowing Rose personally, gave her the benefit of the doubt.

"If he stops in there I'll miss him," said Tex. "But he's bound to go on to Twin from there. If we come together in the trail, it's no harm done: Dave will never suspect me until he looks into my gun. Bet a hat he thinks I'm a pretty good friend of his." He chuckled, recalling the arguments for and against Gerken on the night of the shooting. The consensus of opinion seemed to be that Dave had been within his rights but "some hasty." This was not Tex's opinion. He chuckled again as he recalled the lurid outspokenness of Sandy McQueen's opinion which had turned the perfunctory trial into a farce and had kept Twin River on the grin for two days. "And all is fine when Sandy comes marching home," he hummed. "I'm glad they found the gun on Dutch. Peck of trouble if he hadn't been heeled. There's me, just naturally obliged to pull out Dave. If he goes under I lose touch with the old thief who stops at home. Funny they don't get at it. There's enough material in Twin River alone to wipe three Double Y's off the map, good as Buck is. Give him six months more and half Montana couldn't do it— because the other half would be fighting *for* him. Lordy! The old times! Folks have grown most surprising slow these days."

He had left the foot of the farm road half a mile in the rear when he heard the sound of a horse coming up behind him. The darkness hid Tex until the other was nearly abreast, when he hailed. "He did turn off to see Rose," reflected Tex, as he returned the greeting and Dave rode up.

"That you, Comin'?" said Dave. "I been wantin' to see you. Goin' anywhere particular?"

"No," drawled Tex. "I was just considerin' which of them shanties in Twin'd have th' most loose money."

"Bah!" scornfully exclaimed Dave, drawing along side him. "There ain't no money in Twin River. You an' me could make a good haul over in Wayback but I got somethin' better'n that. Let's go into Ike's. Ike never hears nothin' an' all th' rest is deaf, too. I want to talk to you."

Ike's was primitive to a degree but once removed from a tent. The log walls of the low, single room were weather-proofed in several ingenious ways, ranging from mud to bits of broken boxes. The bar was a rough, homemade table, the front and both ends shut in by canvas on which was painted: "Don't shoot here." Ike was careful either of his legs or his kegs. A big stove stood in a shallow trough of dirt midway between the bar and the door, accepting salival tributes in winter which developed into miraculous patches of rust in summer. Several smaller tables, likewise homemade, a number of boxes, and a few very shaky chairs completed the furnishings. It was the reverse of inviting, even in the bitter cold of winter, but Ike never lacked for customers of a sort and probably made more money than anyone in Twin River. Ike himself was a grizzled veteran of more than fifty years, sober, taciturn, not given to cards but always ready to "shake-'em-up." Dice was his one weakness at any time of the day or night. To be sure, he always won. He had them trained.

The regular *habitués* were a canny lot, tight-lipped, cautious, slow in speech and in movement, except at a crisis. The opening door was a target for every eye and not a straight glance in the crowd; each seemed trying, like the Irishman when he bent his gun-barrel, to make his eyes shoot around a corner. And they all took their liquor alike, squeezing the glass as if it were a poker hand and they were afraid to show the quality or quantity of the contents. It was usually easy to pick out an occasional caller or a stranger: he was drunk or on the way to it; Ike's regulars were never drunk.

The entry of Dave and Tex was noted in the usual manner. Dave had long been recognized as one of their kind. Tex, since his dramatic entry into Twin River, had shown no displeasing partiality for hard

work. Both were welcomed therefore, silently or la-
conically, not to be confounded with sullenly. As
they sauntered over to an unoccupied corner table,
Tex noticed Fanny sitting in a game with Bill
Tregloan, both of them much the worse for liquor,
while their three companions showed the becoming
gravity of sober winners. Fanny closed one of his
wide, woman's eyes and nodded to them with a
cheerful grin, but Bill was too far gone to notice
anything but his persistent bad luck. "Darn this
poker game," he bellowed, banging a huge fist on
the table, "If 't was Nap I might win something, but
here I've been sittin' all night, scatting my money in
the say."

Fanny laughed uproariously but the others eyed
him in silent disapprobation. What "Nap" might be
they did not know, but poker was good enough for
them.

"What'll you drink, Comin'?" asked Dave as a preliminary.

"I ain't drinkin', Dave, not never. But I'm right
ready an' anxious to hear o' that somethin' good
you've got to deal out."

"Y-e-e-a—well, it's this way," began Dave, sam-
pling his liquor in the customary gulp. He set down
his glass to ask abruptly: "Got any friends in Twin
River?"

"Nary friend—nor anywhere else," replied Tex, in-
differently. "Don't need 'em—can't afford 'em."

Dave looked hard at Tex. "What about that bunch
Fanny travels with?" he suggested.

"You said friends," was the significant answer.

"All right—all th' better. I seen you play a mighty
good game o' cards."

Tex snorted. He could not restrain it. Was it possible Dave was aiming to milk him? "I'm allus willin'
to back my play," he declared, drily.

"You won't have to back it. If yo're as good as I

hopes, I'll back it. It's this way: I want to back you agin' a man as thinks he can play. He's considerable of a dealer—considerable—an' he won't play me because he beats me once an' thinks I'm no good. He's got money, a-plenty, an' I don't want a dollar. You keeps what you wins—an' I wants you to get it all." He turned and called across the room: "Ike, flip us a new deck." The pack in his hands, he faced Tex again. "Suppose we plays a few hands an' you gimme a sample o' yore style."

Tex thrust his hands in his pockets and tipped back in his rickety chair. "Lemme get this right," he demanded. "You backs me to play, pockets th' losses, gives up th' winnin's, all to best th' other feller—on'y he mustn't win."

"You got it."

"On'y he mustn't win."

"That's what I said."

"Must be a friend o' yourn."

"Y-e-s," drawled Dave, with a sardonic smile.

"Who is it?"

"Peters o' th' Double Y."

"Ah! I've heard o' him."

"An' you an' me an' a lot more'll hear too damned much o' him if we don't run him out. He's a heap too good for Twin River."

"How'll you rope him?"

"I got a bait—best kind. They allus fall for a woman." Dave's sneering tones, as he broke open the pack, sorely taxed his companion's self-control. "What'll we play?" he continued. "Better make it 'stud.' Th' gamer a man is th' quicker he goes broke at stud an' Peters is game enough."

Tex dropped back into position and took his hands from his pockets. "I shine at stud," he remarked softly, taking the deck Dave offered him. The joker was sent spinning across the room to glance from the nose of Fanny who sat sprawlingly asleep, nodding to an empty table; the Cornishman, swearing strange oaths, had gone off some time previously; two of the others were renewing the oft-defeated attempt to dice Ike to the extent of a free drink; the rest of the inmates were attending strictly to business and if an occasional oblique glance was aimed at Tex and Dave it did not show the curiosity which may have directed it.

"He mustn't win," murmured Tex. The cards rustled in the shuffle. Dave grunted. "An' you mustn't win?" Tex inquired.

"I'm a-goin' to do all I know how to win," warned Dave.

"Oh, that o' course," sanctioned Tex. "Shift this table. I likes to see th' door," he explained.

Dave complied, looking sharply for some other reason. The lamp on the wall divided its light fairly between them. Dave was satisfied.

"Is it for love or money?" asked Tex.

"Might as well make it interestin'," suggested Dave.

Tex thought for a moment. "No," he dissented, " 'Dog eat dog' ain't no good. But we'll keep count so you can see how bad you make out."

It was no game. Tex won as he liked with the deck in his hand and his remarks on Dave's dealing were neither complimentary nor soothing. "Duced bad form, as the Britisher would say," was his plaintive remonstrance at Dave's first attempt; "you palms th' pack like a professional." Sometime later, as he ran his fingernail questioningly along the edge of the cards, he shook his head in sorrow: "You shore thumbs 'em bold an' plenteous, Dave," was his caustic comment. And then, querulously: "Darn it, Dave! don't deal me seconds. Th' top card is plenty good enough for me."

It required very little of this to cross Dave's none too easy temper. He pushed the cards away from him, pleased and annoyed at the same time. "You'll do," he declared, "if you can't clean up Peters there ain't a man in th' country as can." A sudden suspicion struck him. Tex had reached out with his left hand to pick up the deck. "Where'd you get that ring, Comin'? I never seen it before."

A swift movement of the fingers under the idly held pack and Tex extended his hand, palm up. The band of dark metal, almost unnoticeable on the brown hand, was as plain on the palm side as Dave had seen it to be on the back of the hand. "Belonged to my wife," said Tex, the cynical undertones in his voice bearing no expression in his face. "I wear it on our wedding anniversary."

"Excuse *me*," was Dave's hasty apology. He pushed back from the table. "Keep in trainin', Comin'. I'll see Rose an' start things rollin'. Jean will take you in as an old friend when we're ready. We mustn't be too thick; Peters might hear of it. Good night. I'm goin' to roost."

"Night, Dave." Tex sat fingering the cards with something very like wonder on his face. "What sort of a babe-in-arms is this for deviltry? He used to have better ideas. The cold weather up here must have congealed his brains. Break Buck Peters at stud! Maybe he plans to get us shooting. I'll bet a hat old Schatz never hatched that scheme." He took the cards over to Ike and strolled out, unseating Fanny with one sweep of his foot as he went.

Fanny arose to his feet, looking for trouble. He was sober in his legs but his ideas crossed. No one being near him, he surveyed his backless, upended chair with blinking ferocity. "Cussed, buckin' pinto! Think I can't ride you, huh? W'atcher bet?" He righted the chair and took a flying seat, all in one movement. "Huh! Ride anythin' on four laigs," he boasted. Lulled by this confidence in his horsemanship, his head began to nod again, in sleep.

Tex ambled over to the Why-Not where his entry was greeted with boisterous invitations to a game. Four bright boys had come over from the Fort and were cleaning up the crowd. Tex was ashamed of them, and said so, refusing to go to the assistance of such helpless tenderfeet. He borrowed paper and pencil of Dutch Fred and rapidly composed a note to Buck. Much adroit maneuvering secured the services of Cheyenne Charley, not yet too drunk to understand the repeated instructions of Tex. Thus it came about that Buck, without knowing how it got there, found on his table a communication of absorbing interest, signed: "A Friend." It read:

Buck Peters: Don't play cards with strangers, especially stud poker. Dave Owens aims to have Rose rope you into a frame-up. John is in it, too. Mighty easy to plug you in a row.

"A Friend," mused Buck. "An' Rose is to rope me into a crooked game. I'm damned if I believe it." He made as if to tear the paper but changed his mind. "No, I'll just keep this. Mebby there'll be more of 'em. Jake!" he roared.

"—lo!" came the answering roar.

"Who's been here this mornin'?"

"Where?"

"At th' ranch."

A huge, slouching figure with a remarkable growth of hair appeared in the doorway. Jake was a cook because he was too big to ride and too lazy to dig. He ran his fingers through his hair, considering. "At th' ranch?" he repeated. "There was Pickles an' Ned, o' course; and Cock Murray come over to ask—"

"I don't mean them, I mean some stranger."

"Stranger? Where?"

"Right here in this room."

"Ther' ain't been no stranger. What'd he do?"

"Do? Why—why, he stole all th' silver, that's what. It's gettin' so I'll have to lock up all th' valuables every time I go out, yo're that interested in yore cookin'. Course, you need th' practice, I agree. Sling on th' chuck, you blind, deaf elephant. I got to get."

Jake rapidly retreated. In the kitchen he paused and ran his fingers through his hair. He looked scared. "Stole th' silver! Lock up th' valuables! He must be loco." Whereupon he stole out of the back door and concealed two stones in his clothes, where they would be handy. At close quarters he was a very grizzly for strength but if Buck should start to shoot him up from a distance, he did not purpose to be altogether at a disadvantage. Thus fortified he prepared to serve the meal.

CHAPTER IX

Any Means to an End

JEAN LAFRANCE carefully cleaned his boots and stepped into the cabin. *"Bon jour, ma belle Rose. Breakfast is ready, eh? But for why you make three to eat?"*

"Did you not see, on the trail?"

"No." He took up a bucket of water and a tin basin, going to a bench outside, to wash. In a few moments a horseman loped into view and disappeared again, hidden by an intervening rise. At sight of the rider a look of fear flashed across the face of Jean and he smothered a curse, hastily re-entering the cabin to dry his hands. "Dave!" he exclaimed.

"Yes," assented Rose, impassively.

"You know he come?"

"No," as expressionless as before.

"For why he come some early? But yes! Schatz, he send the money, eh? Eh?"

Rose shrugged her shoulders doubtfully and answered the consequent look of anxiety on Jean's face by placing her hands on his shoulders and gently shaking him. "Wait till he comes, *mon pére*," she encouraged him.

He nodded his head, unconsciously squaring his shoulders in response to the subtle appeal to his manhood. At the sound of the horseman's feet he went outside. Dave's smiling cheerfulness relieved his mind and he returned the greeting with new-born good humor, leading the horse off to the stable while Dave went indoors.

The handsome animal glowed with the health of youth; not a trace of his evil nature showed in the sparkle of his eyes and the clear red of his cheeks still stood proof against the assaults of a life of reckless debauchery. "Hello, Rose," he cried, "I couldn't stay away no longer. I come up last night but you'd turned in." Encircling her waist he drew her to him to kiss her on the cheek, laughing good-naturedly at the interposed hand. "All right, have it your own way. But I wants you to know I never aims to kiss a girl yet, as I don't kiss her, come kissin'-time."

"It is not kissing-time for me, Dave—no. Not for any man. Why you stay away so long?" she asked—and could have bitten her tongue for it the next instant.

"Missed me, did you?" commented Dave, delighted. "Well, you see I—" he hesitated.

"You do not want to tell for why you kill that unoffensive man and leave Fritz without a father." The contempt in her voice cut like a whip.

"Unafensive!" he repeated, the color ebbing from his face to leave it the dangerous white of the fated homicide. "He was that unafensive he knocked me off my feet an' started to pull a gun on me. It was an even break. That's more 'n yore dad allows when anybody tries to rush him."

She winced as if struck. "It is not promise you speak nothing of this?"

"I ain't a-speakin' of it. Nobody knows 't was him. Leastwise nobody but me. I wouldn't 'a' dug it up on'y you go accusin' me o' killin' when I has to protect myself."

Jean was heard approaching and Rose made a weary gesture of submission. "*Eh, bien.* Me, I know nothing but what I hear. Do not be angry when father comes."

"Peters, I suppose. Darn him for a liar." His face cleared as Jean entered. "Well, I got bad news for you, Jean. Schatz says he can't let you have that money just now, but he'll remember you."

"Good! Soon, I hope," and Jean rubbed his hands in pleased anticipation as he drew up to the table.

Dave sat silently watching Rose, after Jean had left them to go to his work. She went about her daily duties, patiently waiting. Something in Dave's manner told her he had come for more than the mere pleasure of seeing her.

"Rose, sit down," he said at last. "I want to talk to you." She seated herself obediently and faced him.

"*Allons*," she prompted him.

"You see, it's this way: Here's me, errand boy for Schatz. I draws my time, same as I'm a-punchin' for him, but what is it? Not enough to live on. I can make more with th' cards, a whole lot more, on'y you says no. An' there ain't nothin' reglar 'bout gamblin', anyhow. Schatz is honin' for his ranch. He's bound to get it an' I'm bound to help him. 'Cause why? I strike it rich. Schatz will put me on as foreman or mebby better. Now, how do we get th' ranch? Break that McAllister-Peters combine, that's how. An' how do we break 'em? You."

"Me?"

"You. It's pie. You get him here—Peters—an' I got a man as'll clean him out like a cyclone lickin' up a haystack. You get him here, that's all. You know how. I ain't a-goin' to be jealous of a girl as breaks off a kiss in th' middle an' han's me back my end of it. You ain't woke up yet, Rose, an' when you do, I'll be there."

"You will be there."

"You bet—with aces—four of 'em." He nodded with confident assurance. "You get Peters a-comin' here an' then some night Comin' Thirty drops in casual to see yore daddy. That'll be all. Comin' knows his business."

"Who is Comin'?"

"Who is he?" Dave grinned. "Well, he's th' on'y man can deal a deck between th' Mississip' an' th' Rockies. When Peters gets through with him he won't think so much o' that feller he met in Cheyenne—Hell!" He sprang to his feet, consternation on his face. Rose gazed at him in mute wonder. "It can't be!" he muttered, "he went out long ago." He was silent in troubled speculation for a while. "Rose," he continued abruptly, "you ask Peters, first time you see him—when'll you go? Today?"

"Go where?"

"Over to th' ranch," he explained, impatiently. "You've got to set her rollin'. Go over to see Pickles, can't you?"

"Yes, if you say so."

"All right. Go today. An' ask Peters when he's seen Tex Ewalt. Don't forget th' name: Tex Ewalt."

"Tex Ewalt. I go now. It may be difficult. Men do not come here like before—"

"Before I showed 'em th' way. You'll get Peters, if you try right."

"And you? Is it to Big Moose you ride?"

"No, I got to go to Wayback. Will I throw th' leather onto Swaller?"

"No, Swallow come when I call."

"All right. Then I'll hit th' trail. What, you won't? Wait till you wake up." He went off laughing and in a minute more swung past the house with a rattle of harness and shout of farewell. Rose stood in the doorway, motionless, looking after him.

"If I try right. You beast!" The words came through her lips laden with unutterable loathing. She put her hands before her eyes to shut out the sight of him and turned back into the room, throwing out her arms in despair. "What can I do?" she asked passionately; and again: "What can I do?"

To Tex, grimly watchful in the barroom of the Why-Not, her coming brought a shock. He remembered her as she appeared when publicly denouncing him for a crime he had not committed, a memory that ill prepared him for the all-pervading charm of her beauty. Approaching rapidly, a glorious figure, sitting the powerful black with unaffected grace, her grave loveliness smote him with a sort of wonder. Plunging through the ford in a series of magnificent leaps, the rifted spray flashed about her in the sunlight like bursting clouds of jewels. The solid ground once more under his feet, the black settled into his stride and they were away, the blue sky above the distant hills set wide for them, a gateway of the gods. "When she had passed it seemed like the ceasing of exquisite music," murmured Tex.

Dutch Ford laughed genially at his companion's interest. They two were alone in the room. "Der French Rose, a fine voman, yes," he remarked, with open and honest admiration. "You like her?"

Tex stared steadily out of the window as he answered:

> " 'Had she been true
> If Heaven had made me such another world
> Of one entire and perfect chrysolite
> I'd not have sold her for it.' "

"Sold her! Sold her for a—vot? Vot you talk, anyvay?"

"That, my friend, is what the man said when the shoe pinched. There's a hell of a lot of tight shoes in th' world, Fred."

Fred walked to the door and gazed solemnly after Tex as he rode away; then he walked back to the bar and solemnly mixed himself a fancy drink, which he compounded with the judgment of long experience. He set down the glass and admonished it with a pudgy forefinger: "How *he* know she vear tight shoes, vat?"

But the glass had already given up all it contained.

Swallow, meanwhile, was putting the trail behind him with praiseworthy speed, and brought Rose within hailing distance of the ranch house just as Jake, with his carefully concealed stones, re-entered the kitchen. As she dropped from her horse Buck appeared at the door and sprang forward to greet her, his stern face aglow with pleasure. "Why, ma'am, I'm right glad to see you," he declared, appreciative of the firm clasp of the hand she gave him. "Honest as a man's," was his thought. "Jake! O-o, Jake!" he called.

Jake tip-toed to the door and peered cautiously forth, heaving a huge sigh of relief at the new development. "Better run him in the stable, Jake," advised Buck. "An' take some o' th' sweat off'n him. Take yore time. We'll wait. You see," he went on to Rose, "none of th' boys is up; but Ned ought to be here right soon. An' Pickles, Pickles'll be that pleased he won't eat nothin'. Pickles says yo're a brick an' he likes you 'most as well as Whit."

Her bubbling laughter set Buck to laughing in sympathy and they stood, one at either side the table, looking at each other like two happy children, moved to mirth by they knew not what.

"It is a disappointment I have not come before, M'sieu Peters," said Rose, "you make me so very welcome. But Whit—who is Whit?"

"Whit? Oh, he's th' Britisher we took on when—when we went short a hand. He's willin' an' strong an' learns quick, though he shore has some amazin' ideas about cows."

The momentary clouding of her face as she recalled how he had "gone short a hand," he allowed to pass without comment and went on. "Pickles, he likes to hear him tell stories; fairy stories, you might call them, but they ain't like no fairy stories I ever heard. An' he tells 'em like he believes 'em. I ain't right certain he don't. Pickles does. You wouldn't think a kid like that would take to fairy stories, would you, ma'am?"

"No-o. Always he is for the grand minute—to be a man, to ride, to throw the rope,—like that. And to shoot—he must not shoot, M'sieu Peters."

"Well, you see, ma'am, he—you—I—" he was clearly embarrassed, but Truth and Buck were Siamese twins and always moved in pairs. Hot and uncomfortable as it made him, he had to confess. "Why, he's just naturally boun' to shoot. Yesterday I give him a rifle an' a big bunch o' ca'tridges. He won't hurt nothin', ma'am."

"*Mais non*—I hope not. Make him to be—to be good. A strong man can be good, M'sieu Peters?"

Buck frowned in thought. "Yes," he declared. "But there's more ways than one o' bein' good. Our way'd never do for some places, an' their way'd never do for us. Th' quickest man with a short gun I ever knowed an' one as has killed considerable few, first an' last, he's a good man, ma'am. He wouldn't lie, nor steal, nor do a mean act. An' he never killed a man 'less he was driven to it. I say it an' I know it. I'd trust him with my life an' my honor. An' there's more like him, ma'am, a-plenty." He stood tensely upright, an admirable figure, deep in earnest thought. And she stood watching him, silent, studying his face, absorbing his words with a thirsty soul: the firm conviction of a man who, intuition told her, was sound to the core. "This is a rough country," he continued, "with rough ways. There's good men an' bad men. Th' bad men are th' devil's own an' it seems like th' good men are scattered soldiers with a soldier's work to do. If a bad man takes offense an' you know he means to get you if he can, it's plumb foolish to wait till yo're shot before you begin shootin'. He didn't begin with you an' he shore won't stop with you, an' it's your plain duty to drop him at th' first threatenin' move. Mebby you won't have to kill him, but if you must, you must. I don't say it's right but it's necessary. That's all, ma'am."

He turned to her with a whimsical smile. Her face was alight with a heartfelt gratitude, for Buck, all unknowingly, had exonerated her father, in showing her a new aspect of his doubtful matter from the viewpoint of a man among men. She passed her hand across her eyes in a swift gesture, then laid it for an instant firmly upon his shoulder. *"Merci, mon ami,"* she said quietly. That shoulder, whenever he thought of it, tingled for days later, in a way that to Buck was unaccountable.

A moment later Jake appeared. "Ready in two shakes," he promised, referring to the meal.

"Can't you rustle up somethin' extra, Jake?" asked Buck. "You know we got company."

Jake assumed an air of nonchalant capability. "Well, now, I reckon," he answered; in spite of himself a hint of boasting was in his voice. "What do you say to aigs?"

"Aigs?" repeated Buck, his eyes widening.

"Aigs!" reiterated Jake, complacently.

Rose looked on in much amusement while Buck's

astonished stare wandered down half the length of
Jake's lofty height and stopped. "Are you carryin'
'em in yore pockets?" asked Buck.

"In my pockets!" exclaimed Jake. He glanced
down. What in blazes did he have in his pockets? A
hasty investigation brought forth two large stones.

"What in—what are you carryin' *them* for?" asked
Buck, with lively curiosity.

Jake turned to Rose with his explanation: "You
see, ma'am, it's th' cyclone. I got a' almanac as says
a cyclone is a-comin' an' due today, an' I didn't want
to be blown onto th' top o' one o' these yer mountains an' mebby freeze to death." Rose's responsive
peal of laughter repaid him, and, withering Buck
with a look, he retired to the kitchen to cook his
magically acquired eggs.

The meal was nearly finished when Pickles appeared, late as usual. Ned had been given up by
Buck, who explained his absence as probably due
to the development of some unexpected duty. Rose,
awaiting a more favorable opportunity to introduce
the real object of her visit, had deliberately prolonged the enjoyment of listening to his conversation. His friends would not have known the usually
taciturn Buck. Quite equal to the production of a
flow of language when language was desirable, his
calling and environment seldom found it necessary.
Indeed, if brevity were the sole ingredient of wit,
few men had been wittier. But today he surpassed
himself in eloquence; and it was in the midst of an
unconsciously picturesque narrative that he was interrupted.

There came a scramble of hoofs, the slam of a
door, a rapid padding of moccasined feet, followed
by a yell from Jake and the taunting treble of a boyish voice, and Pickles sped into view, clutching the
door frame as he ran, and swinging himself out of
range. His back toward them and his head craned in

the direction of Jake to insure the full effect of a
truly hideous grimace, he jeered that worthy for his
bad marksmanship: "Yah! you missed me ag'in! W'y
don't you use a *gun* like a man?" and by way of emphasis he shook the light rifle he was carrying. As
Jake directed a missile with unerring skill at anything short of a bird on the wing, it is to be presumed that, with Pickles as a mark, he did not try
very hard. It is certain that he was chuckling gleefully as he went to pick up the dishcloth, a large
remnant of what looked suspiciously like the passing of a blue flannel shirt.

Satisfied there was no immediate danger from the
rear, Pickles wheeled about. "Buck, I near got—" he
stopped short. "Rose!" he exclaimed and looked
sharply from her to Buck and back again. "You ain't
a-goin' to take me back?" he asked, doubtfully.

Rose shook her head as she looked at him. It was
a new Pickles she saw. The roguish mischief had
gone from the eyes which, when he faced them, had
been alive with eager intensity; the air of preco-
cious anxiety, tribute to a happy-go-lucky father
(oftener "happy" than lucky) had vanished completely; motionless as he stood in his hopeful expectancy, he was aquiver with life. "No, Fritz," she
assured him, "M'sieu Peters, he need you—more
than me—yes."

Pickles was at the table in a moment. "Betcher
life he does," he agreed. "You don't want a boy, anyhow. I'd have a girl if I was you. Say, Buck," he informed between bites, "I seen Ned an' he says that
darn bull's broke out again. He's gone after him. An'
Cock Murray says: Can you lend him a hat. That
wall-eyed pinto o' his made b— out o' his 'n."

"You young scallywag! You mustn't swear afore a
lady—not never. An' you must talk polite, besides.
Don't you never forget it."

Pickles looked straight into Buck's stern eyes,

without fear. "I won't," he promised, earnestly.
"Gosh! I'm hungry," and he proceeded to prove it.
And Rose knew then that Pickles would grow up a
"strong man"—and a good man, after the ideas of
M'sieu Peters, which, she had become convinced,
were very good ideas, indeed.

Pickles had long since departed with a hat for the
far-distant Murray; the boys had straggled in and
gone again from the bunkhouse, where Jake minis-
tered to their amazing appetites; and the afternoon
sun was casting shadows of warning before Rose remembered the long ride home which was to come.
A silence, longer than usual, had fallen upon them,
which neither seemed to find embarrassing. Buck's
inscrutable face, as he looked upon her, told nothing of his thoughts; but on hers was a soft wistful-
ness that surely sprang from pleasant imaginings.
She pushed back her chair at last with a murmur of
regret. Jake was glad to hear it. He had begun to
have anxious misgivings regarding his job. Buck
glanced through the window and really saw the outside world for the first time in two hours. He sprang
to his feet and exclaimed in bewilderment. "First
time in my life I ever did it," he declared. Rose
looked an inquiry. "First time th' sun ever stole a
march on me that way," he explained. "Reckon I
must a' been some interested in your talk, ma'am,"
and his humorous smile was deliciously boyish. The
sparkle in her eyes and the flush on her cheeks told
that Rose discerned a compliment higher than the
spoken one. She began to draw on her thick man's
gloves with an air almost demure.

"It is very selfish that I have made you waste so
much time, M'sieu Peters," she apologized, her eyes
intent upon the gloves.

Buck stared. There was a certain grimness in his
humor as he answered: "Hm! Well, I'm a-goin' to
waste some more. That is, I will if you don't run

away from Allday. He's good, but that black o' yourn
has got th' laigs of him, I reckon."

She watched him as he strode away for the
horses, deciding how best to approach the object of
her visit. True to her nature it was less an approach
than a direct appeal. As they set off together she
spoke abruptly: "What time did you see Tex Ewalt
last? I think—I am sure—it is better if you have not
see him for a long time—so."

"Well, I ain't seen him in a long time." He was
plainly surprised. "Do you know Tex?" he asked,
wonderingly.

She shook her head. "No. Someone ask me—but
you have not seen him. That is good. Once I tell you
I am glad if you come to see me about Fritz."

"Shore I'll come," he promised heartily.

"You must not," she warned him. "In the morning,
a little while, yes; at night or to stay long—no."

A light broke in upon Buck, who recalled the mysteriously delivered letter of that morning. The
wholesome admiration for a lovely woman, the natural pleasure in an experience infrequent in his
man-surrounded life, began to concentrate and take
definite shape in his mind at the promised vindica-
tion of his judgment. He tested her shrewdly: "You
don't want to see me," was his brusque comment.

She looked reproachfully at his set profile. "*Mais,
quelle folie*! I am glad to see you always," she assured him, "but it must be like that. It is better." She
hesitated a moment and continued: "It is better
aussi, if you will not play cards. I—I like it, much, if
you will not play cards." Her heightened color and
diffident manner showed what it cost her to make it
a personal request.

"By God! I knew it," cried Buck. He whanged
Allday over one eye with his hat, and that sedate
animal executed a side jump that would have done
credit to a real bad pony. There are limits to all

things and Allday was feeling pretty good just then, anyway.

Rose was startled. "What is it you know?" she asked, doubtfully.

Buck's face was alight with smiling gratification. Oblivious of the fact that at last he had stung Allday into remonstrance, he answered by the card, "I knowed that gamblin' habit'd grow on me so my friends could see it. An' I hereby swears off. I never touches a deck till you say so, ma'am. That goes as it lays."

Still doubtful as to his meaning—such exuberance of feeling could scarcely be induced by swearing off anything—she questioned him in some embarrassment. "Is it I ask too much, that you will not play?"

"Too much! There ain't nothin' you can't ask me, nothin'—" he paused. "It's time I was hittin' th' back trail 'fore I say mor'n I ought. Just one thing, ma'am: I can't never know you better than I do right now. An' I want to say I'm right proud to know you." He drew Allday down to a walk and halted as she stopped and faced him, sweeping her a salute as eloquent in gesture as were his words in speech.

The color came and went in her cheeks as she regarded him. "I am glad," she said at last, "Oh, I am very glad," and turning, she left him at a speed that vied with her racing thoughts.

Buck watched her go, the definite shape in his mind assuming a seductiveness that fascinated while it scared him. "If I was only ten years younger," he muttered. He jerked Allday's head around. "Get away, boy," he cried, and the horse struck his gait at a bound.

Buck was riding wide of the ranch house when a suspicion pricked him and he headed for home. At the door he shouted for Jake.

Jake lounged out. "What's th' noise?" he asked, languidly.

"Say, Jake, where'd you get them aigs?"

Jake looked pained. "I got 'em off Cheyenne Charley," he asserted.

"Cheyenne Charley? Where'n blazes did he get 'em," wondered Buck.

"Well, now, I can't rightly say," drawled Jake, "but I'm certain shore o' one thing: he never laid 'em."

"No," agreed Buck, reflectively. "Did he *give* 'em to you?" he added.

Jake yawned elaborately to hide the weakness of his position. "Not exactly," he admitted. "I got him drunk."

"Oh," commented Buck. He turned to ride off when another question obtruded itself, but Jake had disappeared. Buck slid to the ground and entered quietly by another door, going to where he kept his private stock. A rapid inspection showed where Jake had obtained his supply. He had appropriated Buck's whiskey to pay for eggs which it was very evident he had meant to eat himself. Only his vanity had led to their disclosure. "Th' darn scoundrel!" said Buck, and he hurriedly secured the demijohn in the one place in the house that locked.

CHAPTER X

Introducing a Parasite

IN THE northeast corner of the Cyclone ranch, not far from the Little Jill, and in a hollow, well screened by hills and timber, One-Eye sat on his horse, smoking a brown cigarette and keeping a satisfied watch over a dozen mangy-looking cattle as they grazed intermittently in a restless, nervous way. They were a pitiful-looking handful, weak, emaciated, their skins showing bald patches and scabs, and they continually licked themselves and rubbed against the trees. While they were restless, it was without snap or vim; they were spiritless and drooping, enduring patiently until death should end their misery.

One-Eye beamed upon them, his good optic glowing with satisfaction. He had gone to some trouble and risk to cut these miserable animals out of the herd collected by the hasty round-up, and now that he was about to have them taken off his hands he sighed with deep content. To run infected cattle onto the Cyclone's non-infected northern range was very dangerous, for his foreman was direct and unhesitating in his methods. Discovery might easily mean a bullet above One-Eye's blue-red nose—and this accounts for that puncher's satisfaction. Some men will do a great deal for ten dollars.

"Darn if they ain't beauts," he chuckled. "When it comes to pickin' out th' real, high-toned wrecks, th' constant scratchers, why I reckon I'm some strong. He says to me 'Get th' very wust, One-Eye,'—an' I shore has obeyed orders. That two-year-old tryin' to saw through that cottonwood is a prize-winner when it comes to scabs—his tail looks like a dead tree in a waste of sand, th' way th' hair's gone. Wait till he gets rubbin' hisself through th' brush across th' river, where Peters' cows like to hang out. He'll hang mites on every twig; an' this kind o' weather will boom things. I heard tell that Peters examined that new herd extra cautious afore he bought it— well, boxcars an' pens can hand out itch a-plenty, so he can't prove they got it from us." He pulled out a battered brass watch and gauged where the broken hands would be if they were all there to point. "He's due in ten minutes an' he's usually on time. Yep: here he comes now. I'll get my ten afore I do any more work—wish I could get ten dollars as easy every day."

Dave cantered up, his eyes fastened intently on the cattle, and he laughed cynically as he turned and regarded the puncher. "Well," he grinned, "I reckon you got th' wust that could stand bein' drove. Come on; we'll get 'em off our hands as quick as we can—I don't want to answer no questions right now. It'll be like puttin' a match to dry grass, th' way this dozen will cut down Peters' cows."

"It shore will," replied One-Eye. "Got that ten handy?" he inquired, carelessly.

"Why, they ain't across th' river yet," replied Dave, frowning.

"They'll get across when I gets my ten," smiled One-Eye.

"Here's th' money!" snapped Dave, angrily, as he almost threw the gold piece at his companion. "Fust time I was ever told I couldn't be trusted for ten dollars."

"Oh, I trust you, all right—on'y I worked plumb hard for that coin, an' I want to feel it, like. Come on—take th' south side—I'll handle th' rest."

The herd moved slowly forward into a dry ravine and finally came to the river bank. They hadn't life enough to give trouble until they understood what they were expected to do. Then the everlasting, thick-headed obstinacy, the perverse whims which all cows have to an outrageous extent, asserted itself in a manner wholly unexpected in such tottering hulks of diseased flesh. They did everything but get wet, even showing a returning flash of spirit in the way they swung their heads and kicked up their heels. Time and time again they broke and ran along the bank, and always in Dave's direction, who, until now, had nursed the belief that he was something of a cow-puncher. When half-dead cows unhesitatingly picked him out, time after time, for an easy mark, and simply walked through his defense, it was time to exchange ideas on some things.

At first One-Eye was greatly amused. He liked Dave well enough but he hated Dave's conceit—and to be present at his companion's discomfiture was very gratifying. But gradually One-Eye grew restless unto peevishness and a vast contempt settled upon him, edging his temper with a keenness rare to him. He had been trying to get one dozen imitation cows to cross an ordinarily wide river, and neither coldness nor unusual depth had any bearing on the matter. As he wondered how long he had been engaged in watching Dave's blunders and jerked out the brass watch to see, his voice rumbled and boomed with a jarring timbre and suddenness that made Dave jump.

"What th' hell d'you think yo're doin'?" demanded One-Eye. " 'Allamanleft' an' 'Ladies chain' is all right for a dance, but it's some foolish out here. An' somebody's goin' to lope along this way an' see us, if you don't quit makin' a jackass out er yo'rself."

Stung to the quick, Dave wheeled to face his critic, his pent-up rage almost hysterical. He had held it in, choked it back, and forced himself to be calm, but now—his purpose was never disclosed, for at the instant he wheeled, the watchful cattle leaped through the opening he had made and headed for the hills, their heads down and tails up. Dave hesitated, glancing from One-Eye to the cattle and back again, his face white and pinched. One-Eye's anger melted under his impelling sense of the ridiculous and, slapping his thigh a resounding smack, he burst into roars of laughter, until he was bent in his saddle like a man drunk or sorely wounded.

"This yer's a circus," he finally managed to cry. "Don't get mad, Dave: we'll make 'em cross this time or they'll float down like logs. Come on."

When they rounded up the bunch and started it toward the river again the cows were surprisingly docile and the two drivers exchanged wondering glances. At the river edge the dozen hesitated for a moment while they nosed the water and at One-Eye's wondering command, pushed into the stream, scrambled out on the farther bank, and walked slowly into the brush. Dave's hypnotized senses were all in his eyes and he barely heard his companion speak.

One-Eye prefaced his remarks with a fluent burst

of profanity, and cogitated aloud: "Cows *is* worse than wimmin! They *is*! Of all th' crazy hens what ever a man drove, them dozen mangy critters has got 'em all roped an' tied! What in hell do you *think* of 'em?"

"I ain't thinkin', One-Eye," softly replied Dave. "I'm prayin' for strength an' fortitude. I figgers I can drop th' last six from where I'm sittin', an' it's some temptation!"

One-Eye ironed out his grin. "I'm some tempted myself, Dave. There's things in a cowman's life to drive him plumb loco. I've been part loco more'n once. Mum? You bet I'll keep mum. You don't reckon I'm hankerin' for to collect no cold lead, do you?"

Dave scarcely heard him. He was looking across the river, a smile on his face. Before him was the Rocking Horse, and south of it, so close as to appear a part of it from that angle, lay the Hog Back. He had planned well, he told himself, when he had decided to turn infected cattle on the Double Y at that point.

"Now, they ain't goin' fur to be found while they stops near ol' Hog Back, Dave," One-Eye was saying. "Nobody hardly ever rides that way, an' they'll drift down where th' grass is better, soon as they finds out what they're up agin. Wonder if it was true about that feller ridin' th' Rockin' Horse all day long?" he asked, curiously.

He would have talked all day if given half a chance, but his companion, knowing One-Eye's inability to gracefully terminate a conversation, or effect a parting, mercilessly performed the operation himself. "I'm goin' south, One-Eye. See you in town, some night," and Schatz' *protégé* cantered away, and became hidden by the brush and hills of the rough country skirting the river.

One-Eye looked after him. "Black devil!" he

scowled. "If anybody gets plugged for this, you can bet it won't be little Davy. I wonder what th' Dutch Onion knowed that Dave didn't want told? Well, when me an' him is together my gun hand ain't never far from home—but I'm surprised he didn't pump lead into me when I laughed like I did. I plumb forgot, then. Come on, boss; home for us, an' sudden. I ain't hankerin' none to be seen 'round here, *now*."

CHAPTER XI

The Man Outside

DAVE LOPED through Twin River in no amiable mood. An unreasoning irritability tormented and blinded him to everything but the trail ahead. But if Dave failed to notice his friends, one of them at least bore him no ill-feeling for the oversight; this one was so solicitous for Dave's welfare that he followed all the way to the LaFrance cabin; when Dave went indoors he still lingered, hugging the cabin wall close to a window, while he listened with much interest to the talk that went on inside.

"Where's Jean?" asked Dave, briefly, as he entered.

Rose glanced at him. The even, metallic tones meant temper and she was painfully anxious to avoid crossing him when in this mood. Her voice was soothing as a summer breeze through tree branches when she answered. "He go to the station," she explained; "something about a harrow. He will be late."

"See Peters?"

"Yes."

"What'd he say about Tex Ewalt?"

"He have not see him for many months. He ask me if I know him."

"Well?"

"You forget to tell me what to say. I forget to answer."

"Hm! Beats th' Dutch how a woman'll crawl out of a hole. When's he comin' to see you?"

"I do not know. He—he is very droll, that M'sieu Peters. Always he look at me strange like he suspect something."

"He ain't got nothin' to suspect. Didn't try to kiss you, did he?"

"He never come near me one time—no; only he look at me, straight, without any smile."

"Bah! I knowed you didn't take th' right way with him. You got t' tempt them gray-eyed galoots. They'll follow you easy enough if you show 'em there's somethin' at the end o' th' trail. You go ag'in. Make him glad to see you. Won't be long afore he's hangin' round, then."

"*Quel jour*—when I must go?"

"Oh, whenever you get th' chanst. Soon as you kin. You got Pickles for an excuse, ain't you?"

At this point the solicitous caretaker outside risked a look through the window. His glance traveled over the shoulder of Dave, sitting with his back to the window, and rested on the face of Rose. What he saw there was a revelation: scorn, contempt, loathing, the expression any good woman might bear toward a man with a mind considerably lower than the nobler beasts; it lasted but a moment; placidity swept over the regular features as she replied. *"Mais oui,"* she admitted, "Fritz is excuse."

"Well, you won't need any excuse if you play th' game right. You'll be excuse enough, yourself."

Enthralled by the contradiction between the expression and speech of Rose, the watcher prolonged his stare beyond safety. Rose's level gaze lifted from the unnoting eyes of Dave and rested full on the face in the window. The watcher changed instantly to the listener with one hand on his gun, but not so quickly that he failed to see the brilliant smile that flashed across the face of Rose. The alert tenseness of his attitude relaxed as he realized the significance of that smile and his shoulders heaved in strangling a laugh at the way Dave was being fooled.

Dave's moodiness persisted. He sat glowering at the point of his boot, switching it venomously with his quirt, a thing he had not carried since his experience with the Cyclone cattle at the Hog Back. It reminded him of his proven lack of ability as a driver of cows; but it was "out of this nettle, Chagrin, that he plucked the flower, Complacence"; a cynical laugh announced recovery from the black mood. "Well, there's some as help me better 'n you do," he declared. "If I can't get Peters here, I give him somethin' that'll keep him busy at home."

"*Bien*, but how?" Rose's interest had just the proper amount of congratulatory warmth and a faint wheeze escaped the listener outside as he choked back a laugh of admiration.

"I give him the itch," replied Dave, with dramatic brevity.

"Itch?" repeated Rose, in perplexity.

"Yes—itch, mange, scab! His darn cows'll be scratchin' their hides off afore he knows it. Th' Cyclone had it an' I got One-Eye Harris to save me out some. Mangiest lot o' cows ever *I* saw. We put 'em across th' Jill, up by th' Rocking Horse, a while back."

"But the mange—is it not bad?" asked Rose, wonderingly.

"Shore is. What do I care? Makes 'em trouble, don't it? An' it'll spoil some o' their cows, you bet."

"M'sieu Schatz, he tell you do this?"

"Smiler! The cussed ol' bear! He's been a-layin' up all winter like a bear in a hole an' he ain't woke up yet. Poetry! an' Philosophy! an' some shifty *I*talian named Mac—Mac somethin' or other. Smiler sets a heap by Mac. Jus' sits an' reads an' hol's out his han's an' says: 'Gimme th' Double Y, Dave.' Mus' think I carry it in m' hat."

"But you will get it, Dave—yes."

"You bet yo' boots I'll get it. Peters'll be so sick o' that range afore I'm done with him he'll be glad to quit. But if you get him comin' here, it'll be done quicker."

"I will try," murmured Rose.

The flush that went with the words was wrongly interpreted by Dave. "That's you!" he exclaimed, admiringly, and was at her side before she realized it, bending over her in a swift movement that almost caught her by surprise. He laughed easily at his defeat, in no wise discomfited. "Ain't come kissin'-time yet, eh, Rose?"

She looked up coolly, careful not to give way an inch from the nearness of him. Nothing tempts a man so much as a retreat. "*Mais non, m'sieu.* When the day, then the hour—you go too far unless," was her calm warning.

"All right. Time enough," he rejoined carelessly. "Guess I'll drift back to Twin. Have to see Comin' an' keep him on edge, or he'll get tired o' waitin' for that good thing I promised him. He ain't a feller as you can ask questions or I'd cussed quick find out who he is an' where he come from."

Rose stood in the doorway until the sound of his horse's feet assured her that he was certainly on his way to Twin River. Then she went in, closed the door behind her, darkened the front windows and going to the window at the back called out clearly: "Enter. I want to talk to you, Tex Ewalt."

Tex lounged forward a step, bringing himself into view, his face the picture of mischievous amusement. He rested his arms on the sill and smiled at her. "You are a good guesser," he admitted.

"Enter," she insisted. "Not the door, no; the window—hurry."

He slipped through with the suppleness of a naked Indian and she at once shut out the night at this and the other windows. "We must beware more eavesdroppers," she explained. She motioned to a bench and seated herself near him, looking at him intently.

"I think you kill Fritz' father that night," she began. "I am sorry."

Tex bowed, as if such unjust suspicions were his daily portion, and waited.

"You are M'sieu Peters' friend?" she questioned.

Tex carefully poked two depressions in the crown of his hat and carefully poked them out again, thinking swiftly. "Yes," he replied, meeting her eyes again.

"You are Tex Ewalt. Dave call you Comin'. M'sieu Peters not know you are here. You spy for M'sieu Peters, yes?"

"Buck told you, eh? Did you tell him I was in Twin River?"

She shook her head. "But no. I guess, when I see you at the window."

Tex looked incredulous. "How did you guess?" he asked.

Rose reviewed the incidents from which she had drawn her conclusion. Tex was impressed. "That's not guessing. That's pure reason," he declared.

"You will tell M'sieu Peters about the itch?" she inquired eagerly.

"Why don't you tell him? I can't risk going out to the ranch."

"No! No! Dave must not suspect. You tell him quick so Dave not think it is me."

"Why, Dave is in a hole. Harris will squeal the minute I put my fingers on him."

"He will suspect. He must not—Oh! you do not understand."

Tex indented his hat on the left side; that was Dave: then on the right side; that was Buck: then with careful precision, in the middle of the crown; that was Rose. He studied the result with thoughtful attention. "Like Dave?" he inquired, casually.

"I—" she began with passionate intensity but paused. "No," she answered, more calmly.

"No," repeated Tex. He smoothed out the left-hand depression with an air of satisfaction. "That's good," he continued, "because I shall have to put a crimp, a very serious crimp, in his anatomy one of these days. I can feel it coming. What do you think of Buck?"

"M'sieu Peters is a good man—a good man," she repeated, dreamily. Tex glanced at her and back at his hat, which he eyed malevolently. Then he sighed. "Oh, well, every man has to find it out for himself," was his irrelevant comment. "Where does Schatz stand in this?"

"Dave say he try to get back the range. But Dave he is so much a liar."

"Yes, I should say he was a pretty good liar. Well, I'll be going."

"But no!" she exclaimed. "You must eat supper," and she began hastily to make preparations.

"You didn't offer Dave any," suggested Tex, with a ghost of a grin.

"No," she admitted, seriously. "Sometimes I must, but tonight it is not necessary. I am glad, always, to see him go."

"Well, so am I," agreed Tex. "Here, let me do that."

Tex learned much during the meal that went to confirm the suspicions he had already formed. Also his opinions in regard to women-kind in general seemed less plausible than before. But though shaken, they were not routed; and when he took up his hat in leaving, the two dimples in it looked at him mockingly. "Oh, well, what's the use?" he said. "Good night, Miss LaFrance," and he threw the hat on his head as it was.

CHAPTER XII

A Hidden Enemy

COCK MURRAY had an engagement to meet Schatz at the point where the Double Y's north line touched the Black Jack, and after he had ridden up to the south line to see how the cows were doing, as Buck had ordered, he swung west to the Black Jack to follow it down to the meeting place. As he rode he neared the Hog Back, a vast upheaval of rock, not high enough to be called a mountain, flat on the top except for hollows and gullies, scantily covered with grass and stunted trees. The Hog Back would have been called a mesa in the South, for want of a better name, though it was no more a mesa than it was a mountain. A mile long and a third of that across at its widest point, it made an effective natural barrier between the Double Y and the river, hiding a pasture of great acreage which lay between it and the precipitous cliff which frowned down upon the rushing, swishing Black Jack eighty feet below. While the round-up would, of course, comb this poor-grass part of the range for outlaws and strays, the outfit never gave it any attention because cattle seldom were found upon it.

Cock Murray, knowing that he had an hour to spare, and fond of hard riding where his skill was called into play, suddenly decided to ascend the Hog Back. Antelope were still to be found even on the range itself, along the wildest part of the south line, and he might get a shot at one if he made the climb. It was an easy task to go up the northern end, where the trail arose in a succession of steep grades; but he had no time for that and guided his pony up the rough, rocky east wall. As he gained the top he rested the horse while he looked around. It was a favorite view of his; below him lay the range and the river; he could see, on a clear day, the dot that represented his ranch house; and to the west and south lay the wild, rolling range of the Cyclone. Gradually his gaze sought nearer objects and he thought of antelope. Moving forward cautiously he kept keen watch on all sides, intending if he caught sight of one, to dismount and stalk it on foot. He had ridden nearly to the northern end when he jerked his pony to a stand, and then, gazing earnestly ahead a short distance, went on as rapidly as the broken ground would permit.

"Dead cows! What 'n hell killed 'em? Wolves would clean 'em to the bone. G'wan, you fool!" he growled at his mount. "Scared of dead cows, are you! If you are, I've got the cure for it right here on my heel."

The horse went on, picking its footing, and soon Murray whistled in surprise: "Cyclone brand! Bet they've got the itch, too. Yep! Died from it, by God! Now, how the blazes did they get over here! Cows, and sick ones especially, don't hanker to swim the Jack. Well, that will hold over a little—let's see how many are up here"—and he began the search. Four were all he could find, two alive and two dead. The two that still stumbled weakly in search of food, dropped as if struck by lightning as the acrid gray smoke sifted past Murray's head. "Wonder how many more there was and where they went to? Must have been here some time, judging by the carcasses. Holy smoke! If any cows gone as bad as these are loose on our range may the Lord pity *us*! Come on, bronc; we'll see what Schatz thinks about it. Wish I had time to build a fire over these itch farms."

He was careful to guide his horse on ground barren of vegetation and not let brush or grass touch the animal when he could avoid it. As he plunged down the steep northern trail, a dried water course, he reined up hard, looking closely at the tracks in the soft alluvial soil washed down by the last rain. "Must have been about a dozen; perhaps a few less—then some *did* get where we don't want them—holy cats! as if we haven't got enough with our regular calf round-up!"

When he galloped up to the north line he found Schatz waiting for him. "Schatz," he shouted, "I just found four itch cows on the Hog Back. Six or eight are loose on th' ranch. They was Cyclone, an' they never crossed th' Jack by themselves."

"*Mein Gott!* Did you drive dem back?"

"Two was dead; th' other two was so near it I just dropped 'em. They couldn't stand a drive even to th' river. Shall I tell Peters?"

"Shall you tell him? *Gewiss!* Vat you t'ink—I vant itch on de Double Vy? How dey come?"

"I don't know. But they must 'a' been driven. Th' Jack is cold as ice an' she runs strong by th' Rocking Horse. That's where th' tracks led to. Cows ain't goin' to swim that for fun. Why, these was all et up with th' itch—wonder they didn't drown."

"*Dank Gott!* Sick cows ain't made vell mit ice

vater und schwimmin'. Dey don't lif so long like de vater vas varm. Der shock help kill dem quick."

Murray nodded, his hand resting on his gun, and Schatz noticed it. "*Gewiss*, if dey vas too veak to drive in der river, it vas besser to shoot dem. But ven dey drop dey stay mit all dem parasites. Drivin' dem off de range is besser. *Aber*, you stopped dem de best vay you could."

Murray nodded again. "Yes, yo're right—but I wasn't thinkin' of shootin' no cows," he asserted calmly. "I know all about that. But I was just a-wonderin' if I should ketch some skunk of a cowpunch drivin' itch cattle on us, an' shoot him, if he'd drop any parasites when *he* fell."

"*Ach Gott!* Alvays you shoot, like Dave! Shoot, shoot, shoot! Vy in *Himmel* should you alvays grab dot gun? Brains are in your head, and *besser* as lead in dot Colt. Brains first, and if dey don't do it, den der gun. But alvays der gun should be last. *Verstanden?*"

Murray did not reply and his companion, exchanging a few terse sentences with him, waved him toward the ranch house while he followed the line toward the Little Jill.

Buck was washing for supper when Murray arrived and kept right on with his ablutions as the puncher told his tale. Murray quite expected to see some signs of its effect on the owner, but he met with surprise and looked it. Buck Peters almost made an ally when he turned, after Murray's last word. "Murray, that's good work. Prepare for *hard* work. Send Ned here right away," he said, quietly, no trace of emotion in his voice.

Murray went out, thinking hard. When a man could take such a blow as that one had been taken, then he was clean grit all through. To smile as Buck had done—"By God, he's a man!" swore the puncher. "I can't *help* liking him; wish I didn't have to help throw him. And I wish he didn't trust me like he does—ah, hell!" he growled, savagely. "He's a range thief, after all!"

When Monroe entered the ranch house he found his employer looking out of the window in the direction of the Hog Back, but he turned at Ned's entry. "Got work ahead, Ned. Murray found some Cyclone cows dead and wobbly on th' Hog Back. Bad case of itch. He killed th' wobblers but says th' tracks show that about a dozen was in th' herd. That means eight of 'em are on our range among the cattle. Tell th' boys we start th' round-up at daylight. If we can, we'll make this do for the spring round-up, too; if not, then th' calves'll have to wait till we can go for 'em. Th' north range won't have no itch cows on it yet, so take th' south first. As fast as we can cut out th' cattle that are free from it, we'll throw 'em over on th' north range. Begin in th' Hog Back country an' clean up. Drive everything out of it."

"It's damned funny Cyclone cows swum th' Jack," commented Monroe, a black look on his face "By God, let *me* ketch anybody at that game!"

"That's th' whole thing, Ned," and Buck smiled: "To ketch 'em. I know a man who'd clean up th' mystery if he was here, an' was told he didn't have nothin' else to do." He smiled again quietly and turned to his supper. "But he ain't here, so what's th' use."

"Mebby I—" suggested Ned, nervously.

"No, yo're goin' to help me most by curing th' evil on th' table; never mind th' dealer, nor th' game. We've got as many cards as we're goin' to get—use 'em, Ned. Help me lick th' itch first—th' hows an' whys can wait."

"Yo're right, Peters; an' we *will* lick it! But it makes me fightin' mad, a thing like this. I'll get everything all ready tonight an' th' round-up starts with th' comin' of th' sun tomorrow. Good night."

Buck ate slowly, his thoughts far more occupied with the problem than with the food. This was the firing of the first cannon in the fight Monroe had predicted. Who was responsible? His suspicions, guided by Monroe's warning, were directed toward Schatz, but in his present absence of knowledge they could advance no farther than suspicions. Dave's half-closed eyes sneered at him as he recalled the ambiguous threat made that first night in the Sweet-Echo: still remained suspicion only. McReady, of the Cyclone, might have designs for the Double Y, but he doubted it. They had yet free grass a-plenty, though the time was not far distant when the private ownership of the Double Y would be an invaluable asset. Still, it might be any other cowman in that part of the country—or none of them. Well, he had met problems as great as this one on the Texan range—but he had fought them with an outfit loyal to the last man, every unit of it willing and eager to face all kinds of odds for him. He now recalled those men to his mind's eye, and he never loved them more than he did now, when he realized how really precious unswerving loyalty is. Hopalong, Red, Johnny and the others of the old Bar-20 outfit, made an honor roll that held his thoughts even to the temporary exclusion of the bitterness of his present situation. If only he had that outfit with him now! Even his neighbors and acquaintances on that southern range were to be trusted and depended upon more than his present outfit. His vision, knocking patiently at first upon the door of his abstraction, at this point kicked its way in and demanded attention. Buck became aware that for some time he had been staring unseeingly at a folded paper, tucked partly under his bunk blanket. With a smothered oath he sprang from his seat, strode to the bunk and snatched up the paper. The warning it contained was better founded than the first. It read:

"Buck Peters: Itch on the YY. Crossed the Jack at the Rocking Horse. A Friend."

"If you told me who sent it across, you'd be more of a friend," muttered Buck—in which he was less wise than Tex, who did not see the sense in having the servant removed while the master remained.

Hoofbeats rolled up in the darkness and stopped at the door of the house and a moment later Whitby entered the room, his pink, English complexion aglow with the exercise and wind-beating of his ride.

Buck was glad to see him; he needed a little of the other's cheerful optimism and after a few minutes of random conversation, Buck told him of the latest developments. Whitby's surprise was genuine, and the practicability of his nature asserted itself. This was ground upon which he was thoroughly at home.

"I say, Buck, we can show these swine a thing or two they don't know," he began. "They don't know it in the States, I'll lay, nor north of the line either, for that matter. My Governor is a cattle man, you might say; on the other side of the pond, of course. And I've knocked about farm land a good bit, you know. Now a chap in the same county had a lot of sheep with this what-d'you-call it—scab, they said. He used a preparation of arsenic but a lot of the beggars died, poisoned, you know. He had tried a number of other things and he got jolly well tired of the game; so he wrote to a cousin, chemist or something, and told him about it; and this chap sent him a recipe, after a bit, that killed off the parasites like winking, without injuring a single sheep."

"That ain't goin' to help us none, Whit. You ain't

got th' receipt an' you don't know how to make th' stuff."

"Ah! But I do though. I gave him a hand with the silly beggars and bally good fun it was, too. We passed them through a long trough and ducked their heads under as fast as they came along. But it was work, no end, mixing the solution. There was nothing funny about that part of it."

"See here, Whit, are you really in earnest? Do you think you can make the stuff and show us how to use it?"

"Absolutely certain, dear boy. Cattle aren't sheep, but I'll be bound it'll do the trick."

"How fast can you run 'em though?"

Whitby reflected. "We could do a thousand a day, perhaps more. It depends on how many you do at once, you know." And Whitby went into a detailed description to which Buck gave close attention. At the end he shook his head. "Reckon we'll have to stick to th' old way," he adjudged, regretfully. "There ain't that quantity of lime and sulphur in all Montana."

"Ah, yes; your point is good," drawled Whitby, smiling. "But your partner lives in Chicago where there is any quantity of it. If we wired him tomorrow to get the stuff and ship it at once he would do it, don't you know."

"Take it too long to get here," replied Buck, gloomily.

"Don't you think the railroad will see that such an important consignment gets off and comes through quickly, especially if the consignor is willing to pay the damage? I'll bet you a good cigar it will be here within a week after we wire. Let *me* send the wire and I'll bet you a box. I'm bally good at wires. I used to get money out of the Governor by wire when I could get it no other way."

"Let her go," said Buck. "If it's all you say we'll

show them coyotes we know a few tricks ourselves."

"Yes, I fancy we shall," replied Whitby. "But isn't
this a rummy game? They act like savages, you
know. It is all very refreshing to a sated mind—and
their justice is so deuced direct, right or wrong.
Fancy Blackstone in the discard, as you Americans
say, and a Colt's revolver sovereign lord of the
realm!"

"King Colt is all right, Whitby, when you *know*
who to loose him at," declared Buck, turning toward
the door to the kitchen. "Jake! Jake!" he called.

The sharp, incisive tones told their story and
brought buoyancy to the cook, for he was on his
feet, across the kitchen, and into the dining room in
apparently one movement, which astounded the
soul of that culinary devotee when leisure gave time
for reflection.

"Why, Jake, I believe yo're gettin' to be almost a
human, livin' creature," remarked Buck. "I never
saw you move so fast before. It ain't pay day now,
you know."

"Shore I know, but next *week is*," grinned Jake,
not quite catching the meaning.

"Oh, I'm glad you do," sighed Buck with relief.
"Now as long as you ain't sufferin' no hallucer-
nations, suppose you tell Ned to come in here. You
needn't tell *him*—he knows it ain't, too."

"Knows what ain't?" demanded Jake, his fingers
slowly ploughing through his mass of hair. "If I
needn't tell him, what do you want me to tell him
for?"

"Be calm, Jake, be calm," replied Buck, raising a
warning finger. "There are *two* tells in this; one you
must, th' other you needn't."

"Ah, go to hell an' tell him yourself," retorted
Jake, backing toward a handy chair so as not to be
without a weapon.

"You tell Ned I want to see him—I'll explain th' second tell later. Now—*Will* y'u tell?"

Jake backed into the kitchen, slammed shut the door behind him, and lost no time in getting to the bunkhouse.

"Hey, Ned," he blurted out, "th' boss says to tell you he wants to see you. Th' second tell can wait till later. William Tell?"

"What t'ell!" snorted Bow-Wow, arising.

"You another?" demanded the cook; then he fled, Ned following more leisurely.

Bow-Wow looked at Murray inquiringly: "What did he mean by William Tell?"

Murray put down his mended riding gear. "Why, don't you know?"

"Shore; what is it?" sarcastically responded Bow-Wow. "If I knew, do you think I'd tell?"

"Well I know, all right. It's what he was brought up on, Bow-Wow."

"Huh! Did you know him when he was a kid?"

"Shore! He used to live in th' next street in th' same town, or was it in some other town?" he mused, thoughtfully. "Hell, that don't make no difference, 'cause he lived in th' next street. See?"

"No; I don't; not a damned bit!"

"Bow-Wow, if I was as thick as you get sometimes, I'd drink lots of water an' thin down a bit. This is th' story of William Tell, an' I'll tell it to you if you won't tell: When he was a kid he had a awful yearnin' for apples, like you has for cheap whiskey, Bow-Wow. Nothin' else suited him an' th' bigger he got th' more apples he had to eat. All th' farmers was a-layin' for him with guns, so what did li'l Willie do? Why, he shot 'em down with a bow an' arrer. An' that's why he can throw a stone so straight today. *Now* do you see?"

Bow-Wow threw a shoe after Murray's departing figure and suggested a place to go to. Then he scowled and muttered: "If I was shore of what I suspects I'd give you a sample of *my* shootin', *six* samples so you'd appreciate the real thing." He grinned at the memory of Jake's message.

"You'll say somethin' with sense in it some day if you gropes long enough, Jake. Yo're gettin' warmer all th' time."

When Monroe reached the ranch house Buck met him with some sharp orders: "Send Bow-Wow to Twin River and Wayback first thing tomorrow. Tell him to leave word we want two dozen more punchers for our round-up—fifty dollars a month an' a full month's work guaranteed. Jake's goin' to dig some big holes in th' ground in th' next few days—he ain't fit for nothin' else, not even cookin'.'"

A crash in the kitchen interrupted him. "Jake!" he called. There was a scramble and the cook appeared, much excited. "What's th' fuss about?"

"Fell off my chair," replied Jake. "An' it hurts, too."

"Yo're gettin' too soft, Jake. A little exercise'll toughen you so a chair wouldn't dare to tackle you. I'm goin' to let you dig some holes first thing tomorrow."

Jake had visions of extensive excavations, dug by him, into which thousands of dead cows were being piled for burial. "Wouldn't it be better to burn 'em, or push 'em into th' river an' shoot 'em there?"

"I never saw holes you could handle that way, Jake," gravely replied Buck.

"Why, no," supplemented the foreman. "Most holes would ruther be slit up th' middle an' salted. That's th' way *we* allus used to get rid of 'em."

"I don't mean holes—I mean *cows*!" explained Jake.

"Oh, then it's all right," responded Buck. "I ain't goin' to ask *you* to dig no cows, Jake. But yo're goin' to dig some nice ditches tomorrow; long, deep ones, an' good an' wide."

"I ain't never dug a ditch in my life," hastily objected Jake.

"Why, didn't you tell me how you dug that railroad cut down there in Iowa, an' got a hundred dollars extra 'cause you saved th' company so much money?" inquired Buck.

"Oh, but that was a steam shovel!"

"All right; you'll steam afore yo're at it very long."

Jake backed out again, slipped out of his kitchen, and stood reflective under the stars. He would quit and flee to Twin River if it wasn't such a long walk. "Darn it!" he growled, and forthwith threw two stones into the darkness by way of getting rid of some of his anger.

"Sa-a-y!" floated a voice out of the night. "You jerk any more rocks in *this* direction an' I'll beat you up so you'll wipe your feet on yoreself, thinkin' yo're a doormat! What'n hell you mean, anyhow?"

"Mebby they's *apples!*" jeered Bow-Wow from the bunkhouse. "Hello, William Tell!"

The cook softly closed the door and propped a chair against it. "Gee whiskers! I ain't goin' to stay *here* much longer! *Every*body's gettin' crazy!"

" 'If a body meets a body, comin' through th' rye,' " quavered a voice from the corral and a voice in the darkness profaned the song: "Ever meet yoreself goin' t'other way, after surroundin' th' rye?"

"Never had that pleasure after you'd been at th' booze."

Chesty Sutton entered the bunkhouse and stared at Bow-Wow. "What's eatin' you?" he demanded, curiously.

"I dunno; I've been itchin' ever since Murray told us. Wonder if I've got it?"

Chesty considered: "Well, now I remember that

chickens, cats, and dogs don't get cattle itch. You ain't got it, Bow-Wow. It's yore imagination that's got it. But if you're bound to scratch, do it somewhere else—you make me nervous, keepin' on one spot so long. Wait till I asks th' boys about it."

"Stop!" snapped Bow-Wow, his hand on a bottle of harness oil: "You never mind about askin' anybody! I'll take yore word for it—remember, I'll bust yore gizzard if you gets that pack o' coyotes barkin' at *my* heels!"

"Holy Smoke! We'll have our hands full a while," growled Chesty, dropping onto a box. "Let any o' this crowd ketch anybody throwin' mangy cows over on us! An' right after it comes th' Spring combin'—this is shore a weary world."

"Jake's got to dig some ditches," remarked the foreman, entering the house, and immediately the misery of future hours was forgotten in the merriment and satisfaction found in this news. Jake would have a lot of advisers.

In the ranch house Whitby was laughing gently and finally he voiced a wish: "I say, Peters, what a wealth of character there is out here. I wish Johnnie Beauchamp were here—what a rattling good play he could make. You know, Johnnie's last play was almost a success—and I'm very much interested in him. I backed him to the tune of two thousand pounds."

Invited to spend the night in the ranch house, Whitby accepted with alacrity. In carrying out McAllister's wishes he could not be too near headquarters, he concluded; but added to this, he entertained a sincere admiration for Buck Peters which increased as the days went by.

Some few minutes after the lights were out, Buck was brought back from the shadowy realm of sleep by Whitby's voice coming from the other room. "I say, Peters, did you keep those calculations?"

"Yes," answered Buck. "Why?"

"There's the lumber, you know. It might be a good idea to have McAllister send it on."

"Shore would. You tell him."

"I will," promised Whitby. A few seconds later he broke out again: "Do you know, Buck, the railroad companies of America are cheerful beggars. They take your luggage and then play ducks and drakes with it, in a very idiotic way. Why, mine was lost for two weeks and I was in a very devil of a fix. So it would not be a bad idea, you know, if I tell your partner to send a man with the consignment. He can sit on the barrels and see that they aren't placed on a siding to prove the theory that loss of movement results in inertia. Am I right?"

Buck laughed from his heart. "If there's anything you don't think of make a note of it an' let me see it," he commended.

"What a rummy remark. I say, how—ha! ha!" and Whitby's bunk creaked to his mirth. "That's rather a neat one, you know! I didn't know you were Irish, Peters, blessed if I did! I must tell that to your man Friday—it will keep the bally ass combing his frowsy locks for a week."

Buck had one foot on the Slumberland boundary when he heard the voice again, seeming to have traveled a long distance: "And I believe I should be rewarded for my brilliancy. I'll ask your partner to send some brandy and a box of *good* cigars with the rest of it as my fee. I'll have to learn to smoke all over again," he complained drowsily. A raucous snore bounced off the partition and Whitby opened his eyes for a moment: "My word, if Friday could only cook as well as he snores!"

CHAPTER XIII

Punctuation as a Fine Art

TWIN RIVER was in full blast when Dave rode in, looking for Tex. He dropped off the pony and went into the Why-Not, but his man was not there; after a few unavoidable drinks—Dave could not have avoided one if it had invited from the middle of the Staked Plain—he looked in at Ike's and the I-Call. He sampled the liquor in both places but evidently Comin' Thirty was not in that part of the town and he jogged on up to the Sweet-Echo. He had not been in here since warned off by Slick, but fear of consequences had nothing to do with absenting himself; fear did not enter into his composition. Dave's fundamental fault lay in his hatred of being beaten. It had lead him to cheat at play; to outwit by foul means; to take the sure course to any desired end, deliberately regardless of what anyone might think. The danger of such actions did not deter him in the least; he was always ready, usually overwhelmingly ready, to back them up in any manner his opponents demanded of him. The defeat, sure to be met when he opposed a superior intelligence, he confidently relied upon overcoming by sheer force of personality, mistaking violence for strength, deceit for ingenuity. The bad judgment of his failures ever wore the mantle of bad luck; and the thought and time he wasted in schemes for revenge might have been used more profitably in making success of his failure.

Since his employment by Schatz his mind had been fully occupied by the furtherance, as he considered it, of his employer's plan. Buck Peters, the Englishman, even Slick, at times pricked his memory, but he had resolutely put them aside until a more convenient season. Now, with whiskey spurring his Satanic temperament, he considered it obligatory to go into the Sweet-Echo. He wanted to find Comin' and no fancy barkeep' nor roaring Scotchman should keep him from going wherever he wanted to go. He stepped from his stirrup onto the porch and went into the barroom as if he owned it.

The expected trouble did not develop. Slick gave him a short nod and set up glass and bottle with praiseworthy promptitude. If Dave was without fear, so was Slick, who would have taken him on in any way whatever; preferably, as became his Irish ancestry, with his hands, but failing that, with anything from a pop gun to a cannon. Dave, with his usual habit of ignoring the other man, imagined Slick to be overawed; this leavened his savagery with good nature. What was Slick Milligan, anyhow? Just a barkeep'—Dave turned his back to the bar and surveyed the inmates of the room. Comin' was not there. Where in thunder was he? Maybe bucking the tiger at Little Nell's. Dave had two or three drinks with men he knew and rode back to cross the ford. He was again out in his reckoning. He watched the cards flick from the box. Nell, herself, was dealing and Dave's fingers itched to get down, but he refrained. With the vague hints dropped by Schatz and his consequent hope of speedily winning Rose, he knew he must drop gambling—until he had won to the fulfilment of his desires, at least.

As he watched he suddenly realized he was hungry and strolled into the eating house, run by Nell as a paying adjunct to her other businesses. The whiskey, as it often does in healthy stomachs, was calling loudly for food and Dave answered the call with unstinted generosity. Being genuinely wishful to see Tex he did not linger but, as soon as finished, started to make the round again.

He got no farther than the Why-Not. His entry was met by a roar of laughter and shouts of encouragement: "Bully f' you, gran'pa!"—"Did he ever come back?"—"That's th' caper, Dirty!"—"*Let* him alone, *he* ain't chokin'."

Seated on a box on the top of a table (Dirty would be buried in a box; they would never have the heart to separate his attenuated figure from the object so long associated with it in life), old Pop Snow bent up and down, shrinking, shrinking, until his bony leanness threatened to vanish before their gaze; a wheezing gasp started him swelling again and his "he! he! he!" whistled above the uproar like a hiss in a machine shop.

He was astonishingly drunk—for Dirty. His pervious clay had developed innumerable channels for alcohol in the years of training he had given it; and he was seldom so joyously hilarious as this. For one reason it was seldom that any one would pay for it, and Dirty's means only went far enough to keep him everlastingly thirsty. The explanation appeared to Dave in the shape of a group of miners, whose voices, in their appreciation, were the loudest.

"He-he-he! He-he-he-he!" Pop Snow's shrill pipe

continued, while the others demanded more. "Saw-bones hadn't been gone a week afore he was wanted. He-he-he! eh, dear! eh, dear! Lucky Jones come along—an' stopped. Ther' wearn't nothin' *to* do but stop. He comes to me an' he says: 'Wheer's ther' a doctor?' 'Well,' I says, 'jedgin' from what I hears, if you jest foller th' river north fur about fif-teen mile to Drigg's Worry,' I says, 'you'll find a saw-bones as used to be yer—but when he left he swears as how he ain't never comin' back to th' P'int,' I says. He-he-he! Send-I-may-live if he don't, though. Yep, an' Jones purty nigh goes into th' wet, too. 'Th' P'int?' roars th' Doc, 'No, siree, by God, no, sir! Twenty-eight mile th' last time to tend a stinkin' ole sow, on account o' a misbegotten son o' Beelzebub an th' North Pole they call Snow down there. This time I 'spose 't'ud be a skunk.' 'It's my wife,' says Jones, 'an' if yuh don't come right sud-den I'm a-goin' to blow off th' top o' yore devilish ole head,' says Jones; 'an' if she dies,' he sez, 'I blows her off, anyhow.' He-he-he! Sawbones, he riz up an' come a-kitin'. I ain't much on Welshmen; they biles over too easy. But Sawbones done a good job an' got away wi' his life. We hears all about it nex' day when Jones comes to me an' tells me it is two at once, boy an' a girl. Fust we knowed he'd brung his wife. Not as she stays long. Winter's one too many fur her an' she cashes in. Then Lucky Jones, he tries to cross th' river below th' P'int, 'stid o' th' ford, an' th' ice ain't strong enough, an' Jones, he was some drunk, I reckon. We calls th' river after him an' th' forks after th' kids. Lord, they was bad uns, both on 'em. Black Jack, he hez hisself hung for suthin' or other, an' Little Jill, she turns out just a plain—"

Every one jumped, it was so unexpected. The lead sung so close to Dirty's nose that the backward jerk almost took him off the table and he recovered his seat with a sideways wriggle and squirm that did credit to the elasticity of his aged muscles. Having managed to retain his seat, he continued to retain it. None of the others showed the least desire to move, though every last man of them yearned for absence—sudden, noiseless absence—of a kind so instantaneous as to preclude the possibility of notice: anything less were foolhardy in the face of those blazing eyes and that loosely held gun, its business end oscillating like the head of a snake and far more deadly.

"Don't be afeared, Dirty," purred Dave, in the kindliest tones. "I was jest a-puttin' in th' period. Yore eddication is shameful, Dirty, an' I grieves for you, account of it. You has a generous mixture o' commas an' semi-commas an' things like that, but yore periods is shore some scarce. You was a-sayin' as how Little Jill was a sweet, good gal, as never done wrong in her life, wasn't you?"

Dirty swallowed hard and nodded. Speech was beyond him just then and perhaps he had spoken too much, already. He repeated his former contortion with equal skill and success, and every head in the crowd rose perceptibly and returned to its former level as the gun spoke again and another hole appeared in the wall, close to the first.

"A period comes after that, Dirty," said Dave. "Don't you never forget th' kind o' gal she was—an' then comes th' period. You'll mebby hold yore liquor better." He shoved the gun back in the holster, eyed the crowd insolently for a moment, and turning his back on it, walked calmly from the room.

Pop Snow climbed down from the table in haste and pushed his way through the detaining arms and the medley of questions that assailed him on his way to the door, which opened and closed like a stage trap as he stepped out and sprang to one side; his anger was that of a sober and far younger man and he peered about with keen eyes. His caution was uncalled for: Dave was splashing through the ford and Dirty watched him set out in a swift lope along the Big Moose trail. Dave had no stomach for further company that night.

Dirty rubbed a pair of trembling lips as he gazed. "Black Jack!" he muttered, "Black Jack! He *warn't* hung, then. No, an' he won't never be 'less it's fur killin' pore ole Pop Snow. Pore ole Pop Snow," he repeated, whimpering as he hurried across the bridge toward shelter; "Jest like Dutch Onion. Dead an' gone, pore ole Dutch. Pore ole Pop." He stopped in the middle of the trail and with a flash of his former spirit, shook his fist after the distant Dave: "Shell I?" he jeered: "shell I, then? I been yer afore you, Jack, an' I'll be a-livin' when you rot."

Hoofbeats coming out of the darkness where Dave had disappeared, startled him and he scuttled away like a rabbit.

CHAPTER XIV

Fighting the Itch

MONROE AND the three men left to him after Bow-Wow had departed for Twin River and Wayback, in the company of Whitby, were too small a force to attempt the round-up, so they put in the day riding over those sections of the range farthest removed from the Hog Back, examining every cow they found. At nightfall they had the pleasure of reporting to Buck that the entire portion of the range along the Little Jill, extending from the river to the middle of the ranch, was free from infection; as a matter of fact the conclusion reached in council was that only that portion of range bounded by the Black Jack, the south line, and Blackfoot Creek needed to be cleaned up. This meant that two-thirds of the ranch was free from the itch, and the infected third contained less than a fourth of the Double Y cows.

Plans for the round-up were considered and soon arrived at. All the men with the exception of three, were to be actively engaged in the round-up. They were to start from the south line and drive northwest towards the Hog Back. The Black Jack made a natural barrier on the west and would hold the herd safely on that side. The three other punchers were to ride even with the drive line, but on the other side of Blackfoot Creek, and keep ambitious cows from crossing onto the non-infected portions of the range. This arrangement would constantly force the cattle onto the wedge-shaped range at the juncture of the two waters. Here the herd could be dipped and driven across the shallow Blackfoot onto a clean territory, where they would be held for further observation. Then if the rest of the range showed signs of infection the round-up and dipping could be carried on again at other points. If a strict line could be maintained along the Blackfoot the Hog Back range would be fenced off effectually from the non-infected cattle on the other parts of the ranch. The question of building an actual fence to separate the Hog Back range from the rest was gone into thoroughly and the decision was unanimous that twelve miles of fence was too big a proposition to be attempted at that moment; if necessary it could be put up later when it was found that patrolling the creek was inadvisable. But perhaps a side light can be thrown on this quiet decision when it is remembered how fervently a cowman hated fences. These men were all of the old school and preferred to keep barbwire as a theory and not a fact.

That evening Bow-Wow returned with a crowd of cow-punchers of varying degrees of fitness, all eager to take cards in any game at fifty dollars a month. The majority of them were not up to the standards Buck cherished; if they had been, they would not have been waiting for a job. But it was certain they knew how to punch cows, enough for the demands of the moment—and Jake waxed eloquent and sarcastic when he hazarded a guess as to when they had eaten their last square meal. Perhaps, after all, digging huge ditches would not be so bad, for cooking three meals a day for twenty-odd hungry men was more of a task than he cared to tackle. But Bow-Wow had exercised some intelligence of his own, as after events showed. Two of his squad were ex-cooks. The "ex" is used advisedly, for if ever cooks were "ex" it was these two; this was the decision voiced simultaneously by twenty hungry men at the first meal prepared by the two. Sam Hawkins suggested that they had quit cooking to save their lives, and regretted that they had so made their choice.

The drive went ahead without more than the usual bluster and confusion, and the end of the first day found the round-up well under way. Outlying free range had been thoroughly combed, in which assistance had been given by neighboring ranches; Buck, in carrying out his policy of supplying his own help, had not failed to notify other owners and foremen that they could rely on the Double Y for its contingent of men when the general round-up should take place. The drivers were divided into two squads for day work and three for night riding around the herd; the two-squad arrangement was made for meal times, one squad eating while the other worked. There was no time lost at meals because each of the ex-cooks, in a chuck wagon allotted to him, preceded the drive and was never very far from the field of operations. Thus were system and order gained the first day, which meant time saved in the end.

Buck intended to spend his nights in the ranch house as usual, and when he gained it the first night he found two things of interest. The first announced itself by sending him to his hands and knees within three feet of his front door; the second was a telegram from McAllister saying that a special had the right of way, and from the wording Buck could see it pounding into the Northwest, over crossings and past switch towers, its careening red tail lights bearing a warning to would-be range-jumpers if they did but know it. The message further stated that the consignment was under the personal attention of a puncher who, having grown sick of the stock yards, was cheerfully availing himself of the opportunity of getting back to the open range at no expense. Buck sighed with relief as he realized that the ingredients of the dip were already on the way, and could not be sidetracked or lost without the subduing of a very irritable cow-puncher. As he put the message away he remembered the first thing that had impressed itself on him, and went out to take a look at it.

The light in his hand revealed the sodless strip fifty feet long and four feet wide. Its depth was to the under side of the grass, a matter of two or three inches. There was a stake at each corner of the bare rectangle and these supported a one-strand fence made of lariats.

Buck scratched his head and then growled a profane request to feel the head of the man who was responsible. He strode into the house and stopped in the kitchen door; and Jake very wearily turned around on his chair and looked at him with intent curiosity.

"What'n hell is that scalped grass for?" demanded Buck, evenly.

"That's th' beginnin' of ditch number one," replied Jake. "How'd you like them lines, eh? Straight as a die. Took me all mornin' to lay 'em out like that."

"Did it? I congratulate you, Jake—likewise I sympathize with you. I reckon you'll get it down a foot in a couple o' weeks, eh?"

"Oh, quicker'n that," modestly rejoined Jake.

"Didn't I tell you to dig them ditches close to where th' Blackfoot empties into th' Jack?" demanded Buck. "Are you figgerin' on extendin' it from here to there? I don't want a trench no fifteen miles long. Tomorrow mornin' you ride with me an' I'll show you where to dig. An' don't you bother stakin' it off exact, neither. I want them ditches all finished in *three* days. Did you reckon I was goin' to drive two thousand head of itch cows fifteen miles so I could dip 'em bang up agin my own front door!"

Pickles bounced in, his rifle under his arm. "Hullo Buck!" he cried. "Shot a coyote today!"

"Good, Pickles," smiled Buck. "Want a job shootin' a *man* tomorrow?"

"Betcher life! Is it Dave?"

"No, it's Jake, here," replied Buck. "You take yore rifle an' come with me an' Jake tomorrow. If he don't dig fast enough to suit you, you shoot him in th' laig."

"Betcher life! Which leg?" asked Pickles, agog with anticipation.

"I'm leavin' that to you, Pickles. You're gettin' big enough to figger things out for yoreself."

"Will he limp like Hopalong?"

"Worse, mebby."

Jake, grinning, feared Pickles might be carried away with his zeal, and he put in a laughing objection; but he sobered instantly at Buck's sharp reply.

"I mean it. He'll shoot if he's a friend o' mine. I ain't goin' to lose a lot of cows 'cause I've got a man too lazy to dig. You've got yore orders, Pickles: obey 'em like a real Bar-20 puncher."

"Betcher life I will. Just like Hopalong Cassidy!"

Jake groaned at the intense earnestness in Pickles' declaration; to emulate the great Hopalong Cassidy was enduring honor in Pickles' eyes, and from past performances and several duels with the boy, Jake reached the conclusion that he was slated to do some very rapid digging on the morrow.

"Lemme use *yore* rifle, Buck!" asked Pickles, his eyes shining with the joy of living. He knew he could do a great deal better with Buck's repeater, and the thought of exploding .45–70 cartridges was a delight beyond his wildest dreams.

Jake's heart stopped for the reply and he sighed with relief as Pickles' face fell; but the boy's spirits rose like a balloon. "All right, Buck; I can get him with my gun, though I ought to have a repeater."

The round-up went forward swiftly and the day that McAllister's special puffed into Wayback and snorted onto the siding, found the Hog Back country swept clean of cattle, the herd being held close to Jake's two big ditches. Buck had known the magnitude of the task he set for Jake and when the cook showed he was anxious to do his share of the work, Buck had told off men enough to help him get through in time. The digging was hard and unaccustomed work and the men were changed frequently, all but Jake; he seemed to consider it a matter of pride to stick to the job and made a point of throwing the last shovelful of dirt as well as the first; as a consequence his altitude was below normal for a week afterward, and it was a month before he forgot to grunt with every breath.

The hauling of the lumber exercised the ingenuity and strained the resources of Jean LaFrance, the only man in the locality who possessed anything on wheels capable of carrying it. Inasmuch as he could ill spare the time, although sorely needing the money, it exhausted Jean's stock of oaths to the point where his own language failed him; even English, which he understood, seemed singularly tame and unworthy the occasion; so that he fell back on his carefully reserved specimens of German expletives, which he did not in the least understand, and these with constant repetitions carried him through. Two men, driving the two borrowed chuck wagons, succeeded in transporting the rest of the shipment, and Whitby, to his great satisfaction, found that McAllister had not forgotten his fee.

The junction of the Blackfoot with the Jack presented a busy scene. The close-packed blue-clay, which had made hard work for the diggers, now proved a help, the timbers fitting snug without backing. Meanwhile the more important part, the preparing of the solution, went on under the direction of Whitby; his calm handling and frequent active cooperation without becoming warm or soiled was a wonder to see. Under the huge caldrons, which had been the first of the consignment to arrive, wood had been piled ready for the match; on bases made of logs stood rows of whiskey barrels; shallow troughs were filled and refilled with water until the swelling wood took up and became watertight. Far into the night they worked, and now the crackling fires were giving the night shift trouble with the snorting cattle. Weird shadows darted out over the ground, lengthened and vanished as the men moved about the fires, worked over the lime-slaking troughs or poured off the compound paste into the steaming caldrons. When the barrels were filled with the first lot of the mixture, Whitby relented and the men stumbled off to rest.

With the dawn they were at work again; and now the dipping troughs came into use as the saturated solution was drawn off from the barrels, leaving the sediment at the bottom, and dumped into the troughs, where water was added to reduce it to the required strength. Night was approaching again before the water arose to nearly the required level; the men were thoroughly tired and Whitby, reluctantly and as a result of a direct order from Buck, called a halt. Buck knew the temper of his men better than Whitby: at anything directly connected with range duties, provided they were familiar with it, they would work until they dropped; but this was something whose usefulness remained to be proven. Buck was too wise to push them in such a case, but he grinned cheerfully as he turned away from the reluctance on Whitby's face. The Britisher was surely a glutton for work.

The prudence of Buck's reasoning was shown by the eagerness with which the men responded to the call next morning. In less than an hour Whitby announced all ready and the men entered upon a scene which they individually and collectively swore repaid them for their trouble. At Whitby's shout, two of the men riding herd cut out the first bunch of cattle and drove them toward the dipping trough; the flimsily constructed horse corral swarmed with laughing, joking punchers who roped their mounts with more or less success in the first attempt, while outside the wranglers darted forward and back, wheeling on a pie dish, checking the more ambitious of the ponies that resented a confinement limited to a single line of lariats; saddles dropped onto recalcitrant backs and were cinched with a speed nothing short of marvelous to a layman, and the whooping punchers were jerked away to the herd.

The first lot of cows, some twenty in number, flirting their tails and snorting in angry impotence, entered the wide opening between a wedge-shaped pair of fences and galloped toward the narrow vent which led to the trough. And now was seen Buck's wisdom in continuing the fence along the edge of the troughs a few feet, both at entrance and exit: the first brute, a magnificent three-year-old, appeared to realize the crush that would come and spurted for the opening; the significance of the situation did not appeal to him until he was close to the edge; he slid to the very brink and gathered himself for a leap, but the fence was too high; the next instant the cattle behind, urged on by Cock Murray, whooping like an Indian, bumped into the hesitating brute and he fell forward into the trough with a bellow of rage and started on his swim to the other end.

When Cock Murray, with Slow Jack close behind, had followed the bunch between the fences, they were assailed by a chorus of shouts to which they paid no heed whatever. Slow Jack, being in the rear, caught a glimpse out of the tail of his eye of Whitby running and waving his arms; he looked around for the cause of so much excitement and was in time to see the second bunch, instead of being driven over to the other trough as they should have been, come thundering into the wedge and drive down upon him. Slow Jack shot up to the fence, threw one leg along the neck of his pony and skimmed through the opening he made for, with nothing to spare and a scratched saddle; after which he spent several profane seconds in telling the chaffing drivers what he thought of them. His annoyance was forgotten when they suddenly doubled up, shrieking with laughter, and pointed toward the shoot.

Slow Jack looked and then looked at them. The second bunch had gone galloping madly on to the narrow opening, against which they were wedged and dropping one by one as a third bunch pressed in after them. They were coming too rapidly and Ned Monroe, riding past from the other trough, was sending the next bunch in the proper direction and going on to the herd to put some sense of order into the heads of the rollicking punchers. Slow Jack quite failed to see anything funny in all this and said so with force and directness; he added, moreover, a prophecy regarding idiots, the fulfilment of which was due to take place in the near, in fact immediate, future, which threatened complete derangement of the internal economy of said idiots. The idiots were entirely oblivious. Jack was puzzled. He glanced ahead and noticed a lot more idiots. Disgusted with his vain attempt to get an explanation, he rode forward to see for himself.

Cock Murray, having quirted the last of the first bunch into the trough, became aware of the shouting, gesticulating men who had left their duties to run toward the fence to attract his attention. In the cross-fire of warnings he failed to understand any of them, but the rumbling rush behind brought him suddenly to a realization of his position. One glance and he saw it was too late to retreat. There was just one thing to do. "Holy mackerel!" gasped Cock. He put the quirt to his pony in a frenzy of blows and landed in the dipping mixture with a jump that carried his pony's feet to the bottom of the trough. Sputtering and swearing Cock went through to the end; it was useless, as he knew, to try to climb out over those smooth abrupt walls, and he was too obstinate to leave his saddle. Which was madder, Cock or the pony, it would be hard to say. It was when he went climbing up the cleated incline at the farther end that Slow Jack got his first inkling of the cause of mirth. He gave one astonished stare, made two or three odd noises in his throat, and then, gravely and in silence, dropped from his saddle to the ground. It was not until he lay at full length, the long reins of the bridle drooping from the bit and his pony gazing at him inquiringly, that he exploded—but then he laughed steadily for half an hour.

The cattle, which had not awaited these developments, were dropping into the trough with praiseworthy regularity and making their way to the other end; when about half way there and swimming re-

signedly, a kind-hearted puncher, wearing a delighted grin in addition to his regular equipment,
and armed with a strong pole, forked at the business end, leaned forward swiftly, jammed the fork
over the unsuspecting cow's head, and pushed zeal-
ously. The result was gratifying to the few onlookers, and disconcerting to the cow so rudely ducked;
just before the unfortunate bovine touched the
sloping runway to dry earth, another grinning
puncher repeated the dose. The cows, reluctant to
enter the bath, showed no reluctance to leave it and
the scene of their humiliation, and they lumbered
away with a speed surprising to those whose ideas
of cows are based upon observation of domesti-
cated "bossies" in pasture in the East. But they
were not allowed to run free, being driven slowly
across a roughly constructed bridge to the farther
side of the Blackfoot, onto the non-infected range,
and held there.

"This yere trough is shore makin' some plenty of
Baptists," grinned Chesty Sutton.

"Yep; but with Mormon inclinations," amended
Bow-Wow.

"Bow to th' gents," reprimanded Chesty, ducking
a cow. "You look like a drowned rat," he criticized.

"Bow agin," requested Bow-Wow, and the cow
obeyed, with a show of fight when its head came
up.

"Some high-falutin' picklin' factory," chuckled
Chesty. "Messrs. Bow-Wow Baker an' Chesty Sutton,
world's greatest mite picklers. Blue-noses, red-noses
an' other kinds o' cow inhabitants a specialty. Give
you a whole dollar, Bow-Wow, if you fall in."

"Is that just a plain hope, or a insinooation?" demanded the cheerful Bow-Wow. "I sleep next to you,
so don't get too blamed personal. But we might put
Jake in—though mebby his ain't th' right kind. Hey,
Jake; come here."

"If you wants to see me, you come here," retorted the cook. "I've seen all of them ditches *I* wants to. An' I ain't takin' no chances with a couple o' fools, neither."

"Hey, Chesty!" called Bow-Wow, delighted. "Here comes that LX steer we had such a hell of a time with in th' railroad pens. Soak him good! Ah, ha, my long-horned friend; you was some touchy an' peevish down there in Wayback. Take *that*—don't worry, Chesty's been savin' some for you, too. *Hard*, Chesty! That's th' boy—bet he's mad as a rattler."

"Look at that moth-eaten scab of a yearlin'," laughed Chesty, pointing. "Th' firm could declare dividends on th' mites we'll pickle on her. *Souse* she goes! Once more for luck—look at her steam up! Hell, *this* ain't work—it's fun. Under you go, Alice dear. Next!"

"Here comes Kinkaid o' th' Cyclone," announced Cock Murray, riding up to take a hasty look at the operations before he returned to the herd for another bunch of cows.

Chesty handed his pole to Murray, grabbed up a lariat, and started for the newcomer, shouting: "Here comes some itch! Dip him, fellers! Quick!"

Kinkaid maneuvered swiftly, grinning broadly. "If that stuff is warmer 'n th' water in th' Jack, why, I might be coaxed into it. Howd'y, boys; thought I'd come over an' pick up some points."

"How you makin' out on th' Cyclone?" asked Buck.

"Bad—*very* bad. We tried isolatin' th' mangy ones, but they're dyin' like flies in frost time. Lost forty million so far an' I reckon th' other two'll die tomorrow. We thought our north range was free, but they're on that, too. We drove clean cows up in th' Rockin' Horse territory an' now they're showin' signs o' havin' th' itch. Beats all how it travels."

Cock Murray listened intently, but held his peace.

He thought he might explain how it had traveled toward the Rocking Horse.

"That's where we noticed it first," said Buck. "We found some o' yore cows on th' Hog Back, an' their trail left th' river just below th' Rockin' Horse."

Kinkaid looked surprised and asked questions. He sat very quietly for a few moments and then looked at Buck with a peculiar expression on his face. "Sick cows don't swim th' Jack, cold as it is now. I wonder who in hell—?" he muttered, softly.

"We're wonderin', too, Kinkaid," replied Buck, slowly. "It's lead or rope for anybody we ketch at it." Kinkaid nodded his emphatic endorsement of this.

Whitby was keeping a close watch on the tally of cattle as they emerged, comparing it with the amount of fresh mixture constantly being added to that already in the troughs, and he found reason to be thankful that he had ordered more than he expected to use. Any left over would make all the less needed at the fall shipment when, as he knew, the dipping would have to be repeated; not until then could they be assured that the disease was stamped out.

The first day's work finished less than half the herd, but they continued, the following day, until the last cow scrambled out. After which, as a matter of precaution, Buck gave the boys the fun of driving every pony through the mixture. What had been entertaining before now became side-splitting, for tired as they were, the savage natures of the furious victims drew energy from unexpected sources and made a scene well worth watching, and a little risky for those men waiting with ropes at the end of the dripping board. The cows were angry, but had neither the intelligence nor the fighting ability of the maddened animals who had only a short time before seemed to enjoy the discomfiture of the animals they were accustomed to drive and bully; and it was only agility and good luck that the flying hoofs landed on nothing more substantial than air.

While this did not take long it was too late when finished, and the men too weary, to break camp; but the next morning saw the chuck wagon piled high with barrels and caldrons on the way to the ranch house. Some of the extra men, having in mind the wording of the guarantee of a full month's pay, cherished the hope that there was no further use for their services and that they would be paid off and told to leave. They were disappointed, for instead of loafing or leaving, half of them were set to planting posts for the fence which it was found necessary to erect along the creek, while the others rode over the range on the look-out for cows with signs of itch. A small herd of about a hundred, found scattered along and near the creek, were dipped as a precautionary measure, and after a week had elapsed without finding further signs of the disease, Buck ordered the second squad to begin the Spring or calf round-up; the fence division patrolled the creek to effect a quarantine until the wire arrived. They had a two-strand fence extending along Blackfoot Creek from its source to the river, when the round-up was half over, and were immediately put to work with the others. When the last calf was branded, the extra force was let go and Buck waited for some new deviltry. It came, and turned his hair grayer and deepened the lines of care on his face. Calves had totalled up well and proved to him that there was lots of money to be taken out of the Double Y under fair conditions, but the next blow cut into his resources with crushing effect and made him waver for a moment.

CHAPTER XV

The Slaughter of the Innocents

THE ROUND-UP was still under way when Cock Murray was taken off and sent to Twin River in a chuck wagon to get provisions for the ranch. He had loaded his wagon and left town behind him when he saw Dave riding hard to overtake him. He drew rein and nodded when the horseman pulled up beside him.

"Howd'y, Dave."

"Howd'y, Murray," replied Dave. "Spring round-up over yet?"

"Nope; 'bout half."

"Itch all cured good?"

"Can't find no more signs of it. That dippin' play was a winner an' it's a good thing to remember."

"I've got a little job for you an' Slow Jack," Dave remarked, after a moment's thought.

"Yeh? Hope it's better'n some o' yore schemes."

"What do you mean? I never had no schemes."

"All right—my mistake," drawled Murray. "What's th' new one?"

"New nothin'. I just want you an' Slow Jack to drive a couple o' thousand head up in th' Hog Back country some'rs an' hold 'em hid till I can take care o' 'em."

"If yo're goin' to start up in business for yoreself, I'd keep away from th' Hog Back," replied Murray gravely. "Better try down on th' southeast corner. There ain't no itch hangin' 'round there."

"Business nothin'!" snapped Dave, not liking his companion's levity. "I've got somethin' in my head that'll make a fortune for you an' Slow Jack. I don't want no profits—just th' joy o' takin' a good punch at Peters'll do for me. But you two ought to split 'bout twenty thousand dollars a-tween you."

"Music to my ears!" chuckled Murray. "Slow Jack's goin' to work on a salary basis on *this* job—th' profits 'll be mine. Whereabouts is this gold mine located, did you say?"

Dave did not heed him but continued hurriedly: "There's a good pasture atween th' Hog Back an' th' river, an' th' only way to it or out of it is up that ravine. You an' Slow Jack can drive cows to it whenever you gets a chanct, an' a couple o' ropes acrost th' ravine'll hold 'em in. When you get a couple o' thousand there we'll drive 'em north o' th' Cyclone's line to Rankin, put 'em on th' cars there an' get 'em south into Wyoming. There's good money in it, Murray."

The driver was staring at his companion, blank amazement on his face. "Gosh! That sounds easy! 'Bout as easy as me an' you capturin' th' Fort an' makin' th' Government pay us a big war indemnity. Slow Jack's goin' to get th' wages an' profits, too. I'm too generous to cut in an' spoil his chance to make a fortune. I suppose we're goin' to tie th' herd to balloons an' get 'em to Rankin that way?"

"You collect th' herd an' I'll attend to all th' rest o' it," declared Dave. "I've got this thing all worked out an' it's goin' through."

"Can't be did, Dave," emphatically replied the driver, dazed by the signs of insanity manifested by his companion.

"You say that because it ain't never been done," retorted Dave, angrily. "It *can* be done, an' I'm goin' to do it. Put that in yore pipe."

"All right—you ought to know," responded Murray, tactfully. "Who are th' miracle-men that are goin' to get th' herd off that table-land an' to Rankin without bein' seen or leavin' a trail?"

"Big Saxe, th' hunchback, is one," Dave explained. "Th' trail we'll leave ain't botherin' us any. They won't be missed till it's too late to look for tracks—an' by that time th' cows'll be sold."

Murray thought of one objection that would kill the plan without mercy: the railroad was not in the habit of accepting unaccredited cows for shipment; curiosity would be shown as to the brand, where it came from, who owned it, and other pertinent facts. But Dave was so hopeful, so earnest, that Murray decided to talk the matter over with Schatz before dispelling Dave's dream.

"Well, that's true, Dave," he soberly replied. "When you think it over ca'm like, it ain't so plumb foolish. Me an' Slow Jack'll see what we can do—let you know as soon as we can. I got to poke along. But say, Dave; it's shore death to anybody tryin' to fool with *Cyclone* cows along th' river—tell th' boys so they won't try to throw over any more scabby cattle on us. Kinkaid is some peevish 'bout his north range gettin' th' itch. Got any more plans you want to tell about? All right—don't get mad at *me*, Dave; I'm only foolin'. So long."

Murray had crossed the north line of his ranch before he emerged from his trance. Then he shook himself, laughed and looked around, urging the team to livelier efforts. He nursed his secret until after dark and then slipped away from the ranch and struck out toward Twin River. When he had gone a mile in this direction he wheeled sharply and urged his pony toward the trail along the Little Jill. Arriving at the Schatz domicile he reconnoitred a little and then slipped up to the kitchen door and drummed lightly on it. Schatz opened it and dragged the visitor inside.

"You must nod come to see me more as iss necessary," began the German. "It iss such carelessness as puts peoples in chails. Vat iss it dis time?"

Murray, grinning, unfolded Dave's plans to the astonished German, who could only grunt his surprise and disgust. Suddenly Schatz brightened and a faint twinkle came into his eyes. "Dot iss a goot plan, Murray. A very goot plan. *Aber* it goes too far. Dose railroad peoples vould spoil it quick. You get der herd like Dave says, more if you can; und hold it till *I* say somet'ing. Neffer mind vat Dave say—he iss *ein verruchter Mensch.* But ven *I* say somet'ing, den you do it. *Verstanden?*"

"All right, Schatz," agreed Murray, smiling. "I'll back yore play to th' limit, every time. But what'll I say to Dave when he gets anxious?"

"He von't ged anxious. I vill speak der vord before he haf time to ged anxious. I vill tell vat to do mit dot herd, und it von't be vat Dave vants."

"Then I'll tell Slow Jack that th' collection takes place. Anything else?"

"*Nein*—careful you go. Alvays you must be careful. *Goot nacht!*" and the door closed quickly.

"Ach! Dot Dave!" exclaimed Schatz, his hands upraised.

Slow Jack must have been told of Schatz's wishes, because during the week following Murray's visit to the German's house, cattle had been disappearing from the southwestern part of the range; this was not strange enough to cause worry even if it had been observed, because cows go where they please; and it was not observed by any one but Cock Murray and Slow Jack. The fence, extending to within a short distance of the south line, was regarded as barrier enough to keep the cattle off the infected range, and Buck gave no particular thought to it. Slow Jack rode along the fence every few days to see that there were no breaks in it and as Cock Murray had the south line under his care, it was an easy matter to round up small herds and drive them over the Hog Back, down the ravine on the river side, and hold them on the plateau pasture by the means Dave had suggested. The grass was heavy and the water plentiful along the line patrolled by Murray and there were always large numbers of cows grazing there—so many, in fact, that those driven off could not be missed under ordinary circumstances. Thus the hidden herd grew rapidly and it was not long before a large herd grazed close to the edge of the precipitous cliffs frowning down on the cold, hard-looking Black Jack.

Murray, fussing around the horse corral, had put in a hard day's riding and had no desire to stray far from the bunkhouse that chilly, windy night. He had been engaged in driving cattle onto the range he had been thinning, so as to cover the missing cows, and over five hundred extra head grazed near the springs that made the swampy headquarters of the creek.

Slow Jack was getting nervous because Schatz had not been heard from and he was grouchy and touchy even to his partner in the business on hand. He and Murray would be likely to have unpleasant questions asked of them if the herd should be discovered. They were in charge of that part of the range and it would not be easy to excuse the presence of so many cows on the infected section. The fence was intact and if it were not, then it would be squarely up to them; Buck would be profanely curious how it was that a respectable herd had managed to get past Murray and go around the end of the fence. And it would be hard to explain how the cattle willingly left the best grass on the ranch and wandered up the Hog Back, all finding the ravine and herding on the cliff-top pasture. And if the rope or the tracks of the two punchers' horses should be seen, gunplay would follow with deadly certainty.

"Darn that Dutchman!" growled Slow Jack to Murray, as they met and strolled away a short distance; "Seems like we ain't got enough cows up there to suit th' hog. He wants that pasture *covered* with 'em, I reckon. Word or no word, them cows has got to get back on th' range. An' th' itch is among 'em, too, Murray."

Murray smoked in silence for a while and then looked up, a frown on his face. "Smiler has got to be quick. Dave, th' fool, was out to see me again today. I asked him when he was goin' to rustle that bunch an' he says he's got it all fixed—mebby th' first black night. Is it black tonight?" he asked, ironically.

"Black as hell!" growled Slow Jack. "If Dave beats th' ol' man to it, an' gets away with that herd, I'll be plumb tickled to death. An' if he gets away with it good an' clean, without bein' caught, it'll go down in th' history o' cattle stealin' as th' greatest miracle since th' Dead Sea was walked on. Holy Cripes! Wouldn't it be a sensation?"

"Th' laurels will remain with th' Dead Sea," grunted Murray. "Dave's shore goin' to be fertilizer for th' daisies some o' these days if he don't get sane." After a moment he growled: "An' if he don't

stop comin' to see me like he has, Smiler 'll have to
dig up another ass to be father to."

"He was lookin' for me, yesterday," grinned Slow
Jack, "but I seen him first. He ain't goin' to *sic* no
lead *my* way if I can help it."

"Jack, did you ever figger out why Smiler lets
Dave mess around like he does?" suddenly asked
Murray. "Th' Dutchman is one clever individual, but
every clever crook makes one mistake that ropes
him. I hereby prophesy that Dave is Smiler's mistake an' will make th' Dutchman lose. Want to bet
on it?"

"What you allus lookin' for shore things for?"
jeered Jack. "You ain't got no sportin' blood in you!
In course I know it—an' that's just th' reason I've
got my stuff ready to move quick an' my trail all
mapped out. I might want to leave before breakfast
some day. Tell you one thing—*you* can drive cows
over th' Hog Back but I'm *all through*! Darn if I drive
another one!"

"I'm th' good little boy, too, from now on," replied
Murray. "An' I'm goin' to be awful busy farther east
on that line. Savvy? I ain't goin' to be able to even
guess how they got over th' Hog Back, an' I'll take
th' blame for bein' careless. I'd ruther lose my job
than house any lead under my skin. Aw! I'm goin' in
an' get some sleep."

"Me, too; I'll come right soon," and Slow Jack
drifted off into the darkness as his companion
started for the bunkhouse.

When Slow Jack entered the bunkhouse half an
hour after Murray, he paused in the door and
looked at the western sky, where lightning zig-
zagged occasionally. The barely audible roll of thunder told him how far off the storm was and he
noticed that the wind was blowing less steadily,
coming in gusts from varying points. Even while he
stood, the sound of the thunder increased in vol-

ume and the long, thin lightning reached out nearer
to him, a livid whip that lashed the heavens into
roaring anger.

"Huh! Reckon Spring is shore nuff here now," he
muttered. "Fust real lightnin' I seen this year." Five
minutes later he was asleep.

The Hog Back loomed up like a condensation of
the surrounding night, its huge bulk magnified and
made soft in its rugged outlines. A restless wind
scurried like a panic-stricken animal, sighing
through the brush and whispering through the
rocks. At intervals the silence was so intense that
the scraping of a twig, yards away, could be plainly
heard; and at other times the bellow of a steer
would have been lost in a few rods.

Something moved across the plain, slowly and
carefully as if feeling its way, and toiled up the pre-
carious trail, rolling pebbles clattering down; in the
noise of their fall was lost the soft thudding that
marked the course of the moving smudge. The lightning in the western sky flashed nearer and gave
brief illumination of the scene. Four men rode single
file up the dark trail, silent, intent, wary, the leader
picking his way as though he knew it well; in reply
to a low-voiced question from his nearest companion, he stretched out an abnormally long arm in a
sharp gesture. He did not like to have his ability
doubted.

Reaching the top, the procession strung along
and finally dipped into a ravine, following the
steeply slanting water-course until stopped by a lariat stretched across the way. Tossing aside the
rope, the leader led the force onto the walled-in
pasture where each man went swiftly to work without instructions. The fire at the leader's feet, fanned
by the high wind, leaped from him through the sun-
cured bunches of grass in a rapidly widening circle,

the heavy smoke rolling down upon the restless cattle in pungent clouds, sparks streaming through them. Every cow on the pasture was on its feet, pawing and snorting with fear at this most dreaded of all enemies. While they stood, seemingly hypnotized for a moment by the low flames, the darkness to the east of them was streaked with spurts of fire and the cracks of revolvers on their flank sent them thundering toward the river. The confusion of the stampede was indescribable as the front ranks, sensing the edge of the cliff, tried in vain to check itself and hold back against the press of the avalanche of terror-stricken animals behind. The change was magical—one moment a frenzied mass of struggling cows lighted grotesquely by the burning grass, and then only the edge of the cliff and the swishing grayness of the river below. The wind was blowing the flames toward the edge of the cliff and they would die from lack of material upon which to feed, though the four cared little about that. Their horses stumbled with them along the ravine, leaving behind a blackened plain across which sparks were driven by each gust of wind, to glow brilliantly and die. Below, once more wrapped in impenetrable darkness, swished the Black Jack, cold, cruel, deep, and fugitive, its scurrying, frightened cross currents whispering mysteriously as they discussed the tragedy. Suddenly the rain deluged everything as if wrathful at the pitiable slaughter and eager to wash out the stain of it.

In the middle of the forenoon of the following day Slow Jack loomed up in the fog of the driving rain and the vapors arising from the earth and slid from his saddle in front of the ranch house, his hideous yellow slicker shining as though polished. Buck opened the door and instinctively stepped back to avoid the wet gust that assailed him. "There's a lot o' cows floating in the backwater o' th' Jack where th' creek empties in—I roped one an' drug it ashore. Just plain drowned, I reckon. There was signs of itch, too," Slow Jack reported.

Buck hastened into his storm clothes, got Monroe from the corral, and started through the storm to see for himself. When he reached the river he saw a score of Double Y cows drifting in circles in the backwater, and at intervals one would swing into the outer current and be caught in the pull of the rushing river to go sailing toward Twin. The stream was rising rapidly now, its gray waters turning brown and roiled. Sending Monroe to follow the stream to town, he and Slow Jack rode close to the water toward the hazy Hog Back. When he met Monroe at the ranch house that afternoon he learned that most of the inhabitants of Twin River were swarming upon the point behind Ike's saloon, busily engaged in roping and skinning the cattle as fast as they drifted by; the count varied from one hundred to five hundred, and he knew that the fight was on again.

There had been no clues found upon which to base action against the perpetrators. True, the pasture behind the Hog Back had been burned since he last saw it, but Slow Jack's tardy memory recalled that one morning, several days before, he had detected the smell of grass smoke in the air. He was going to investigate it but hesitated to go through the quarantined range for fear of bringing back the itch. During the day the smell had disappeared and he had seen no signs of smoke at any time. He had meant to speak of it when he returned to the bunkhouse but had forgotten, as usual.

When left alone Buck stared out of the window, not noticing that the storm had ceased, burning with rage at his absolute helplessness. The loss of the cows was not great enough to cripple him seriously but this blow, following hard upon the other, showed him what little chance he had of making the Double Y a success without a large outfit of tried and trusted men. Even while he looked at the plain with unseeing eyes his cattle might be stolen or driven to death in the swollen waters of either river—and he was powerless to stop it.

To his mind again leaped the recollection of Ned's warning regarding Schatz: he was a "hard nut," Ned had said. Buck was beginning to think he would have to crack him on suspicion. He looked in the direction of the German's cabin and a curse rumbled in his throat.

Whitby opened the door and reported that everything was all right on his part of the range and asked for orders for the next day. After a few minutes' conversation he moved on to the bunkhouse, troubled and ill at ease at the appearance of his employer. In a way Whitby had certain small privileges that were denied to the other members of the outfit. He was a gentleman, as Buck had instantly realized, and he could make time pass very rapidly under most conditions. He paused now and finally decided to thrust his company upon Buck for the evening; in his opinion Buck would be all the better for company. He had almost reached the ranch house door when behind him there was a sound of furious galloping and Bow-Wow flung himself from his horse and burst into the room excited and fuming, Whitby close upon his heels.

"They've shot a lot of cows on th' southeast corner, close to th' Jill. I'd 'a' been in sooner only I went huntin' for 'em. Lost their tracks when they swum th' river. Three of 'em did it, an' they dropped nigh onto fifty head." Winded as he was, Bow-Wow yet found breath for a string of curses that appeared to afford him little relief.

A look came into Buck's face that told of a man

with his back to the wall. The piling on of the last straw was dangerously near at hand. His fingers closed convulsively around the butt of his Colt and he swayed in his tracks. No one ever knew how close to death Whitby and Bow-Wow were at that moment, by what a narrow margin the range was spared ruthless murder at the hands of a man gone fighting mad. The Texan was cut to the heart by this last news, and only a swift reaction in the form of the habitual self-restraint of thirty years saved him from running amuck. The grayness of his face gave way to its usual color, only the whipcord veins and the deep lines telling of the savage battle raging in the soul of the man. He waved the two men away and paced to and fro across the room, fighting the greatest battle of his eventful life. One man against unknown enemies who shot in the dark; his outfit was an unknown quantity and practically worse than none at all, since he had to trust it to a certain extent. He thought that Ned Monroe was loyal, but his judgment might have become poor because of the strain he had undergone; and was not Monroe one who had lost when the ranch was turned over to its rightful owners? Bow-Wow was more likely to be honest than otherwise, but he had no proof in the puncher's favor. Chesty Sutton had no cause to be a traitor, but the workings of the human mind cause unusual actions at times. Cock Murray and Slow Jack could be regarded as enemies, but there was not enough proof to convict them: they had been in charge of the western part of the ranch when the herd had been stampeded into the Black Jack—yet Buck realized that two men could hardly handle so large a tract of land; and again, the stampede had occurred at night while they were asleep in the bunkhouse. If he got rid of every man he could find reason to doubt, he would have no outfit to handle the routine work of the ranch. There remained Jake and Whitby. The cook could be dismissed as of no account one way or the other, since he was a fool at best and never left the ranch house for more than a few minutes at a time. The Englishman seemed to be loyal but there was no positive assurance of it; while he had undoubtedly killed the itch, it was so dangerous a plague that every man's hand should be turned against it.

When he tried to reason the matter out he came to the conclusion he had reached so often before: the only man in Montana whom he trusted absolutely was Buck Peters. If he had some of his old outfit, or even Hopalong, Red, or Lanky, one man in whom he could place absolute trust, he felt he could win out in the end—and he would have them. He ceased his pacing to and fro and squared his shoulders: He would give his outfit one last tryout and if still in doubt of its loyalty, he would send a message to Hopalong and have him pick out a dozen men from the Bar-20 and nearby ranches and send them up to the Double Y. Lucas, Bartlett, and Meeker could spare him a few men each, men friendly to him. It would be admitting preliminary defeat to do this but the results would justify the means.

When he thought he had mastered himself and was becoming calm and self-possessed, Chesty Sutton and the foreman entered with troubled looks on their faces. Monroe spoke: "Chesty reports he found a dozen cows lyin' in a heap at th' bottom of Crow Canyon, and Murray says th' fence has been cut an' stripped o' wire for a mile on th' north end."

Buck lost himself in the fury of rage that swept over him at this news. The fence had been intact that noon when he rode out to look over the floating cows in the Jack; this blow in daylight told him that the battle was being forced from several points at once; and again he realized how absolutely helpless he was—there was no hope now. When Ned and Chesty returned to the bunkhouse, drawing meager satisfaction from the clearing weather, they left behind them a man broken in spirit, weak from fruitless anger, who shook his upraised arms at Providence and cursed every man in Montana. A desperate idea entered his head: he would force the fighting. He slipped out of the corral, roped his horse and led it around back of the ranch house, where he tethered it and returned to the house to wait for night. Night would see him at Schatz's cabin, there to choke out the truth and strike his first blow.

Jack came in, muttering something about lights and supper, to retreat silently at the curt dismissal. The long shadows stole into the room, enveloping the brooding figure, and deepened into dark. The time was come and Buck arose and went out to his horse. With his hand on the picket he paused and listened. Across the Jill a broad moon was beginning to cast its light and from the same direction, a long way off, came the sound of singing. The singer was coming toward him and Buck stepped into the house again to await his arrival. He might be the bearer of some message.

While he paced restlessly the singing died down and in a few minutes the squeaking of a vehicle caught his ear. He wondered who cared to drive over that trail when there were so many good saddle horses to be had for the asking and he started toward the door to see. Suddenly he stopped as if shot and gripped his hat with all his strength as another song came to his ears. He doubted his senses and feared he was going crazy, hoping against hope that he heard aright. Who in Montana could know that song!

" 'Th' cows go grazin' o'er th' lea—
Pore Whiskey Bill, pore Whiskey Bill.
An' achin' thoughts pour in on me
Of Whiskey Bill.
Th' sheriff up an' found his stride,
Bill's soul went shootin' down th' slide—
How are things o'er th' Great Divide,
Oh, Whiskey Bill?' "

"Hello th' house! Hey, Buck! Buck! O, Buck! Whoa, blame you—think I'm a fool tenderfoot? Hey, Buck! B U C K!"

Buck leaped to the door in one great bound and ran toward the creeping buckboard, yelling like an Indian. The bunkhouse door flew open and the men tumbled through it, guns in hand, and sprinted toward the point of trouble. Bow-Wow led and close upon his heels ran Whitby, with Murray a close third. When the leader got near enough he saw two men wrestling near a buckboard and he maneuvered so as to insert himself into the fracas at the first opportunity. Then he snorted and backed off in profound astonishment, colliding with the eager Englishman, to the pain of both. The wrestlers were not wrestling but hugging; and a woman in the buckboard was laughing with delight. Bow-Wow shook his head as if to clear it and began to slip back toward the bunkhouse. This was against all his teachings and he would have no part in it. The idea of two cowmen hugging each other!

Whitby strolled after and overtook the muttering puncher. "I fancy that's one of those Texans he's been talking about; or, rather, two of them. Perhaps we shall see some frontier law up here now—and God knows it is time."

Slow Jack veered off and swore in his throat.

"*Texas* law, huh? We'll send him back where he come from, in a box!" he growled.

He stopped when he heard Buck's laughing words, and sneered: "Hopalong Cassidy an' his wife, eh? She'll be his widder if he cuts in *this* game. But I wonder if anymore o' them terrible Texas killers is comin' up? Huh! Let 'em come—that's all."

CHAPTER XVI

The Master Mind

FOR A while, at least, Buck seemed to cast his troubles to the four winds and was a picture of delight; his happiness, bubbling up in every word, kept his face wreathed in one vast smile. At last he had a man whom he could trust. Jake was summoned and prepared the best meal he could and the three sat down to a very good supper, Buck surprised to find how hungry he had become. His visit to Schatz was forgotten as he listened to Hopalong and Mary chatter about old times and people he wished he could see again.

After a little, Hopalong noticed how tired his wife was and sent her to get a good night's rest. The long railroad journey and the ride in the buckboard had been a great strain on her.

When left alone, Buck demanded to know all about the Bar-20 and its outfit and laughed until the tears came as he listened to some of the tales.

"What deviltry has Johnny been up to since I left?" asked Buck.

"Well, it's only been six months," replied Hopalong, "so you see he ain't really had much time; but he's made good use o' what he did have. He fell in love again, had th' prospectin' fever, wanted to go down to th' Mexican line an' help Martin. I had th' very devil of a time stoppin' him. Him an' Lucas had their third fight an' Lucas got licked this time; then they went off to Cowan's an' blew th' crowd, near havin' another scrap 'cause each wanted to pay. He dosed Pete's cayuse with whiskey an' ginger, chased Lee Hop clean to Buckskin, so we ain't got no cook. Red licked him for that, so Johnny tied all th' boys together one night, tied chairs an' things to 'em an' then stepped outside an' began shootin' at th' stars. It was some lively, that mess in th' dark, judgin' from th' hair-raisin' noises; it scared th' Kid all th' way to Perry's Bend—leastways, we has no news for a week, when we hears he'd pulled stakes there, leavin' th' town fightin' an' th' sheriff locked up in his own jail. Th' Bend has sent numerous invitations for him to call again. From there he drifts over to th' C80, wins all their money an' then rides home loaded down with presents to square hisself with th' boys. He wanted to fight when I made Red foreman while I was away—it's Red's first good chance to get square."

"That's th' Kid, all right," laughed Buck. "Lord, how I wish he was up here!"

"Red, he's th' same grouch as ever but he's all right if Johnny 'd let him get set. As soon as Red calms down th' Kid calls his attention to somethin' excitin' an' th' trouble begins again. They all wanted to come up here an' give you a hand till you got things runnin' right. I told 'em I could get a better crowd in two days, so they stayed home to spite me. From what I've heard I wish I'd told 'em they

could come—things 'd run smoother for you with
them wild men buckjumpin' 'round lookin' for trouble. Like to turn Red an' Johnny loose up here with
a good grudge to work off. Th' railroad would report that Montana was jumpin' east fast."

"What was that your wife called you?" asked
Buck, curiously.

"Billy-Red," laughed Hopalong. "That's her own
name for me."

"Billy-hell!" snorted Buck. "Billy-goat would suit
you better."

"Say, Buck, Pete saw som'ers there was lots o'
money in raisin' chickens, so he borrows all our
money, gets about a hundred head from th' East, an'
starts in. For a week there was lots of excitement
'round our place—coyotes got so they'd get under
our feet an' th' nights was plumb full o' hungry animals with a taste for chicken. We put up a bomb-
proof coop but they tunnelled it th' first night an'
got all that was left o' th' herd 'cept about a dozen
what was roostin' high. Pete, he was broken-hearted
an' give up. He makes Mary a present o' what was
left of his stock, an' what do you think she give him
for 'em? Two days' work diggin'. He dug a ditch,
four-sided, for th' foundations of a new coop. Then
he has to sink posts in it in th' ground an' fill th'
ditch with stones. Johnny got th' stones in th'
chuck wagon from th' creek, so as to square hisself
with Mary, an' she give him a whole apricot pie for
it. He's been a nuisance ever since. Well, th' posts
rose four feet above th' ground an' when that hen-
corral was roofed over, you could see, any moon-
light night, plenty o' coyotes trottin' 'round it,
prayin' for somethin' to happen. We got some fine
shootin' for a while. But I got other things to talk
about, Buck—Texas can wait."

"Kind of a dry job, Hoppy," replied Buck, going to
a cupboard and returning with a bottle.

"Better stuff than Cowan ever sold," smiled the visitor, and then plunged into what he considered real news.

"When we got off th' train at Wayback, I went huntin' for a wagon an' purty soon we was on our way to Twin River. I knowed we'd have to spend th' night there: Mary couldn't stand forty miles in a buckboard after that train ride. We hadn't got very far from town when I hears a hail an' looks around to see Tex Ewalt comin' up. He spotted me when I left th' train but he didn't want to show he knows me there."

"What!" exclaimed Buck, in great surprise. "Tex Ewalt! Why, I thought he went East for good."

"He thought so, too, at th' time," and Hoppy gave a brief history of their friend's movements. "When he got back to th' ranch he was restless an' decided to come up here an' help you. He's been very busy up here in a quiet way. He tells me he knows th' man that put th' itch on yore range. Tex says he could 'a' stopped it if he knew enough to add two an' two. But he says there's another man behind him, slicker'n a coyote. Tex's been hopin' every day to rope an' tie him but he ain't got him yet."

"Who is it?" asked Buck, with grim simplicity.

"Tex won't tell me. He says you can't do no good shootin' on suspicion. He's tried watchin' him but he might as well be goin' to church when he does leave home, his travels is that innocent."

"Why didn't Tex come here? I been wantin' one man I could trust, an' me an' Tex could 'a' wiped out th' gang."

"He says different—an' he was afraid o' bein' seen. You see, that would kill his usefulness. Just as soon as he could get to th' bottom o' th' game an' lay his fingers on th' real boss, *then* he'd 'a' come out for you in th' open, put th' boss in th' scrap-pile for burial, an' burned powder till you had things where you wanted 'em. We about concluded you ain't makin' good use o' th' punchers you got, Buck, though I shore hates to say it."

"How can I make use o' men I don't trust? You don't know th' worse, Hopalong—"

"About th' couple o' thousand head went swimmin'? I ain't heard much else in Twin River. How'd it happen?"

Buck ran over the day's occurrences graphically and without missing a single point. Hopalong's thoughtful comment was characteristic of the man upon whom Buck had unconsciously leaned in crises not a few.

"The two men on yore south pasture is liars," he declared. "Yore foreman is some doubtful: 'pears like to me if he's honest an' attendin' to business, no point o' yore range ought to go shy o' him for long. Th' Britisher figures it's no part o' his business to help you, th' way Tex tells me; if he ain't square he just does his work an' don't offer no suggestions. Th' other two is all right if they ain't just fools what'll do as th' foreman says 'cause he's th' foreman, right or wrong. That's how I reckons you stand. Now we got to prove it."

"Fire away," said Buck, earnestly. "I agrees to every word. Provin' it's th' horse I ain't been able to rope."

"Th' outlyin' free range don't count. You ain't missed no cows in th' round-up, has you?"

"No, they tallied high."

"Goes to show there's a head to th' deviltry. You don't get no losses on'y right on yore home range. Now, we divide th' range in sections, a man to each section, an' work 'em that way a few days. There won't be no night ridin' at first. Then we set 'em night ridin' when they ain't expectin' it an' shift th' men every night. We soon know who to trust, don't we?"

"Yo're right—plumb right—an' it's so simple I ought to be fed hay, for a cow. I got a map som'ers—or I'll make one. We'll lay out them sections right now."

"That's th' talk! There ain't no time like right now for doin' most things, Buck."

They were not long in laying out and perfecting their plans and had said good night when Buck suddenly remembered the picketed pony. He turned it into the corral and went to bed. Smiler Schatz, sleeping the sleep of the very wicked and the very innocent, did not dream how near he had come to an incident more exciting than any he had ever passed through.

CHAPTER XVII

Hopalong's Night Ride

HOPALONG, PASSING the bunkhouse on his way to the stable, paused to listen. Through the open window Pickles' voice had reached him quite clearly: "I don't guess I'll ever get him, Whit, but if I do, it'll be for keeps, you betcher."

Hopalong was interested. The death of Gottleib Gerken was an old story and so many things of pressing moment having occurred about the time of Hopalong's arrival, he had not been told of this. The finality of decision in Pickles' murderous intention was so evident that Hopalong wondered how the boy came to conceive so deadly a hatred. He stepped to the window and stood looking at the two figures within. They neither saw nor heard him.

Both were deep in thought. Whitby's inherent regard for due process of law had received numerous shocks since he left Chicago. Like many another square man finding his niche in a raw country, he was beginning to see that right must be enforced by

might, until such time as wrong became subdued by
the steady march of the older civilization. And this
face-about in opinion is not accomplished in a day,
even when on the spot and a personal sufferer. It
was this new feeling that led him to listen with respect to Pickles' confidences, boy though he was.
Boys imbibed men's ideas early in this country; too
early, thought Whitby, recalling his own play-time at
this lad's age. He stole a look at the glum face beside him and began to draw circles with the point of
the switch he held in his hand—he was never without one. "It's a pity," he said, "a pity."

"What's a pity?" asked Pickles, a note of indignation in his voice at the implied suggestion.

Whitby ignored the tone. "It's a pity you never
heard of the Witch's Spell," he explained, reminiscently.

"What's that?"

"But then, of course," reasoned Whitby, "if you
can't find a Witch's Ring, you can't work the Spell;
and I rather fancy there isn't a Witch's Ring in all
the world outside of Yorkshire."

"What's it like?" demanded Pickles, with the practical insistence of Young America.

"Why, the Old Witch makes it, you know. She runs
around in a ring and blows on the grass and it
never grows anymore. Inside the Ring and outside,
the grass is just the same, but the Ring is always
bare."

Pickles was silent. He was picturing to himself the
process of the Ring in the making. So was Hopalong.
It seemed very matter-of-fact as Whitby told it; still,
there was something—

"What's she do that for?" asked Pickles—the very
question Hopalong was asking himself.

"It's the bad fairies, you know, and Wizards, and
that sort of thing; she's afraid of them. But they
can't pass the Ring, no matter how deep they dig,

so the Witch is quite safe, you know. They're a bad lot, those others, no end. But the Old Witch is quite a decent sort. She lives inside the Ring, under the ground, and that's where you go to get your wish."

Pickles pondered. His eyes began to glow. "Any wish?" he questioned, in subdued excitement.

"All sorts," declared Whitby. "There was Jimmie Pickering: he always got his wish; he told me so, himself; and Arthur Cooper: he wished to be a minister and he got his wish; and George Hick: he wished to see the world and he's always traveling up and down the earth; and Allen Ramsey, who wished to be an athlete, strong, you know: he got his wish; then there was Maggie Sheffield, who wished to marry a soldier: she married a soldier; and Vi Glades, who wished to be a singer: she can sing tears into your heart, lad, so sweet you're glad to have them there; so she got her wish. And ever so many more: they all got their wishes. She was a rare good one, that Witch."

"Did you get yore wish, Whit?"

"I could only count to seven," explained Whitby.

Pickles' lips moved silently. "How many do you have to count?" he asked, dubiously.

"Nine," said Whitby, with a regretful sigh. "You run around the Ring nine times, holding your breath and saying your wish to yourself over and over again. Then you run into the middle and lie down. You mustn't breathe until you lie down. When you put your ear to the ground you can hear the Old Witch churning out your wish. 'Ka-Chug! Ka-Chug! Ka-Chug!' goes the churn, away down in the earth. Then you know you will get your wish."

Pickles straightened up and looked fixedly at Whitby. His voice was very solemn: "Whit, I take my oath there's a Witch's Ring right here on the range!"

"Nonsense!"

"Hope I may die! I'll show you, tomorrow. An' I'm a-goin' to wish—"

"I say! You mustn't tell your wish, you know. That breaks the Spell. If ever you tell your wish, it doesn't come true."

"Jiggers!—I won't tell. Nine times 'round the Ring an' hol' yore breath an' say yore wish fast an' then to th' middle—"

Hopalong lost the rest as he continued on his way to the stable. Pickles' Ring puzzled him only for a moment, for as he turned away from the window, he was chuckling. "Means some place where th' Injuns used to war-dance, I reckon," was his conclusion. "But the Britisher seems like he believed it himself."

Two minutes later and he was in the saddle and riding south, edging over toward Big Moose trail. He melted into the surrounding darkness like a shadow, silence having been the evident aim of his unusual preparations earlier in the evening. Not a leather creaked; an impatient toss of his pony's head betrayed no clink of metal on teeth; the velvety padding of the hoofs made as little noise as the passing of one of the larger cats, in a hurry. Hopalong meant to quarter the section of range allotted him like a restless ghost and, if the others did as well, he had a strong conviction that night-deviltry would lose its attractions in this particular part of the country.

It was not long before he began to test his memory. To a man of his experience this guard duty would have presented but little difficulty in any case, but Hopalong had been careful to make a very complete mental map of this section when riding it by daylight. He went on now like a man in his own house.

He turned abruptly to the left, heading for the Jill and taking the low ground between two huge buttes. Just short of the Big Moose trail he halted, listening intently for five minutes, and then, turning

west again, began to quarter the ground like a
hound, gradually working south. With the plainsman's certainty of direction his course followed a
series of obliques, fairly regular, though he chose
the low ground, winding about the buttes, to the
top of which he lent a keen scrutiny. He stopped for
minutes at a time to listen and then went on again.

It was during one of these pauses that he espied
a dark shape at rest not far from him. He eyed it
with suspicion. It should be a cow but there was
something not quite normal in its attitude. He rode
forward cautiously, being in no way desirous of disturbing the brute. Circling it at a walk a similar object loomed up, some little distance from the other.
"Calf!" he decided. A few steps nearer and he
changed his mind. "No, another cow. I don't know
as I ever see cattle look like that. 'Pears like they
was shore enough tuckered out—an' I bet they ain't
drifted a mile in twenty-four hours." They were very
still. There was no reason why they should not be
and yet—the wind being right, he hazarded a few
steps nearer.

And then there came to his ears a sound that
stiffened him in his saddle. His pony turned its head
and gazed inquiringly into the darkness. "Injuns!"
breathed Hopalong, doubt struggling with conviction. He slipped to earth and ran noiselessly to the
nearest recumbent figure. A single touch told him: it
was a dead cow; warm, but unquestionably dead.

With his horse under him once more, Hoppy
crept forward. Careful before, his progress now had
all the stealth of a stalking tiger. There it came
again: the unmistakable twang of a bow-string. The
pony veered to the left in response to the pressure
of Hoppy's knee, when there sounded a movement
to the right and he straightened his course to ride
between the two. His spirits began to rise with the
old-time zest at the imminence of a fight to the

death. Mary, back yonder in the ranch house, with her new proud hope, Buck and his anxieties, Tex in his indefatigable hunt for evidence, the far-distant Bar-20 with its duties and its band of loyal friends, all were forgotten in the complete absorption of the coming duel. Indians! Rebellious and treacherous punchers were foemen to beware of, but these red wolves, savage from the curb of the reservation and hungry with a blood lust long denied—a grin of pure delight spread over his features as he foresaw the instant transformation from cattle-killing thieves to strategic assassins at the first crack of his Colt.

The odds could not be great and he expected to reduce them at the opening of hostilities. Warily he glanced about him as he moved slowly forward, casting, at the last, a searching look off to the right. He saw that which brought him up standing, his breath caught in his distended lungs; it escaped in a long sigh of pleased wonder: "Great Land of Freedom! Please look at that," he pleaded to his unresponsive country.

Broadside on, head up and facing him with ears pricked forward, alert yet waiting, stood a horse that filled Hopalong's soul with the sin of covetousness. So near that the obscurity failed to hide a line, the powerful quarters and grand forehand betrayed to Hopalong's discerning eyes a latent force a little superior to the best he had ever looked on. "An' a' Injun's!" sighed Hoppy, in measureless disgust. "But not if I sees th' Injun," he added hopefully. Wishing that he might, his thought back-somersaulted to Pickles and Whitby and the Witch's Spell. A whimsical smile wrinkled the corners of his mouth and at this very moment the thing happened.

A nerve-racking screech, the like of which no Indian ever made, lifted the hair on Hoppy's head, and his pony immediately entered upon a series of amazing calisthenics, an enthusiastic rendering no doubt enhanced by the inch or two of arrow-head in his rump. Hopalong caught one glimpse of a squat, misshapen figure that went past him with a rush and let go at it, more from habit than with the expectation of hitting. When he had subdued his horse to the exercise of some little equine sense, the rapidly decreasing sound of the fleeing marauder told him that only one had been at work and with grim hopelessness he set after him. "Might as well try to catch a comet," he growled, sinking his spurs into the pony's side and momentarily distracting its attention from the biting anguish of the lengthier spur behind.

The pony was running less silently than when he left the ranch. Portions of unaccustomed equipment, loosened in his mad flurry, were dropping from him at every jump. This, and the straining of Hopalong's hearing after the chase, allowed to pass unnoticed the coming up of a third horseman, riding at an angle to intercept the pursuit. The first intimation of his presence Hopalong received was the whine of a bullet, too close for comfort, and Hopalong was off and behind his pony to welcome the crack of the rifle when it reached him. "Shootin' at random, darn his fool hide!" snorted Hoppy; "an' shootin' good too," he conceded, as a second bullet sped eagerly after the first. Hoppy released a bellow of angry protest: "Hey! What'n hell do you reckon yo're doin'?"

There was an interval of silence and then a voice from the darkness: "Show a laig, there: who is it?"

"Show you a boot, you locoed bummer! It's Cassidy." He mounted resignedly and waited for the other to ride up. "Couldn't 'a' caught him, nohow," he reflected. "Never see such a horse in my life, never. Hope to th' Lord it don't rain. Be just like it."

The unknown rode up full of apologies. Hopalong

cut him short. "Whatd' they call you?" he asked, curtly.

"Slow Jack," was the answer.

Hoppy grunted. "Well, you camp down right here," he ordered, "an' don't let nobody blot that sign. I'm a-goin' to be here at daylight an' foller that screech-owl th' limit. Good night."

He headed for the ranch house, satisfied that his section of range would remain undisturbed during the next few hours, at the least.

"Sweet birds-o'-paradise! Would you—would you oblige me by squintin' at that!"

Straight north, from the few dead carcasses where the trail started it led to the creek bank, east of the ranch house; and like hounds with nose to scent, Hopalong, Buck, and Ned had followed it from the point where Slow Jack had been found doing sentry-go and sent, in profane relief, to breakfast and sleep. Hoppy was in the lead and as he came to the creek he raised his eyes to look across at the other bank for signs of the quarry's exit from the water. It was the sign on the north bank, coupled with that on the somewhat higher bank where they stood, that had made him exclaim.

Ned Monroe's face cleared of the frowning perplexity that had darkened it at first sight of the hoofprints they tracked. "Must be a stranger," he affirmed. "Dunno th' country or he'd never jump when he could ride through."

"Jump!" exclaimed Buck, startled. "Why, of course," he conceded. "Hoppy, that's shore one scrumptious jump"; and the dawning admiration grew to wonder as he mentally measured the distance.

Hoppy nodded his head. "*I* never see th' horse could do it right now; an' that bird flew over there last night. He was right on it afore he knew an' he didn't stop to remember how deep it was; he just dug in a spur an' lifted him at sight of th' breakin' bubbles: they'd show purty nigh white last night—an' th' horse, he doesn't know how much he has to jump, so he jumps a good one—a darn good one, though Ned, here, don't think it so much. Mebby you know a horse as could do it right easy, eh, Ned?"

With Hopalong's sharp eyes on his face, Ned shook his head in denial, gazing stolidly at the sign. "Too good for any in these parts; wouldn't be no disgrace for a thoroughbred."

Buck glanced quickly at Ned and then, pulling his hat low over his eyes, struck up the brim with two snappy blows of the back of his hand.

"Well, Buck, I reckon I'll leave you an' Ned to foller this. I got a feelin' I'm wanted at th' ranch. So long." Hopalong rode off in obedience to one of the signals that had helped to simplify affairs among the Bar-20 punchers.

Buck had signified his desire for Hoppy's absence. He pushed Allday to the creek and set off at a lope. "Easy as follerin' a wagon, Ned," he remarked.

"Yep," agreed Ned.

"Stopped here," observed Buck. "Listenin', I reckon. Goin' slower, now."

"Some," replied Ned.

"Right smart jump acrost the creek," said Buck, questioningly.

"Uh-huh!" consented Ned, with non-committal brevity.

They rode a couple of miles before Buck hazarded another remark. "Seems like I oughta know that hoof," he complained. "Keeps a-lookin' more'n more like I knowed it. Durn thing purty nigh talks."

Ned threw him a startled glance and then gazed

steadily ahead. "Be at th' Jill in a minute," he announced.

"Yeah. Thought he was driftin' that-away. Lay you ten to two he don't *jump* th' Jill, Ned."

"Here's Charley," was the irrelevant response. The Indian was a welcome diversion. Buck slowed to a walk, raised his eyes and waved Charley an amiable salute. The Cheyenne promptly left the trail and rode to join them.

"Hey, Charley, whose horse is that?" asked Buck, pointing to the hoofprints.

The Indian barely glanced at them. "French Rose," he declared. "Cross trail, swim river before sun. Heap good horse."

"Where goin', Charley—ranch?" asked Buck, evenly. He did not question the Cheyenne's conclusions. *He knew.* Buck was satisfied of that.

Charley grinned sheepishly and shifted uneasily under Buck's stare. "That's all right," assured Buck, "tell Jake to give you—no, wait for me. I'll be there as soon as you are." He turned away and Charley accepted his dismissal in high good humor, riding off with cheering visions of a cupful of the "old man's" whiskey, which was very different from that dispensed over the bar in Twin River.

"Well, Ned," said Buck.

"Well, Buck," returned Ned.

"You knew it was Rose's horse."

"I was a-feared."

"You knew it, you durn ol' grizzly."

"Look a-here, Buck. You ain't goin' to tell me as how Rose—"

"Not by a jugful! That's a flower without a stain, Ned, an' I backs her with my whole pile."

"Here, too," coincided Ned, in hearty accord.

"We lost th' trail, Ned."

"You bet!"

"In th' Jill."

"Took a boat," suggested Ned, solemnly.

Buck concealed his amusement. "Or a balloon," he offered.

"Mebby," assented Ned. "Couldn't pick her up agin, nohow."

"Not if we'd had a dog," declared Buck.

"Or a' Injun," supplemented Ned. They gazed at one another for a second and, of one mind, spun their horses around and off for the ranch like thoroughbreds at the drop of the flag.

"I just thought o' Charley," explained Buck.

"Here, too," grunted Ned.

"Might talk," said Buck.

"You bet."

Charley heard them coming. When he saw them, the explanation to his untutored mind was a race. Determined to be in at the finish, he laid the quirt to his pony with enthusiastic zeal, casting a rapid glance over his shoulder, now and then, to see if he were holding his own. It was a sight to see the tireless little pony wake up under punishment. He had covered twenty miles that day and over forty the day before, but he shot forward on his wiry legs like a startled jackrabbit and in one-two-three order they thundered up to the ranch house with a noise that brought Mary to the door.

"Well, Buck Peters!" she exclaimed, "ain't you *never* goin' to grow up? Yo're worse'n that loco husband o' mine, right now."

Buck grinned at the abashed Ned and winked knowingly at Mary. He and Mary were very good friends, Buck long ago having gauged her sterling worth and become aware of her mischievous propensity for teasing. As he led Charley indoors he asked for Hopalong and learned that he had set off for Twin River soon after his arrival at the ranch house.

• • •

Hopalong had taken his cue from Buck without question but not without curiosity. On his way to the house he decided, not without a longing thought in the direction of Red Connors, foreman *pro tem* of the Bar-20, that Tex Ewalt would be all the better for a knowledge of recent events. Therefore he paused only long enough to inform Mary of his intention before starting in search of him. At Twin River he pulled up at the Why-Not and went in for a drink. Tex was standing at the bar and ten minutes after Hopalong left, Tex had overtaken him on the Wayback trail. They struck off through the undergrowth until secure from observation, and Tex was soon acquainted with the latest attempt at stock reduction.

He listened silently until Hopalong mentioned the kind of man who had done the killing. "Big Saxe," he exclaimed. "So, that's his game. Well, we got 'em now, Hopalong. I can lay my hands on that cow killer right soon, an' he'll squeal, you bet. An' I got a long way to go. *Adios.*"

"Blamed grasshopper!" grumbled Hopalong. "Never even guessed where that horse come from. If Big Saxe is on him yet, you shore got a long journey, Tex."

CHAPTER XVIII

Karl to the Rescue

DAVE, HARBORING a fermenting acerbity beside which the Spartan boy's wolf was a tickling parasite, lay hidden behind a stunted pine, his glasses trained on the Schatz cabin. Sourly he reviewed his several plans, each coming to nought as surely as if Peters had been made aware of it in its inception. The last grand coup, from which he had expected to derive immediate benefit, had arrived prematurely and mysteriously at its unexpected denouement; and that fool Saxe, upon whom he had relied to create a diversion, must needs keep himself hidden, to turn up when his efforts would be worse than useless. And then to come to Dave to be paid for making a fool of himself! He cursed aloud at the recollection. "It was a good scheme, too," he asserted savagely. No use telling him all those cows had stampeded and hurled themselves to destruction—"When the money for 'em was as good as mine." It had never been his real intention to allow Murray and Jack to divide the profits and by a curious mental strabis-mus he readily saw how he had been robbed. But losing the money was not the only nor the greatest blow. The injury to his sorely tried vanity hurt the most. He had been beaten, not so much by the enemy as by one of his friends.

Clouded by that same vanity his reason had ac-quitted all those who might have betrayed him, ex-cepting Schatz. Rose, a woman who loved him—he had dismissed the thought with scorn; Comin', Cock Murray; they had all to lose and nothing to gain by treachery: and all the others were bound to him by ties, the weakest of which was stronger than any Buck could have formed in the time. Schatz alone might prove a gainer. He did not know in what way, but purposed to discover. That was why he was watching now. He knew Schatz was at home: he had seen the smoke of his breakfast fire. "Allus *is* home," he grated. He anticipated the calling of Schatz' agents at the cabin and when Schatz came out and finally rode off on the Twin River trail, Dave was disconcerted. He followed with much care, making good use of his glasses. The sight of Schatz turning off the trail and riding toward the Double Y ranch house filled him with a cold fury. He deter-mined to intercept him on his return and have it out on the spot.

But Dave, intent upon the unconscious back of Karl, had been careless of the surrounding country; and only his luck in choosing to wait in a place re-mote from cover, saved him just then from a rude awakening. Dodging about in the vain effort to ap-proach to a point of vantage, was Pickles; he had finished certain mystic incantations involving the running at speed in circles, and was returning to await the fulfillment of his wish. Filled with awe as he was at this swift response, it did not prevent him from acting upon it.

His arrival at the nearest possible point showed
him that Dave was still out of range. For the first
time a doubt of Buck's omniscience assailed him: it
was no part of wisdom to arm a man with a rifle of
that sort. With cautious speed he retraced his
steps, mounted the Goat, and scurried for the ranch
by a roundabout route. There was nothing haphaz-
ard about this; his ideas were clearly defined: didn't
Red Connors always borrow Hopalong's Sharps for
long range? That showed. Pickles had implicit faith
in the rifle. All that worried him was that Dave
might not wait long enough.

Karl rode leisurely up to the ranch house and
called. Mary came to the door and behind her Buck,
whose brow was wrinkled in the effort of compos-
ing a letter to McAllister. It was not an easy letter to
write and Buck had enlisted Whitby's services. He
asked Karl to climb down and come inside. Mary
had disappeared with a promptitude due to instinc-
tive dislike. Karl was not a man to invite the admiration of any woman at the best of times and now
his appearance gave abundant proof of its being
long past "chipping-time."

Karl entered with the unexpected lightness of
step so often a compensating grace in fat men,
shook hands with Whitby, accepted the proffered
chair, and plunged into the reason of his visit with
but little preamble. Whitby sat making idle marks
with his pen; soon he began to write swiftly.

"Big lot of cows you loose, ain'd it?" he asked.

"A few," replied Buck.

"Vat you t'ink: stampede?"

"Looks like it."

"*Look* like it? *Donnerwetter*! Look like a drive."

"You seen it?"

Karl nodded. "Look like a drive," he repeated.

"Wouldn't surprise me none," admitted Buck. "We
had Injuns shootin' 'em on th' range last night."

"*Himmel!* Vat fools!"

"Looks like they're tryin' to drive me off'n th' range."

"*Yah, aber* not me. Ten years und no trouble come."

"Huh! Well, what would *you* do?"

"Fight," advised Karl. "I vill fight if you let me in. I haf a plan."

"In where?" asked Buck, in some wonder.

"In der ranch—a partner. Look! Cows you must haf, money you must haf, brains you must haf: I bring dem. I bring shust so much money as you und your partner togedder. Der money in der bank *geht.* You buy der cows, goot stock, besser as before. Goot cows, goot prices, ain'd it? You pay for everyt'ing mit der money in der bank. I stay here and stop dot foolishness mit precipices und parasites und shooting. Vat you dink?"

"Let me get you. You want to buy in on the Double Y, equal partners. I put in so much, McAllister puts in so much, and you put in as much as both of us. Th' money goes in th' bank an' I have th' spendin' of it. You do yore share o' th' work an' yo're dead certain you can stop th' deviltry on th' range. Is that it?"

"*Yah!*" assented Karl, emphatically.

Buck was astounded at the audacity of the proposal. His gaze wandered to Whitby, whose pen was moving over the paper with a speed that impressed Buck, busy as his mind was. Outside, a horseman clattered up to the house and Mary, from the kitchen door, motioned Hopalong to come in that way. The door had no sooner closed behind him than Pickles sped from the security of the stable, slipped Hoppy's rifle from the saddle holster, and half a minute later the Goat went tearing away, bearing the triumphant boy and the coveted rifle to another scene of operations. For tenacity of purpose

and facility of execution, Pickles was already superior to most men.

Buck recovered his wits and faced the expectan͟t
Schatz. "I just been a-writin' to McAllister," he informed him. "You'll have to give me time to see
what he says. Let's liquor."

Buck stood in the door watching Karl ride away;
the expressionless face gave no hint of his feelings
unless it were found in a certain cold hardness of
the gray eyes in their steady stare, fixed upon the
broad back of the receding German. Leaving this
mark, his glance fell on the horse, waiting patiently
for its late rider, and he turned back into the room
and called: "Hoppy!" Hopalong came in from the
kitchen and Buck met his entry with the question:
"What do you think that Dutch hog come for?"

Hopalong glanced meaningly at Whitby, who still
appeared to be writing against time. "That's all
right," asserted Buck, "I'm a-copperin' my bets from
now on. Schatz wants to buy in as a partner an'
reckons he can stop th' Double Y from losin' any
more stock, long's he's in on th' deal."

"What'd *you* say?" asked Hopalong.

"Nothin'. I wanted a chance to get my breath."

"Well, I wouldn't flirt with that proposition, not
any."

"Why, curse his fool hide, what do I want with
him or his money? If he can stop th' deviltry mebby
he's at th' bottom of it; an' if he is, it won't be long
afore we know it. Next time he comes I'll tell him to
go plumb to hell."

"I wouldn't, Buck."

"What's that?" asked Buck, staring hard at
Whitby.

"I wouldn't," repeated Whitby. "I fancy it's time
you learned what I know. This German chap, now.
You can't fight him yet, Buck; you can't, really."

"Oh, can't I!" exclaimed Buck. "What do you know about it?"

"I know all about it, I should say all that can be found out. Do you mind if we have in Mrs. Cassidy? Clever woman, Mrs. Cassidy."

He left the room while Buck and Hopalong eyed each other helplessly. "Damned if he ain't tellin' me what kind of a wife I've got," complained Hopalong. Mary came in, followed by Whitby.

"Now if you two boys'll only listen to Whitby, you'll learn somethin'," promised Mary.

"It began in Chicago," said Whitby. "Beastly hole, Chicago. I wasn't at all sorry to leave it, except— but that's neither here nor there. McAllister is a friend of mine and he rather thought Buck underrated the difficulties here; so he asked me to run out and look it over. I soon found it was jolly well too big for me so I wrote to the Governor—my father, at home you know—and he said he'd foot the bills. So I put it in the hands of a detective agency; very thorough people, 'pon my word. They tell me this German chap is at the bottom of the mischief but they can't prove it. He is always behind somebody else. If Ned Monroe had not been honest and given up, McAllister would never have won his case in that court: Schatz owns the judge, so they tell me. Amazin' country, isn't it? And then he is far too clever to wage a losing fight: you would have won at the last, despite his efforts. Now he's come with his offer of partnership. Clever idea, really. He'll jolly well use you if he can't beat you; and no doubt he expects to trick you, Buck, in some way, perhaps lending you money—then, you out of it, he has McAllister at a disadvantage.

"My idea is this: take Schatz in as a partner and he'll grow less careful. We shall be able to trip him up. Remarkable man, really. Not one of those he employs can be made to talk; they're entirely loyal. But

sooner or later he will make a mistake: rogues all
do, even the cleverest of them; and if they continue
to escape, it is merely because no one happened to
be watching and catch them at it. I'll lend you the
money, Buck—"

"But what in—what do I need money for, Whit?
Ain't th' range an' th' cattle enough?"

"Of course they are. But the German wants to see
some cash capital and it will do no harm to give
him plenty of rope, will it now?"

"But, Whit," objected Hopalong, "if yo're shore
it's th' Dutchman, we can drive him out of th' country so quick he'll burn his feet. Men 's been shot for
less'n he's done."

"You can't do it, Cassidy. The agency hasn't been
able to get a bit of proof. And McAllister is set
against anything rash. I thought at one time he had
put on another man. There's a chap who makes his
headquarters at Twin River who's busy, no end. The
agency rather suspected he was one of Schatz's
men. Sharp chap, that. And he can't be working on
his own hook, can he?"

He glanced at Buck as if expecting a reply.

"That's Tex Ewalt, Whit," informed Mary. "He's on
our side."

"Ah! do you know, I thought as much. My word,
I'm thirsty; wish I had a brandy and soda here." He
paused to take a drink of water, shaking his head
when Buck motioned to the whiskey. "I'm afraid I
shall never get used to that rye of yours," he declared, mournfully.

Buck turned to Hopalong. "What do you make of
it?" he asked.

"If it depended on you alone, Buck, it would be
easier to answer. But McAllister is in th' game an' it
shore ain't Frenchy: we both know what he'd 'a'
done. What does McAllister think o' this partnership deal?" he asked Whitby.

"He hasn't heard of it, but I'm sure he would agree with me."

"All right!" exclaimed Buck. "We'll let Mac make th' runnin'. If it looks like he's goin' to lose th' race it will be all th' easier to drop th' winner if we got him in gun range. But I shore hates to pay big interest, like I must, a-puttin' up money that way."

"Let me lend it you, Buck," advised Whitby. "The Governor will cable it fast enough when I ask for it. You won't have to pay me a penny interest. And when things settle down a bit you can turn it over to McAllister. I shall stop in this country. I like it, by Jove! And I'm jolly well sure McAllister will sell out to me particularly if—I say, Buck, have I made good out here in the West?"

Buck laughed as he grasped Whitby's hand. "Made good!" he repeated. "Yo're th' best Britisher I ever knew an' I've met some good ones in my time." With Hopalong's slap on his shoulder and Mary smiling at him from her chair by the window, Whitby felt that it was likely to prove a very pleasant country "when things settled down a bit."

"Let's get at that letter to Mac," suggested Buck. "Th' sooner I hear from him th' easier I'll be in mind."

"I've written it," answered Whitby. "If you like I'll get it to Wayback tonight and stop over until morning."

"Go ahead," agreed Buck.

When he had left, Hopalong turned to his wife with the query: "How did he find out yo're a clever woman, Mary?"

"Because he's a clever man, only he hides it," replied Mary. "He was a-gassin' 'bout you an' Buck an' I naturally found out a thing or two myself. That's how he came to tell you. He regular confided in me an' I advised him to tell you-all."

"It was a safe bet you'd find out more'n you'd let go," complimented Hopalong.

"Oh, you Billy-Red!"

When Pickles, mounted on the Goat, had left the ranch by a roundabout way he headed for the bottom of one of the range's many depressions and followed it until close to the Jill, where he turned south and began edging nearer and nearer to the place he had seen Dave. Pickles had listened to many tales of hunting and as his associates had been grown men, experienced in stalking, the boy had absorbed a great deal of healthy knowledge which he made use of in his playing, in the great outdoors. With a grave thoughtfulness beyond his years he now proceeded to put his knowledge to a sterner use and worked cautiously toward his objective without loss of time. When he rode up the bank of a draw, alert and wary, and saw the solitary horseman still keeping his patient vigil, he swiftly dismounted, picketed the Goat and, taking the heavy rifle, crept forward, crouching as he went.

He had come to the edge of the cover and saw Dave still very far away; and after vainly trying to find some way to get closer to the man he was after, he carefully opened the breech of the heavy Sharps to be again assured it was loaded. A bigger cartridge than he had ever used confronted him: four inches of brass and lead, throwing a 500-grain bullet by the terrific force of one hundred and twenty grains of powder. The forty-five Sharps Special raised Hopalong another notch in Pickles' estimation—truly it was a man's weapon.

"Gosh!" he gloated, and then glanced thoughtfully across the open plain toward the horseman. "Twelve hundred, all right," he muttered, regretfully, for one hundred would have suited him better. But a swift smile chased away the scowl. The rifle belonging to Hopalong never missed—he had Buck's word for that—and besides, he had made his wish. One last look around for a cover nearer to Dave, and the big sight was raised and set. The gun went to his shoulder and the heavy report crashed out of a huge cloud of gray smoke as the Sharps spoke.

Dave's sullen temper was rudely jogged into fierce and righteous anger. Something hit his face. Something else screamed past him, struck a rock and whirred into the sky with a sharp, venomous burr. The pony, resenting Dave's painful appropriation of part of his ear, went up into the air and came down on stiff legs, its back arching once as it landed. The instant the hoofs were firmly on the ground it stretched out and ran as it never had before, Dave helpless to check it. The heavy, sharp report of the huge rifle in Pickles' hand had no sooner reached him than he had all he could do to hold his seat. But the sound of that bullet passing him, lingered in his mind long after he had regained control of his terrified mount.

Pickles, swallowing hard and holding one shoulder with a timidly investigating hand, blinked his dazed eyes as he looked about, inquiringly. He remembered pulling the trigger—and then the Goat had reached out thirty feet and kicked him in the neck—and if it wasn't the Goat, who threw the rock? Dave! He sat up and then struggled to his feet, looking eagerly out to see the remains of Dave scattered carelessly over the landscape. Dave was fast getting smaller, a cloud of dust drifting to the south along his trail.

"Darn it!" cried the boy, tears of vexation in his eyes. "He got away! I missed! I missed!" he shouted. "Buck lied to me! Th' old gun ain't no good!" and in the ecstasy of his rage he danced up and down on the discredited weapon. "Whitby's witches ain't no good! Nothin's no good; an' I missed him!"

Meanwhile his injuries were not becoming easier: his head displayed a large, angry lump, and ached fit to burst; his shoulder wasn't broken, he decided, as he exercised it tentatively, but not far from it; and a piece of skin was missing from his bleeding cheek.

"I ought to 'a' got him," he muttered sullenly, picking up the rifle and moving slowly back to where his horse was picketed. "Well, anyhow, he was awful scared—I *knowed* he was a coward! I knowed it! If this old gun was as good as its kick I *would* 'a' got him, too." Pickles had gauged the distance perfectly and his hand had not even quivered when he pulled the trigger—but he had yet to learn of windage and how to figure it. Dave owed his life to the wind that swept the dust of his pony's feet southward.

When Pickles had turned the horse into the pasture he reloaded the rifle before slipping it back into its long leather scabbard. It must be found as he had found it and, besides, he was plainsman enough to realize how serious it might be for Hopalong if he believed the weapon was loaded and found it empty in a crisis.

"Never missed, hey?" he growled savagely as he moved away. "Huh! *Next* time, I'll use *Buck's* gun!"

CHAPTER XIX

The Weak Link

THE LITTLE buckskin pony stood with wide-planted feet and hanging head; his splendid bellows of lungs and powerful abdominal muscles sent the wind in and out of the distended nostrils in the effort to overcome the effect of that last mad burst of speed demanded of him; in his eyes alone, battling against the haze, shone his unconquerable spirit. Bearing saddle and bridle Dave strode away from him to the cabin.

Straight in from Wayback, without a stop, the game little buckskin had carried Dave. Jealousy consumed him. Rumors of Smiler's defection were floating about the town and, though no one but those intimately concerned knew the actual agreement made, the presence of the principals and their several places of call had been noted and fully commented upon. From such premises the town's deductions came near the truth.

The facts as known were enough for Dave. Whatever Schatz might be planning, Dave was satisfied that *he* had no part in it. That Schatz intended to treat him fairly was beyond the angle of his narrow mind. He was very calm over it, his face smooth of wrinkles, his movements slow and assured. He had passed through all the stages from irritation to rage—and beyond: Calm is always beyond.

"Mein gracious, Dave, you vas in a hurry?" asked Schatz, as Dave entered.

He hung saddle and bridle on a peg in the kitchen and strode through into the other room before replying. "No," he drawled, dropping into a chair and stretching his legs full length.

"No? Schust try to kill a horse, *vas?*"

"Yes. Played a trick on me this mornin' an' I'm showin' him who's boss."

"*Dummer Esel!* Und vor a trick you kill him! Den no more tricks, *vas?*"

"Oh, to hell with th' cayuse! What's all this I hear o' you an' Peters in a lovin' match?"

"*Ach! 'Nun kommt die Wharheit'!* If you not come today, I send for you. Vy you stay avay like dot?"

"I'm busy tryin' to make Peters good an' sick o' th' range, tryin' to drive him back to Texas, where he come from. What are you doin': payin' his passage or backin' him to win?"

"Paying his passage, Dave; vere, I am not sure. Look: here iss Herr Peters," stabbing a finger into the palm of his extended right hand, "und here iss McAllister," duplicating with his left; "und ven I do so," closing both hands tightly, "nobody iss left but Schatz."

"Easy as that, eh?" said Dave, skeptically.

"Schust so easy like dot. Look! I make me a pardner by der Double Y."

"Fine," drawled Dave, with hidden sarcasm.

"Vine as gold. Peters, he get all der money vat he can. McAllister, he send der same as Peters. Me, I got dot money, already. Der money vas in der bank. Der range iss my property schust so much as Peters und McAllister."

"Fine," repeated Dave.

"Peters, he dink he spend der money. Soon he go to buy cows. Now iss de point: tomorrow I go by der bank, I dake oud all der money. Four men iss guard. I say I go over by der Bitter Root vere der Deuce Arrow herd for sale iss; und I take all der money. Because dot bank in Vayback too small. I leave der bank und stop by der Miner's Pick saloon. Ve drink. A man vot vears a mask comes in. He cover us mit a gun. He take der money, ride away to Coon River by der Red Bluff. Dere iss man und boat. Der man mit der boat take horse und ride to first relay and pretty soon he iss in Rankin. A relay every ten miles. Der man mit der money go down river in der boat five mile und dere iss man mit two horses; he ride to Vayback und den here mit der money. Vat you tink?"

"Fine," said Dave, for the third time. "An' who's goin' to do all that ground an' lofty tumblin' with th' money?"

"Dave Owens," replied Schatz, with an air of conferring a great favor.

"Me!" exclaimed Dave. He laughed cynically. "Why, Karl, if I had somebody to do all th' hard work, I can make plans like that, myself. Talk sense."

"Hard vork! It iss easy, like a squirrel up a tree. Everybody iss by der station ven der train comes. You take all der guns und ve not make noise, *aber* some thief know you got all der money and catch you first und rob you. Ve got no horses ven ve go by train, und most run, and must run, get horses to run after you. So you get avay. You come here mit der money und who know it?"

"Who's makin' th' blind trail?"

"Denver Gus."

"I don't envy Gus none."

"Vy? I pay him goot. He vas go to Texas, anyvay, pretty quick."

"How you goin' to get out of it?"

"I don't get out of it. Peters, he gets sick und I say: 'Vell, some money I got yet, I buy you out'; *aber* he tink it iss a trick und get mad. Four men I got, gun-men, all. Dey shoot him so soon he get mad."

"An' then McAllister jumps on you with both feet for takin' that money out o' th' bank in th' first place."

"*Ach!* Vat you dink? Am I a fool? Ain'd I a pardner already?"

"What's that got to do with it?"

"I have schust so much right to take der money as Peters. I don't steal der money—it iss steal avay from me. Can I help it?"

"Is that th' law?"

"Der law iss my part. For der law, brains you must haf. Brains I got. To ride, you know. Vat you dink?"

"I go you," declared Dave. "But you shore take a big chance with th' money. I *might* get plugged an' have to drop it."

"*Mein lieber Gott!*" moaned Schatz, in despair. "Brains! Brains!" he roared. "*Ach!* Vat use? Alvays it iss der same. Von day Canada iss der United States; so England iss *gebunden*; South America iss Deutchland; soon all der continent iss Deutchland. Vat fools! No *Verstand—blos* for money. Und to make money iss der little part. Vat fools!"

"Wake up! Who's th' fool if I drop that bundle an' somebody on a good horse gets away with it? Because you can bet yore whole pile I ain't aimin' to stop an' stand off th' beginnin' of a Judge Lynch party, not any."

"Dave, if a veek you sit und a veek you tink, und

schust about von ting, you know somethings about it, *vas*?"

"Shore would."

"Und mit *your* head you must tink. Many days mit *my* head I tink und tink, everythings, possible und not possible. Den ven der plans iss made, *you* mit *your* head mistakes find. Der money vat you steal, it iss no matter, *aber* don't lose it—besser you burn it, as lose it."

"*Burn* it?"

"Yah! Paper it iss, schust paper."

"Paper!" Dave stared in doubt. "Paper," he repeated, struggling to grasp the idea. He gave it up and quite humbly asked for light. "What th' blazes am I a-goin' to run away with paper for?"

"Maybe somebody smarter as I tink. Two men, already, much questions ask. Maybe Peters take all der money before me. So I go by der bank und get der money first. Dey can't help it. It iss my bank anyvay und der check iss dere."

"You've *got* th' money!"

"Yah, here in der house I got it. Everythings iss *vollkommen*. All der mistakes vat come I know, possible und not possible. Noding can slip, noding can break."

"Yo're a wonder!" congratulated Dave, "th' one an' only original, sure-fire, bull's-eye wonder." He leaned forward suddenly, head bent in listening. "Somebody outside," he warned, softly. Gun in hand, he sprang to the door and passed out. The gloom of the coming night lay in wait in the valleys but it was light enough to detect any skulker. Dave made a systematic search, satisfying himself that no one was within a mile of the cabin, before returning. "It's all right," he assured, as he entered the room again. A deafening roar followed his words. Schatz gave a convulsive start and slid slowly from his chair to the floor; on his face was an overwhelming surprise.

"Huh——Huh! Huh!——" the grunting laugh spoke immeasureable contempt. "Brains!"

The half-open drawer of the sideboard revealed in the lamplight a number of packages, the wrappings of several being torn open. Dave sat thoughtfully contemplating them. He had removed them from their hiding place and put them in the drawer before lighting the lamp, both acts due to precaution: spying upon Karl had discovered to Dave the hiding place; he was distinctly opposed to finding himself in the same predicament regarding his suddenly acquired wealth. The still figure, resting under two feet of earth, close to the river bank, gave him no concern whatever. His mind was busy with the best way to pack the money; small bills were difficult to trace but bulky to carry. He shoved the drawer to with his foot and re-lit his pipe.

His plans were already made. He had reasoned them out swiftly while hunting the supposed skulker. The disappearance of Karl would be associated with the disappearance of the money. The bank would maintain that the money had been drawn on the day the check was dated, which necessarily must be tomorrow. The four men who were to act as guards would conclude some difficulty had arisen and await further orders; it would be the same with all the others involved. The way was clear for him. There remained only Rose. He knocked the ashes from his pipe and went to bed.

CHAPTER XX

Misplaced Confidence

PICKLES WAS hungry. He cocked his eye anxiously at the sun and sighed. He gazed in discouragement over the widespread furrowed earth where his best efforts left so small a trace and dropping the hoe, sighed again. With all his soul he wished he had not fled from the Double Y. Sudden resolution armed him. He shoved his hands in his pockets and marched manfully in the direction of the house. He refused to go hungry for anybody.

Topping a rise, his head barely showed against the skyline when he dropped as if shot. The horseman making for the house might be Jean; his glance had been too hasty for recognition. Flat against the earth, Pickles pushed himself backward until he felt it safe to turn and gallop clumsily down grade on hands and feet. Far enough, he sat and thought. He could gain the barn unseen and if he ran, would have time to dash into the house, grab some chuck, and get away again before the horseman got there.

He sprang to his feet and ran like a long-horn steer, gazed upon by the stock in pasture with interest: they were not accustomed to this style of locomotion in trousers.

Pickles made excellent time on the level but when he turned to breast the slope it was harder going; and Pickles was tired; he had been at work since sun-up with a short rest at breakfast. He gained the barn winded but went through and crossed to the house without pausing. Back of the house he stopped to listen. He had cut it too fine. The horse was coming up to the door. "Darn it!" said Pickles, with bitter emphasis.

The snap of the catch on the front door and Rose's voice told him she had gone outside. Maybe the rider wasn't coming in; they couldn't see the end window if they did and if he were quick—he squirmed over the ledge, dropped noiselessly to the floor, sped through the doorway—and almost dislocated his spine with the ferret-like turn he made in trying to get back into the room the same instant he left it: he had barely escaped the other's entry; if Rose came to the bedroom she would be certain to exclaim at sight of him. Pickles breathed a short—a very short—prayer. He put his hands to the window ledge—and stiffened.

"No, I can't stay. Rose, I'm pullin' my freight. How soon can you come along?"

It was Dave—he was going away—and he wanted Rose to go, too. Pickles knelt silently by the bunk and muffled his rapid breathing in the blankets, while he listened.

"Where?" asked Rose.

"Anywhere you say. I'm a-goin' to clean up a gold mine in a few hours an' yo're goin' to help me spend it. We'll get married first stop."

"A gold mine?"

"More money than you ever saw."

"And you want—me—to go with you?"

"Not with me. I got to get th' money first. I'll get th' train to Helena tonight. You get on at Jackson. You can make it easy on Swaller."

"I must know more. Perhaps you tell true. Perhaps you run away. Tell me."

"Got a good opinion o' yore future husband, ain't you? Quit foolin', Rose. Have I got to show you the cards afore you take a hand?"

"Yes," was the decisive answer.

"All right. It's this way: Schatz deals to Peters from a cold deck. He gets all th' money out o' the bank, Peters', McAllister's, an' his. Then he lets me lift it, him not knowin' who I am, o' course. I do th' mysterious disappearance act an' Schatz makes foolish noises too late. A posse takes after me an' runs into a blind trail. I circle back to town. Right there is where I fool Schatz. He thinks I'm driftin' along the Big Moose trail to hand th' money over to him graceful. 'Stead o' that I'm snortin' along the track to Helena with you. Schatz dassent make no holler an' we leave him an' Peters to fight it out. Do you get me?"

"They will kill you."

"Oh, not a whole lot, I reckon. I'm gettin' so used to bein' killed thataway, I sorter like it. Talk sense. Where's th' ole man?"

"I will leave a letter for him."

"Hip hooray! Mighty nigh kissin'-time, Rose. *Would* be, on'y I can't leave this blasted cayuse: 'fraid to trust him. Which way you goin'? Don't show in Wayback. Hit th' river farther west."

Pickles had heard enough. His exit through the window was rapid and silent. His retreat from the house, made along two sides of a triangle, was prompted by his knowledge of the positions of Rose and Dave and he maneuvered so they should not be able to see him. Nevertheless the security of the

barn was very welcome, although he gained it only
to recall that the Goat was at pasture. Then Swallow
must be in the corral. He looked from the rear door.
Yes, there he was, close to the fence, gazing across
the grass at the field stock and no doubt wishing he
were with them. Whimpering with suppressed delight the boy ran silently to his rope, hanging in
long loops over two pegs in the wall; he coiled it
ready to hand, crept out the door, and was at Swallow with the rush of a bob-cat. The great stallion
made one mighty bound, lashed out one foot and
stood with flattened ears; he knew the meaning of a
rope in that position as well as any cow-pony in
Montana and the indignity vexed while it subdued
him. Pickles never bridled and saddled so rapidly in
his short life. Keeping the barn between him and
the house, he rode a mile or more out of his course
before he dared to turn; then he took his bearings,
set a straight line for the Double Y ranch, and gave
Swallow his head. The good horse, scarcely feeling
the boy's light weight, went forward with a rush,
but responded to the light hand on the bridle and
settled down, traveling mile after mile with the tireless stride and ease of movement that had won him
his name.

Greatly as he wished for the journey's end, Pickles rode with judgment. The first doubt assailed him
as he neared the Jill: would Swallow take the water?
He was not kept long in doubt. Swallow knew better
than to refuse. A master rider had put him through
this stream, close to that very spot, in the dark of
a not long distant night. The sight of the water sent
the horse's ears pricking forward; he entered readily and swam for the opposite bank the moment the
ground left his feet. Pickles shouted his delight; it
would have broken his heart to have been compelled to go back to the ford. Swallow scrambled
out onto the bank with little trouble and stretched

out once more in his sweeping gallop; he knew now
where he was bound and pulled impatiently against
the restraining touch. The pace was a source of
wonder to Pickles; seven miles and a swim at the
end of it and here he was asking for a loose rein, demanding it, and going faster than ever. "Darned if I
believe he *can* get tired," said Pickles; "go on then,"
and he gave him his head and smiled a tired smile
to note how the powerful limbs quickened their action and the horse gathered pace until Pickles was
traveling faster than ever before in his life. Only the
smoothness of the motion gave him confidence in
his own ability to hold out. "I could never 'a' made
it on th' Goat," he reflected. "Go on, boy! Eat 'em
up!" One slender black ear slanted toward him and
away again. Swallow was eating 'em up the best he
knew how.

Having made her decision, Rose listened carefully
to Dave's advice. The more he talked the better she
understood the situation; and Dave had scarcely
mounted to ride away before she began her own
preparations. They appeared to be very simple,
merely the apparelling for a ride and keeping watch
after Dave to see that he kept on his way.

Dave's disappearance sent her hurrying to the
stable. She was surprised to find her bridle missing.
On the next peg was Pickles' bridle, the only one
ready for instant use. She hesitated a moment at
sight of the heavy bit, but took it down and hastened to the edge of the pasture, sending a clear
call for Swallow as she ran. There came no answering hoofbeats and she waited to reach the fence before calling again. A glance to right and left and she
put her hands to her mouth and sent forth a ringing
summons that carried to the far corner of the enclo-
sure. The wait of a few seconds told her that Swallow was not in the pasture. Vexed and wondering

she glanced from one to another of the animals near her: two draft horses, a brood mare, its long-legged colt close by, all watching her with that spellbound intensity of gaze frequently accorded the sudden appearance of a human among domestic animals running free. Swallow would never be turned in the same field as these; then where was he? Jean was riding the only saddle pony—no, there was the Goat. Suspicion awoke in Rose: was it possible Pickles had dared to ride away on Swallow!

The Goat had ideas of his own; he had positively no use for a bridle just then, but Rose had ideas of a distinctly superior order of intelligence and but little time was lost before the Goat was plunging away to where Pickles should be, carrying Rose astride and bareback. Her suspicions were confirmed in part: Pickles was not where he should be. She swung the Goat through a half circle on his hind feet and started back for the barn with a rush. Ten minutes later, the Goat, properly saddled, turned short out of the farm road with a catlike scramble onto the Twin River trail. He had not carried so much weight since his old master rode him and he did not like it, but knew better than to shirk; he had tried that, and the spurs, two of them, clanking loosely on Rose's small boots, had ripped his sides with quite an old-time fervor. Rose had found time to adjust them after saddling; the last hole barely held them but they served. How she longed for the free-striding gallop of Swallow! The tied-in gait of the Goat was irksome to her but she kept him to his work and Twin River drew rapidly nearer. With Dave's instructions in mind she knew there was plenty of time but it would be foolish to lessen the margin of safety by loitering.

A quarter of a mile from the ford she passed the stage from Wayback. The driver was just whipping up to enter Twin River in style and the stage occupants had opportunity to appraise Rose as she forged ahead. "My heavens, what a beauty!" exclaimed a young lady on the seat beside the driver, herself no mean specimen of God's handiwork. "Who is she?"

The driver shifted his whip and swept off his hat with a flourish. He gazed admiringly after the rider. "That, ma'am, is the French Rose; an' this is certainly my lucky day. I ain't seen two such pretty women before in one day, not in a dog's age. I ain't *never* seen 'em," he amended with enthusiastic conviction.

The coach cut through the ford to the hiss of the swirling water and turned into the straight in time for them to see a man run out from the Sweet-Echo to meet Rose, standing with his hand on the bridle while Rose leaned forward in what looked suspiciously like a warm greeting.

Another exclamation escaped the young lady on the stage: "Whitby!" and the blush called forth by the driver's frank admiration paled as she watched the two whom they rapidly approached.

"Know him, ma'am?" asked the driver politely; but his companion was oblivious to all but the scene before her.

Rose's imperious gesture and call had brought Whitby running. They had achieved a warm regard for each other during Rose's numerous visits to the Double Y, made at Dave's instigation; visits that had not ceased until the arrival of Hopalong and Mary, when Dave had declared it was no use to try longer. Whitby grasped the significance of Rose's hurried words in very brief time. "By Jove!" he exclaimed, thinking rapidly. "By Jove! he will do it, too. They can't refuse to honor his check, you know. Buck is the only one can stop it. Lucky Pickles was gone and you came here instead of going to the Wayback bank. Buck hasn't long left me. I can catch him." He

ran around to the shed at the rear and was going
fast when he turned into the trail, astride his pony.
His reassuring wave of the hand to Rose stopped in
mid-air as he caught sight of Margaret McAllister,
standing on the footboard of the coach and looking
at him with an expression he did not in the least understand. He made as if to pull up, thought better of
it, and sweeping off his hat, dug the spurs into his
pony and shot out over the Big Moose trail at a
speed that promised to get him somewhere very
soon.

Dave had not left the LaFrance cabin far behind
when he pulled up with an oath and after a short
period of consideration, turned back, riding at fair
speed. He found cause to congratulate himself in
starting early: it gave him time to go back to Rose
and furnish her money in case of need. He saw her
sooner than he expected. Turning a slight bend in
the trail, he had full view of the Goat, not two hundred yards away, and saw him bound forward like a
racer as the spurs ripped into him; Dave gripped a
shout in his throat at sight of this act: why was
Rose in such a hurry? Suspicion ebbed and flowed
in his mind. If she were in such a hurry, why wasn't
she on Swallow? But the spurring had been for
speed, not for punishment. Maybe she was saving
Swallow for the longer journey. But if content to tell
her father by letter of her going, who in Twin River
needed a personal call? She could not be going farther than Twin River—to the Double Y, for example:
there was not time for that. And why should she
want to go there, either? Dave shook his head impatiently. Either she was square or she wasn't. If she
wasn't, there would be a group of hard-riding boys
pounding along the trail in time to cut off Schatz at
the bank. He decided to ride to within a short distance of town, lay off the trail, and wait. If no one

showed up, he would stick to the original plan. If Rose played crooked, he would take a train East. If too hard pressed, he could use the relays south in place of Denver Gus. Denver might put up an argument but he had one answer to all arguments that had always silenced opposition the moment he produced it. "Get on, bronc," he commanded, heading for Wayback.

Buck had got farther south than Whitby suspected; so far, that Whitby was beginning to hope he had not struck off from the trail, when he sighted him. Buck was riding head on shoulder, as if he had heard the coming of his pursuer, and he pulled up at the other's wild gesture. "What's eatin' him?" said Buck, smiling for the thousandth time at Whitby's manner of riding; it was a constant wonder to Buck that a man could sit a horse like that and stick to the worst of them as Whitby did. "He shore ain't meanin' to swim the Black Jack to get to the Fort." The smile faded as he suddenly realized the appeal in the Englishman's frantic waving; he rode forward rapidly and they were soon near enough together for Whitby to be sure his words would be heard and understood.

"Twin River, Buck! Twin River! And ride like hell!"

Buck's quirt bit into his pony's flank. Never before had he known the Englishman profane; it must be serious. Whitby turned and raced ahead of him, rapidly overtaken by Buck who rode a fresher and speedier mount. As they ran side by side, Whitby rapidly repeated Rose's news.

"I can make it, Whit," declared Buck. "They won't try to work th' game till closin' time at th' bank. Train bound west is due at Wayback about then. Wish I had Allday under me. So long."

Whitby slowed to a lope and Buck drew away rapidly. His duty accomplished, the Englishman's thoughts turned to the puzzling expression on Margaret McAllister's face, as he had last seen it. He tried in vain to analyze it and unconsciously pressed his tired horse into a faster pace in his anxiety for an explanation.

Buck did not spare his pony. He *must* be at the bank before the money was paid over. The stringing up of Schatz by Judge Lynch would not bring the money back; and Buck had grave doubts of his ability to accomplish this retribution. Schatz appeared to grow stronger the more he knew of him. Nobody but a man very sure of himself and his power would dare such deviltry. Well, it would come to a personal straightening of accounts. Buck's grim face was never sterner. But first he must get to the bank. Resolutely putting aside all other considerations he gave his whole mind to his horse. Presently he shook his head: "Never make it," he muttered; "have to relay at Twin." Even as he said it he saw ahead of him another rider approaching at an easy lope; an expression of gratified pleasure appeared on Buck's face as he saw the other dismount and begin to lengthen the stirrup leathers. It was Rose. "By God! What a woman!" exclaimed Buck. "She thinks as quick as Cassidy an' never overlooks a bet."

He urged his pony to its best speed. With a fresh mount in sight, his object was practically assured. As he drew near, Rose called out: "Horse wait for you at Two Fork Creek."

He pulled short beside her in two jumps. "Rose, I love you," he declared, his eyes sparkling with pleasure; "you'd oughta been a man!" He sprang to the ground while speaking and was astride the Goat at a bound, turning in his saddle to call back to her: "But I'm most mighty glad yo're not." A wave of his hand and he faced about, settling in his seat for the run to Two Fork, five miles beyond Twin River.

The crimson flood that burned in her face at his first remark, to recede at his second, returned in full tide as she stood with lips apart and eyes wide, watching him ride away. A trembling seized her, so that she clung to the saddle for support. The moving figure became blurred as the tears gathered in her eyes; she brushed them away impatiently with the back of her hand. "He is not mean it that way," she murmured; "it is only that he is glad I think about the horse."

She mounted and rode soberly toward Twin River. The pony, awaiting the customary notice to attend to business and finding it long in coming, began to entertain a sneaking affection for skirts, which until then he had regarded with suspicious hostility.

CHAPTER XXI

Pickles Tries to Talk

MARY SAT at the window sewing—a continuous performance with her these days. The sound of a horse approaching caused her to glance up just as a faint call for "Buck" reached her. One look and the sewing fell to the floor as she sprang to her feet, crying out for Jake as she ran. With Swallow nuzzling at her dress, she supported Pickles until Jake came to aid; he lifted the boy from the saddle and carried him into the house.

Mary hastily got out the whiskey and Pickles gulped down a mouthful before he realized what it was. He choked, and pushed away the cup. "Don't want it," he declared, weakly; "ain't never goin' to drink."

"Good boy," encouraged Mary, patting his head. "You stick to that."

"Where's Buck?" asked Pickles.

"He ain't come back yet," answered Mary.

"Where is he?" insisted Pickles.

"I don't know," was the patient reply.

"I gotta find Buck," the boy declared, starting to rise.

Mary pushed him back. "How can you find him when you don't know where he is?"

"Ain't he som'er's on th' range?"

"No; him an' Whit rode off Twin River way this mornin' an' they ain't neither of 'em back yet."

"Well, I gotta find him, an' I gotta find him now," declared Pickles. "Lemme go."

"What's eatin' you?" demanded Jake. "*You* ain't fitten to ride *no* place an' I'm mortally certain you can't walk."

"Shut yore trap, Woolly-face. What's a sheep like you know, anyhow? Nothin'! Can't even dig holes less'n yo're prodded with lead. Lemme go."

The whiskey was having an effect on Pickles or he never would have shown malice like this. Besides, it was not true and Pickles knew it. To all questions he had but one answer and Mary was in despair when Hopalong strode into the room. Hoppy wanted to know things—"Where'd you get that horse?" he asked, sharply.

"Huh?" queried Pickles.

"Where'd you get that horse—that horse you was ridin'?"

"That's Rose's horse—where's Buck?"

"Rose who?"

"Huh? French Rose. Say, where's Buck?"

"French Rose, hey? Say, Mary, that's th' horse got away from me with that cow-killin' screech-owl th' other night."

"That horse? Rose LaFrance's horse? Oh, Billy!" It seemed that Mary was deeper in Buck's confidence than his old friend Hopalong, in this matter, at all events.

"Say you, blast you! Where's Buck? Lemme go! What's eatin' you? Ah, hell!" Pickles relaxed under the grasp of Jake's hands and limply essayed to retrieve his reputation. "I asks yore pardon, ma'am. I promises Buck I won't never swear afore a lady an' here I goes an' does it, first time I'm mad."

Hoppy eyed the penitent keenly. "Say, Bud: what's wrong?" he asked quietly. "Buck ain't got no better friend than me and I'll find him for you; but there ain't no good huntin', less'n I got somethin' to say when I get there."

"Will you? Bully for you! Tell Buck th' Dutchman's goin' to get all th' money—then Dave's goin' to get it—it's in th' bank—on'y Schatz don't know who it is—nobody catches Dave runnin' into a blin' trail thataway—then Dave takes th' money to th' Dutchman—but right here's where he fools him—he don't take it—he keeps it—an' he marries Rose on th' train to Helena—Rose rides Swaller to Jackson to get th' train—on'y she has got to get another horse 'cause I rode Swaller here. D'you get me?" Pickles stared expectantly at Hopalong, who turned to Jake.

"Put that horse in th' barn. Saddle Allday. Rope a cayuse an' set that smoke a-rollin'—take a blanket an' ball th' smoke three times at th' end o' every minute—go through th' Gut an' up th' north side. *Pronto!*"

Jake went out of the door on the jump. He moved fast for Buck on occasion—rare, it is true—but there was a volcanic danger in Hopalong's eye that put springs in Jake's boot-heels.

"That's th' way to talk," sighed Pickles, happily. Hopalong went to the rack and took down his rifle. "Reckon yo're going to want that?" asked Pickles.

"Reckon I might," admitted Hopalong, gravely. "You see, after I find Buck I'm a-goin' to look for Dave an' th' Dutchman."

"Jiggers! I shore hopes you find 'em. I'd sooner you get Dave than any man I know, 'ceptin' me."

"Well, I sorter count on gettin' Dave. So long, Pickles."

"So long," echoed the boy.

Mary followed her husband outside. "Don't get hurt, Billy-Red," she warned him.

"That sort o' vermin never hurt me yet, Mary. When th' boys get here send 'em after me to Wayback. Tell Ned, rifles. Let me have all th' money you got; if I miss Buck I might want it."

Mary watched him until he rode by on Allday, waving to him from the corner of the house. Then she went indoors to Pickles.

"That's a bully man, that Hopalong, ain't he?" was his enthusiastic greeting.

"He shore is; an' you're a bully boy, Pickles," replied Mary. She took up her sewing again. The boy watched her curiously and was about to ask a question, when Sleep floated past and Pickles forgot to ask it.

CHAPTER XXII

"A Ministering Angel"

MRS. BLAKE surveyed her surroundings with the surface calm which comes from seeing and disbelieving. These were depths to which she never had expected to descend. She allowed herself half a moment of speculation on the possibility of there existing, somewhere in the world, a real lack of accommodations as appalling as her imagination could now conceive. "I have often thought Mr. Blake somewhat careless in his choice of a hotel during our wanderings, but the worst of them never even suggested—Margie, did you ever in your life imagine such a room could exist?"

"It is only for an hour or so," returned Margaret, listlessly.

"Oh, I don't complain, my dear. You are an equal sufferer. And I am distinctly relieved at the thought of removing some of this terrible dust before we—before—we—"

Her voice trailed off into silence as she caught

sight of a motto over the door; it was one of those affairs worked in colored worsted over perforated cloth; the colors had been chosen with less regard to harmony than is usually exhibited by an artist; perhaps it was contrast that was sought; as a study in contrasts it was a blasting success. Mrs. Blake glared at it with the fascinated interest of a spectator within the danger zone of a bursting bomb. " 'God bless our home,' " she read, in awed undertone. "Perhaps He will, but it is more than it deserves." She mounted laboriously onto a chair and turned the motto to the wall, hastily facing it about again with a suppressed scream: if the front were chaos the back was a cataclysm. In a spasm of indignation she jerked it loose from its fastening and dropped it out of sight behind the evil-looking washstand. In this position her glance fell on the crude specimen of basin provided. She picked it up doubtfully and struck it against the side of the washstand. "Tin!" she exclaimed. "A dishpan!" and went off into peals of laughter, banging the pan and calling "Dinner!" in an unnaturally deep voice, when she could speak from laughing.

Margaret turned a sullen face from the window. She had seen the French Rose in animated conversation with a tall, good-looking man in flannel shirt and overalls, who had ridden away up the road, evidently in obedience to her orders; while Rose, herself, rode in the direction taken by Whitby. The soft, broad-brimmed hat, the waist but little different from the flannel shirt of the man, the ill-fitting skirt, the mannish gloves and clumsy boots—the superb health of the splendid figure proclaimed itself through all these disadvantages. The woman was a perfect counterfoil for Whitby, and Margaret hid the ache in her heart under a sullenness of demeanor that a less astute companion might have attributed to the annoyances and inconveniences of the journey.

"For heaven's sake, Aunt, don't make such a noise," she insisted; "my head aches as if it would split."

"Your head aches! I'm sorry, my dear. Still, there are worse things than headaches, now aren't there?"

Margaret stared. "No doubt," she admitted, tartly; "but it is the worst I have to submit, at present. When a greater evil befalls me I will tell you."

"Why, that's honest," said Mrs. Blake, cheerfully; "and as long as we are to be honest, you are sure it is not your conscience that is at fault?"

"My conscience?" asked Margaret. "What has my conscience to do with a headache?"

"First class in Physical Geography, rise. Jessie, what is the origin of the islands of headaches that vex the pacific waters of the soul? They are due to volcanic action of bad conscience."

"Oh, Aunt! how can you be so absurd?"

"I would rather be absurd than unjust, Margaret."

"I don't understand you."

"You understood me very well. Because you see Whitby talking to a pretty woman, is that a reason to condemn him?"

"Talking! He kissed her before my very eyes, in the public street."

"You cannot say that, Margaret. I saw the meeting as plainly as you did."

"How could you? You were inside! Why has he never mentioned her in his letters?"

"Has he ever mentioned anything but business? He would scarcely mention her to George, and you know he has not written to you."

"No, he had something better to do. This is an unprofitable discussion. I am utterly indifferent to Mr. Booth's actions, past, present, and to come, as

well as the reasons for them. If you intend to use
that basin for something other than a dinner call,
do so. I'm not hungry, but we might as well get it
over with. We have a long drive before us."

"With all my heart, my dear; unless the water is
on a par with the other—er—conveniences."

"Seems like Buck Peters might be in a hurry," observed Slick Milligan, sufficiently interested to come
from behind the bar and walk out onto the porch.
"Which it's th' first time I see him use a quirt."

"None o' thea punchers think aucht o' a horse,"
was Sandy's opinion, based on a wide experience.

If Margaret had chanced to overhear Slick's remark it would have explained much. Mrs. Blake was
resting, preparatory to sallying forth on the last
stretch of their journey, and Margaret was about to
make inquiries regarding a conveyance, when the
rapid drumming of a horse's feet drew her to the
window as Buck went past. Margaret had never met
Buck but she was far too good a horsewoman to fail
to recognize the pony. She had noted every detail
when she had first seen Rose and you may be sure
no point, good or bad, of the Goat as a saddle pony,
had escaped her critical judgment. Her first
thought, as the Goat went past, was one of surprise
that he should make so little of the weight of his
rider, a full-grown man and no lightweight, either;
lean and hard as Buck was, Margaret's estimate of
the number of pounds the pony carried was very
near the mark; and then, in a flash, she knew him:
the very animal that the French Rose had ridden.
Margaret knew it to be out of the question that he
had traveled to the Double Y ranch and back; they
must have exchanged horses on the road. But, why?

The consideration of this enigma and the many
possibilities it offered as collateral questions, occupied her fully, to the very grateful content of Mrs.

Blake, who was genuinely tired and ashamed to say
so. It was a consideration so perplexing that Margaret was prepared to allow Whitby to explain, when
he was so unfortunate as to appear in company
with Rose. He had overtaken her, a half-mile down
the trail, but Margaret could not, of course, know
this. They remained in earnest conversation for two
or three minutes, when Rose went on and Whitby
went around to the shed to put up his pony. Margaret ran down stairs and went out onto the porch.
She felt better able to face him in the open.

It was thus that Whitby, coming in at the back
door, was directed out through the front one. Rapidly as Margaret moved, she was too great an attraction to escape instant notice. Whitby advanced
with outstretched hand. "Ripping idea, taking us by
surprise, Miss McAllister. Awful journey, you know,
really."

"We wished to avoid giving trouble. You are looking very well, Mr. Booth."

"Fit as a fiddle, thank you. But—I say—you'll excuse me,—but aren't you feeling a little—ah—seedy,
now? I mean—"

"I quite understand what you mean. Am I looking
a little—ah—seedy, Mr. Booth?"

"No, certainly not! Very stupid of me, I'm sure.
I—ah—rather fancied—but of course I'm wrong.
This confounded dust gets in a chap's eyes so—"

"Do you mean that my eyes look dusty, Mr.
Booth?"

"Oh, I say! Now you're chaffing me. As if—"

"Not in the least. Chaffing is an art in which I fail
to excel. But if you mean that I look a little pale and
dragged with the journey, you must remember that
I do not pretend to have the vitality of a cow-girl."

"Ah! Just so. And Mrs. Blake—she is with you, I
presume."

"The presumption is justified. Aunt's vitality was

even less equal to the journey than my own. She is resting and begs to be excused until she can say 'How-do' at the ranch."

"Why—ah—how did Mrs. Blake know I called in?"

Margaret bit her lip. "I happened to be looking from the window as you rode up," she explained, carelessly.

"Ah! Just so. Miss McAllister, you don't know me very well, not really; perhaps no better than I know you. I'm no good at this sort of thing, this fencing with words, you know; I discovered that long ago; and I long ago adopted the only other method: to smash right through the guard. My presumption doesn't presume so far as to imagine you are jealous; I am not seeking causes; all I know is, you made me a promise when I came West, a conditional promise, I grant you: I was to make good. Well, I haven't done half bad, really. I fancy Mr. McAllister would admit as much. Buck Peters admits more; and one has to be something of a man, you know, to merit that from Peters. He's the finest man I ever knew, myself, bar none. It is very good of you to hear me so patiently. I'm coming to the kernel of the difficulty just now:

"Rose LaFrance, the cow-girl you mentioned, is the right sort. She brought word this morning that will save Peters a goodish bit of money; incidentally Mr. McAllister, also. Buck had to be in Wayback at the earliest possible moment and I was fortunate enough to overtake him. Miss LaFrance not only was thoughtful enough to ride to meet Buck and give him a fresh mount and to send a man ahead with whom Buck will change again, but she insists that we follow him, which is a jolly good idea; these fellows are very careless with their fire-arms and he might require help. If the blackguard he is after succeeds in withdrawing the entire deposit from the bank and it is given to him in cash, before Peters gets there, he will certainly require help. I leave you to reflect on these facts, Miss McAllister. Give my kindest regards to Mrs. Blake."

He stalked back the way he had come, in the characteristic wooden manner which precluded any appeal, if Margaret had felt like making one; but her mind was too fully occupied with what she had heard to understand that he was actually leaving. He was splashing through the ford before she realized the significance of this part of his defense. Thoughtful, and without resentment, she went to rejoin Mrs. Blake.

Whitby pushed his horse sufficiently to overtake Rose who, he knew, was riding slowly. Just outside the town he met Cock Murray, astride the Goat; the Goat was a very tired pony and showed it.

"My dear man! Why aren't you following Peters?" asked Whitby, in surprised remonstrance.

"My dear Brit! I sorta allowed it wasn't healthy," answered Cock. "I tells you th' same as I tells th' French Rose: 'When Buck says "Scoot for th' ranch an' tell Cassidy to hit Wayback *pronto* an' he'll get news o' me at th' bank," ' it 'pears like, to my soft-boiled head, that's what I oughta do."

"I beg your pardon. Of course. Rather odd Peters didn't tell me."

"He meant to. I'm sorry he didn't. So long."

"So long," echoed Whitby, mechanically. He pulled up to shout after Cock: "You won't get far on that horse; he's done, you know."

"I ain't goin' far on that 'oss," Cock shouted back: "an' they're never done till they're down, you know."

"Impudent beggar, but a good man. They grow 'em good out here. I fancy the bad-plucked ones don't last." And Whitby hastened on to overtake Rose.

He had left Two Fork Creek four miles behind him

before sighting her; in her impatience she had gone faster than she knew. Whitby had almost caught up, when he saw Rose bend forward, wave to him, and then dash away, as if she were inviting him to a race.

"Buck!" exclaimed Whitby, with intuitive conviction. "It's Buck as sure as little apples Kesicks." Fifty yards' advance showed him that he was right. The figure lying huddled in the road was certainly Buck, and beside him was his dead pony. Rose flung herself from the saddle and ran to him; and Whitby, wearing the terribly savage expression of the man slow to anger, was not far behind. Together they laid the unconscious figure at full length.

"It is there," said Rose, dully, pointing to the right thigh.

"Ah," breathed Whitby, in a sigh of relief. He cut the cloth but forbore to tear it away, the coagulated blood having stopped the bleeding. "Drilled through!" he exclaimed. "Why, the swine must have been near enough to do better than that. How ever did he miss? We'll bandage this as it is, Miss LaFrance, and do it properly at—now, should you say take him to the doctor at Wayback?"

"No. He is a drunken beast. I will nurse him."

"Very well. A good nurse is better than a drunken doctor. Just cut this sleeve from my shirt, will you?"

Rose took the knife and cut, instead, a three-inch strip from the bottom of her skirt, Whitby meanwhile producing a flask, from which he carefully fed Buck small quantities of whiskey. Rose tendered him the bandage. "Well rolled, Miss LaFrance! Have you been taught this sort of thing?" Rose silently nodded her head. "My word! Buck is in luck. You apply the bandage then, while I give him this. You'll make a better job of it than I should."

Buck slowly opened his eyes to see Whitby's face bending over his. "Got away, Whit," he whispered, weakly; "ambushed me, by God," and relapsed into unconsciousness.

"Much blood! He have lose much blood," murmured Rose.

"Yes," assented Whitby. "How shall we carry him? He can never ride."

"Travois," said Rose. "I show you."

Buck again regained consciousness and his voice was distinctly stronger. "Get after him, Whit. He mustn't get away."

"Oh, nonsense, Buck. They know the cat's out of the bag by this time and they will never be such asses as to try it on now. As for Dave, he can't get away. The agency will be jolly glad to do something for the money they have had by turning over Dave if I ask it of them. And McAllister will think you are worth a good bit more than the money, I lay. I know I do."

Buck was attempting feeble remonstrance when Rose returned from her survey of the timber available and swiftly placed her hands over his lips. "Do not talk," she commanded. "It is bad to talk, now."

"What price the nurse—eh, Buck? Oh, you lucky beggar!"

"Rose," murmured Buck. "Why, that's right kind."

Admonishing him with raised forefinger, Rose gave instructions to Whitby and he hastened away to gather material for the travois.

When Margaret returned to Mrs. Blake she was carrying a pair of driving gloves and a jaunty sailor hat which Mrs. Blake knew had been packed in one of the trunks. "Are we going to start, Margie?" she asked, with languid interest.

"*I* am going to start but I am going the other way. We shall not be able to leave for the ranch before morning, probably."

Mrs. Blake sat up with a suddenness that sur-

prised even herself. "The morning!" she echoed. "If
you think that I shall stay in this horror of a room
until morning, Margaret, you are mistaken. I will go,
if I walk."

"It's a long walk," commented Margaret, carelessly.

"'And may I ask why you are going the other way
and when you purpose to return?"

"I am going to Wayback to telegraph. Some thief
has planned to get all of papa's money from the
bank there, and of course he will try to escape on
the train. We shall catch him by telegraphing to the
officers at the next town."

"If you do he is a fool. And who are 'we'? How did
you learn all this?"

"Whitby told me."

"'When?"

"Just now."

"Was Whitby here?"

"Yes."

"And never asked for me?"

"I told him you begged to be excused."

"You told him I—now see here, Margaret. There *is*
such a thing as going too far, and this is an example
of it. 'Beg to be excused'! What will he think of me?
Where is he now?"

"He has gone on to Wayback. But he never will
have the sense to telegraph. That is why I am going."

"Did you quarrel?"

"Well—we weren't exactly friendly."

"Oh!—oh!—oh!" The three exclamations were
long-drawn, with pauses between them and in three
different keys.

"Aunty!" cried Margaret, furiously, stamping her
foot. "How dare you insinuate—I said I was going to
telegraph!"

"All right, my dear. Have it your own way. I'll immolate myself on the altar of friendship: in this case, a particularly uncomfortable bed. Please remember, Margaret, as you speed away on your errand of avarice, I said a *particularly* uncomfortable bed."

Margaret went out and slammed the door. Mrs. Blake chuckled until she laughed, and laughed until she gasped for breath and was obliged to loosen her corsets. "I am as bad as Margie," she sighed; "I don't know when I am well off. Now I shall have to stay marooned in this pesky room until Margie returns. I never can fasten these outrageous things without help."

In her fetching gown of figured brown cloth, bordered with beaver fur, with slanting drapery of plain green, above which a cutaway jacket exposed a full vest, and topped by a high beaver toque—with flush due to the recent passage-at-arms still in her cheeks and the fire of indignation in her eyes—Margaret presented a *chic* daintiness that met with the entire approval of the burly Sandy, who hastened from the barroom at the sound of her descent.

"I want a hitch of some kind," requested Margaret; "something with speed and bottom, and the sooner the better."

"A hitch?" queried Sandy. He had ominous visions of the dainty figure being whirled to destruction behind a pair of unruly bronchos.

"A horse, a team, a rig, something to drive, and at once," explained Margaret, impatiently.

"Oh, ay! I ken ye meanin' richt enough. I ken it fine; but I hae doots o' yer abeelity."

"Very well, then I will buy it, only let me have it immediately."

"It's no' th' horses, ye ken. What would I tell yer mither, gin ye're kilt?"

"Bosh!" said Margaret, scornfully. "I can drive anything you can harness."

"Oh, ay! Nae doot, nae doot. But it willna be ane o' Sandy's, I telt ye that."

Here a voice was heard from out front, roaring for Slick and demanding a cayuse, in a hurry.

"Losh! yon's anither. They must theenk I keepit a leevery," and Sandy hastened out to the porch to see who was desirous of further depleting his stock. When he saw the condition of the Goat his decision was quick and to the point: "Ma certes! Ye'll no run th' legs of ony o' my cattle, Cock Murray, gin ye crack yer throat crawin'. Tut, tut! Look at yon!" He shook his head sorrowfully as he gazed at the dejected appearance of the Goat.

"Won't, hey!" shouted Cock, slapping back the saddle, "then I'll borrer Dutch Fred's, an' Buck Peters'll burn yore damned ol' shack 'bout yore ears when he knows it." A man, watching interestedly from the barroom, left by the hall exit, running.

"Buck Peters! Weel, in that case—Slick, ye can lend him yer ain."

"I was just a-goin' to," declared Slick, hurrying off; "which yore damn very generous when it don't cost you nothin'."

Cock loosened the cinch. "Generous as—Miss McAllister!" he exclaimed, aghast.

"Why, of all the people! How delightful! What on earth are *you* doing out here?" Margaret ran down to him, extending both hands in warm greeting.

Cock took them as if in a dream. "Miss McAllister—Chicago—Oh, what a fool I've been!"

The man who had left the barroom tore around the corner of the hotel on a wicked-looking pinto which lashed out viciously at the Goat when brought to a stop, a compliment the Goat promptly returned, though with less vigor. "Here y'are, Cock. He'll think he's headin' for th' Cyclone an' he'll burn th' earth." The Cyclone puncher pushed the straps into Murray's hand and led away the Goat to a well-earned rest.

"I have to go, Miss McAllister. See you at the ranch. I'm punching for the Double Y. They call me Cock Murray. It—it's a name I took."

"I'll remember. Cock Murray: it fits you like a glove," and Murray mounted to her ripple of laughter. "We shall be out there tomorrow. Aunt is with me," she called to him, while the pinto worked off a little of its superfluous deviltry, before getting down to its work. She watched him admiringly, Cock sitting firm and waiting, until presently the pony straightened out and proceeded to prove his owner's boast. "Tip-top, Ralph," praised Margaret; "but you always could ride." She turned and faced the dour Sandy. "See here! Do you *ever* intend to get out that rig?"

"Weel—gin ye're a relative o' Buck Peters, I jalouse ye'll gang yer ain gait, onyway," and he went grumbling through the hall to do her bidding.

A roaring volley of curses, instantly checked and rolling forth a second time with all the sulphur retained to add rancor to the percolator, drew Margaret curiously to overlook the cause. Seeing, she thought she understood Sandy's reluctance to let his team to her: a pair of perfectly matched bays, snipped with white in a manner that gave to their antics an air of rollicking mischief, they were lacking the angularity of outline Margaret already had come to expect in Western ponies, and their wild plunging seemed more the result of overflowing vitality than inherent vice. Drawn by the uproar, Slick appeared beside her.

"No team for a lady to drive," he declared, shaking his head.

"Ridiculous!" asserted Margaret. "Go help them." A devitalized imprecation from Sandy hastened his

steps. Margaret was in doubt which amused her
most: the trickiness of the ponies or Sandy's heroic
endeavor to swear without swearing. She understood him far better than either of the others, who
worked silently and with well directed efforts.

With Slick's invaluable assistance their object was
soon accomplished, the team being hitched to a
new buckboard that was the pride of Sandy's heart.
" 'T is a puir thing," he protested, eying it sourly. "I
hae naething better."

"Why, it is perfect," declared Margaret, "but I
shall want a whip."

"Ye'll want nae whup," denied Sandy, shaking his
head ominously.

The Cyclone puncher at the head of the nigh
horse called to her: "Take 'em out o' th' corral,
miss? They'll go like antelopes when they start."

Margaret laughed in excitement. "No, no! please
don't," she entreated, drawing on her gloves. "I
could drive that pair through the eye of a needle."

Sandy glanced from her to the team and back
again.

"Havers! I'll gie ye ma ain whup," he promised. He
was back in half a minute with a lash whip whose
holly stock never grew in America.

"What a beauty!" exclaimed Margaret. She ran
down the steps, gathered up the lines, and sprang
into the buckboard, bracing herself for the inevitable jerk. "Ready," she warned. "Let go."

It was lucky for Mrs. Blake that she had loosened
her corset strings and was confined to her room;
had she seen the start—and she knew Margaret's
skill as well as any one—she certainly would have
burst them in her fright. With the three men it was
otherwise; they vented their admiration in a ringing
cheer. The ponies, gathering speed in the short
stretch to the ford, were coaxed over so near the
I-Call that Dirty Snow tumbled precipitately from his

box and fled around the corner of the saloon; missing the box by a foot, the wheels began a wide arc toward the water through which the rig whirled in an avalanche of spray, to shave the front of the Why-Not as closely as it had the I-Call. To the delighted astonishment of Twin River—by this time the entire inhabitants, excepting only Mrs. Blake, were more or less interested in the proceedings—the team was no sooner going in the straight than Margaret cracked the lash to right and left and the startled ponies bellied to the ground in their efforts to escape an unknown danger. Sandy guffawed in pride of ownership; Slick gazed with his soul in his eyes; the puncher danced up and down in his joy, thumping first one and then the other.

"Did you see it?" he demanded, "Did you see it?" The others admitted eyesight equal to the occasion. "Say," asseverated the puncher, "if I owned all Montany, from here to th' line, I gives it to get that gal. That's th' kind of a hair-pin I am. You hear me!"

Margaret's sudden exclamation hastened the speed of the ponies but she drew them firmly in and approached the group on the trail at an easy lope. Whitby ran up from the river bank as she pulled the team to a stand.

"Who is it, Miss LaFrance? How did it happen?" asked Margaret, guessing the answer to her own questions.

"It is M'sieu Peters, ma'am'selle. He is wounded," replied Rose.

"Just in time, Miss McAllister," said Whitby, coming up at that moment. "We'll commandeer that wagon as an ambulance."

"Miss McAllister!" exclaimed Buck, wonderingly. Then, energetically: "Whit, you get after that polecat. I can get to th' ranch, now. Get a-goin'."

"Buck, I'm like Jake: 'sot in my ways.' There is no

necessity to follow that pole-cat, as you so aptly call him. And you are not going to the ranch, you know. Miss LaFrance has kindly volunteered expert service in nursing and I intend that you shall get it. Miss McAllister, Miss LaFrance, whose services you already know; and Mr. Peters, your father's partner."

"You must not think of going on to the ranch, Mr. Peters," persuaded Margaret. "I only hope it is not too far to Miss LaFrance's home. If we could lift you—I'm afraid these horses won't stand."

"Lift! I reckon I got one good laig, Miss McAllister—" he fell back with a grunt.

"Dash it all, Buck! Do you want to break open that wound? 'Pon my word, I don't envy you your patient, Miss LaFrance. You lie still, you restless beggar. I've packed more than one man with a game leg and gone it alone. Do you think you can manage those dancing jackasses?" He looked doubtingly from them to Margaret.

Margaret dimpled. "Ask Sandy," she advised, demurely.

"Ou, ay!" quoth Whitby and Margaret broke into bubbling laughter that reflected from Rose's face in the faint shadow of a smile.

"Too bad of me to be laughing this way, Mr. Peters," apologized Margaret, correctly interpreting the expression of Rose, whose glance had turned to Buck; "but I have so much cause to be merry when I least expected it that I forgot for the moment you are wounded."

She resolutely avoided looking at Whitby who, thus unobserved, displayed a grin more fittingly adapted to the countenance of the famous Cat of Cheshire. Rose glanced swiftly from Whitby to Margaret and the two women were already aware of that which the men would never guess in each other.

"Shucks! I been shot up worse'n this, Miss

McAllister," assured Buck; "if that pig-headed Britisher would on'y take orders like he oughta. He's obstinater nor a cow with a suckin' calf."

"Right-o!" assented Whitby, who had finished his preparations for the lift. "Now, Miss LaFrance."

He had managed to pass the blanket under Buck's middle, looping it over his own neck; while this arrangement eased but little weight from Rose, it had the advantage of keeping Buck comparatively straight. Whitby, backing up into the buckboard, his hands tightly grasping Buck beneath the arms, was ably assisted by Rose, who moved and steadied her load without apparent effort. Margaret was genuinely surprised. "How strong you are!" she exclaimed, admiringly.

"Gentle as rain," commended Buck. "If you got that flask handy, Whit, I'd like to feel it."

CHAPTER XXIII

Hopalong's Move

HOPALONG, NURSING Allday with due regard to the miles yet to be traveled, was disagreeably surprised to recognize Cock Murray in the horseman approaching. The explanation offered did not improve his temper. He turned on Murray a hard stare that was less a probe than an exponent of destruction to a liar. There was that about Hopalong which spelled danger; no strong man is without it; and a few men, honest, or not, fail of the impression when in the presence of it. Cock Murray was no coward. He was distinctly not afraid to meet death at a moment's notice or with no notice at all, if it came that way; yet he was grateful to be able to face that stare with an honest purpose in his heart.

"Murray, down Texas way hell-raisin' on a range means sudden death. It's a-goin' to stop on th' Doubly Y. Which side are you on?"

"If it depends on my say-so, th' Double Y is as peaceful as a' Eastern dairy from this out."

"Let 'er go at that. How's that cayuse?"

"Good, an' fresh as paint. I on'y breathed him, comin' from Twin."

"Swap. This bay has come along right smart for twenty miles. I ain't goin' to lose you much, either. Th' boys is after us but they won't catch you."

Hopalong was well past the Sweet-Echo before the pinto was recognized. Slick let out a yell of surprise. The Cyclone puncher sauntered to the window, where Slick was pointing, glanced up the trail and laughed. "That's a friend o' Buck's," he explained, "an' he's certainly aimin' to get there, wherever it is, as quick as he can."

"Ain't that yore pinto?" queried Slick.

"Less'n I'm blind," agreed the cow-punch.

"Seems to me there's a lot o' swappin' goin' on som'ers along th' Big Moose," hazarded Slick. "Which they can't *all* be backin' winners," he added, thoughtfully.

They were still seeking light in useless discussion when the long-striding Allday went past. Slick shouted to Murray for news but Cock waved his hand without speaking. Twin River was beginning to show a languid interest. Day-and-night *habitués* of the I-Call lounged out into the open and gazed after Cock inquiringly, irritated Pop Snow into a frantic change of base by their apparently earnest belief in his knowledge of these events and their demands for information, and lounged back again; Dutch Fred soothed the peevish old man by talking "like he had some sense"; having sense proved an asset once more as Dirty, no one being near, suddenly discovered a thirst. Ike, wise old wolf, though unable to solve the riddle, smelled a killing. "Stay around," he advised several of his own trustworthy satellites. Little Nell alone, who looked on and read as the others ran, came near to supplying the missing print: "The French Rose has shook Dave," she decided.

"Dave has pulled his freight and the Double Y is on the prod after him. Smiler ought to show for place but the minute he looks like a winner the Texan'll pump him full of lead. The Double Y will win out. Maybe Ned—" Little Nell's wild heart had regretted bluff, kindly Ned, these many days.

The passing of the Double Y punchers, strung out half a mile, confirmed Nell's guess. The Cyclone puncher, hurriedly throwing the leather on the Goat, loped along beside Slow Jack, the last in the string, obtaining from him such meager information as only whetted his curiosity. He returned to the Sweet-Echo and Slick, disdaining to reply to the I-Call loungers. Ike was too wise to risk a rebuff; he already knew enough from what he had seen. "Pickin's, boys," was his laconic comment; and soon a company of five Autolycus-minded gentlemen took the Big Moose trail, openly. The break-up of this chance foray was largely due to the simple matter of direction.

Hopalong, knowing nothing of the wagging tongues at Twin River, drove the pinto for every ounce there was in him. A vague uneasiness, risen with the delivery of Buck's message by Cock Murray, rode with Hopalong; he could not shake it off. Ten minutes beyond Two Fork he saw the buckboard and the curse in his throat had its origin in a conviction as accurate as Whitby's had been. He turned and rode beside them. "Well, they got you, Buck," was his quiet comment.

"Shore did," admitted Buck. "Ambushed at four hundred—first shot—bad medicine. I lit a-runnin' an' caves in just as th' next ball drops th' bronc. I lays most mighty still. He thinks I kicked th' bucket but he's afraid to find out. I was hopin' he'd come to see. He gets away quiet an' I lay an' bleed a-waitin' for him. Rose an' Whit here wakes me out of a sweet dream." He smiled up at Rose whose anxiety was evident.

"Too much talk," she warned him.

"Dave?" asked Hopalong, looking at Whitby, who nodded.

"How far?"

"Two miles; possibly less," answered Whitby.

"I'll get him," said Hopalong, with quiet certitude. "So long, Buck."

"So long, Hoppy. Go with him, Whit. Can't afford another ambush."

"Very well, Buck. You will find a medicine-chest in my kit, Miss McAllister."

Whitby turned and rode hard after Hopalong who, nevertheless, arrived at the dead pony considerably in advance, and after a searching look around, rode straight to the ambush. The signs of its recent occupancy were plain to be seen. Hopalong got down and squatted under cover as Dave must have done, from which position his shrewd mind deduced the cause of the poor shot: a swinging limb, which had deflected the bullet at the critical moment. The signs showed Dave had led his horse from the spot, finally mounting and riding off in a direction well to the east of Wayback. Minute after minute Hopalong tracked at a slow canter; suddenly his pony sprang forward with a rush: even to the Englishman's inexperienced eyes there was evidence of Dave having gone faster; very much faster, Whitby thought, as he rode his best to hold the pace, wondering meanwhile, how it was possible to track at such speed. It wasn't possible: Dave had set a straight line for Wayback and gone off like a jackrabbit. Hopalong was simply backing his guess.

Exhaustive inquiries in Wayback seemed to show that Hoppy had guessed wrong. No one had seen Dave. No one had seen Schatz, either; the bank president had gone to Helena and his single clerk, single in a double sense, was an unknown number of miles distant on a journey in courtship. The station agent declared Dave had neither purchased a ticket nor taken any train from the Wayback station. Whitby became downcast but Hopalong, with each fruitless inquiry, gathered cheerfulness almost to loquacity. It was his way. "Cheer up, Whit," he encouraged: "I'd 'a' been punchin' cows an' dodgin' Injuns in th' Happy Hunting Grounds before I could rope a yearlin' if I'd allus give up when I was beat."

Whitby looked at him gloomily. "I'm fair stumped," he admitted. "D' you think, now, it would be wisdom to go back and follow his spoor?"

"Spoor is good. He came to Wayback, Whit, sure as yo're a bloomin' Britisher. Keep a-lookin' at me, now: There's a bum over by th' barber's has been watchin' us earnest ever since we hit town; he's stuck to us like a shadow; see if you know him. Easy, now. Don't scare him off."

Whitby won his way into Hopalong's heart by the simplicity of his maneuver. Taking from his lips the cigar he was smoking, he waved it in the general direction of the station. "You said a bum near the barber-shop," he repeated. His pony suddenly leaped into the air and manifested an inexplicable and exuberant interest in life. When quieted, Whitby was facing the barber's and carefully examining the bum. Hopalong chuckled through serious lips. Whitby had allowed the hot end of his cigar to come in contact with the pony's hide. "No, can't say I do; but he evidently knows me. Dashed if he doesn't want me to follow him," and Whitby looked his astonishment.

Hopalong's eyes sparkled. "Get a-goin', Whit. Here's where ye call th' turn. What'd I tell you?" He wheeled and rode back to the station. Whitby followed the shambling figure down the street and around the corner of a saloon, where he discovered him sunning himself on a heap of rubbish, in the rear.

"Well, my man; what is it?" asked Whitby.

The crisp, incisive tones brought him up standing; he saluted and came forward eagerly. "Youse lookin' f'r Dave?" he responded.

"What of it?"

"I seen him jump d' train down by d' pens. She wuz goin' hell-bent-f'r-election, too. W'en Dave jumps, I drops. Dave an' me don't pal."

"Why not?"

"Didn't he git me run out o' Twin? Youse was dere. Don'tcher 'member Pickles an' Dutch Onion—Pickles' old man—an' dat Come Seven guy w'at stopped d' row? Don'tcher?"

"Yes; I do. Are you the man who shied the bottle?"

"Ke-rect. I'd done f'r him, too, but dey put d' kibosh on me."

"And are you sure it was Dave? Did the train stop?"

"Stop nothin'! 'T was a string o' empties. Dave jumped it, all right. An' I'd hoof it all d' way to Sante Fe to see him swing."

"Deuced good sentiment, by Jove. Here, you need—well a number of things, don't you know."

Boomerang gazed after the departing Englishman and blinked rapidly at the bill in his hand. Did he or did he not see a zero following that two? With a fervent prayer for sanity he carefully tucked it out of sight.

Whitby returned to Hopalong as much elated as previously he had been cast down. "We have the bally blackguard," was his glad assurance.

"Where?" asked Hopalong; "in yore pocket, or yore hat, or only in yore mind." Whitby explained and Hopalong promptly appealed to the station agent.

It was a weary wait. Whitby, a patient man himself, found occasion to admire the motionless relaxation of Hopalong, who appeared to be storing energy until such time as he would require it. To Whitby, who was well acquainted with the jungle of India, it was the inertia of the tiger, waiting for the dusk.

The station door opened again but this time with a snappier purpose that seemed promising. Whitby turned his head. The railroader nodded as one well satisfied with himself. "Got your man," he announced, with a grin of congratulation. "He dropped off at X—. Don't seem a whole lot scared. Took a room at th' hotel. Goin' to turn him over to the sheriff?"

"No," answered Hopalong, "an' I don't want nothin' to get out here, *sabe*? If it does, yo're th' huckleberry. When's th' next train East?"

"It's past due, but it'll be along in twenty minutes."

"I'll take a ticket," and Hopalong rose to his feet and followed him into the station. He returned shortly, to apologize for leaving Whitby behind. "I know you'd like to go, Whit, but you ought to find out about that money. Better stay here an' see them bank people in th' mornin'."

Whitby acknowledged the wisdom of this and agreed to call on Buck at Jean's on his way back to the ranch. "You tell Buck Dave is at X—," said Hoppy. "An' that's where he stays," he added, grimly. "Here she comes."

Long before this, the usual crowd of idlers had gathered; and now the rest of Wayback began to ooze into the road and toward the station. As the train drew in it attracted even a half-shaved man from the barber's, hastily wiping the soap from his face as he ran; after him came the barber, closing the razor and sticking it in his pocket. The first man off the cars was a fox-faced little hunchback, whose deformity in no way detracted from his agile strength; after him, with studied carelessness, came Tex. Hopalong grunted, turned his head as the clatter of hoofs sounded through the turmoil, and signaled Chesty Sutton, first man of the rapidly arriving Double Y punchers.

"Don't you stray none, screech-owl, or I'll drop you," he warned the captive, who shot one impish glance at the speaker and froze in his tracks. "Chesty, tell Ned to take this coyote to th' ranch, an' don't let him get away, not if you has to shoot him."

"Hold hard, stranger. He looks mighty like Big Saxe to me, an' if he is, I wants him. I got a warrant for him in my clo'es." The deputy sheriff started forward.

"Wait!" commanded Hopalong. The deputy waited. "Tex, hold that train. You an' me are goin' th' same way. Mr. Sheriff, I got a warrant ahead o' yourn an' *I* wants him. You'll find him at th' Double Y ranch when I gets through with him."

Slow Jack, the last of the Double Y punchers, loped up to the station, swung from his saddle and joined the interested group surrounding the disputants.

"If that's Big Saxe I wants him now an' I'm goin' to take him."

"Don't you, son." Kind as Hopalong's tone sounded, the deputy halted again. "Bow-Wow, hit th' trail an' have eyes in th' back of yore head. Straddle, boys." The crowd scattered as the mounted punchers moved their ponies about, to open a clear space. Hopalong met the eye of the hunchback, whose clear, shrewd glance recognized the master of the moment. "Screechy! that pinto's a-waitin' for you an' if any son-of-a-gun gets there first, *you* won't need no bracelets. Git!"

Struggling between indecision and duty, the deputy saw the group of punchers, the pinto in advance, turn into the Twin River trail. "Looky here!" he began fiercely to Hopalong, " 'pears to me—"

"Bah! Tell it to Schatz"; and Hopalong sprang up the steps, followed by Tex, to the outspoken regret of Wayback's citizens there assembled.

CHAPTER XXIV

The Rebellion of Cock Murray

THE BUCKBOARD, wheeling off the trail, was lost to view almost as soon as Murray saw it. Rose and Margaret he had recognized at a glance but whose figure had been the second in the wagon? Suddenly misgiving assailed him. Forgetting Hopalong and his orders, he turned and followed them. Every step of his horse increased his anxiety and urged him forward; and twin-born with it smoldered a growing anger that held him back: he hesitated to have his fears confirmed in the presence of two women, one of whom—well, that was done with but it had left a scar that was beginning to throb again with the old pain. He rode slowly but gaining steadily on the trio ahead. When they reached the cabin, Rose called; receiving no answer she was about to go for help when she saw Murray and pointed to him. Margaret motioned and he hurried to obey the summons.

He recognized Buck while still some distance away and the smolder burst into a blaze. This was the game then? Schatz had emphatically stated it was to be one of freeze-out; when they found it wouldn't work then the good old way was good enough. The jauntiness of carriage which had earned him his nickname (he was responsible for the surname only) was gone when he joined the others; the insolence of his speech was gone also, and some of his good looks. The successful concealment of his feelings had lost him much but it had gained him more: Margaret thrilled to a sense of power she had not expected in him. Rose's gesture of finger to lips was superfluous: Murray never felt less like talking.

"How'd you get here, Cock?" asked Buck, dully. The strain of the drive was telling even upon his iron frame.

"Orders," answered Cock, briefly; and Buck was not sufficiently interested to inquire further.

The team was effectually secured and they got Buck from the wagon and into the cabin with but little difficulty; Murray, though he did not look it, was a far stronger man than Whitby; and Buck was laid gently in the bunk, his head brushing the spot where Pickles had muffled his breathing a few hours before.

The removal of the bandage brought a gasp to the lips of Margaret, who pressed her hand to her heart and stared with horrified eyes. She touched Rose on the shoulder: "Can you—can you dress the wound without me?" she asked, breathlessly.

"But certainly," answered Rose, mildly surprised.

"Then I will go—back—and send on the medicine chest. I am sure you will need it."

"That is good," commended Rose, looking curiously after Margaret, who swayed as she went out of the room.

Murray hurried after her. "It is nothing, Miss

McAllister, except for the pain and possible fever. Buck will tell you so himself. Drink this."

The cold water made her feel better. "I never realized before—what fighting means," she murmured. "It may be nothing but it looks—terrible."

"Nothing dangerous, I assure you, and perfect health will bring him through. Shall you go on out to the ranch?"

"Why, I must send the medicines."

"Then wait for me to join you at Twin River. I shall not be long."

He controlled the restive team until she was ready and watched her start. When he returned to Rose she had bared and was bathing the wound from which but little blood came, now. When a fresh bandage had been put in place she turned to him with expressive gesture: "Remove all," she commanded, indicating Buck's clothing. She left the room and Murray heard her moving about in the attic while he busied himself in obedience to her orders.

"Who was it, Buck?" he asked, somberly.

"Didn't see him. Dave, I reckon."

"Was it Dave you was after?"

"That's him. Didn't you know?"

"No." Murray slit viciously through the waistband of the trousers and raised Buck with one powerful arm while he eased away the severed cloth. He said nothing more until Rose came with a garment such as Buck had not worn for more years than he liked to remember. When it was donned and Buck made comfortable, Murray spoke with decision. In his earnestness he unconsciously reverted from the slip-shod manner of speech to which he had habituated himself.

"I have a confession to make," he began; "and I want to make it now. I don't think it will harm you to hear it."

"Let 'er go," said Buck, with awakened interest.

"I am a hypocrite. I am indirectly responsible for the loss of your cattle. I have been taking your money and working for another man. I am not at all proud of it. In fact, as things have turned out, I'm damned sick of it. All that I can say for myself is that I honestly thought the other man was in the right; now I know better. If it will be any satisfaction to you I would give my life this minute rather than have it known by—by certain people who are bound to know of it if you talk. So it has not been easy to tell you. I have only one thing more to add: I can't be treacherous to the other man although he has been treacherous to me; but if you are not afraid to trust me, I guarantee to make the Double Y sound on the inside, at least—that is, if they don't kill me."

"By th' Lord!" breathed Buck. "I'm right glad I got that pill. Trust you? You bet!" He reached out his hand to Murray and the grip he felt confirmed his belief that the canker was surely healed on the Double Y.

Softly as Buck spoke, the sound of his voice brought Rose to the door. She looked sternly at Murray: "You must go," she declared; "So much talk bring fever."

"All right, ma'am," assented Murray, carefully keeping from her his tell-tale face, "sure you won't need help?"

"No, my father come soon." She advanced to the bunk and improved comfort and appearance with a few deft touches.

"Good-day, then, ma'am. So long, Buck. I'm ridin' to th' ranch with Miss McAllister."

"So long, Cock. Get at it, son. Th' Double Y needs you, you bet," and the smile on the stern face was so winning that Murray left hastily, with long strides.

CHAPTER XXV

Mary Receives Company

MARY'S HEART skipped a beat and then pulsed ninety to the minute as her first suspicion became a certainty: a wagon was coming through the dark to the ranch. With a prayer for her husband on her lips she went slowly to the door. She recognized Murray's voice and Jake's in conversation and stood with her hand on the door until Jake's rough command was followed by the sound of the wagon going to the stable. No one wounded! Her relief was so great that she walked unsteadily in crossing back to her chair. Mary was nervous and easily upset, these days.

Surprise acted as a tonic when the two ladies entered, followed by Murray. A glance at Margaret's face stirred memories in Mary. She stammered: "Why—why—I know—who—"

Murray supplied the name: "It is Miss McAllister, Mrs. Cassidy."

"Why, of co'se," said Mary; "I'd know Miss McAllister anywhere; she favors Frenchy like she was his own daughter."

"Did you know Uncle John?" asked Margaret, breathlessly.

"Yes, indeedy. I took to him first sight," and Mary smiled at the girl's eagerness.

"Aunt Jessie! Isn't that just glorious? Mrs. Cassidy, this is my aunt, Mrs. Blake—and I want you to tell me everything you can remember about Uncle John."

"Now you have done it," declared Mrs. Blake. "You will get no peace from Margaret while she thinks there is a wag of your tongue left about her Uncle John."

"Margaret—that's a right sweet name. But I'm afraid Billy would insist—" she flushed a dull red as Mrs. Blake sharply addressed Murray: "Ralph, see that some one gets those trunks in, will you? That is, if they did not drop off into the bosom of this blessed wilderness, somewhere *en route*."

"They didn't. But it's all Montana to an incubator Jake took them to the stable," and Murray promptly vanished.

"Certainly he would insist," agreed Mrs. Blake, resuming the thread of Mary's unconscious soliloquy. "And quite right, too. It would have to be—what did you say your name is, my dear?"

"Mary"—the shy smile made her seem very unlike the self-reliant H2 girl.

Mrs. Blake took her in her arms and mothered her. "Mary is every bit as sweet as Margaret," she declared. "And now you must come over here and sit down. That is six for me and a half dozen for myself. *How* I shall rejoice to land in a seat that neither shakes nor bumps!"

"I shore begs you-all's pardon; but I ain't got over my surprise yet."

"Shall we put you to very much trouble, Mrs. Cassidy?" asked Margaret. "Perhaps if you get that lazy Murray to help—"

"Why, Murray ain't lazy. There ain't none of the boys lazy, 'cept maybe Jake. An' it's shore a pleasure to have you here."

"May heaven forgive my vegatative emotion in the cessation of motion," and Mrs. Blake carefully refrained from moving her foot forward one enticing inch; it was good enough as it was.

"You ain't use' to traveling, Mrs. Blake," suggested Mary.

"On the contrary, my dear," that lady assured her. "Mr. Blake hauled me over the entire country from the Mississippi to the Atlantic; but he never subjected me to the churning discomfort of a devil-drawn buckboard driven by a heartless madcap in petticoats." Mrs. Blake shifted the faintest imaginable distance to the left and back again immediately: the first position was the more comfortable, as she might have known.

The two younger women exchanged a smile, Margaret's a merry one, Mary's more sober as she thought how easily the buckboard might have carried a load indifferent for all time, to jolts. "Did you see anything o' th' boys?" she asked.

"I saw them all, I believe," answered Margaret. "They went through Twin River just before we started."

"Cock Murray came back with you. Did you see my husband? He started out to find Mr. Peters."

"Mr. Cassidy and Mr. Booth went after that Dave brute."

"Where was Buck?"

"He was wounded, Mrs. Cassidy. Not badly, they say. Dave shot him from ambush. We found him lying in the road."

"Oh! I ought to go to him," and Mary started from her seat.

"Certainly not," declared Mrs. Blake. "It is quite evident that you do not appreciate the comforts of inertia. Besides, from what Margaret tells me, he is well taken care of."

"Oh! and I forgot the medicine chest," exclaimed Margaret. "Yes, he has an attentive nurse, Mrs. Cassidy. We took him to the LaFrance place. And I must get that medicine chest from Whitby's kit and send it over. Where are Whitby's things, Mrs. Cassidy?"

"They're in th' bunkhouse. Murray will get them for you. So Buck is there? Did you see the French Rose, Miss McAllister?"

"Yes, haven't you? She is lovely; so serious and calm and strong. In some way she makes you feel that she is sure to do the right thing at the right time. Oh, I like her, immensely."

"Liking goes by contrasts," sleepily reminded Mrs. Blake. Mary smiled no less at Margaret's grimace than at Mrs. Blake's pointed sarcasm.

"She hasn't been to the ranch since we-all came," said Mary. "Buck says she rid over quite often afore that. I'm glad Rose is 'tendin' him; from what I hear of her he couldn't be in better hands."

"Mr. Peters seemed glad, too," said Margaret, suggestively; "and Miss LaFrance did not seem at all sorry."

Before Mary could respond to Margaret's unspoken question, the door opened with a bang and Pickles rushed in. "Been a-helpin' them sheep with th' trunks," he informed them. "Where's Hopalong? Did he find Buck? That cacklin' Murray has forgot how to crow; he on'y grunts."

"Hopalong has gone after Dave. He shot Buck," answered Mary.

"Not dead!" Pickles was aghast.

"No, only wounded."

"I just *got* to kill that Dave. Rose has got to lemme off on that promise. I bet she will now he's gone an' shot up Buck."

Mrs. Blake stirred in her chair and opened one eye. "Out of the mouths of babes and sucklings—"

"Sucker yoreself!" retorted Pickles. "Reckon you think I don't know nothin'. You wait." He slammed the door behind him and stamped off, greatly incensed. His advice to Jake, who told him to open the other door while he carried in a trunk, was impossible to follow, involving a journey from which no one, not even Jake, would ever be likely to return.

When Margaret, insisting that Mary direct operations from her chair, was satisfied with domestic arrangements, she asked Murray's advice about sending the medicine chest to Rose. Obeying Whitby's wishes seemed the most important thing in life at present. Cock demurred to her plan of sending him before morning; and he was opposed to leaving the ranch at all before Buck himself took charge again. Margaret was vexed at his stupidity. They had gone together to the bunkhouse and argued the matter with the object of dispute on the floor between them. Glancing at them from his own especial bunk was Pickles, trying in vain to make sense from a jumble of sounds unlike any he had ever heard. Pickles' vocabulary was very limited. His snort of disgust as he gave it up and turned his back on the disputants, gave Cock an idea. "Pickles," he said, "Buck's sick and he needs this box. Buck told me to stay at the ranch. Will you take it if I saddle Swallow?"

"Shore will," and Pickles shoved one entirely nude leg from the bunk; before he could follow it with the other, he was much surprised and more embarrassed to find himself swooped upon, seized and swiftly kissed by Margaret, whose brown-clad form fled through the door like the flirt of a wood-thrush, vanishing into the dim recesses of the forest.

Ned Monroe and the boys, Big Saxe with them, came straggling up to the bunkhouse in the early hours of the morning, Ned having acquired a change of mounts at Twin River. They secured their prisoner by the simple expedient of tying him in a lump—and a cowpunch makes knots that are exceedingly hard to struggle out of. Big Saxe didn't try.

Cock Murray was first out and he awoke Ned. In the open, safe from being overheard, they held conference, Monroe nodding his head understandingly as Cock made his points. After breakfast, Monroe delivered a speech, short and to the point, and when they separated to their duties, Cock and Slow Jack rode away together. Big Saxe, very effectually hobbled at the ankles, was put in charge of Chesty Sutton who tersely informed him that the first false move he made he would find himself humpbacked all the way to his feet.

Cock bent his powers of persuasion to the converting of Slow Jack. It proved an easy task. Secretly admiring Cock and his ways, Slow Jack also perceived the trend of events to be putting Schatz out of the running. The unbending will of Hopalong was over them all and Slow Jack was not averse to throwing his services to the winning side.

It was the middle of the afternoon when Whitby appeared. The women listened to his news with varying degrees of interest. Buck was doing well and had declared it would not be long before he was at the ranch; in the meantime, as he was obliged to be quiet, he seemed well contented where he was. Pickles had arrived safe and had constituted himself body-guard and messenger-at-need for Rose. As for Hopalong he could tell them no more than they had already learned from Monroe. Mary was not worried. She had supreme confidence in Hopalong's ability to take care of himself and would have smiled if any one had suggested danger.

The end of Whitby's budget was punctuated with a huge sigh from Jake, whose ear had never been far from the kitchen door. He now entered diffidently and addressed himself to the Englishman: "I wrastled some chuck for you, Whit; reckoned you might want some." His lumbering exit was closely followed by Whitby's, whose strangled appetite slipped the noose at Jake's invitation.

In the lively conversation of the three women, Margaret's voice groped about in Whitby's consciousness like a hand searching in the dark for a hidden spring; her sudden ringing laugh awoke him to his purpose and hastily finishing his meal he made his way to the barn. After an hour's delay, spent in selecting a pony for Margaret and taking the edge off the temper of the quietest—a favor that Margaret would have repudiated with scorn—he appeared at the house again with the offer to show her over the range if she cared to go.

It was the very thing Margaret most wanted to do and they set out with but little time lost. When she became accustomed to the saddle she suggested a race but Whitby had no intention of running any such risk. He easily held her interest in another way.

"I say, Miss McAllister, there's one thing I didn't mention just now," he began.

"Not bad news?" questioned Margaret.

"Can't say it's good. That beastly German had the cheek to get away with the money after all. He checked against the blessed lot yesterday forenoon. I was at the bank this morning. It's right enough.

They produced the check. Seems a bit odd, you know, they should be carrying that amount and pass it over in cash. I said as much; but the president—rummy chap, by the way—he explained it; something about big shipments of cattle. However, it's gone."

"Dear me! it seems very careless of somebody. Papa ought to know. What shall you do?"

"Oh, I notified the agency at once; they've taken it in hand. But it won't do any good, you know. That bounder Schatz had it all planned out and if he loses it, why, there you are, you know."

"Yes, so it seems; but, to all intents and purposes, he steals it. Do you intend to let him triumph in such brazen robbery?"

"I rather fancy I shall have very little to say in the matter. That Cassidy chap who is trying to catch Dave, went off without knowing the money was gone. My word! I shouldn't care to be Schatz when Cassidy hears of it. Deuced odd no one saw him in Wayback but the banking people. However, the German will have to go. I wrote the Governor and Mr. McAllister this morning. Between them they can come to an agreement with Peters and we can buy the German out—or perhaps I should say his heirs. It's a good sporting chance that it will be his heirs. Cassidy has a proper amount of suspicion in his character and no one will ambush him, I'll lay."

"Good gracious! But you can't afford to lose all that money, can you?"

"It is a bit of a facer. But what of it? The range can stand it. In twenty years it will bring ten times the money for farm land, or I'm much mistaken. I'm sure the Governor will chance it and Buck will be glad to have me an active partner. He said as much."

"Mr. Booth, didn't you advance the money to Peters in the last partnership agreement?"

"Oh, I say! Did they tell you that? Then you should know it was my advice that brought on his loss. But Buck isn't obliged to put up any money with us; his experience and services are quite equal to the money I shall put up. I fancy Mr. McAllister will agree with me in that. All Buck wants is fair play, don't you know."

Margaret pulled her pony so that she had the advantage of a few feet nearer the house when she spoke. "Whitby," she said, very clearly, "you are a dear."

Both ponies swung their noses toward home in the same moment. The burning blush on Margaret's face streamed from it on the air-currents and settled on Whitby's determined countenance, to leave him and float away to the rose clouds in the western sky. Whitby had the faster mount but Margaret rode a far lighter weight and the chase might have been a long one had she been very anxious to keep away. As it was a short half mile found them on even terms. Whitby's arm went about the girl's waist as the ponies ran stride for stride and she felt herself leaving the saddle. With reckless abandonment to the law of might she yielded and lay in his arms; their pace slowed to a walk, Whitby looking solemnly into the brilliant eyes that mockingly regarded him.

"The good old rule, the simpler plan, that he shall take who hath the power," quoted Margaret.

"And he shall keep who can," capped Whitby. "I can, Margaret, and I will," he declared, a deep note of earnestness in his voice.

Margaret reached up and covered the steady eyes whose searching threatened the unconscious secrets of her heart. But her voice reached him, fainter, fraught with the vibration of sureness: "Whitby, you are a dear."

CHAPTER XXVI

Hunters and Hunted

A STRING of empty cars backed onto the siding at X—, bumping and grinding and squealing as the engine puffed softly; a running rattle and crash told of the shivering line coming to rest and the sibilant sighs of the engine seemed to voice its protest at being side-tracked for the passing of an engine of a higher caste. While it panted and wheezed, its crew taking advantage of the opportunity to look to and oil journals and rods, a man made his way through the brush several hundred yards down the track, swearing mildly as he brushed cinders and dust from his clothes. His only possessions besides his clothes were a revolver swinging in its buttoned holster, and a tightly rolled and securely tied gunny sack, to which he clung in grim determination.

"Hell of a ride," he growled as he headed in a circuitous course for the town a short distance away. "But it breaks th' trail. They'll figger I went north to cross th' line, or up to Helena. Lucky they told me

Denver Gus's relay was relieved. Brains, says Smiler—huh, devil a lot of good his brains done him. He is out of it, an' so is Peters, darn 'em. Brains!"

He entered the town, looking for a place to put up. The Come-Again looked good and he entered it, securing a room on the second floor, which was under the roof. He was explicit to the proprietor: "It's got to be a back room, an' I want it for a couple of days, an' I don't want no noise,—I'm out here for my cussed nerves an' as soon as I can get a good job we'll see about terms. Oh, I expect to pay in advance—will two days' pay keep you from layin' awake nights?"

"Reckon somebody made a mistake," replied the proprietor. "Yore nerves is purty strong."

"Have a drink and forget it," Dave smiled. When he had paid for the drinks he asked a question: "Who's got th' best horse in town? I'm a-goin' to buy it if it's good enough."

The proprietor looked him over and nodded toward a table in the farther corner: "That's him."

Dave sauntered over to the lone drinker: "Just been told you got th' best horse in town. That right?"

The other looked up slowly: "I might," he replied.

"I want to buy him. I don't give a darn about th' price if he's good. Interested? Thought you'd be."

The other also looked the cocky stranger over: "Yes—I'm interested—a little. I ain't hell-bent for to sell that horse. He's th' best ever came to these parts—that's why he's good—he *came* here."

Dave was impatient: "Is he where I can see him?"

"Shore," drawled the horseman, arising languidly. "Come along an' you can see him if yore eyes is good."

The owner of the "best horse in town" studied Dave as they walked along and his mental comment was not flattering to the *protégé* of the late Herr Schatz. "Fake cow-puncher," was his summing up. "He don't know a *hoss* from a hoss—but he thinks he does."

When they came to the corral the owner pointed to a big gray in the corner: "That's him, stranger. He's part cow-horse an' part Kaintuk, an' too good to be out here in this part of the country. *That's* th' hoss Bad Hawkins rid from Juniper Creek to Halfway in ten hours—one hundred an' forty miles, says th' map, an' Hawkins weighed a hundred an' seventy afore they got him. He weighed so much he broke off th' limb of th' best tree they could find. Why, *he's* th' cuss what held up th' Montana Express down at Juniper Creek bridge—reckon you *are* a stranger to these parts."

"He don't look like no miracle to *me*," asserted Dave, closely scrutinizing the horse.

"No? Mebby you ain't up on miracles. If you want a purty hoss why didn't you say so? Dolly's slick as silk an' fat as butter—you can have her if you wants her. Cost you about twenty-five dollars less. But you won't save nothin' on her if you wants a hoss for hard ridin', one that gets there quick, an' gets back quick."

"I ain't said nothin' 'bout savin' no money," retorted Dave. "An' it seems to me yo're purty darn high in yore prices, anyhow."

"Well, I sees you wants a hoss right bad; an' when a man wants a hoss bad he wants a *good* hoss—an' good hosses come high. Dolly's gentle as a kitten," shrewdly explained the owner. "Big Gray, there, he's some hard to ride, onless you can sit a saddle good as th' next."

"How much for Big Gray?" snapped Dave.

"One hundred dollars."

"I ain't buyin' a herd," remonstrated Dave.

"I ain't sellin' a herd," smiled the owner. "I told

you good hosses come high. Mebby Dolly'd suit you better. She's my daughter's hoss."

"Here's th' hundred," replied Dave, nettled. "Got a bridle or halter or piece of rope? An' I want to buy a saddle—one that's been broke in."

"There's a halter on him—good enough? All right; I got a saddle that's in purty fair shape—don't need it, so you can have it for twenty."

When Dave rode from the corral he was headed for the general store and bought a rifle, a rope, and sundry other necessaries, including food. Returning to the hotel he put his horse in the corral, had a drink, and went to his room carrying the saddle, the gunny sack, and his other purchases with him. The gunny sack had not been from under his arm an instant while he had been in town. The erstwhile owner of Big Gray drifted back to his table shortly after Dave's return and settled himself for another drink.

"Did you sell him one?" asked the proprietor, digging down for change.

"Yep," was the reply.

"Fifty, sixty, seventy-five—there's yore change. I wonder who he is an' where he's goin'?" remarked the proprietor, in lieu of something better.

"Dunno; but he ain't no cow-punch, an' likewise he ain't no tenderfoot. Looks like a tin-horn to me. His fingers was purty slick gettin' th' bills off his roll. They was so slick I counted 'em to be sure he wasn't robbin' hisself. But there wasn't no folded bill there. Here, have a drink with me—business is pickin' up."

When the east-bound accommodation pulled into X—— at dusk two men jumped off and started toward the nearest hotel. The proprietor of the Come-Again assigned them a room and spoke of supper, to which they intimated their ability to do justice to "anythin' you got." As they turned away carelessly toward the "washroom" one of them halted: "We're expectin' a friend," and he gave a concise description of the third man.

"Why, he's upstairs now—first door to th' left at th' top of th' flight—got in this afternoon. But he said he didn't want to be bothered none," hastily warned the proprietor.

"That's right—you can let that go for th' three of us," replied Hopalong, smiling.

"Said his nerves was all stampeded," commented the host, dubiously.

Hopalong winked, grinning: "Didn't act none that-a-way, did he?"

"Oh, I *told* him somebody was stringin' him," laughed the proprietor.

"Reckon we'll go up an' hustle him down to his feed," Tex remarked, leading the way, with Hopalong stepping on his heels.

The proprietor studied the three names on his register, and spoke to the horseman, who now was playing solitaire in a negligent way. "Wonder what's up, Dick?"

"Dunno," replied Dick, holding aloft a queen of hearts and studying the layout. "Reckon you better let this deal go by. Keep yore chips out, Joe; don't like th' looks of th' pair of 'em. That redhead looks like a bad customer, if his corn's stepped on. Mebby their nervous friend has did somethin' they don't like."

The knocking upstairs now reverberated through the house and a peevish voice threatened destruction to the door unless it opened speedily.

"That's th' redhead," remarked Dick. "What did I tell you?"

The proprietor hastened from behind the bar and went up the steep, narrow stairs with undignified haste. "Don't bust that door!" he cried. "Don't you bust it!"

"Aw, close yore face!" growled a voice, and Dick nodded his head wisely. "Both of 'em bad customers," he mumbled.

There was a crash and the sound of splintering wood, followed by disgusted exclamations. Dick arose and sauntered up to see the show: the host was nervously clutching a bill large enough to pay for several broken doors. The redhead was looking out of the open window while the other man rapidly searched the room.

"He dropped his belongings first," audibly commented the man at the window. "Then *he* dropped." He turned quickly to the proprietor: "Did he have a horse?"

"Yes; bought one first thing after he registered."

"We want one apiece," crisply demanded Hopalong, "with speed, bottom, an' sand. Got 'em? No? Then where can we get 'em tonight?"

"What'd he do?" blundered the host, rubbing the bill with tender fingers and looking for information instead of giving it.

"He dropped out th' winder," sharply replied Tex. "We never stand for that."

"Never, not under no circumstances," endorsed his friend. "It allus riles us. How 'bout them horses?"

"I reckon I can fix you up," offered Dick. "I sold him th' hoss he's got. He wanted th' best in town, which he didn't get for bein' too blamed flip. But he paid for it, just th' same. I got a roan an' a bay that'll run Big Gray off'n his feed an' his feet. If yo're comin' back this way I'll buy 'em back again at a reduction—I'd like to keep them two. I don't reckon I'll get no chance to buy back th' other."

The horseman fell in behind the descending procession and lined up with it against the bar on

Hopalong's treat. Then they left the proprietor to swear at the cook while they departed for the corral.

Dick chuckled. "Th' gray I sold yore missin' friend carried Bad Hawkins from Juniper Creek to Halfway in fourteen hours—ten miles an hour. Th' roan an' th' bay did it in ten hours even—which puts a period after th' last words of Hawkins. Bad Hawkins weighed less 'n you," he said to Tex, "an' th' gray shore sprains a laig a-doin' it. It don't show—that is, not when he was sold it didn't. That feller was too damned flip—one of them Smart Alecks that stirs my bile somethin' awful."

Tex wearied of his voice: "Yore discernment is very creditable," he replied, with becoming gravity.

The horseman glanced at him out of the corner of his eye: "Yes—I reckon so," he hazarded.

When they reached the corral the two strangers looked in critically. Nearly a score of horses were impounded, among them several bays and roans. Hopalong pointed to one of the roans. "That looks like th' horse," he remarked, quietly, at the instant his friend singled out the bay.

"Them's th' hosses—they'll run th' liver out of Big Gray even if his laig does hold out," smiled their owner, glad that his first customer had not been as wise as either of these two men. The horses were cut out and accepted on the spot.

"How much?" demanded Hopalong, brusquely.

"Eighty apiece."

"That's a lot of money. But we got to have 'em. How 'bout saddles? We can do without 'em if we has to, but we ain't hankerin' very strong to do it."

"I got a couple of good ones," responded the horseman. Then he yielded to a sudden burst of generosity. "Tell you what I'll do—I'll sell you them saddles for forty apiece an' when I gets 'em back, you gets yore money back. An' if you don't kill th' hosses, we'll have a little dicker over them, too. I wouldn't sell 'em only for a good price an' you won't have nothin' to complain about if I buys 'em back again."

"Yo're a fair man," responded Hopalong. "Now we all oughta have a drink to bind th' deal. An' I reckon supper'll go good, too. We'll be right glad to have you join us." The invitation was accepted with becoming alacrity.

After the meal, and a game of cards, during which both punchers had learned much about the surrounding country, they went on a tour of investigation. They had discovered that the only way south likely to be taken by a man not perfectly familiar with the several little-known mountain trails, was through Lone Tree Pass. A walk about the town, before turning in, disclosed to them the kind and amount of Dave's purchases: these showed that he expected to be in the saddle more than a few hours. Returning to the hotel they went at once to their room. Sitting on the edge of the bed Hopalong asked a question: "You've got me on t' lay of th' land in this part of the country, Tex. Why do you figger he'll head south?"

Tex blew out the light and settled himself snugly in his bed before replying. "Because anybody else would figger he'd strike north for th' Canadian line, or up to Helena an' West, where a man can get lost easy. I've sort of palled with Dave, an' I know th' skunk like a A B C book. His trail will show us th' way, but it won't tell us about th' country ahead of us. I allus like to know what I'm goin' up against when I can."

"Shore; good night," muttered Hopalong, and in a moment more soft snores vibrated out through the open window, to be mildly criticized by the cook in the cook shack below.

Down in the barroom the proprietor, having said

good night to his last customer, pushed the column of figures away with a sigh of satisfaction and rested his chin on his hand while he reviewed the events of the day. "Why," he muttered, pugnaciously, coming out of his reveries and pouring himself a liberal drink on the strength of the day's profits; "why, now I know what that coyote wanted his room at the back of the house for—good thing I got th' money ahead of time! Well, he's got a hell of a lot of trouble chasin' him, anyhow, th' beat."

With three days' rations fastened to their saddles Hopalong and Tex whirled away from the Come-Again as the first streak of gray appeared in the eastern sky and after a short distance at full speed to take the devilishness out of their mounts, they slowed to a lope. Heading straight for the Pass, they picked up Dave's trail less than two miles from town and then settled into a steady gait that ate up the miles without punishing their horses. They had not made any mistake in their mounts for they were powerful and tough, spirited enough to possess temper and courage without any undue nervous waste, and the way they covered ground, with apparently no effort, brought a grim smile to Hopalong's face.

"I don't reckon I'll do no swappin' back, Tex," he chuckled. "I've allus wanted a cayuse like this'n, an' I reckon he'll stay bought, even at th' price."

"They look good—but I'll tell you more about 'em by night," Tex replied. He glanced ahead with calm assurance: "I don't figger he's so very far, Hoppy?"

"Why no, Tex; he couldn't ride hard last night, not over strange country—it was darker'n blazes. We didn't leave very long after him when you figger it in miles, an' he ain't reckonin' *shore* on bein' chased. He drops out th' winder an' sneaks that way 'cause he ain't takin' no chances.

"We've got th' best cayuses, we've had more sleep than him, we know this game better, we're tougher, an' we can get more out of a cayuse than he can. I reckon we ought to get sight of him afore sundown, an' I wouldn't be surprised if we saw him shortly after noon. We'll shore get him 'bout noon, if he's had any sleep."

"I'd ruther get him this side of Lone Tree Pass—I ain't hankerin' for no close chase through th' mountains after a cuss like Dave," Tex replied. "What do you say 'bout lettin' out another link?"

Hopalong watched his horse for a minute, glanced critically at his companion's, and tightened the grip of his knees. "That feller said a hundred an' forty in ten hours—how far is that pass? Well, might as well find out what this cayuse can do—come on, let 'em go!"

Pounding along at a gait which sent the wind whistling past their ears they dipped into hollows, shot over rises, and rounded turns side by side, stirrups touching and eyes roving as they searched the trail ahead. The turns they made were not as many as those in the trail they followed, for often they cut straight across from one turn to another. The ability to do this brought a shrewd smile to Hopalong's thin lips.

"Let his cayuse pick its way, Tex—told you he couldn't go fast last night. Bet a dollar we come to where he slept afore long—an' say! luck's with us, shore. Notice how he was bearin'—a little off th' course all th' time—that gray of his must a' come from som'ers up north. He had to correct that when he could see where th' Pass lay—come on, we'll try another cut-off, an' a big one."

"Yo're right—we'll gain a hour, easy," Tex replied as they shot off at a tangent for the distant mountain range on a line for the Pass. The sun was two hours higher when Tex laughed aloud, stretching his hand across his friend's horse and pointing some distance ahead of him. "There's th' track again, Hoppy," he cried, "you was right—see it?"

Hopalong waited until they swept up along the fresh trail before he replied and the reply was characteristic of him. "Pushin' th' gray hard, Tex. Them toe prints are purty deep—an' damned if th' gray ain't havin' trouble with his bad laig! See that off fore hoofmark? See how it ain't as deep as its mate? Th' gray's favorin' that laig, an' only for one reason: it hurts him more when he don't. Move away a little, Tex; don't do no good to be bunched so close where there's so much cover. He ain't a long way off, judgin' from them tracks. We don't know that he ain't doubled back to pick us off as we near him."

Tex tightened his knee-grip and rowelled his spurs lightly along the side of his mount, darting ahead with Hopalong speeding up to catch him. It was a test to see how the horses were holding up and when the animals took up the new speed and held it with plenty of reserve strength, the two men let them go.

As they shot down a rough, sloping trail to a shallow creek, flowing noisily along the bottom of a wild arroyo, Hopalong looked ahead eagerly and called to Tex to slow down to a walk. Tex, surprised, obeyed and took the reins of the bay as Hopalong went ahead to cross the stream on foot. But Tex's surprise was only momentary; he quickly understood the reason for the play and he warmed to his sagacious friend while he admired his skill.

Hopalong waded the stream and looked carefully around on both side of the tracks where they left the water. Motioning Tex to come ahead, he grinned as the other obeyed. "Didn't want to splash no fresh water around here till I saw if th' water Dave splashed was all soaked up. It is; but th' spots is moist. An' another thing: see th' prints o' that hoof

where he takes up an' sets down—where is he
lame?"

"Shoulder," replied Tex with instant decision.

"Shore is. An' he's been a-gettin' lamer every
step. Bet he ain't an hour ahead, Tex."

"Won't take you—an' he'll be above us all th' way
till we cross th' top of th' range, so we better keep
under cover as much as we can," Tex replied.
"We've trailed worse men than Dave, a whole lot
worse, an' far better shots; but he ain't really due to
miss twice in two days. Th' Pass ain't so far ahead
now—there it is, with th' blasted pine stickin' up
like a flagpole. Half an hour more an' we'll be in it."

Ahead of them, toiling up the Pass on a tired and
limping horse rode Dave, not so fresh as he might
have been with the four hours' sleep he had secured in the open at dawn. The night ride over
strange, rough country had been hard and his rage
at the shabby trick played upon him by the horse
dealer had not helped him any. To win up to the
point where success was almost his; and then to
have a half-breed horse coper—one who had absolutely no connection with the game—threaten to defeat him! To fool all the players, to gain, as he
thought, a big handicap and then to be delayed by
a man who sought only to gain a little money and
be well rid of a poor horse! Dave's temper was like
that of a rattler hedged in by thorns and the
rougher part of the mountain trail had been saturated with profanity. There was not much chance of
meeting any one on that trail and by the time he
reached a place where he could get another horse,
the need for one would have gone. Let him see a
horseman and he knew who would ride the horse.
He struck the limping gray savagely as it flinched
over a particularly rough part of the trail and he
was growling and swearing as he rounded a turn in
the Pass and came to a place where, by climbing a

boulder just above him, he could get a good view of
the way he had come. Dismounting, he made the
climb and looked back over the trail. Miles of country were below him, the trail winding across it, hidden at times and then running on in plain view until
some hill concealed it again. The sun was half down
in the western sky and he swore again as he realized how much farther he should have been—how
near the end of his ride.

"A hundred an' forty miles in ten hours!" he
snarled, squirming back to descend to his horse.
"No wonder Bad Hawkins got caught! Served th'
darn fool right; an' it'd serve me right for being
such a ——" the words ceased and the speaker flattened himself to the rock as he peered intently at a
hill far down the trail, waiting to be sure his eyes
had not deceived him.

The slanting sun had made a fairyland of the
rugged scenery, bathing the rocks until they
seemed to glow, finding cunningly hidden quartz
and crystals and turning them into points of flame.
The fresh, clean green coat that Spring had thrown
over the crags as if to hide them, softened the
harsher tones and would have thrilled even Dave,
who was sated with scenery, if it had not been for
his temper and the desperate straits in which he
found himself. He lay like one dead but for the
straining eyes. An eagle, drifting carelessly across
the blue, missed him in its sharp scrutiny, so well
did his clothes blend with the tones of the rock.

"Hell!" he muttered, for far below him something
moved out into the trail again where it emerged
from behind the hill, and two mounted men came
into sight, riding rapidly to take advantage of the
short run of level country.

Dave could not make them out—they were only
two men at that distance, but he wasted no time
nor gave heed to any optimism. He wriggled back-

wards, dropped to the trail, and looked around for
a place to hide his horse. Not seeing one at hand he
mounted again and forced the limping animal forward until he saw a narrow ravine cut into the
mountain side by the freshets of countless years.
Leading the gray into this and around a turn in the
wall, he picketed the animal and then hastened
back, scurrying to and fro in search of a hiding
place that would give him a view of the trail for the
greatest distance. His mind worked as rapidly as his
feet. The coming horsemen might be innocent of all
knowledge of him or of his need. If so, he preferred
to ride behind them. If they were in pursuit—and he
could not believe it to be a mere coincidence that
any but an enemy would be following him so close
through Lone Tree Pass—they had not started from
the town he had just quitted—unless they had
traced him by telegraph! Dave cursed softly and settled himself a little more at ease in his ambush.

Hopalong and Tex, enjoying that friendship that
sets no embarrassment on silence, rode forward
side by side when the trail permitted it, grim, relentless, dogged. They represented that class of men
who can pursue one thing to the exclusion of all
tempting side leads, needing nothing but what they
themselves can supply; who approach all duties
with cool, level-headed precision and gain their goal
without a thought of reward and with small regard
for danger. Danger they had both met in all the
forms it took on the range and trail, dance-hall and
saloon; both had mastered it by the speed and certainty of their hands and guns, and neither found
anything exciting or fearful in this game of follow
and take; on the other hand it was tiresome to have
to follow, and one man, at that. If some bold, daring
stroke of strategy or a reckless dash could have
been hoped for, it would have made the game inter-
esting. So they jogged on toward the opening of the

pass, taciturn and somber, but with the cold patience of Indians.

The trail narrowed again and Tex took the lead. "Closer now," he remarked, more to himself than to his companion, whose reply was a grunt, presumed to be affirmative. When they entered the pass itself it was Hopalong who led, and to see him as he sat slouching in his saddle, apparently half asleep, one would have wondered that a man whose wariness was the basis of so many famed exploits could ride thus carelessly, allowing his horse to pick the way. But in the shadow of his straight-brimmed hat, two hard, keen eyes squinted through the narrow lids, among the wrinkles, and missed nothing that could be seen; under the faded red shirt sleeve was an arm ready for the lightning draw that had never yet been beaten, and the hand-worn butt of the heavy Colt rubbed softly against the belt-strap of its holster.

Hopalong rolled a cigarette and took advantage of the movement to speak: "Goin' back to Texas, Tex?"

"Why," replied Tex, pausing to reflect. "Why, I said as how I would to all yore boys, but I reckon mebby Buck needs me worse'n you do. What think?"

"Stay up here an' run for sheriff," was the crisp reply. "This country's sick with crooks."

"Reckon so."

"Good place for undertakers, while th' boom is on," continued Hopalong, smiling grimly at the truth in his jest. He knew Tex Ewalt.

"Th' boom'll be busted flat afore you go home," Tex responded. "It's fallin' now. Dave was its highwater mark."

They were riding side by side now and Hopalong growled a suggestion: "Go slow, Tex; mebby he's holin' up on us, like he did on Buck. He ain't more'n a million miles ahead of us now."

"Uh-huh; an' if he is he ought to get us easy in this place. Got to take a chance, anyhow. Gimme a match—*Look out!*"

As he spoke he hurled his horse against Hopalong's and his left arm dropped to his side with a bullet through it, while his right hand flashed to his hip, where a pungent cloud of smoke burst out to envelop his horse's head. Off his balance from the unexpected shock, Hopalong's shot went wide, but the next five, directed at Dave's head-long rush as he came crashing down through the underbrush, gave promise of better aim.

"I owed him that, anyhow," muttered Tex, his ears ringing from the fusillade so close to him. "An' I owed you th' play, Hoppy, ever since that day in th' brush—"

"You don't owe me nothin' now, Tex; that's as close as any in ten years," returned Hopalong. "Well, he showed hisself a damned ambushin' snake just as we thought he would. He could a' got us both if his nerves hadn't got th' chills an' fever. We was some careless!"

"We was a pair of blasted kids," Tex remarked. "Now what'll we do with him? We can't take him back, an' buryin' in solid rock ain't been in my schoolin'."

"We can cover him with rocks, I reckon, but we ain't got time—besides, how'd he leave Buck?" demanded Hopalong sharply. "Why, he got you, Tex! Here, you close-mouthed fool, lemme fix that hole."

Tex stood quietly thoughtful until Hopalong had finished his task. "We'll just chuck him off th' trail, Hoppy; then we won't have to answer no question or shoot sense into no thick skulls. How 'bout it?"

"Uh-huh, go ahead," grunted Hopalong and the two walked over, picked up the unresisting bulk and placed it in a fissure in the rock wall.

"By th' Lord!" swore Tex: "Five shots out of five

when you got yore balance—*that's* shootin'! *You* better run for sheriff."

"I hadn't ought to 'a' done it when I knowed th' second got him—but he kept a-comin' an' I was a-thinkin' of Buck. Come on, let's get goin'." He mounted and waited impatiently for Tex, who was still standing beside his horse as if unwilling to leave the scene. "His pot-shootin' is over, so let's start back."

"Uh-huh," muttered Tex, still lost in thought. Hopalong waited, having acquired increased respect for his friend's brain capacity in the last few days.

"Hoppy, why did Dave ambush Buck an' have to run, just when he was goin' to skin Schatz for a pot of money?"

"Give it up," answered Hopalong.

"Well, why didn't Schatz turn up when everything was set for the play?"

"Got to pass again, Tex," was Hopalong's indulgent reply.

"Dave had plenty of chances to kill Buck—better chances than that one—an' no need to run, if he was careful. Th' Twin River trail is traveled some—it was shore risky—no time to waste in Wayback waitin' for Schatz after that, huh?"

"Mebby th' kid didn't get it right," suggested Hopalong.

Tex nodded his head convincingly. "Yes, he did. Told a straight story. Hoppy, Dave knew Schatz wasn't comin'. Hoppy, I got—I got a feelin'—Hoppy, what'll you bet Dave ain't got th' money right now?"

"By God!" exclaimed Hopalong, staring at his friend, his mind racing along the scent like a hound to the kill. "By God!" he repeated, softly, as he dropped from the saddle and became hidden in the crevice. "No money, Tex; only a few—"

"Where's his horse?" demanded Tex, eagerly.

"*Yo're* goin' to run for sheriff," came the retort,

and Hopalong followed the track of Dave's horse and turned into the ravine, out of sight of Tex, who waited impatiently.

Tex was surprised at the result of the quest when a crazy man came buck-jumping into sight, yelling like an Indian and frantically waving a tightly grasped saddle pad of sacking. He would have come out with more dignity if the money had been his, but belonging as it did to his old foreman, the big-hearted man who had been for so long a time on the verge of despair and defeat, allowed himself the luxury of free expression to the bubbling joy within him.

"Come on, Tex!" he cried. "Th' hell with goin' back—we'll take a chance of meetin' th' Dutchman as Dave Owens' personal executors an' ambassadors. If Schatz has got a wad like this, he's th' man I want to see. Come on! We'll bust all Montana records for hold-ups—come on, you wise old devil!"

"Now who's goin' to be sheriff?" grinned Tex, and then allowed himself the relief of working off his joy in a short jig, which informed him that Dave had made a hit; not a bull's eye, but a hit just the same.

"Here, you drunk Apache," Hopalong cried, "let's count up an' see what we got."

Had any one drifted along a minute later he would have been torn between duty and discretion: duty to provide a sane guardian in himself for that part of the Government treasury strayed to the wilds of these western mountains, and discretion in facing the two capable-looking highwaymen who sat cross-legged on the trail with guns on the ground close to their hands.

"Um-m-m," murmured Tex, who knew of the size of the joint account. "Schatz is lucky if he's got carfare—th' capital of th' Peters-McAllister-Schatz combine is spread reckless under our gloatin' eyes; all except th' few miserable bills that Dave spent

Come on, you greedy hog—we'll let Schatz have his
two-bits an' be glad to get rid of him. I'd hate to
shoot any man as fat as him—no tellin' what'd happen. Stick yore roll where it won't jar loose, load
that right-hand gun, an' see that nobody holds you
up."

"I've allus been plumb a-scared o' hold-ups,"
grinned Hopalong, facetiously. "We all was. Lead
costs money, an' there ain't no use wastin' it." The
grin disappeared and a hard look focused in his
clear eyes as he thought of what a lovely time any
hold-up squad would have when Buck's money was
at stake.

They mounted and rode away down the pass. As
they came to the first bend, Tex glanced back and
saw Big Gray peacefully cropping the scanty vegetation along the trail by the ravine. He was without
bridle or saddle and Tex glanced covertly at the
happy man at his side who could put five bullets in
a falling enemy without a pang, and immediately after release a limping horse so that it could live and
grow strong, to roam free among the mountains.

Hopalong rolled both guns at once to end the cel-
ebration, the bullets striking a rock down the trail
as fast as one could count and at intervals as regular as the hammer-stroke of a striking clock. To a
man who looked upon a gun only as a weapon to be
pointed and discharged at an object, this would
have been sufficiently wonderful, but to a real gunman, one acquainted with the delicacy of manipula-
tion and absolute precision required to effect this
result, it was far more wonderful. There are many
good gun-men who never have acquired this art,
and the danger of practicing it is enough to deter
most men from attempting it. To hold a six-shooter
by a finger slipped through the trigger guard and
make it spin around like a pinwheel, firing it every
time the muzzle swung out and away from the body,

is risky; and when two guns are going at once, it is trebly risky, while accuracy is almost impossible. Hopalong was accurate, so was Johnny, but the latter could work only one gun. Tex, being something of a master of gun-play, was capable of appreciating the feat at its true worth and his eyes glowed at the exhibition. To him came the memory of a day far back in the years when this dexterity had worked to his dishonor, yet it brought with it no malice and it was with the deep affection that a man has for a man friend—and usually for only one—that he playfully advised his companion to "load 'em up again." "Hoppy, there's only one hand I ever see that I'm more afraid of than that'n o' yourn," he remarked.

Hopalong looked at him in mild surprise: "Whose is that?" he asked.

"Yore other one," and Tex grinned at his jest.

CHAPTER XXVII

Points of the Compass

THE LONG-SLANTING shadows found Hopalong and Tex far from Lone Tree Pass, riding straight for the Double Y ranch. Their chase after Dave had taken them well to the west of south and they had concluded to keep the horses and equipment and strike for the ranch. As Hopalong sagely remarked: "Eighty dollars is eighty dollars, Tex, but these here two bronchs 'pear to me purty good stock; besides, what's eighty dollars 'longside the money-bag I'm a-sittin' on?" and he eyed, complacently, the bloated gunny-sack that hid its wealth under so innocent an exterior.

They went ahead with that unerring instinct of the plainsman whose sense of direction seems positively uncanny to a tenderfoot, especially if the tenderfoot has ever been lost. There was no sign of a trail nor did they expect to see one, until they struck the Big Moose, north of the Reservation. This in itself was a source of gratification to them;

they were quite content to meet with no one and all they asked was to be let severely alone until such time as the money was turned over to Buck and they should cease to be responsible for it.

The stumbling of the tired horses led them reluctantly to make camp. Hopalong was loath to be away from Mary longer than was necessary; only the grim determination to get Buck's money to him with as little risk as possible had decided him to ride to the ranch instead of taking the train from X—, which would have been hours quicker. They had discussed this matter, even to the thinking of a possible train hold-up, and Hopalong expressed his very decided preference for the open. "I was in a train hold-up once," he told Tex, "an' seven of th' boys wasn't none too many to break it up. Skinny got plugged—not bad—but it might be us this time, an' it might be a whole lot worse."

He entertained Tex with the story while they made their simple preparations for their supper. Tex listened with the ear of a good listener, giving voice to his amusement, or endorsement of an action, or profanely consigning the whole troupe of train robbers to that region where go the "many who are called but not chosen." But all the while, though interested in the tale which concerned so many of his old friends, his analytical mind was pondering over the reason of Dave's action: How had he got the money from Schatz? Why had no one seen Schatz in Wayback? Where had the transfer of the money been made from Schatz to Dave? What had happened to change the plans of the fake hold-up, when Dave was to relieve Schatz of the money? His busy mind approached the riddle from many angles, as in the dark of night, a man with a lantern might cover a big stretch of country, searching everywhere for the track which would lead him to the finding of a hidden treasure. Farther and far-

ther afield went Tex, examining, comparing, and rejecting every possibility that presented itself to his
inward vision. Disappointed at the failure of his efforts to discover the solution, he cast from his mind
all his useless speculation and adopted the slower
but surer method which he should have tried at
first: He put himself in the place of Dave—little by
little he cast off his own personality and changed to
that of the other, picturing to himself the effect
upon Dave's cupidity when told of the part he was
to play in the stealing of the money. So sensitive
was his intelligence, so receptive to the shadowy
suggestions that beckoned to him, perhaps from
that lonely, unmarked grave beside the upper waters of the Little Jill, that presently his eyes began
to gleam, his lips parted, and he stretched out his
hand to Hopalong in unconscious emphasis. "Th'
gunny sack, Hoppy! Where did he get th' gunny
sack?"

The ghost of Schatz smiled. Tex was a man after
his own heart.

Tex's abstraction had not escaped Hopalong. The
end of his tale reached, he had put away the balance of the food, seen to the secure picketing of the
two horses, put out the fire by the simple expedient
of kicking over it sufficient sand, and had arranged
the saddles in such a way that they completely hid
the sack and could not be disturbed without arousing both him and Tex. From time to time he glanced
at his silent companion, smiling to himself at the
sight of such complete absorption. He could see
himself over again in Tex, who was almost as old a
man, recalling how he had been wont to ponder on
the probable movements of an enemy and the pleasure he took, after a victory, in reviewing what had
gone before and checking the mistakes and the suc-
cesses in his reasoning. He wondered idly why it
had lost its attraction for him and he concluded,

with a whimsical grin, that marriage gave a man other things to think about.

But however lost Hopalong might be to inward speculation, no outward manifestation of the unusual or unlooked-for failed to appeal to his always active and alert senses. The pipe he had been smoking contentedly was held between his fingers, out and almost cold, his head was bent to one side and he was listening intently. He put his head to the ground and then arose to his feet, his ear turned to the stray breeze that was bringing to him faint and disagreeable sounds. When Tex's hand went out to him and Tex's voice broke in upon those barely audible sounds, he grasped the hand and gripped it hard to enjoin silence. Tex listened with all his ears but the ground noises had ceased and he was not high enough to have the advantage of the wind that was vexing Hopalong's hearing. Hopalong silently dragged him to his feet; they stood thus for a few seconds and then the look they turned upon each other was pregnant with significance.

"Makin' quite a noise," said Hopalong. "An' we ain't near th' trail yet. What do you make of it?"

"Dunno," answered Tex. "Hadn't ought to be a man within twenty miles of us, Hoppy, 'less it's a Injun—an' them's no Injuns. Sounds to me like singin'."

"Same here," agreed Hopalong. "Can't be a drive herd, can it?"

"Not as I knows of. No herd ever come this way since th' railroad put through, an' then they stuck to th' trail."

"We got to find out, Tex," declared Hopalong, decisively. "Can't roost with a noisy bunch of coyotes like them runnin' 'round an' howlin' for gore."

"I'll go, Hoppy," said Tex, "an' if I ain't back in an hour, you take both cayuses an' hike out for th' ranch."

"An' leave you afoot?" asked Hopalong. "Not by a darn sight."

"You must, Hoppy. I got a reputation that'll serve me with either honest men or thieves. I can't come to no harm. 'Tother way, you might get hurt. Two of us can't get away on them bronchs, they did too much today already. You'll have to go at a walk, if you do go. 'Course I don't stop with that bunch 'less I has to. It's that bag I'm thinkin' about, Hoppy. If I has to stop, you want to put as much ground as you can between them an' you. I'm damned glad they didn't see our fire."

"All right, Tex. I gives you an hour. 'Tain't more'n a mile. Get a-goin'.'"

Tex started away and Hopalong began to get ready for a possible flight. Even if Tex did return they might decide that another location for their camp would be healthier. As he fastened the saddles to the two animals they each turned and looked at him with a disgust as expressive as if spoken.

Tex made for the spot from which the sounds had come, walking easily but silently, his form a mere shadow in the starlit night and invisible on the lower levels, to which he carefully kept, at a distance of two hundred yards. At the end of ten minutes he was able to distinguish words and knew that Hoppy's and his surmise had been correct: they had heard the singing of night riders around a herd. It was the un-called-for presence of a herd in this vicinity which, more than all else, had led Tex to insist upon the reconnoiter being left to him. "Honest men or thieves," he had said. He was very doubtful of finding honest men. Only the condition of the horses had checked him from advising a departure on suspicion.

He was skulking along now, bent double; in his

hand, the blade lying along his arm, was a knife
such as few men in the West carried at that day and
in the use of which Tex was unusually expert. It was
entirely characteristic of him that he should possess such a weapon: silence in action is desired by
the worst class of man, and Tex had been of that
class before the enforced association of better men
and the heroically magnanimous action of an opponent had changed him to the man he was. He slunk
forward with the stealthy prowl of a wolf, glancing
to right and left as he went, hoping to sight the
camp of the cattlemen and get near enough without
being seen, to learn what he had come to find out.
He dropped flat to earth as a sudden snort startled
him: he had come upon the herd without knowing
it. A disquieted animal sprang to its feet and did not
lie down again until the soothing voice of the
herder was raised. The song floated down the wind
and Tex listened as well as the cow:

> " 'Now then, young men, don't be melancholy;
> Just see, like me, if you can't be jolly;
> If anything goes wrong with me
> I never sulk nor pout;
> In fact I am and always was
> The merriest girl that's out.' "

If the cow were soothed it was quite otherwise
with Tex: his hair almost bristled as the rider went
past, near enough for the heavy knife to have sped
through the air and sunk haft-deep between his
shoulders. "Chatter Spence!" sprang to Tex's lips.
"Who's he driving for?" a question that he was still
asking himself when another herder neared him,
whose choice of lullaby was probably influenced by
that of his companion, for he was calling out in
most lugubrious voice:

> " *'Buffalo gals, are you comin' out tonight,*
> *Comin' out tonight, comin' out tonight?*
> *Buffalo gals, are you comin' out tonight*
> *To dance by th' light of th' moon?'* "

"It's all wrong," the singer broke off to say in a sing-song voice, that, as far as the cattle were concerned, had all the effect of a melody. "It's all wrong," he repeated. "There ain't no moon. 'To dance by th' light of th' stars,' " he corrected, and then: "Gentlemen, I rises to a question of order. I don't want to dance. I'm too blasted sore to dance—I'm too sore to be a-sittin' on this cross-eyed, rat-tailed, flea-bitten son-of-a-dog, too; an' if I ain't relieved pretty soon, Shanghai is a-goin' to hear—" his voice trailed away and the words were no longer distinguishable.

Tex cautiously sat up. "That's Argue Bennett. And Shanghai is with them. Why, darn it! There must be a whole brood of Ike's chickens roosting around here. I'm going to find them, even if I miss Hoppy in doing it."

He started to arise and back away before the first singer should approach again, only to drop back into his former prone position at the sound of a third singer, coming from his right. Bennett and Spence heard him too and were more than ready to resign the herd by the time he and his companion arrived. Bennett did not hesitate to announce his bitter condemnation of the way things were being done.

"That you, Ship?" he called.

"That's me," came the answer.

"Shore it's you," agreed Bennett, in sarcastic acknowledgment. "I'd a' bet every cow I own it's you. An' I goes on record as bettin' every cow *you* own that Cracker is a-ridin' 'longside you. Do I win?"

"You win with yore own stock but I objects to you winnin' with mine. It *might* a' been Shanghai."

"Yes, it *might*; but if it was I'd a' dropped dead from surprise. What I want to know is: what call has Shanghai got to hold down all th' soft snaps? Is he any better'n we are? Echo answers no—Echo bein' Chatter Spence, who hasn't got pride enough to disagree with a hen."

"Aw, what's eatin' you! This ain't no regular drive. An' did you ever know Shanghai to get left on a deal? How'd we ever got through th' Cyclone if it hadn't been for Shanghai? You make me tired. Did you ever know a herd to get over th' ground so fast? Been you, we'd be some're near Big Moose right now. You leave Shanghai alone an' we'll have th' herd in our pockets afore Peters knows they're gone. Nice little bunch, too. Go an' get yore chuck an' you'll feel better. 'Jennie, my own true loved one, Wait till th' clouds roll by' "—he rode on to circle the herd.

"Did you ever hear such a pill? He thinks nobody knows nothin' but Shanghai. What do you say, Cracker?"

"Well, I kind o' sides with Ship. We ain't done as much as Shanghai, if it comes to that, 'ceptin' night herd."

"Hell! I'm wastin' my breath talkin' to you. Come on, Chatter, we—why, th' greedy hog's gone a'ready." Bennett made haste to get back to camp. He knew the supplies to be none too plentiful. So did Chatter Spence.

Tex stole away as silently as he had come, leaving the cattle-thieves happy in their ignorance of his discovery. He pushed himself hard on his return, fearful of having overstayed the time. Hopalong was waiting for him, however, and listened to his news with quiet interest.

"Buck's cows, Hoppy," was Tex's greeting, as he

arrived on the run. "We got to get 'em but it's one
sweet little job. Old Ship o' State is a holy terror in
a row; Chatter Spence ain't bad, an' Argue Bennett
an' Cracker impressed me as bein' good men to
have around. But th' one we got to watch out for is
Shanghai. He never falls down an' it wouldn't surprise me none to know he was watchin' them four
same as I was. There's two of 'em ridin' herd an'
three in camp. How do we go at it?"

"Got to get th' two night-ridin'. Tie 'em up an' th'
other three is easy. Hol' on a minute till I get th'
bank."

Ship o' State was beginning the twenty-seventh
stanza in the melodious history of an incorrigible
reprobate who deserved death in every one of
them, when he was utterly confounded to hear a
voice, almost at his ear, command him to "throw up
his hands an' climb down off'n that cayuse, *pronto*."
Contrary to what all his friends would have expected him to do, he obeyed the command instantly and to the letter. He was relieved of his gun
and was being very effectually secured when the
strangely quavering voice of Cracker was heard and
came near. Ship eyed his captor in wonder. If
Cracker were to be captured in the same manner,
then this was the coolest man in the country.
Nearer and nearer came the voice until Ship actually found himself worrying over the narrowness of
the margin of safety. It was not until Cracker went
by that he understood. The grotesque shape could
only be accounted for in one way: Cracker's captor
was straddling the same pony.

It was just when Ship had reached this conclusion
that a very unpleasant bunch of rags was thrust
into his mouth and he was lifted and thrown face
down across the back of his horse. Hopalong got
into the saddle and they rode away from the herd.
They had not gone far before another horseman

joined them and Ship could hear the singing
Cracker as he circled the herd. "There's three of
'em anyway," was his thought, wherein he was
wrong. Cracker, with his hands trussed high behind
his back and his feet hobbled, was stumbling slowly
along with the threat in his memory that if he
stopped singing until he was told, his head stood a
good chance of being separated from the rest of his
carcass, when he would never be able to sing again;
and the further information that, if the herd should
stampede, he was in a fair way to be crushed to a
pulp. The latter he knew to be true and he was
equally convinced that the other would be quite
likely to take place.

Fifty yards from the herd, Ship was quietly
dumped to the ground. Far enough away from him
the horses were picketed and two forms crept carefully upon the three men in camp.

Dark as it was, there was no difficulty in finding
two of the three. Spence and Bennett, the latter
agreeably surprised to find that Shanghai had depleted the general treasury to the extent of one
cow, had both eaten a large and satisfying meal;
their hunger appeased, weariness had asserted itself in double force and nothing less than a determined kick would have awakened either of them.
But Hopalong and Tex prowled around looking for
Shanghai without success.

Shanghai was living up to his reputation. Having
made his plans and given orders to insure their
carrying out, he then stayed around and saw it
done. Argue Bennett might grumble to the others
but he knew the futility, as also the danger, of grumbling to Shanghai. When his two subordinates had
eaten their fill and gone to sleep, Shanghai still sat
hunched before the dying embers of the fire, smoking a meditative pipe. When the smoke ceased to
float lazily from his nostrils he knocked the warm

ashes onto the palm of his hand, got to his feet and slipped quietly away from the camp.

Any one who knew Shanghai well would have reasoned that he was probably going to look over the herd because he started away in the opposite direction. Going straight to his objective point was entirely too elemental for Shanghai. He fetched a wide circle before drawing near the herd, his approach being unheralded and made with the suspicious caution which marked all his movements. He listened inattentively to the husky voice of Cracker who was mourning the demise of somebody named Brown, and moved a little nearer. Presently he became vaguely uneasy at the silence of old Ship-o'-State. It was not the lack of song on Ship's part that troubled Shanghai—the cattle were resting easy enough—but where was he? When Cracker came around again Shanghai was near enough to see him and he craned his neck in wonder at the sight: Cracker on his two feet, staggering along like a man about three whiskeys from oblivion, and Ship off post. Here was something very wrong and Shanghai cursed softly to think how far away his horse was. What in blazes made him come afoot, anyway? He started back to camp to repair the oversight and to have Chatter and Argue behind him before making an investigation of Cracker's astonishing preference for night-herding on foot.

His descent upon the camp would have been creditable to an Apache. First making sure of his horse and leaving him in shape for instant departure, he circled the two sleeping forms, viewing them from all sides. There was something wrong. Shanghai did not know what it was but the figures of his two companions seemed actually to exhale menace and the longer he hesitated the stronger the feeling became. Shanghai stole quietly back to his horse, mounted and rode off with the settled conviction that sunup was the proper time for investigating these unusual circumstances and that the proper spot was several miles distant from below the skyline of some convenient knoll.

At the unmistakable sound of retreating hoofbeats the figures in camp came to life. They sat up and listened and then Tex looked at Hoppy with frank disapprobation. "Hoppy, my way was best," he declared. Hopalong nodded, in silent agreement, and Tex continued: "I been a-hearin' considerable talk about this here Shanghai an' I'm bound to say I believe all I hears. Darn if he ain't got second sight."

Hopalong nodded again. "Let's round up th' rest of th' roosters, anyhow. We got four, an' four's a plenty to take care of."

"Shore is," admitted Tex. "Let's bring 'em in an' hog-tie 'em. Them cows wouldn't move for anythin' 'less'n a Norther after th' way they've come across country."

A half hour later Ike's four pets were lying side by side in camp, trussed to the point of immovability and all apparently, in spite of their discomfort, taking advantage of the opportunity to secure the sleep they so much needed after their unsuccessful exertions.

"Hoppy," said Tex, "I think that with that Shanghai party still runnin' at large, it'd be some wise to split up that wealth. Better take a chance of losin' half of it than all of it. What you think?"

"Same here," agreed Hopalong. He opened the sack and dumped out the packages, dividing them roughly into two parts with a sweep of his hand, and proceeded to rip up the sack, preparatory to making two parcels of the money.

" 'With milk an' honey blest,' " faltered a voice and they turned to find Argue Bennett's eyes almost starting from his head at the sight he beheld.

"Playin' 'possum, eh? It'd do you no harm to stretch hemp right now," and Tex's meditative air was fringed with ferocity.

"No offense, Comin', no offense. You woke me movin'. Is that what Dave got away with?"

"Yes—an' there won't no more Daves get away with it, you can bet all th' cows you own on that."

"An' me a-riskin' my neck rustlin' that bunch when all that beautiful wealth was a-leavin' th' country easy an' graceful an' just a-shoutin' to be brought back. Excuse me, Comin'. I ain't got no call to talk. I reckon I never did talk. Th' best I ever done since I was born is bray."

Thus it came about that Shanghai suffered the acute misery of seeing his four-footed fortune headed back the way it had come. Not that he lost heart all at once. After some hours of following he had decided that a bold stroke might put him again in possession and was perfecting the details of the stratagem his ready mind conceived, when a sudden check was given by a rapidly approaching cloud of dust from the northwest. The check became check-mate when the useful field-glasses disclosed to his pained vision the hilarious meeting that took place. A certain jaunty carriage, a characteristic swagger that did not forsake him even in the saddle, made Shanghai look hard at the leader of the newcomers and suspect Cock Murray. And his suspicion was well founded. Cock Murray had already redeemed his promise to Buck and it may be pardoned him if in the joy of his heart, his swagger became so pronounced as to disclose his personality across some miles of country.

Shanghai closed his glasses and moved slowly to his horse. "Well, it had to be," he conceded, philosophically. "An' I reckon it's about time I pulled my freight."

CHAPTER XXVIII

The Heart of a Rose

AND THE evening and the morning were the second day. At a time when, through the diffused and fading light of the sun-vacant sky, the silver-pale stars blinked one by one in their awakening; when the protesting twitter of disturbed birds seeking their rest sounded sweetly clear above the steady rumble of the marshland frogs; when the velvet-footed killers stretched and yawned and gazed with dilated pupils at the near approach of night; when the men who persuaded luck to their advantage, in various ways, began to gather about the tables in cow-town and mining-camp, and there was a lighting of lamps by the foresighted and a trimming of wicks by the procrastinators—the French Rose faced her father, Jean, and did battle for love and happiness, though she knew it not.

The easy-going Jean had known nothing of the manner in which their guest was wounded, nor by whom; and Rose had not thought it wise to tell him, even if it occurred to her in the stress of that first day. But Jean had heard many rumors in Twin River, many disquieting facts and equally disturbing inferences. He had hurried home beset with fears for the outcome, alarmed at the reckless step Rose had taken and vainly asking himself why. Immediately upon his entry he had set Pickles at a task which would occupy him away from the cabin. Standing moodily at the window he watched him go. Then he turned to his daughter for an explanation.

"Is Dave here yesterday?" he asked.

"Yes," replied Rose, non-committally.

Jean turned over in his mind this new fact and fitted it into the pattern. "For why you go so fast to Twin?" he questioned.

"No one is here but me. Fritz, he go to the Two Y's ranch."

"You tell him?"

"No. He hear Dave talk an' go to tell M'sieu Peters Dave have stole all his money."

"*Diable!* Steal?"

"Yes."

Jean knitted his brows in the effort to understand the reason for this; quite naturally he came back in a circle to his first inquiry and repeated it: "For why you go to Twin?"

"I go for men to catch Dave when he steal the money." This, while not strictly true, was the nearest to truth that Jean could understand.

The trend of his thoughts was shown by his next question. "Dave—he know?" he asked, and his anxiety was apparent.

"Yes," was the brief answer.

"*Mon Dieu!*" exclaimed Jean. He turned from her and stared with unseeing eyes over the land he had struggled hard to make his own. And now he must lose it. Rapidly calculating how long his slender resources would support him until Rose could dispose of his stock and follow, despair came upon him as he realized that the vengeance of Dave was not to be escaped. "For why," he asked, hoarsely, "for why you do this?"

"For why?" repeated Rose and the thrill in her voice caused him to turn and look at her in surprise. "Figure to yourself, then: That devil he come here and he sneer at you, and he insult me—yes. Many times he insult me that I have to hold myself, so! that I do not kill him. I endure. He send me—*Dieu*! that I should say it—he make dirt of me to walk on, to arrive at a man who is high, good, ah, a man! *mon père*, a man like you, one time when you have no fear. He send me. I say nothing. Many times he try, like a dog, to spring at his throat, but always, it is nothing but snap at his heels. Like a dog which he is. Then he come to me and say he is triumph. He get much money. And he tell me go with him. Me! me! he command like he is master and me slave. He steal money from M'sieu Peters and him and me, we go away together, like that, like man and his squaw. And I say nothing. Ah, *mon père*! it is too much—too much. If it be some other man—not M'sieu Peters—then I go. I save you, *mon père*, though it kill me. But—it is too much."

She bowed her head, filled with self-reproach, with a knowledge that her father could never see this thing as she did. Jean stared at her, motionless; but his dumb amaze slowly lifted. He came to her and rested his hand lightly on her bowed head. "*Ma Rose—ma belle Rose*—when you have for a good man so big love as that, I would die, with gladness, to know so big happiness is come to you." And he went swiftly from the cabin.

At the closing of the door she sprang to it and threw it wide again. "You will not go—now—tonight?" she called.

The answer, low, determined, in the tones of the father of that other time, reassured her: "No. We stay. Maybe—who knows?—God is good."

She went back and with steady hand lit the lamp and placed it on the table. The noble face was aglow with hopeful pride: he would face it at last, this thing that had embittered both their lives.

"Rose!"

She started and turned in dismay toward the inner room. He was awake—how long?—and calling her.

"Rose!" the call came again, gentle but insistent. "Rose, I—I want you."

She stood a moment longer, both hands pressed against her heart, her breath coming in great gasps and in her eyes the frightened look of a child. Then she caught up the lamp and with swift step went in and stood beside the bunk. "Is it then you rest ill, my friend?" she asked softly, and then bent to rearrange the pillow. Buck's hand closed over hers.

"Rose," he whispered, "Rose—I heard."

She slipped to her knees, hiding her face in the pillow, her figure shaking with great tremors and sobs breaking from her so that she could scarcely speak. "Oh, I am ashamed," she said brokenly, "I am ashamed."

"Ashamed! And I——" he stopped, drawing in a deep breath at the wonder of it; then raising himself to rest on bent arm, he laid his cheek against her hair. "I'm th' one as ought to be ashamed, Rose: a man o' my age, an' feelin' th' way I do—an' you a girl. But I've got to have you, Rose. I just got to have you. An' if you don't say 'yes' I swear to God I'll give up an' pull out o' this country. I don't want to stop another day if you say 'no.' "

She drew away from him and raised her head to look at him doubtfully, appealingly, believingly. A wonderful smile broke through her tears and stilled the trembling of her lips. "You mean it, Buck. Oh You do! You do!" Her arms were about him and she lowered him gently back again. "Rest you, and get well quickly, wounded man," she murmured. "My man—my man until I die—and after."

SKYE'S WEST
BY RICHARD S. WHEELER

☐ 51071-2 SKYE'S WEST: BANNACK $3.95
Canada $4.95

☐ 51069-0 SKYE'S WEST: THE FAR TRIBES $3.95
Canada $4.95

☐ 51073-9 SKYE'S WEST: SUN RIVER $3.95
Canada $4.95

☐ 50894-7 SKYE'S WEST: YELLOWSTONE $3.95
Canada $4.95

☐ 51305-3 SKYE'S WEST: BITTERROOT $4.50
Canada $5.50

☐ 51306-1 SKYE'S WEST: SUNDANCE $3.99
Canada $4.99

☐ 52142-0 SKYE'S WEST: WINDRIVER $3.99
Canada $4.99

WESTERN ADVENTURE
FROM TOR

☐	58459-7	THE BAREFOOT BRIGADE *Douglas Jones*	$4.95 Canada $5.95
☐	52303-2	THE GOLDEN SPURS *Western Writers of America*	$4.99 Canada $5.99
☐	51315-0	HELL AND HOT LEAD/GUN RIDER *Norman A. Fox*	$3.50 Canada $4.50
☐	51169-7	HORNE'S LAW *Jory Sherman*	$3.50 Canada $4.50
☐	58875-4	THE MEDICINE HORN *Jory Sherman*	$3.99 Canada $4.99
☐	58329-9	NEW FRONTIERS I *Martin H. Greenberg & Bill Pronzini*	$4.50 Canada $5.50
☐	58331-0	NEW FRONTIERS II *Martin H. Greenberg & Bill Pronzini*	$4.50 Canada $5.50
☐	52461-6	THE SNOWBLIND MOON *John Byrne Cooke*	$5.99 Canada $6.99
☐	58184-9	WHAT LAW THERE WAS *Al Dempsey*	$3.99 Canada $4.99

Buy them at your local bookstore or use this handy coupon:
Clip and mail this page with your order.

Publishers Book and Audio Mailing Service
P.O. Box 120159, Staten Island, NY 10312-0004

Please send me the book(s) I have checked above. I am enclosing $ _____
(Please add $1.25 for the first book, and $.25 for each additional book to cover postage and handling.
Send check or money order only—no CODs.)

Name _____
Address _____
City _____ State/Zip _____
Please allow six weeks for delivery. Prices subject to change without notice.

MORE WESTERN
ADVENTURE FROM TOR

☐	58457-0 **ELKHORN TAVERN** *Douglas Jones*	$4.95 Canada $5.95
☐	58453-8 **GONE THE DREAMS AND DANCING** *Douglas Jones*	$3.95 Canada $4.95
☐	52242-7 **HOPALONG CASSIDY** *Clarence E. Mulford*	$4.99 Canada $5.99
☐	51359-2 **THE RAINBOW RUNNER** *Cunningham*	$4.99 Canada $5.99
☐	58455-4 **ROMAN** *Douglas Jones*	$4.95 Canada $5.95
☐	51318-5 **SONG OF WOVOKA** *Earl Murray*	$4.99 Canada $5.99
☐	58463-5 **WEEDY ROUGH** *Douglas Jones*	$4.95 Canada $5.95
☐	52142-0 **WIND RIVER** *Dick Wheeler*	$3.99 Canada $4.99
☐	58989-0 **WOODSMAN** *Don Wright*	$3.95 Canada $4.95

Buy them at your local bookstore or use this handy coupon:
Clip and mail this page with your order.

Publishers Book and Audio Mailing Service
P.O. Box 120159, Staten Island, NY 10312-0004

Please send me the book(s) I have checked above. I am enclosing $ _____
(Please add $1.25 for the first book, and $.25 for each additional book to cover postage and handling.
Send check or money order only—no CODs.)

Name _____
Address _____
City _____ State/Zip _____
Please allow six weeks for delivery. Prices subject to change without notice.